An Aria for Nick

Part 2 of the Song of Suspense series

A Novel by

Hallee Bridgeman

Published by
Olivia Kimbrell Press™

Olivia Kimbrell Press™
Fort Knox, Kentucky 40121

PUBLISHED BY: Olivia Kimbrell Press™*, P.O. Box 470 Fort Knox, KY 40122-0470 The Olivia Kimbrell Press™ colophon and open book logo are trademarks of Olivia Kimbrell Press™.

*Olivia Kimbrell Press™ is a publisher offering true to life, meaningful fiction from a Christian worldview intended to uplift the heart and engage the mind.

Some scripture quotations courtesy of the King James Version of the Holy Bible.

Some scripture quotations courtesy of the New King James Version of the Holy Bible, Copyright © 1979, 1980, 1982 by Thomas-Nelson, Inc. Used by permission. All rights reserved.

Cover Art and graphics by Amanda Gail Smith (amandagailstudio.com)

Library Cataloging Data

Names: Bridgeman, Hallee (Bridgeman Hallee) 1972-

Title: An Aria for Nick; Song of Suspense Series book 2 / Hallee Bridgeman

452 p. 5 in. × 8 in. (12.70 cm × 20.32 cm)

Description: Olivia Kimbrell Press™ digital eBook edition | Olivia Kimbrell Press™ Trade paperback edition | Kentucky: Olivia Kimbrell Press™, 2015.

Summary: The Only Man Who Can Save Her Life Has Been Dead for a Decade.

Identifiers: ePCN: 2017950544 | ISBN-13: 978-1-68190-081-0 (hardcover) | 978-1-68190-093-3 (trade) | 978-1-68190-092-6 (POD) | 978-1-939603-12-8 (ebk.)

1. suspenseful thriller 2. clean romance love story 3. Christian fiction mystery 4. women's inspirational 5. music songs recording 6. spiritual warfare family 7. military nuclear spy

PS3558.B7534 A753 2013   [Fic.] 813.6 (DDC 23)

An Aria for Nick

Part 2 of the Song of Suspense series

A Novel by

HALLEE BRIDGEMAN

Table of Contents

Dedication

Lovingly dedicated to...

My Dad, William "Bill" Poe, U. S. Army Sergeant Major (Retired), who so patiently served as an advisor to me when I wrote the first draft of the book many years ago.

I love you, Daddy, and am SO proud to be your daughter. Thank you for constantly supporting and encouraging me.

Chapter 1

Columbus, Georgia
Near Fort Benning
Twelve Years Ago

"Wake up, birthday girl!" Aria Suarez buried herself deeper under the covers. "Aria, honey, time to wake up!"

With a groan, Aria stretched and slowly sat up. She could hear her mother at the base of the stairs and knew that if she didn't get up, one of her brothers would soon arrive to retrieve her. They could be relentless. A few minutes of extra sleep were not worth the torment that would cause, especially on her eighteenth birthday.

She stumbled from her bedroom and into the bathroom where she turned on the shower and closed the shower curtain, letting the hot water make the long morning journey up the old pipes from the water heater in the basement. She leaned against the wall and waited for the mirror to start to steam. As she looked out through the window and noticed the dark pre-dawn sky, she made a silent resolution that she would take only afternoon classes in college, and find work that never required her to wake before dawn.

Aria showered quickly, then stumbled back to her room and threw on a pair of jeans and a sweatshirt. She heard a tap on the door and looked up as her mother walked in, carrying a cup of coffee. Aria gratefully accepted the hot cup and eagerly enjoyed the first sip. "Thanks, Mom."

Doris Suarez regarded her youngest child, a little grin playing about her lips. Aria imagined what her mother must be feeling. Perhaps a little tug at realizing that the last of her babies had grown into adulthood. Out of four children, Aria was not only the baby but also the only girl—so very different from her brothers. She even looked different.

Her brothers had all inherited their father's dark looks and height, while Aria was petite with blonde hair, more like her mother. The only traces of her Hispanic heritage were her caramel brown eyes and skin that looked just dark enough to imitate a healthy tan.

Aria ran her hands through her short blonde hair and sat on the side of her bed to wiggle her toes into her shoes. "Is Daddy still here?" she asked.

"No. He left a couple of hours ago. He tried to wake you, but said you wouldn't budge." Aria's father served in the United States Army. He had made the Army his career and a way of life for his family. They currently enjoyed the duty station at Fort Benning, Georgia.

Aria rubbed her eyes and put her head in her hands, trying to banish the cobwebs from her brain. "No big deal.

We had such a big party Saturday."

"He said to tell you, and I quote, 'God has truly blessed this family with such an amazing daughter.' He prayed for you this morning, thanking God for your talent with music and for your sharp mind."

Aria smiled despite her drowsiness. Sometimes she thought she could listen to her father pray all day. She started to feel the caffeine hit her bloodstream and willed it to help her wake up. She hated mornings, especially Monday mornings. "How many more days until Spring Break?"

Doris Suarez laughed and kissed the top of her only daughter's head. "Another cup of coffee, and you'll be ready to face the day, dear." She started to walk out of the room but stopped at the door. "Your brothers are all downstairs, awake, and waiting to wish you Happy Birthday," she confided. Aria groaned, making her mother laugh. "John is even making you waffles."

John was Aria's eldest brother, eight years her senior, and a police officer in Atlanta, home on vacation for five days past New Year's Day, having worked over Christmas. Then there was Henry, who was twenty-five and a third-year medical student. Finally, Adam, who was twenty-one and going to college in California learning to make movies and write screenplays. Henry and Adam each had another week before school started back for them.

"Tell them I'm on my way," Aria said and bent to gather her books. She packed up her backpack, grabbed her coffee cup from her dresser, then made her way downstairs. She walked through the living room and pushed open the kitchen door, ignoring Henry, who made some laughing comment about it being a beautiful morning. John stood at the counter, pouring batter into the waffle iron as Adam poured a cup of coffee. She walked up behind Adam, rested her forehead against his back, and she set her coffee cup in front of him for a refill.

"It's not good for you to be so dependent on caffeine. You're barely eighteen," Henry said, crossing his arms.

"I wouldn't have to be if they didn't start school around here at the ungodly hour of seven-twenty," Aria mumbled. "I miss Washington. They didn't start there until eight-ten." Her cup full, she grabbed it and flopped down at the table. She crossed her arms, resting her head on her folded wrists as the coffee cup warmed her palms. She heard someone set a plate on the table, and the smell of waffles with softened butter and real maple syrup filled her senses. Her mouth started watering, so she lifted her head and saw all three of her brothers standing around the table, staring at her and grinning. "What are you staring at?" she asked. She put a hand to her hair to make sure nothing was sticking up anywhere.

"Happy Birthday, Aria," Adam said. Henry pulled a small box wrapped up in a page from the Sunday comics out of his pocket. The large pink baby-shower style bow adorning it looked slightly crushed.

She took the box and stared down at it for a moment. "You guys already gave me presents," she said. For some reason, she felt tears tickling the corner of her eyes and an unexpected tightness in the back of her throat.

"Didn't you wonder why we got you things like socks and stationery?" Adam asked.

"I didn't really think about it," Aria whispered as she

ripped the paper off the box. She opened the lid, and her mouth dropped open in shock. The tears had moved to cloud her eyes and threatened to spill over. Her hand shook a little as she retrieved the single key nestled in a bed of tissue paper.

"Come outside, Aria," John said.

She flew out of her chair and into the arms of the closest brother, laughing and crying. She went to each one, kissing and hugging them in turn, then dashed outside. Parked at the curb under a streetlight was a shiny little black sports car with a big pink ribbon around it. She turned back around to look at them. They all stood on the porch with grins on their faces, watching her. "How...?"

"Adam and I had extra money after last semester was over with, and John here has good credit," Henry said.

"Real good credit," Adam said, elbowing John in the ribs. "Besides, when you become a world-famous pianist, you can buy us all cars."

"Make mine a Viper!" John enthused.

She went back to them and kissed each one of them on their unshaven cheeks again. "You guys are awesome," she said. Then she ran to the car and stood at the driver's door. "Come on. Let's go for a ride."

♫ ♫ ♫ ♫

"And there it sat all shiny and black," Aria bragged. She stood at her locker, talking with her best friend, Carol Mabry.

"We're still talking about *your* brothers, right? The Brothers' Suarez? I didn't know they had it in them to be that sweet," Carol teased.

"Every once in a while, they throw me a bone," Aria said. "Apparently, my parents didn't have anything to do with it." She glanced up and felt her pulse pick up. Nick Williams walked toward her.

She remembered how she had smiled for days after discovering that his locker was next to hers this year. Since her sophomore year, she'd had a very strong, very serious crush on him. Aria had even joined JROTC to try to get him to notice her. It hadn't worked. Other than barking orders of a military capacity at her, he never even looked at her of his own volition. He reached his locker and spun the dial without even glancing in her direction. "Hey, Nick," she greeted, a little breathless.

He looked down at her, an annoyed look on his face. She could have sworn that she had to swallow around her heart when his eyes met hers. Ice blue was the only way she knew how to describe them, nearly silver, with lashes any woman would envy. His dirty blond hair was cut military short, his nose slightly crooked, and he had a little scar on his chin. It served to give him a daring, somewhat dangerous bad-boy look. Also, he was tall. She barely reached his shoulder. When she noticed he had a fresh bruise on one cheek, unexpected anger surged through her mind. The black eye he had last week had barely faded, and now he already had another bruise.

"Suarez," he answered evenly, responding to her greeting. "Don't be late again this afternoon," he cautioned as he grabbed his U. S. History textbook and slammed his locker. She watched him walk away without a backward glance.

They served on the JROTC rifle team together and had

a match on Friday. Nick was the best shot in the state, and Aria had been hoping that he might finally notice her if she joined the team, too. So, she'd joined, despite her intense piano lessons and practice schedule. Apparently, the time and sacrifice hadn't worked, because he still only called her by her last name.

"You need to give up on that boy," Carol said.

Aria shook her head sharply. "Never."

Carol slammed her locker shut. "He thinks you're too good for him."

Aria pursed her lips, considering. "Seems like I should be the judge of that," she concluded as she and Carol made their way to Physics class.

Chapter 2

Aria lay her head on the thick chemistry book and felt little fingers of frustration mingled with dawning panic work their way up and down her spine. How could she possibly understand this stuff?

She heard the heavy footsteps of one of her brothers come into the room and looked up, feeling her cheeks flush with color when she saw her brother, Henry. He had always had a mind for science and was apparently excelling in medical school.

"Why the long face and, you know, the defensive body language?" He pulled a bottle of soda out of the fridge and sat across from her.

"Because I am sinking in Chemistry. I just can't—I just don't get it. And the school I want to go to is going to look at academics as much as my music."

He twisted the top of the bottle off and took a long pull of the cold drink. "Which school did you decide on again?"

"Eastman. At the University of Rochester."

He whistled low under his breath. "Then I guess it's

good you're not only a musical prodigy, but also a straight-A student besides."

"Was."

"Was?"

"Yeah. Was. I *was* a straight-A student. Now I have a B."

"Ah," he said with a nod. "Chemistry."

"Which I know is your best subject, so I don't even want to hear how easy you think it is." She slapped the book closed and leaned back in her chair with her arms folded across her chest.

He too leaned back and stared at her with their father's dark brown eyes until she wanted to fidget under his gaze. Finally, he said, "Maybe you need to look at it from a different angle."

Sarcastically, she spun the book around, knitted her eyebrows at the upside-down text, and announced, "I'm not seeing how that helps."

"Cute." He took another pull of the drink. "When you look at music, do you think, 'C-note plus F-sharp equals whatever'? Or, do you hear the music in your head?"

Aria spun the book back around and opened it up to the center page, which contained the periodic table of elements. Maybe she understood where her brother was going. "I hear it."

"You hear it. What's that like? How does that work in your head?"

Aria considered. "I don't just hear it. I can kind of see the entire piece like a road map in my head. The base and treble staffs are different colors, and the sharps and flats are bright or dark, you know?"

Henry nodded. "What you're saying is that you can

visualize the information that the sheet music is conveying. Like a code."

Aria sat up a little straighter. "Okay. That seems right."

Confidently, Henry said, "It seems right because it is right. When I see a list of elements, like H_2O, I think 'water,'" he waved his hand and conceded, "or ice or steam—but I don't ever think, 'two parts hydrogen, one part oxygen equals water.' I don't decode it. I already know the code just like you already know how to read music."

Aria leaned forward, suddenly interested. Her brother said, "Look." He spun the book back around to face her. "You don't say in your head each letter like C-H-E-M-I-S-T-R-Y then announce 'chemistry!' You see that word on that textbook, and your mind translates the entire word into a symbol. Then your mind visualizes something. Maybe your classroom, or your teacher, or a recent experiment, or a pop quiz you just choked on. You visualize the information. Right?"

Aria nodded. "Go on."

"Every good boy does fine. Face." He recited the anagrams for musical notation. "In every combination on that musical staff, all the 'letters' in the musical octaves, whether sharp or flat; they don't convey notes. They convey music. They convey information."

He gestured toward the book. "The alphabet? Sheet music? Computers? Chemistry? It's all just code. The code is not the information, baby sister. *Information* is information. The code just *conveys* the information. The combination of musical notes, or the combination of letters in words, or the elements from the periodic table, in the end, it's just a code. You're sitting here so wrapped up in the code you're missing the information."

He leaned forward and clapped. "Try this. Try to think of the elements in the periodic table as music, or try to think of music as elements. Try to compose with them. See where that takes you."

She stared at the chart in the book long after he left. As she considered what he said and redirected the way her brain looked at the chart. Suddenly the elements came to life for her. Going back to the beginning of the book and working forward toward her current chapter, the chemistry started to make sense. No longer did it feel like this worthless jumble of letters and numbers that made no sense to her. As she looked at it from another angle, it all became much clearer.

Excited, she pulled a sheet of paper toward her and began writing as quickly as she could, unscrambling a semester's worth of information and restructuring it so that she understood it. She was completely unaware that the entire time she wrote, she hummed what an outside observer would hear as a completely tuneless song.

♫ ♫ ♫ ♫

Nick opened his eyes, instantly alert. A glance at the clock revealed that it was barely after six, and he relaxed slightly. He had feared he would sleep in after last night. His old man rarely got that violent anymore, not since Nick had gotten big enough to hit back. As he lay there, he took inventory, slowly testing his body for any permanent damage. He had a nasty bruise on his left cheek, and his right arm was bruised from the wrist to the elbow. He winced a little when he touched his ribs, but after a more thorough examination, decided nothing was broken this time.

Nick got out of bed quietly and made his way to the bathroom. Roaches scurried toward the corners when he turned on the light, and Nick shuddered at the sight of them. He hated the filth in which he lived. If the Army took recruits with a GED instead of a high school diploma, he would have already joined. Four more months.

He went back to his room and threw on a pair of jeans and a T-shirt, then grabbed his bag and his jacket. He moved through the tiny trailer as quietly as possible, trying not to kick one of the many beer cans that littered the floor. In the front room, he automatically wrinkled his nose at the smell of old urine, unwashed sweat, and stale smoke. More cans and bottles littered the floor in that room, mingled with takeout cartons and cigarette butts.

His father lay stretched out in the recliner, snoring in an alcohol-induced sleep, a nearly empty bottle of cheap whiskey in the crook of his arm. Nick sneered at him, and not for the first time, the thought crossed his mind that the old man would never wake up if he happened to set the trailer on fire. Knowing that the Army didn't take convicted felons either, whether or not they had a high school diploma, kept him from acting on the notion.

Nick snagged his father's pack of cigarettes off the table beside the chair, then went outside, quietly closing the door behind him. He started the long walk to school. Nick cut through the back lots and pitted driveways until he left the trailer park and entered the bordering neighborhood. This neighborhood had streetlights and fences, and the houses weren't propped up on bricks and jacks. Without a backward glance, Nick tossed the cigarettes in the general direction of a storm drain and started whistling a jaunty tune.

"Hey, kid!" A deep voice bellowed. Nick froze and glanced back. He saw the man—the soldier—who occupied the little ranch number with the garage that faced the storm drain. "I don't smoke. Neither should you."

Nick realized that the pack of cigarettes had landed in the soldier's yard. The soldier wore fatigue pants bloused into the tops of his combat boots. He also wore a brightly colored yellow T-shirt that was emblazoned with a black Ranger tab and a black baseball cap with a red scroll on the front. So, he was cadre at one of the schools on the fort, Nick surmised. He had apparently been doing pushups or something in his dimly lit garage.

"Hey, man. Sorry," Nick offered lamely. "I got it." He walked over to pick up the discarded pack, and the soldier strolled down to size him up.

As Nick reached for the cigarettes, the soldier's hand flew out and grabbed his wrist. In a moment, he had the arm turned upright, and Nick winced at the uncomfortable contact with his bruised flesh. The soldier then took his left hand and tapped Nick's chin, making the boy look up, bringing his face up into the light. He watched the soldier's eyes slit. "Thought so."

Realizing that the soldier had just assessed all of Nick's visible injuries, Nick felt his cheeks heat in shame. "It's nothin', man."

The soldier's thumb pressed harder on the bruise on

Nick's wrist, and Nick hissed in sudden pain. The soldier said, "Doesn't look like nothing to me. You limp by this house about every other day. I see black eyes and hunched shoulders. Care to explain, kid?"

Nick jerked his arm out of the soldier's grasp and took a step back. The soldier followed him, keeping eye contact. Nick said, "I said it's nothing. I got it. I don't even know you, man."

The soldier cocked his head, then nodded once, sharply. "Don't remember me, then?" He stuck his hand back out, this time extended in an offered handshake. "Staff Sergeant Ahearne, Thomas E. And your name, son?"

Nick stared at the hand the soldier offered in friendship. He slowly extended his own and shook the older man's hand. "Nick." The man did not release his grip, but he did cock an eyebrow. "Nick Williams."

Still holding Nick's hand in his gloved grip, the soldier nodded and said, "You have a strong grip, Nick Williams. So I doubt you're accident-prone. That means you either applied all those bruises to yourself for some insane reason—or else you have a serious bully problem." The soldier stared significantly at the pack of cheap cigarettes. "Either way, I want to help. You willing to give it a shot?"

This soldier was an Airborne Ranger, one of the U. S. Military's elite special forces infantry shock troops. He represented everything Nick aspired to become one day. He had no business even talking to Nick, much less offering him something for nothing.

As the soldier released his hand, Nick felt something in the center of his chest that he hadn't felt in a very long time. It felt sharp and achy, like a saddle burr, an uncomfortable and unfamiliar feeling. In later years he would recognize this feeling as the birth of hope.

"What's in it for you?" Nick challenged.

The soldier smiled an ironic grin. "Well, Nick Williams, that is a very fair question, but I am afraid that at this point in time, you just wouldn't understand the answer. Not that I think you're dumb. You just don't have all the facts. Let's just say I would be paying off a debt there is no other way I can settle. I can't have some kid limping around in front of my house all bruised up and littering up my neighborhood, can I?"

Nick shrugged, and then to his very great surprise, heard himself blurt out, "How can you help me? I don't want any cops involved. If he goes to jail, I got nowhere to go except maybe foster care. I don't want anything to get between me and a solid enlistment after I graduate."

The soldier's eyes darkened, and his expression hardened a little with his unintentional confirmation of the abuse Nick endured at home. "Why don't you come inside, Nick." It wasn't a question. "We'll discuss it over breakfast. Getting some decent food into your body is going to be key in the weeks ahead. I'll introduce you to my wife before she heads over to the hospital for her shift. Maybe she can take a look at you."

He started walking toward his garage. After a few heartbeats, Nick followed. When he caught up, the soldier gave Nick a friendly slap on the shoulder. It made Nick jump as if startled, like a spooked stallion. The soldier nodded again. "PTSD," he observed clinically.

"You're going to be fine, Nick. I think there are some things we can do that will fix your situation and make it just as right as the mail in short order. Tell me something, ever see a movie called *The Karate Kid*?"

The morning Tom had invited Nick to join them at their breakfast table, Patricia Ahearne, Tom's wife, had set a plate of pancakes in front of him. The stack towered in front of him, covered in butter and real maple syrup. She quickly added fresh-squeezed orange juice and strips of turkey bacon, a cup of yogurt, and a tall, ice-cold glass of whole milk.

Nick stared at the feast before him and bit the inside of his lip to keep from shedding a tear. He made no move to reach for his silverware as if waiting for permission, or unsure that all this food was his to take. Patricia said, "We already blessed the meal, lad. Go ahead and eat."

Patricia was a Physician's Assistant who pulled shifts at the Martin Army Community Hospital on Fort Benning. In the next room, Nick heard a little argument between her and her husband. She was saying words like "social services," and he was saying things like, "just give me a month. Then we'll do it your way."

Over the course of the next month, Nick ate better breakfasts and dinners than he ever had before in his entire life. She fed him things he had never even heard of before; corned beef and cabbage and savory stews made with lamb and lentils for dinner; fresh fruit, lean meats, and whole grains with whole milk and juice for breakfast. As Patricia nourished his body and treated his injuries, Nick felt himself growing stronger. His mind cleared of cobwebs and shadows. In fact, he began to see things much more clearly.

Though he refused to acknowledge it, the hope that

had clawed its way into his heart in the Ahearne's front yard that first morning began to grow and blossom as the days passed.

In the afternoons and evenings, Thomas Ahearne instructed Nick in something called close quarter grappling. In addition to holding a few belts in various martial arts, the Staff Sergeant was a U. S. Army Combatives Master Instructor, and Nick became his star pupil. Under the dedicated instruction of Staff Sergeant Thomas Ahearne, Nick learned to ignore inconsequential pain inflicted on his own body and how to leverage his speed and size to deliver pain that could not be ignored to his opponent.

♫ ♫ ♫ ♫

Aria felt a trickle of sweat go down her back between her shoulder blades. Eight minutes into the piece, her arms felt fatigued, and she wondered if she might run out of energy. Hot, unbelievably bright lights beat down on her as she sat at the grand piano on center stage at Atlanta's Symphony Hall and played the third movement of Prokofiev's 8th Sonata, the most complicated piano piece she'd ever played. The music made her think of an ant bed all stirred up while ants scurried to-and-fro putting it all back together. It was a busy, crazy, hard piece to play, and that was exactly why she chose it.

This recital had filled the Atlanta Symphony with over 1,700 people, dressed to the nines in formal attire, watching a concert put on by all of Georgia's most gifted high school musicians. Here, they vied for scholarships from the top music schools in the country. Here, they made their mark as graduating seniors about to enter the adult music world.

Aria was a favorite among the colleges. A brilliant performance tonight would allow her the opportunity to pick any school she wished. She knew where she wanted to go. It was her prayer, as she reached the end of the piece, that a representative from Eastman was in attendance and would be impressed by her choice of music and her skill at playing it.

As she added a flourish to the end and stood to face the audience, her first thought was that her arms felt like rubber, and her stomach muscles ached at her core. Her next thought was one of absolute surprise and amazement as all 1,700 people in the audience surged to their feet in ovation. They clapped and yelled, some even whistled. The whistle made her feel certain that at least one of her brothers had managed to make her recital.

Breathing hard and heavy, she put a hand over her heart and curtsied, bending at the waist. As she straightened, she caught sight of the stage manager in the wings motioning for her to walk toward him. Gracefully, as gracefully as she could in three-inch black heels and the long black gown, she crossed the stage and made her way into the wings.

Even back there, they applauded. Other kids her age, all vying for those scholarships, applauded her and her skill.

"Amazing!" Dr. Bridgett West proclaimed, striding straight up to her. Dr. West, a petite woman with straight black hair cut to her chin and big brown eyes that always looked too big for her face, had instructed her in piano for three years on the recommendation of her tutor from Washington state. Dr. West realized the prodigy she had on her hands within the first week. She encouraged Aria's parents not to let their daughter hold anything back, and worked Aria with a drive that sometimes made the teenager hate the older woman. "I have never heard you play so well. Beautiful job, Aria."

Aria dabbed at the sweat that dripped from her temple and smiled. "I messed up a chord at the Coda."

"I honestly didn't hear it, and you know I'd tell you if I did." She gripped Aria's upper arms, the most physical contact she'd ever given her student. "I am incredibly proud of you."

Nearly a hug and some hefty praise? At that moment, Aria knew she'd done a good job. "Thank you," she said, smiling. "I mean it. Thank you for everything."

"Let's go find your parents. I have a feeling you're going to be getting a lot of phone calls tonight and tomorrow morning."

Giddy, excited, Aria grinned and spun in a circle, tottering a bit in her ridiculously high heels. "I'm so happy this is over." She put her hands to her cheeks and felt the heat. "Do you think I could get some water?"

An hour later, Aria milled through the crowd in the reception area above the lobby. She had left her parents and her brother Henry talking to the director of the school of music for the University of Georgia and made her way to the glass balcony. Down below, on a platform in the lobby, a string quartet from a local high school provided chamber music ambiance while over a thousand people rubbed elbows. Aria smiled as she took a sip from the water glass in her hand and knew, without a doubt, that this was what she wanted in her life. This feeling of euphoria after an amazing performance, concert halls, symphony halls, people dressed in tuxedos and pearls. She loved this.

As she scanned the crowd below, something caught her eye—the flash of perfectly polished brass on a military uniform reflecting the light. Curious, she turned her head until she saw it again, then felt her heart start beating a little faster. Nick?

She rushed toward the staircase and flew down it to the lobby. She'd seen him by the doors. He hadn't left, had he?

She rushed to the entrance and saw him again, in his Army JROTC uniform, hat under his arm, hand on the push bar to exit.

"Nick!" She watched him pause before he turned to look at her. His entire stance tensed as if deciding whether to flee or attack. She nearly skidded to a halt in front of him, quietly cursing the three-inch heels. Even in them, though, the top of her head barely reached his chin. "I can't believe you came!"

Nick looked her up and down, from the toe of her shiny black heels to the top of the blonde hair she had pulled back off of her face with a black ribbon. Around her neck, a strand of pearls gleamed in the light. He'd bet money they were real.

He didn't tell her that from the moment he met her, he'd attended every public concert and recital she'd ever given, including the one at her church. When she'd cornered him at the locker yesterday and nervously handed him a ticket to that night's performance, he'd almost let it slip that he'd seen her play a dozen times already. For some reason, he didn't want to tell her that. Instead, he borrowed a friend's old Volkswagen Bug and limped it from Columbus to Atlanta on borrowed gas money.

"Suarez," he said, calling her by her last name, his voice flat and absent of any emotion, "you did amazing."

He watched her cheeks flush with color. "Thanks." She gestured at him. "Why the uniform?"

Maybe he wanted to shock her. Maybe he just wanted to see what her reaction would be. Maybe he had never lied to her, and he wanted to keep that record intact. "It's the only suit I own."

Whatever his motives, her response surprised him. "It's perfect. My dad wore his dress uniform, too." She leaned forward and whispered. "I think he wanted to sway the more patriotic minded college scouts."

"Any college that doesn't pick you is stupid and not worth your time."

She opened her mouth as if to say something, but closed it again. Then she spoke. "Thank you," she said. "I really appreciate that."

It felt like the air had been sucked out of his lungs. He did not belong here, with these people, talking to this amazingly beautiful and unbelievably talented girl. He put his hand on the push bar to open the door. "I need to get going, Suarez."

"Nick, wait!" She put her hand over his. Suddenly, every nerve ending in his body, every brain cell in his head, every molecule of his being, was focused on that one hand on top of his. A two-hundred-pound man could no longer stop him from moving his arm, but her feather-light touch stopped him dead in his tracks. He froze, not even looking back at her as she spoke. "Please stay. Come upstairs with me. I want to introduce you to my parents. I talk about you all the time."

He looked up through the throng of people in their expensive suits and sequined gowns, wearing earrings and watches that could buy ten of the trailers he lived in and the lot besides. Then he finally looked back down at her. "I don't think so," he said quietly. "Not tonight." He turned his hand so that their palms touched and closed his hand so that it completely engulfed hers. She was so small.

"I'll see you Monday," he said, looking into her brown eyes. Not understanding where the motion came from, but recognizing how right it felt, he brought her hand up to his lips and brushed a kiss over the back of it, maintaining eye contact the entire time. He recognized her surprised look as her eyes widened, and her chest stopped rising and falling. To break some of the tension, he winked and released her hand. "Only a few weeks of school left."

She didn't say a word as he left the building.

Chapter 3

Aria closed her eyes against the bright Georgia sun, feeling it bake into her skin. She was lying in the middle of the track field, half-asleep. What a wonderful feeling, she thought, knowing she didn't have to do anything she didn't want to for the next three months.

She smiled and stretched when a shadow suddenly fell across her. She opened her eyes, startled. Nervous energy slowly replaced the fear when she realized that Nick Williams stood over her. She sat up slowly, brushing the grass out of her hair as she did. She shielded her eyes and looked up at him. "Hey, Nick."

"Suarez." Nick acknowledged, thrusting his hands into his pockets. "Saw you lying out here motionless. Got worried something had happened to you."

"I'm just getting into the summer relaxation mode," she said with a smile. She patted the ground next to her, inviting him to sit.

Nick hesitated, but finally sat next to her on the soft grass, the sun beating down on them. "Why are you out here? School's out now, remember?"

"Carol had to come get some stuff from the band room. I drove her." Aria picked a stem of grass and twirled it in her fingers.

"Big plans this summer?" he asked.

Aria smiled and leaned back on her elbows. "Nothing at all. I'm sleeping until noon every morning, then I'm going to put on a bathing suit, go down to the pool at the NCO Club, and sleep in the sun every afternoon."

"Sounds boring," Nick mumbled.

Aria laughed. "I worked my fingers off for the last ten years to get that scholarship to Eastman. For the first time since I sat down at a piano, I'm taking a break. I plan to relax and catch up on all the sleep I missed for last week's finals before I have to go back to school in the fall." She had graduated third in her class of two hundred. "What about you? What are you doing this summer?"

"Basic training here at the Fort," Nick simply said.

"You aren't going to take the summer off?"

He looked like he wanted to say a lot more than, "Why? I got no money and nothing to keep me here."

Aria shrugged, a little sad that there wouldn't be an opportunity to see him over the summer. She heard a sharp whistle and looked up. Carol waved at her from the school building before she walked toward Aria's car. "I have to go. Two of my brothers come in town today for tonight's graduation, and I'm supposed to pick one of them up from the airport."

She didn't want to leave, though. She wanted to sit here in the warm sun with Nick Williams. Before she realized what happened, Nick reached out and brushed a strand of hair off her cheek. She felt her breath catch in her throat. "Nick—"

"Aria," he said. It was the first time he had ever called her by her first name. Whatever else he intended to say remained unsaid. Instead, he leaned closer to her and pulled her to him. He let his lips brush hers softly, then leaned back and looked into her eyes with his very pale blue and very sad eyes. He stared into her gaze like he was desperately searching for something, maybe the answer to some question he never asked or maybe something he only dared hope to find.

She thought maybe her heart would beat itself out of her chest. He started to pull back, but she grabbed the front of his T-shirt and pulled him to her again.

He kissed her, cupping her cheeks with his hands, the strong, calloused fingers of his right hand supporting the back of her neck while the fingers of his left hand cradled her face so very, very gently. Aria heard a buzzing in her ears, a rush, as he deepened the kiss.

She had wanted his attention for so long, and now, in his arms, it felt so perfect and so right. Continuing to grip his shirt with one hand, she let her other arm go around his neck, trying to bring him even closer to her. Every part of her felt alive. Even her fingertips tingled. Her head spun, and she had no thought outside of the feel and sound and smell of him.

Until he pushed her away. Out of nowhere, suddenly, he stood, hands fisted at his sides. He looked down at her and cleared his throat. "Sorry, Aria. I have to go." He stuck his hands in his pockets and turned away.

"No, Nick. Wait!" Aria demanded, pushing herself to

her feet and running after him. She grabbed his arm, and he spun around.

"Forget it, Aria. I'm out of here tomorrow morning," Nick said. He looked down at her and put his hands on her shoulders. "You don't want me. I'm no good."

Aria felt the tears welling up in her eyes. "Don't say that, Nick. Of course I want you. I always have."

He cupped her cheeks with his hands. "No, you don't. You have better things to do with your life and better men to do them with. Besides, you're so little. I could hurt you so easily," he said. He dropped his hand and turned and walked away from her.

Aria watched him go and felt a tear slip down her cheek, crying for something she had lost that she'd never really had.

♫ ♫ ♫ ♫

Throngs of students in their blue and yellow graduation gowns milled around the football stadium. Graduates took pictures with groups of other students, with parents, with siblings, or with favorite teachers or coaches. Aria smiled with Carol, her brothers, her parents, her entire family—dozens of pictures until she thought her face would permanently stay in that excited "I've graduated!" grin she sported for all the poses.

Finally, she extricated herself, promising her parents she'd be right back. She could see Nick, still in his blue gown, walking away from the crowd.

She kicked off her shoes and ran after him, holding the hem of her yellow gown up, so she didn't trip on it. "Nick!" she yelled, clutching the package. She saw him pause before he kept walking. "I know you heard me. Please wait!"

He turned, a fresh bruise on his cheek shining in the evening sun. "Not now, Suarez. I need to go sign in to my unit. I'm finally free."

She skidded to a stop in front of him. "I know you're going. I just wanted to give you something." She held out the package.

He stared at the small cloth-wrapped square. "What's this?"

Nervous butterflies flew up to her stomach and threatened to cut off her breathing. She felt the hand she held out tremble with nerves. "It's a graduation present, sort of. It's a gift. It's like a tradition. For luck." And love, she added to herself, annoyed that she didn't have the courage to say it out loud.

He finally took it from her. "I don't believe in luck."

Aria sighed, a bit exasperated. "Just open it, okay?"

Giving her a long stare, his blue eyes reflective, he finally pulled the ribbon loose. The handkerchief slid open, revealing the small, palm-sized Soldier's Bible.

When he looked at her again, she nearly took a step back at the intensity of his expression. Instead, she gestured toward her gift. "My dad often said how his favorite gift going into Basic Training was his Soldier's Bible. I hope you don't already have one."

"I—" Nick had never even held a Bible. He looked down at it and looked back at her again before clearing his throat. "I don't. Thank you." He shifted the Bible out from under the handkerchief and held it out. "You can have this back."

Instead of taking it from him, she took his hand in both of hers and closed his fingers over the linen cloth. "That's yours, too. Traditionally, a lady would give the knight of her choosing her handkerchief as a favor before he went into battle. It's like a talisman. A token of her..."

His eyebrows knitted.

"... of her affection for her favored warrior." She was such a coward!

Aria could feel his hand tense under hers as he tightly clutched the handkerchief in his fist. He closed his eyes, and a muscle ticked near his jaw. Finally, he opened his eyes and pulled her to him. Instead of kissing her, like she hoped, he just wrapped his arms around her and hugged her to him.

It felt like they stood that way forever. She leaned into him and inhaled his scent, memorized the feel of his body against hers. Why did it take this long to finally get to this point? Right when he would have to leave?

She felt him rest his cheek on top of her head, and she wondered if she felt as perfect to him as he felt to her. When he spoke, she thought maybe she felt the rumble of his voice before she heard it.

"I'm not who you need."

"You don't know that," she said quietly.

He lifted his head but did not step away. Instead, he cupped her face with his free hand and lowered his mouth to kiss her. It was such a sweet, beautiful kiss that it stole the breath from her chest. She slipped an arm around his neck and tried to get him to deepen the kiss, but he did not. Instead, he broke contact and lifted his head, brushing her hair off of her cheek.

"Goodbye, Aria," he said. He searched her face, for what she did not know, then stepped back and completely broke contact with her.

"Bye, Nick," she said in a whisper.

Without another word, he turned and walked away. Aria watched Nick walk all the way out of her field of vision without so much as a backward glance.

Chapter 4

Mosul, Iraq
Twenty-Three Months Later

The stars had faded, and now an empty palette of light gray spread out above the desert from horizon to horizon, waiting for the strokes from God's brush that would create colors and beauty unlike that found anywhere else in the world. Just on the eastern horizon, the first slash of pink began to work its way through the dark, signaling the beginning of a new dawn. In the blink of an eye, yellow streaks shot through the pink, coming forward like trumpeters heralding the arrival of a king, pushing away the blackness of the night. The colors created a breathtaking image that stretched for as far as the eye could see, and the edge of the horizon began to burn as the white-hot globe inched itself upward.

Sergeant Nick Williams sat on top of his bunker, absorbing every moment of the breaking dawn. The mild fatigue he felt as a result of the late-night mission from which he'd just returned faded away at the sight. He felt light and free and in communion with God.

Nick's first taste of God had come from the Chaplain in Basic Training, who had told him about his Soldier's Bible and showed him how to read it. It had amazed him, in hindsight, how empty he felt until he came to know God. What he discovered was a hunger unlike anything he'd ever experienced, and only the Word of God could sate him. Over the past several weeks since he'd arrived here from Afghanistan, during these quiet moments on this bunker every morning, he had even considered the possibility of becoming a Chaplain himself.

After the war, of course. For now, other things required his attention, training, and expertise.

"Williams!" He turned when he heard his name, then scrambled off the bunker, sliding his Bible into the cargo pocket on his pants leg, right next to the linen handkerchief in which it had first come into his possession. First Sergeant Martinez headed in his direction from the headquarters building. Many men before him had made the mistake of assuming that Martinez was a weak man because he was a short man. It had taken Nick less than a week to learn that Martinez didn't have a weak bone in his body.

"Had chow yet?"

Nick glanced toward the structure that housed the mess hall. "No, First Sergeant."

"Get in there and get some chow. I want you on that prisoner transport in an hour. We aren't keeping him here. Apparently, he's too high visibility a prisoner. Intel squirrels think they'll try to eliminate him rather than risk him talking, so we're shipping him out to Baghdad right away. Since you were instrumental in the mission that brought him in last night, I want you on that transport. They need a gunner."

Nick stopped the grin he felt threatening his cheeks. "Yes, First Sergeant," he barked, then took off at a run. He went quickly through the mess line, grabbing some scrambled eggs and a slice of toast. As he sat down, he thought of the mission the night before, and their unexpected capture of one of the most wanted Iraqis in the nation.

Nick had recognized him, captured him, secured him, and brought him to his commander. He didn't expect to be given credit for the capture. He knew his unit would get the credit, but he didn't think anyone would pay attention to a new member of the unit. They had, and that impressed him. It made him feel really proud of himself, something he rarely had an occasion to feel.

As quickly as he could, he ate breakfast then rushed to the armory, where he secured a flight rigged helmet and side plates for his body armor. He reported to the airfield and hopped on board the double-bladed CH-47 Chinook. The copilot helped Nick and two other gunners strap into the gunners' harnesses and then strapped himself into his seat. Nick positioned himself at the gun and waited. The pilot started the aircraft, and, about five minutes later, two civilians in khaki pants and body armor vests came out of the aircraft hangar escorting a hooded prisoner between them. They were actually wearing brown shirts which made Nick grin a private grin.

The brown shirts did not condescend to speak to Nick as they boarded the aircraft and secured the prisoner. As soon as they gave the all-clear, the pilot took off. The crew chief broke out his M249 SAW and deployed it using snap links on the legs of the bipod to secure it to the lowered ramp. He performed a function check, then lowered himself into a prone position and peered out the back of the aircraft over the gun sites.

The beauty below was not lost on Nick as the helicopter sped across the desert; it was just placed in the background so that he could examine it later. Little stabs of insecurity and maybe a little bit of fear threatened his confidence and initial burst of excitement, but he fought them down. He knew his job, and he did it well, but failure here would mean the loss of lives. Another stab of fear clawed its way to the top, and before he was able to give in to it, the helicopter banked a hard turn and went over a rise. On the ground, about two dozen armored vehicles began firing vehicle-mounted Soviet-built antiaircraft guns at the helicopter.

Nick sighted his gun and began returning fire in conjunction with the other gunners, doing his best to eliminate all the threats. The pilot moved the large craft evasively, but there were just too many of them, and they were under the guns. Nick couldn't get the angle for even a deflection shot most of the time.

"Stinger!" The crew chief announced in Nick's helmet.

When the first turbine took a direct hit from the American made state-of-the-art antiaircraft missile, the pilot banked hard enough to nearly send Nick flying out of the helicopter. Only his harness caught him and kept him from sliding all the way out. Momentarily off his gun, he was unable to stop the enemy combatant below who lifted a machine gun and fired into the aircraft. Nick actually felt bullets whiz by his face and heard the single cry from one of the civilians who took a hit directly in the chest. The medic on board rushed to his side and unstrapped him from his seat, dragging him over to the side where he laid him on the deck of the helicopter. It didn't take him long to stop working on him.

Nick regained his balance and took back control of his gun, returning fire with a roar he unintentionally broadcast over his helmet microphone. The helicopter wobbled and, as the wind shifted, black smoke from the damaged engine blinded him.

Through the helmet speakers, he could hear the pilot and copilot frantically talking to each other and knew they were going down. They were doing their best to get them as far away from the enemy combatants below as possible before they crash-landed. Nick looked out and saw that they were temporarily clear. He looked behind him. The prisoner fought against his restraints. The other civilian, a tall, salt and pepper haired man, struggled to keep the prisoner contained. The door gunner on the opposite side of the aircraft from Nick hung suspended in his harness, dead. The medic kept him strapped to his harness and just secured the slack so that he didn't fall out of the aircraft.

The copilot was broadcasting while the pilot struggled with the large helicopter in an attempt to get them to safety. "Hammer, this is Arrow Four. We are taking fire. I say again, we are taking fire. Hostiles in the area are danger close. I say again this is Arrow Four. Come in, Hammer."

"Arrow Four, this is Hammer Actual. Send sitrep over."

The crew chief announced, "Incoming on our six!"

The pilot simultaneously jinked the entire aircraft and released flares and chaff. The inside of the helicopter filled with blinding light from the flares and the smell of the burning cordite reminded Nick of the fourth of July fireworks the kids in the trailer park usually started setting off in May or June. The missile followed the flares down, and the pilot instantly descended to treetop altitude, hoping to take advantage of ground effect and reflected desert heat.

The copilot picked up his radio broadcast as if nothing had happened, "Roger, Actual. Line 3 is Arrow Four and supercargo listed on manifest. Get with SCIF for itemization. Line 7 is approximately one-four klicks north by northwest of Log Base Zulu, and beacon is hot. Line 8 is a company-sized element with armored vehicles, archie, missiles, and a truckload of small arms. Over."

They never saw the missile come up on the far side of the aircraft opposite Nick. The dead gunner who still hung suspended in his harness never reported incoming. It struck the remaining engine on their blindside, and the turboprops began to slow almost immediately.

The pilot gripped the sticks with both hands and broadcast, "Any station this is Arrow Four. Mayday, mayday. We are going down. Hostiles in the area danger close. I say again this is Arrow Four. Mayday, mayday. We are going down."

The copilot broadcast, "Line 10 we are auto-rotating. Nine line to follow shortly, break."

Nick unhooked himself from the door and rushed to

the rear of the aircraft, taking the empty cargo seat next to the prisoner. Grabbing the back of the prisoner's neck, he forced the man's head between his knees, fighting against him as he struggled.

The pilot interjected, "Brace yourselves!"

"Be still!" Nick yelled in Arabic, using the phrase he'd picked up from the translator in last night's mission. Then he bent at the waist himself and braced for impact.

It felt like the entire world suddenly moved in slow motion. He felt like he could see every molecule in the helicopter. The smell of the smoke burned his nostrils. The blood on the deck from the civilian casualty reflected the sunlight outside. The sound of the whirring blades above barely penetrated the panicked voices of the pilot and copilot echoing in his helmet speakers. The feel of the back of the prisoner's neck against his hand, of the cold sweat and the pounding pulse under his fingers. All of that became crystal clear for a split second before impact. The thirty-thousand-pound beast of an aircraft—with overhead blades moving at well over two hundred miles per hour when they began to splinter and fly apart—struck the ground in stages that Nick felt in the very soles of his boots.

♫ ♫ ♫ ♫

Aria inspected the envelope that had contained the letter. As always, it had no return address, not even a postage stamp. Just the handwritten words FREE APO where a stamp should be. For two years, she'd received letters from Nick Williams, detailing his growing and changing thoughts about God, his feelings about the world, his hopes to one day go into ministry. It thrilled her, this precious contact with him, yet it frustrated her because she had no way of replying to him.

One thing not in the letters—ever—was anything about *them*. No promises for the future. No hopes for serving God together. Aria told herself that the more he wrote to her, the more he thought of her. One day, they'd see each other again in person. Maybe looking at her through the eyes of a fellow believer would remove any of his silly notions about not being the man she needed.

He was all she ever wanted from the first time she ever spoke to him. She couldn't imagine even wanting to spend time with a man other than Nicholas Williams. As far as she was concerned, he just needed to catch up to her way of thinking, and then the two of them could go forward together.

She glanced at the ticket she had taped to her mirror. Aria would perform tonight at the Kilbourn Hall in Rochester. It was her first solo performance since she started school at Eastman. Every time she performed, she got bombarded with phone calls, e-mails, and texts from agents and music industry representatives. However, she had no desire to leave college to pursue a professional music career. Not yet. First, she had other musical aspirations. Having seen them perform, Aria hoped to play with the Rochester Philharmonic Orchestra at the Kodak Hall. Mainly, she wanted to wait; wait for Nick to come back to the States, wait until she graduated, wait until she could talk about her options with him. Because, as far as she was concerned, her future included him, and he had a say in it.

Whenever she had an upcoming concert, she kept a ticket back. In case he just showed up, as she fully anticipated him to do at any time. She just knew the first time she didn't save a ticket for him, he'd need one.

With a grin, she put the letter into the box in which she saved all of his letters. She had to get to class before she was late and then meet her coach for warm-ups before tonight's concert.

♫ ♫ ♫ ♫

The armored vehicles surrounded the crash site. The helicopter had split in half. The fire at the rear of the helicopter would soon force them to evacuate, but the blades still spun dangerously overhead. The survivors would have to move into the open away from the blades, and that meant they would surely die at the hands of the enemy.

The remaining crew and the lone civilian barely held their positions, firing short bursts from SAWs and M-4 carbines while trying to take cover within the burning aircraft as the enemy bore down on them from all sides.

Nick reloaded for what felt like the tenth time and sighted his gun again, but before he began to fire, he watched the pilot lift the copilot to his shoulders in the cockpit across a patch of desert from them. They were very exposed so far from the others. If they didn't get to cover quickly, they would certainly be killed. Nick wondered why they weren't moving until he saw that the man had no legs.

Dear God, Nick prayed, *please protect us, God.*

The pilot struggled to lift his copilot in a fireman's

carry, but it didn't really work out since the copilot's legs had been severed at the knee in the crash.

Apprehension overwhelmed Nick, tightening around his neck like a noose. The pilot looked up and met Nick's eyes. Suddenly, he found his strength again. These men needed Nick. Everyone needed to just hold, just keep fighting, until help arrived. Or else they wouldn't survive this day. With a roar that came from his soul, he sighted his weapon and started firing. Training took over, and the scared kid from Georgia became a soldier again.

As the medic leaped out of the helicopter, Nick saw another vehicle carrying enemy combatants coming over another rise. He called for the crew chief to cover him, and unstrapped, grabbing an M-4 as he jumped out of the burning Chinook. As he ran, he fired in the direction of the enemy and heard the loud and ironically comforting sound of the M249 SAW being fired from the helicopter. He reached the medic, who was trying to apply a tourniquet to one of the copilot's legs.

"We have more company coming. You need to get on board now. Do that there," he yelled to them. "I'll cover you."

The pilot helped the medic lift the copilot to his shoulders, and they ran to the broken Chinook. The new group of enemy combatants reached the high ground and started firing. Nick surmised their operational objectives and priorities. They would either kill every American and rescue their prisoner, or else they would kill the prisoner. In either scenario, they were clearly willing to keep trying until they achieved either outcome or else they all died in the attempt.

Nick found partial cover behind the fractured cockpit of the helicopter and returned fire until his clip ran dry. He managed to pick two of them off before he saw the medic and pilots had made it to relative safety. The pilot waved him forward, and he reloaded and started to run in that direction.

Suddenly, he felt as if a truck had slammed into his chest. His individual body armor deflected the bullet, but the force of the hit knocked him backward. The impact knocked the breath from his body, but years of living with his father trained him to move even then, and he managed to get back on his feet. Thirty feet to go. Thirty short feet, and he was there.

Everything around him moved in slow motion, and the smallest of details seemed so absolutely clear—the brightness of the sun, the insidious grit of the powder-fine sand, the acrid smell of the desert soaking up the spilled aircraft fuel.

Then something ripped his helmet off, jerking his head backward, and it felt as if his whole head had exploded. From the corner of his eye, he saw red blood spatter on the ground, and his helmet landed on top of it then bounced away. Was that his blood?

He put his hand to his head—it took hours to reach up and touch his temple—it came away covered in crimson. He didn't feel his knees give out, but somehow, he was lying on the ground, watching his helmet roll down an incline. The crew chief fired his SAW again, the noise of the rounds vibrating Nick's chest and throat. Then blackness enveloped him.

Chapter 5

The knock on her dorm room door surprised Aria. Her roommate and most of her friends would be in class right now. When she opened the door and saw two officers in military dress uniform, the first thing she thought of was her father.

The very tall black man with the light blue cord around his shoulder spoke first. "Pardon the intrusion, ma'am. I'm Captain Kahan with the 173rd Infantry. This is Chaplain Noble. Are you Aria Suarez?"

The smile melted from her face as her eyes widened. "No, no, no," she breathed, feeling the blood drain from her face.

The Captain looked confused. "You're not Miss Suarez?"

She nodded. "I'm Aria Suarez."

"Miss Suarez?" The Captain stepped forward.

"Daddy?" she whispered. "Is it Daddy?"

The other man with silver crosses of the Chaplain's corps on his shoulders held up a hand and shook his head.

The Captain spoke again. "No, ma'am. As far as I know, your father is just fine. We have the unfortunate duty to inform you of the death of Sergeant Nicholas Williams."

The roaring in her ears blocked out anything else he might have said. "No," she said again, backing up and holding up a hand. "You can't be right. I just got a letter from him today."

The Captain retrieved a green folder with the U. S. Army symbol embossed in gold leaf on the outside of it. He began to quietly read, his voice low but steady, almost calming. "During Operation Arrow Feather, Sergeant Williams was sent to Ramadi, Iraq with his unit and assigned to train Iraqi Army soldiers. Five days ago, Sergeant Nicholas Williams was detailed as a machine-gunner on an aircraft transporting a high-profile prisoner.

"The aircraft was attacked in flight and forced to crash land. During the subsequent engagement with enemy combatants, two crewmen were killed. The copilot was badly injured. Sergeant Williams ran into the open while under continuous insurgent gunfire to help rescue his injured comrade. He personally engaged ten insurgents in that firefight, killing four and injuring six before he, himself, was shot and killed. Due to his valor and selfless sacrifice, his comrades survived and were subsequently rescued.

"We're very sorry, Miss Suarez," the Captain concluded.

The Chaplain stepped forward, "Ma'am, I know this is a shock. Do you have any questions at this time? Is there anything we can do for you? Is there anyone we can for you?"

"He can't be dead," Aria said. "He just can't be. I know he isn't dead. This isn't right."

Chaplain Noble nodded and said, "Miss Suarez, his remains will arrive in Dover tonight, and he will be interred at the National Cemetery of your choosing. In his last will and testament, he specifically asked that you accept his honors. Sergeant Williams was awarded the Purple Heart and the Silver Star, posthumously, for his service in Iraq. He was also awarded the Bronze Star for his earlier service in Afghanistan.

"Were you aware that he left his Soldier's Group Life Insurance entirely to you? You are named as the sole beneficiary. Do you understand?"

Aria's head spun. "What?"

Chaplain Noble handed her an envelope. "He wrote this before he deployed. It was also in his proof of life kit. It's for you."

The letter was addressed to her in Nick's handwriting. There was no doubt. She tore it open and could not read beyond the first line. It said, "Aria. If you are reading this, that means I am dead." She fumbled behind her for her desk chair and collapsed into it as the world in her peripheral vision turned gray.

♫ ♫ ♫ ♫

The sun streamed brightly through the trees that shaded the ceremony spot at the National Cemetery. Aria's mind whirled with the last several weeks... the visit from the captain and Chaplain, finding out she was the benefactor of Nick's will and his life insurance, making the funeral arrangements. She had no idea what to do or how to do it and spent the time relying on her mother to help her with the arrangements while desperately trying to finish the school semester.

Now she sat at his graveside surrounded by her parents, her friend Carol, and a few JROTC friends from high school. In a large military town, it had become almost a common occurrence for a military funeral during the war. Nick Williams was the first combat death from their school, their class, and it hurt now that it was so personal. She watched as if from a distance while the military burial team went through the ceremonial motions.

Aria couldn't believe it. For five years, she'd pined for Nicholas Williams. Now all she had left of him was the urn of ashes she was having interred at the National Cemetery and the precious memory of a few stolen kisses.

Thinking back to their graduation day almost exactly two years ago, she felt her heart twist before actual physical pain from her chest overwhelmed her. She sat on the little folding chair next to her mother and accepted the flag from the white-gloved uniformed man, feeling sobs well up from deep inside her. "On behalf of a grateful nation, we present this flag in memory of Sergeant Nicholas Williams."

She bent, clutching the flag, and rested her forehead on her knee, her whole-body trembling as grief completely overtook her. The officer who had presented the flag came to rigid attention and rendered a parade ground perfect salute. The instant his fingertips touched his temple, seven rifles fired in unison. The loud noise made Aria jump in absolute shock. Then the rifle team fired yet another volley, and she let out a little cry. Her mother patted the back of her hand as the rifle team of seven fired the third and final volley.

No sooner had the echoes of the twenty-one shots died on the hot summer breeze than a lone bugler began to play the long, slow, mournful notes of *Taps*. A deep sob surprised her, and she choked her emotion back.

When her father put his hand on her back at the conclusion of *Taps*, she pulled herself together and sat up. Everyone milled around now, talking about high school Nick because no one present ever knew soldier Nick.

Her mother encouraged her to stand. All she could keep thinking was, What now? Until this moment, when the reality of Nick's death washed over her, she'd always hoped and prayed that her future would be *their* future. What now?

She saw a man enter the courtyard, and her breath caught in the back of her throat. Could it be? Was it Nick?

She rushed toward him, but as she drew closer, she realized that it wasn't Nick but rather an older version of him. Only—darker, angrier. He wore a gray mechanic's uniform stained with black grease, the front unbuttoned to show a dirty and ripped white T-shirt. His unshaven face sported a vicious scowl as he scanned the crowd, then honed in on Aria, the young woman in the black dress carrying the folded flag.

As she approached, he drained a beer bottle and tossed it on the ground. The shattering of the glass on the concrete courtyard silenced the crowd around them.

"And just who are you, then?" he yelled at Aria, approaching quickly. She held her hand up in an almost defensive gesture and heard the sound of her father and brother, John, rushing toward them. "Who are you that you get what's mine?"

"I don't understand what you mean," she said.

"I mean I'm Nick's father," the man said, grabbing her upheld hand and twisting it painfully, the smell of beer on his breath so strong that it made her gag, "and any money you got from that no good fer nuthin' boy ain't yours. It's mine."

Aria yelled aloud as pain rippled up her arm. "You're hurting me," she gasped.

"You don't know what hurt is," he said, twisting. The crack of bone sounded like it echoed around her even louder than the rifle shots from before. The pain sent her to her knees just as her father tackled the man.

Chapter 6

Portland, Oregon
Present Day

Aria made the mistake of watching the morning news. The lead story was about a military transport that had crashed just outside of Joint Air Base Lewis-McChord, killing all thirty-one American service members on board. The flag-draped coffins on her television screen had instantly taken Aria back to that terrible day ten years ago when she had buried Nicholas Williams. That day had changed the very course of her life in so many ways. Thoughts of how her life had changed and what lay before her filled her mind during her morning run.

She jogged up the street to her little bungalow nestled in the trees just a block away from the Willamette River. She always felt a sense of calm and relief when she saw her home. The stress of work, the demands and pressures of a project, it all melted away when she curled up on her front porch swing and listened to the birds cry to each other from high above. An easy walk or jog down to the waterfront could provide shopping, food, entertainment, people, or solitude—anything she could wish for. Even her church was just two short blocks from her door, built out of beautiful cedar, and tucked away in Oregon greenery.

Aria pulled the key out of her armband and opened the front door. She'd spent three years worth of weekends remodeling and redecorating her home. Hardwood floors gleamed in the bright sunlight streaming through the big bay window of the main room. Where a wall once separated that room from the second bedroom, now one large room housed a baby grand piano that sat on a platform in a nook. Against the far wall, a small couch and wing-backed chair surrounded a low coffee table in front of a stone fireplace. A small, delicate desk was against the wall opposite the door, and her laptop sat closed on top of it.

She moved through the room and into the kitchen. It was long and narrow, the length of the house, with a large wooden table at one end. The entire wall was glass and looked out at the woods behind the house. The small kitchen sat at the other end of the room, with white cabinets and white counters. She reached over the bar and pressed the button to start the coffee, grabbed the bottle of water she'd left out before her run, then left the kitchen and headed for her bedroom. A glance at her watch told her she only had about an hour before she had to be at work. She still needed to review her notes before her ten o'clock meeting. Since nothing could leave the office, she didn't have the ability to work from home in any capacity.

After she got out of the shower, she powered on her computer. While her laptop booted up, she went back to her room and quickly threw on a blouse and skirt.

She returned to the front room and sat at the computer. She activated the program she had written to hide her IP address and the MAC address of her computer. Even with the three levels of encryption she randomly employed, Aria knew that whoever was on the other end of the e-mail she sent would be able to eventually trace her, but she didn't want to make it too easy.

She accessed the e-mail account she'd set up under a ghost name, and her hand shook a little on the mouse when she saw that she had incoming mail. She opened the mail folder and pulled up the message.

We need proof of your suspicions before we can proceed.

That was it? It had taken her two months to work up the courage to do this, it took them a week to write her back, and this was the response that she got? She clicked the icon to reply and sat there with her fingers poised over the keyboard. What did she say now? Inspiration struck her, and she typed the message and sent it before she could change her mind.

I have proof. You have to meet me in person to see it. You don't want to pass this up.

Aria sat back in her chair and stared at the computer screen for a few minutes. What if they called her bluff? She had hard proof, but national security didn't allow her to take anything in or out of the secure facility where she worked. She'd hoped she could be interviewed in some clean conference room by some suited agents of the government, and *they* could go collect evidence. What could she do? She then leaned her head back and closed her eyes, offering a quick prayer for continued courage and a touch of wisdom or inspiration. She was nervous and more than a little scared. What happened next had the ability to affect her entire career.

She rubbed her wrist, trailing a finger over one of the fine scars left behind by a talented surgeon. Then she shook her head and pulled herself out of her reverie. Speaking of her career, she had a meeting in too short of a time to be sitting there staring off into space. She pushed herself out of her chair and gathered her purse and car keys. As she left her house, she paused to look back at her main room, her eyes trailing over the piano sitting in the corner. Releasing a heavy sigh, she shut and locked the door, then raced to her car.

♪ ♪ ♪ ♪

"Hey, Benson. How's that new grandkid of yours?" Aria asked. She had pulled up to the security gate leading to the main parking lot of NWT, Inc. She had just celebrated her fourth anniversary with the company. The acronym stood for Northwestern Technologies, but the common joke around the cafeteria was that it stood for "Nuclear War Trappings" or "Nit Wit Takeover."

"Pretty as a picture, Dr. Suarez. I tell you, after three sons, granddaughters are like a breath of fresh air," Benson said, taking her ID badge and scanning it. The little handheld device gave her clearance, so he returned her badge and stepped back away from her car. "Have a good day, Dr. Suarez." Proper procedure would have him look in the trunk of her car, but he didn't. Aria was counting on all the little skips in security procedures.

She smiled and waved back at him, then drove into the parking lot. The clock on her dash told her she didn't have time to go to her office before the meeting, so she called her secretary, Julie, from the parking lot and asked her to bring her laptop to the administrative building. She tossed her phone onto the car seat, locked the car, and headed in the direction of the security building that provided a gateway into the facility.

Because she often came in so much later in the morning than a lot of the employees there, she rarely had to wait in line at the security station. It was usually very quick, with an X-ray to scan any purses or lunch bags that came into the facility, and a metal detector body scan. This morning, Aria only had to wait in line behind three people, and while there, she chatted with Dave, the head of security.

"Morning, Dave. Did I see your boat out on the Willamette last night?"

"You sure did, Doc. It was a beautiful night."

Aria set her purse on the conveyor belt for the X-ray machine. "I know. I ate dinner at the Fresh Catch Restaurant next to the dock. I love spring. I'm looking forward to the dry summer months."

"That eastern blood of yours isn't used to all this wet now, is it?"

"It rained a few times in New York," she said with a smile as she walked through the metal detector. With the all-clear, she picked her purse up on the other side of the X-ray machine.

She left the security center and headed straight for the main administration building. In the main lobby, an armed guard checked ID cards and gave clearance to those allowed passage. He knew her and chatted with her while he checked the list for the morning's meeting, then handed her a security badge that would allow her access to the floor where the meeting would be held. To save time, she used the elevator instead of her standard run up the staircase. When she arrived on the third floor, she showed the temporary badge to another security guard and informed him her secretary would be arriving with her laptop.

She entered the conference room and stopped short when she saw Peter Harrington already seated at the table. He wasn't on the list of attendees she'd seen yesterday, and she hadn't been prepared to see him. She'd managed to maintain a *façade* of calm for two months now. She didn't understand why, in the final decision last week to report what she knew, she suddenly felt nervous. Nothing had changed.

Except for everything.

Just as she was about to go greet him, Julie rushed in carrying her laptop. Aria intercepted her, whispering a desperate, "Thank you," when she took it from her. The pale, brown-haired, very pregnant woman smiled back with a wink, then left the room.

Aria's hands trembled slightly when she set her computer down, but she kept her face composed. Peter would expect her to go straight to him, so she dredged up a warm smile and sat next to him.

He had a lean face with thin, dark hair that he wore

rather short. His dark-rimmed glasses made his brown eyes look intense. He wasn't very tall, maybe five-six, and had a lean, runner's body that saw regular workouts.

She had started dating him about nine months ago. While she was the project manager, Peter was in charge of the administrative and security portion of her project, along with three other projects at the facility.

Despite being fifteen years her senior, he had thoroughly charmed her and spent a year asking her out. She started off just sharing a lunch break with him, but the more time they spent together, the more comfortable she felt until she was a regular part of his weekends with his daughter and an occasional date with just the two of them. Peter never pressured her for any kind of intimate relationship, and that relieved her because she truly wasn't interested in one.

Until recently, the biggest problem she had with him was that despite his profession of faith, he didn't seem to live as a man of faith. She never saw him pray, he never engaged her about discussions of the Bible, and he did not attend his own church. It made her hesitant to pursue any furthering of their relationship beyond just an intimate friendship. Additionally, for whatever reason, he didn't act like that bothered him.

"Hi, Peter. How was the visit with your daughter?" she asked.

"She wants to get her belly button pierced," Peter said with a dry humor that had helped spur Aria's initial attraction to him. "Unfortunately, there isn't a whole lot I can say about it, because her mother got hers done last year." He pulled the carafe of coffee towards him and poured each of them a cup. "What can you do with a fifteen-year-old?"

Aria didn't pick up the cup. Her hands weren't quite steady enough yet. "I imagine that it's hardest when both parents aren't on the same page."

He took a sip of his coffee and looked at her over the rim. "I wouldn't know any other way, sadly."

"I know. I have no experience with broken families, but looking at it from the outside, I imagine it must be so hard."

One of the project leads interrupted her to tell her good morning and ask about an e-mail that had gone out the day before. As they finished speaking, she realized the room had filled with men until every chair at the table, and most seats against the wall were taken.

She looked at her watch, then moved to the head of the table. As she connected the projector cable to her laptop, she smiled at the room full of rocket scientists. "Gentlemen, shall we begin?" She nodded to an associate near the door, who dimmed the lights for her. "I just want to begin by saying that our testing last week was amazing. I think we all deserve a round of applause."

While the team gave each other an ovation, Aria clicked a few keys on her laptop and pulled up a report that projected onto the screen. "One of the chief complaints during proving trials was the weight of the pack. As sympathetic as I am to those who would have to handle it for transport, the user will be in zero gravity, so I don't think the issue is going to require changing anything in the design."

A question came from someone at the table. "Isn't

weight an issue during launch?"

Aria shrugged. "I imagine it is. But our specs don't ask for a pack that weighs a specific amount. At this point, I'm sure they're thinking it was an oversight in the specs. I bet Peter can speak to that," she said, gesturing in his direction, "and they may eventually issue a change order. But for now, our mission is simply to design a working pack, and as far as the results look on my end, we are so very nearly there that the tweaking should be minimal."

Peter sat forward. "It's too late in the project to make any major changes, but the issue NASA has is that it costs about $10,000.00 per pound of payload to get anything into space. You guys are better at math than me so you can see how quickly that will add up in terms of tax dollars, so you can expect a change order. A change order will ultimately cost less than delivering the system as is. Bottom line, if there's any way to cut weight now, without cutting corners, and it fits into your hours and project plans, you may want to get ahead of the inevitable change order."

Aria said, "The nuclear material is going to weigh what it weighs, and additional shielding is going to add weight, not subtract."

Peter nodded. "I don't disagree with you. The priority is shielding. We have to keep the astronaut safe, and if that means we add weight, then so be it. All I'm saying is we should all remain cognizant of the weight issue moving forward. Lighter is going to be better. So, what is the progress of the shielding? Any good news to report to the government?"

Aria clicked a button and pulled up another chart

showing radiation leakage. "This is over a six-hour period. As you know, these numbers in a single exposure aren't dangerous, but with long term exposure, we could be looking at some issues. We need to figure out how to tweak it to get these numbers down further. We have RFIs out to JPL and DoE that they haven't answered, so we'll follow up on that this week."

With a gesture toward the associate by the lights, she shut her laptop lid and spoke as the lights came up. "This is intended to be a brainstorming session since we know the design best. Keeping weight considerations in mind, if you have any ideas at this point, I'm opening the floor to suggestions."

♫ ♫ ♫ ♫

After Raymond Williams broke her wrist at his son's funeral, any future Aria could have looked forward to as a musician vanished; permanently destroyed. While only a highly trained ear could distinguish the difference in the quality of her present skill from her ability before the assault, her dominant hand simply no longer had the stamina needed to perform professionally.

It had taken Aria an entire semester to face that fact, and the two additional surgeries on her wrist only fully confirmed it. She had some hard decisions to face on her twenty-first birthday, the first being, "What now?"

Now no future with Nick. Now no future in music. Her entire life plans and expectations disappeared in a short six-month span.

She spent hours praying about it, trying to battle resentment, trying not to feel angry. Good things had come out of it, and she clung to that. During his time in jail for the assault, Raymond Williams sobered up for the first time in his adult life.

He experienced such remorse for hurting Aria, and for the years of abuse his own son had suffered at his hands, that he willingly sought God. With Aria's father and oldest brother John present, he gave his life to Christ. He left the jail, then went straight into rehab and never drank again. Now he volunteered at a children's home, teaching teenaged boys how to work on car engines, trying to make up for abusing Nick by helping as many boys as he could.

Aria clung to that. Every boy he mentored and helped was one more reason she accepted her new future. Seeing the difference Raymond Williams was able to make reminded her that even if she couldn't play professionally, she could still play in ministry and for personal enjoyment and relaxation.

In the meantime, Aria reluctantly left the School of Music and was accepted into the School of Science and Engineering where she bounced between a computer major and a math major, and finally decided to study engineering. She'd changed her major so many times that it should have taken her five years to earn her degree. Instead, she sweated and studied and cried and prayed, and didn't take a summer off ever again, then ended up graduating not only with her class but near the top of her class.

Four years later, in pursuit of her Ph.D., Aria had published several times. In one article, she had taken on jet propulsion principles in a vacuum. Part of her thesis dismantled and corrected an opposing hypothesis published in a widely distributed scientific trade and academic magazine by a well-respected name in the field. During the last few weeks of finishing up the requirements for her doctorate, a Washington D. C. based hiring manager with Northwestern Technologies Incorporated read her article, realized it was spot on, and promptly offered A.C. Suarez an interview.

Three days after receiving her doctorate in nuclear engineering, Aria packed her bags and left Rochester, New York behind for Portland, Oregon. The people in Portland had been a bit surprised to learn that A.C. Suarez wasn't a man, but was actually a petite blonde who looked a lot closer to eighteen-years-old than her true twenty-six-years-old. Still, after a weekend of intense interviews and pretty hard-hitting questions, and with the contract with NASA needing an out-of-the-box thinker, they shook her hand, offered her an impressive benefits package, and hired her.

NWT Incorporated designed and manufactured nuclear technology, primarily weapons technology, for the United States Government. After the end of the Cold War, most of their focus centered around improving the current technology they had already developed in order to maintain or renew their patents. In the wake of nonproliferation, the time for the mass production of nuclear weapons had passed. Now, the nuclear powers of the world wanted the most advanced weapons, rather than the highest number of weapons.

Aria's department had nothing to do with weapons technology. Instead, she worked on a contract for NASA, working to develop technology that would help astronauts working outside of a spacecraft or space station—called extra vehicular activities or EVA—work longer, more productive hours in greater comfort and safety. She worked with nuclear technology to create a nuclear power source that could be worn by any person who could then power and operate the suit safely and for a much greater period of time than the current technology allowed. With a small nuclear-powered pack, and with less need for fossil-fueled power, more room could be dedicated to oxygen in the suit, and give the astronaut much more productive time in the suit.

The technology they worked on was classified higher than Top Secret in an already secure facility. The people who worked there were an extremely closely-knit group of exceptionally trained specialists, and Aria currently headed a small team that specifically concentrated on the shielding of the device to protect the person wearing it from any kind of possible radiation dangers.

It had taken weeks to break into the good-old-boy network at NWT. It actually ended up being a lot easier than she originally anticipated. Once people started reconciling the A.C. Suarez who had burned up the industry with her many articles with the woman who worked tirelessly alongside them, they started trusting her.

In a year they made more progress than they had in the previous three years. Within two years, testing on both the power pack and the shielding showed real promise.

"Aria, Peter Harrington is on line three," her secretary, Julie, said from her office. Aria took off her reading glasses, gritted her teeth, and put a smile in her voice.

"Hello, Peter," she said.

"Aria, I tried to catch you after the meeting this morning, but you disappeared before I could. I was wondering if you were free for dinner tonight?"

Aria held the phone in place with her shoulder and rubbed her hands over her arms, trying to ward off the chill she felt. "Sure, as long as we make it an early night. I have a deadline on an article for *Popular Science*."

"Still writing for that science fiction magazine, are you?"

She forced herself to chuckle. "As long as they pay me for my unclassified opinion, I'm game."

Peter cleared this throat before suggesting, "Why don't we meet at the deli on the corner of your street, then?"

"Sounds good. I'll see you there around seven." She hung up the phone feeling grateful that he wanted to meet her there instead of picking her up. That meant he wouldn't have to drive her home, and she could easily beg off and make it an early night.

Chapter 7

Aria let herself into her house, rubbing her temples to ward off the headache that had started the moment she walked into the deli. She had never been very good at lying, and the stress of keeping her smile and laughing at jokes had worn on her over the last hour.

She found her phone where she had accidentally left it sitting on the kitchen counter. She checked it and saw some missed calls. While she put on the kettle for tea, she accessed her messages, annoyed with herself for forgetting it in the first place.

"Aria, this is Henry. You haven't called in two weeks. Call me back tonight, or I'll call you at five tomorrow morning." Aria grinned, knowing he probably would call her that early. She deleted the message as she moved into the bedroom and started unbuttoning her blouse.

"Aria, this is Adam. They loved the soundtrack you wrote. Check your calendar and shoot me a text to let me know when you're free to come down here and sign contracts."

She paused at her bed with a huge smile on her face, her blouse half unbuttoned. One blockbuster movie at a time, her brother Adam was taking Hollywood by storm. She was so proud of him. He always offered her the opportunity and right of first refusal to compose the soundtracks for his films. She'd done it twice now and couldn't believe how much she loved it.

Conducting the orchestra for the recording was an experience she never imagined she'd have. Writing and conducting were not her focus in school. She'd taken classes, of course, but she'd thought she just wanted to play the piano. She never considered the thrill of direction.

She put her hands to her cheeks and grinned then spun in a little circle. They *loved* her soundtrack!

The whistling of the tea kettle interrupted her spontaneous celebration, so she rushed to the kitchen and turned the stove off. She dug through her basket of tea and settled on a spearmint tea. She grabbed a cup and opened the bag, then splashed the boiling water over the bag.

Carrying the cup, she turned off lights and locked doors and windows on her way to her room. Once there, she set her cup on her nightstand next to the alarm clock. She finished unbuttoning her blouse and slipped on a pair of comfortable pajamas. As she took a sip of hot tea, she played her last voice mail message.

The voice caused her to flash back ten years. "Aria, um, hey, this is Carol Mabry. Henry gave me your number. I hope you don't mind. Anyway, I'd really love to talk to you and catch up. Please call me, whatever time you get in. I don't mind the time difference. I'm usually up working late anyway. Okay. Well, bye for now."

Aria sat on the edge of the bed, rested her elbows on her knees, and put her head in her hands. Carol Mabry. They hadn't seen each other or spoken to each other since right after Nick's funeral. Aria never could fully explain the feelings she had for a man who had never—in his lifetime—reciprocated her feelings in the first place, and she didn't know how to defend them. Carol had never understood the depths of Aria's mourning for Nick. She even accused her of using her grief to get attention.

Aria felt betrayed by her friend's criticism and lack of understanding. They'd had a big argument, and the two drifted apart. Aria hadn't thought of Carol in years.

What could she be calling about now? Aria replayed the message. She scrolled through her missed calls and found Carol's number. Carol had the same area code as her brother Henry.

Had Carol become an attorney as she'd always wanted? Had she married the boy from college she'd dated a few times? Did she still play the violin?

Suddenly, Aria couldn't wait to call her. The years seemed to melt away as she thought back to three years of high school and two years of college with Carol Mabry as her best friend. She had so much to talk about and tell her about. The job at NWT, remodeling her cottage, playing in the church orchestra, and even her broken engagement with Brandon Laramore.

She scrolled through the call log again, but as she found Carol's number and started to hit send, the phone in her hand rang, startling her. She answered it on the second ring.

It was Henry, and they talked for an hour. Aria

yawned into her hand as they hung up. Checking the time, she made a mental note to try to give Carol a call the next day when it was not so late on the east coast.

♫ ♫ ♫ ♫

Aria heard the alarm going off, but buried her head under the pillow, ignoring it. She hated waking up, especially on a day like today, when she planned to pilfer top-secret classified information from her office.

Finally, unable to take the constant buzzing, she sat up and reached over to turn the alarm off, forcing herself to stay in the sitting position. Why they had rescheduled the weekly staff meeting to nine o'clock instead of the regular two o'clock remained a mystery to her.

She went to the kitchen and turned on the coffeepot, then pulled on a pair of shorts and a tank top. With the change in the meeting time, she would only be able to run two miles that morning, a fact which only served to worsen her mood. It was her normal day for five miles.

Her annoyance with the disruption of her schedule and her anxiety over what she planned to do, spurred her to run faster than usual. Within fifteen minutes, she arrived back at her house.

She showered and ignored the brewed coffee, deciding to have a cup of Irish breakfast tea instead. The idea of eating made her stomach turn, so she went ahead and prepped for the day. Nervous butterflies in her stomach made her hands unsteady as she packed her purse. She kept going over the step-by-step motions she would need to go through to successfully sneak technology into a highly secure government contractor facility then smuggle information out.

She packed her lunch, careful to keep everything the same as she always did. Tuna salad, ice pack, whole wheat crackers, apple, yogurt, coffee in her coffee mug. Would they search her? When was the last time they searched her? A month, maybe longer? If they searched her, would they find it?

The drive to work felt interminable, traffic a little heavier, and her fellow drivers more intense than usual. All the while, she prayed, whispering helpless prayers to God, knowing she couldn't do this alone.

At a stoplight, with her windshield wipers swiping off the morning drizzle in a regular staggered pattern, she put her forehead on the steering wheel and closed her eyes. Why did they need proof first? Why couldn't they just call her into some cushy little FBI field office and interview her?

If she'd never held her hand up to Raymond Williams, he never would have had the opportunity to snap her wrist. She often had dreams of him just punching her in the face instead. She would have sported a black eye like a badge of courage and still gotten to play on the stage at the London Symphony in a sequined gown and a stunning pair of red-soled Jimmy Choo high heels.

The tooting honk of the car behind her brought her back to reality. Reality reminded her of the imminent danger government leaders of these United States faced if she didn't follow through. Pulling her mind back in, regaining the focus she needed to get through the day, she smiled at Benson as she pulled up to the gate and spent her standard few seconds chitchatting with him as he inspected her ID card. She wondered if her smile looked as fake to him as it felt to her.

After she parked her car, she grabbed her purse and her ceramic travel coffee mug—that contained no metal specifically so that it wouldn't set off the metal detectors. She retrieved her lunch box from the back seat, then locked her doors and rushed to the security line.

The eight-thirty crowd was way larger than the nine-thirty crowd. Aria checked the time often, watching the minutes tick by. She finally got up to where she could put her bags on the belt of the X-ray machine.

"You're in early this morning, Dr. Suarez," Dave observed as he took her badge.

"Rescheduled staff meeting. Big east coast suit on the VTC, apparently." The guards would know if anyone was due to arrive in person but had no knowledge of who joined the video teleconferences. She looked at her watch and waited for her turn to step through the metal detector. "I am in so much trouble if I'm late."

The guard on the other side of the scanner waved her forward. She rushed through, and a red light started flashing as an alarm rang. Aria felt her face fuse with color and turned as Dave approached. Aria set her coffee cup next to her purse then put her hands on her thighs and patted. From her pocket, she retrieved her car keys and did her best to look embarrassed, not terrified. "Dave, I'm so sorry. I forgot to put them in my purse."

"Not a problem, Doc. Just go on back through, please." He extended a hand politely toward the metal detector. Clearly, it wasn't a request. Ignoring her steaming hot coffee cup, Dave placed her keys into a small tray and ran them through the X-ray machine while Aria rushed back around the metal detector, then walked through it again, this time to a green "all clear" light.

"All set, Doc," he said, smiling and nodding before his attention went to the next person in line.

Snatching up her purse, lunch box, and her coffee cup, she waved at him. "Thanks Dave! I'm so sorry!"

She left her lunch box at the guard's station in the lobby of the administration building, and after going through all the procedures and check-ins, she arrived five minutes late to the meeting. She sat in the back of the conference room and offered little input.

All of the details of her plan's execution this afternoon kept swimming in her head. She must have glanced at her watch three times during the hour, and caught her director, Tom Curtis, watching her with a frown on his face. She decided she should probably pay a little more attention to the meeting and turned to watch the speaker.

As soon as the meeting ended, she retrieved her coffee cup from which she had not taken so much as a sip, then grabbed the stack of papers in front of her and left, not stopping to speak with anyone. When she got back to her office, she shut the door. It wasn't uncommon for Aria to work on a difficult project, and when she shut her door, Julie knew she was off-limits unless a family member called. Aria typically didn't like to have her concentration interrupted.

This morning she took a roll of paper towels out of her credenza. She unrolled several and created a little pallet on her desk, then opened the lid to her coffee cup and reached inside the now cooled liquid and pulled out a small disposable cell phone that had been wrapped in three layers of plastic baggies and jammed into her coffee.

She'd already turned off the wireless card on the phone. If it tried to access any kind of wireless network or send any kind of signal out, it would have been detected instantly, and automated geolocation protocols would have led to her discovery. She didn't need it to be a phone. All Aria needed was the camera and the scanner application she'd written and installed on it.

She went to her filing cabinet and pulled out a file she'd started two months earlier. She whispered a quick prayer and started scanning documents. About halfway through the first page, she realized that if she were going to back out, if she were not going to commit a federal crime punishable by up to twenty years in a federal penitentiary, she could stop what she was doing right now. The thought of so blatantly breaking the law gave her some pause, and she felt her heart race for the hundredth time that day.

She took a deep breath, said a somewhat longer prayer, and then got back to work. It was tedious scanning one page at a time, but she had absolutely no other way to do it. No machine in the facility had a plug for any kind of external or backup drive. She could hack one of the boxes and possibly hand-wire a drive, but she didn't know how fast she could do that, and the threat of discovery was much greater than doing it this way. Instead, she tediously scanned a single page at a time.

When she'd copied the entire file, she shredded two pages, put the others back in the folder, and jammed it back into her filing cabinet. She would shred two pages at a time until she had rid herself of the printouts so as not to draw any attention to the amount of waste in her shredder.

Turning to her computer station, she accessed a list of files she'd made the day before and opened them up, one at a time, on the three computer screens at her desk. Using the video capabilities of the phone, she shot a video and, as quietly as possible, gave brief explanations of what she recorded.

It took her about three hours to fill the phone's memory with all of the information she needed. When she finished, she removed the micro-SD card from the phone. She opened her wallet and took out the fake quarter, slid it open, and placed the micro card inside the compartment and closed the quarter. It now looked and felt like a real coin.

Her tasks complete, she wrapped the phone back into one of the plastic bags and set it on the ground next to the leg of her heavy desk. She lifted the desk and let it fall onto the phone. She repeated this five times, moving the phone a few inches with her toe each time, cracking the case and motherboard pretty thoroughly. Once it looked entirely crushed under the force of the impact, she retrieved it and divided the pieces into the three plastic bags, wrapped them up in crumpled paper, and put them in the pocket of her lab coat. After grabbing her keys out of her top desk drawer, she unlocked a drawer in her credenza, grabbed her lab security badges, and left her office.

Julie sat sorting printed documents at the table in the outer office. "I'm going to run to the lab if anybody needs me, Julie. But I'm not expecting any calls."

"No problem, Dr. Suarez. I'll be here until at least four." She rubbed her pregnant stomach. "God willing."

"Yes, please. I need at least another week out of you," she teased, then left her office.

She tossed one of the packets with the pieces of the phone into the garbage can of the break room of her building, which overflowed with breakfast and lunch refuse. She left the building and walked along the sidewalk toward the laboratory, stopping at a smoking area where three benches surrounded a combination ashtray and garbage can. She deposited another baggie there.

Outside the lab building, she threw away the last piece as nonchalantly as possible. When she entered the lab, she smiled at the guard, showed him her credentials, then went to her section of the building.

Chapter 8

Aria slept until ten Saturday morning. She was relatively free to set her own schedule during the workweek, but between morning meetings and the regular jogging schedule she'd set for herself, she still had to get up earlier than she liked every weekday morning. On Saturdays, she never made any plans before noon.

Once she was up and functioning, she decided to tackle cleaning her home. Her schedule was usually so busy during the week that she tended to ignore the clutter. It took a few hours. When she finished, she sat down on her couch—guilt-free—with an organic root beer and her laptop, all set to work on her article for the rest of the day.

An hour later, the telephone startled her out of her essay on jet propulsion analytics using an unconventional power source in a vacuum, and she absently answered. "Hello?"

"Aria, it's Peter. I unexpectedly have Becky for the weekend and wondered if you were interested in pizza and a movie." Becky was Peter's fifteen-year-old daughter. While Peter constantly bragged about his daughter, he never spoke of his ex-wife. Never. Aria wasn't even sure of the woman's name.

Aria bit her lip. She had no desire to spend any more time with him ever again. Except that she knew she had to keep acting as if everything were normal until she heard back from the FBI. "That sounds good. I'm working, but I can spare a few hours, I guess. What time do I need to be ready?" she asked.

"We'll pick you up about... six, maybe? The movie starts at eight-fifteen, so we'll have time to enjoy our meal. She wants to go back to that one place, you know," Peter explained.

"Yeah. Great cheese bread. Okay. I'll be ready. Thanks for calling, Peter." Aria hung up. She still had a few hours, but try as she might, she found she couldn't refocus on her article. Instead, she went to her piano and slid onto the bench.

Not bothering with sheet music, she just played from her heart, her hands and fingers slowly moving across the keys. What poured out was a melodramatic, haunting melody that ended up making the hairs on the backs of her arms stand up. Determined to change the mood all around her, she played a couple of quick show tunes, an old kids' nursery rhyme, and a worship song.

Restless, she grabbed her keys and wallet and left the house, stopping to lock the door behind her. She lived within walking distance of the Willamette River and an eclectic collection of tourist shops and seafood restaurants. The sun was warm, but the breeze blew wintery cold, so she was glad she'd worn a hoodie sweatshirt and a pair of jeans.

She walked down to the dock that served as the front walkway for the Willamette Fresh Catch Restaurant. Arriving after lunch but before dinner made for a light crowd on a spring Saturday afternoon, and Aria opened the wooden door to the familiar sound of the bell jingling announcing her arrival. As her eyes adjusted to the interior, she heard her name on a squeal. "Aria!"

With a grin, she hugged the apron-clad waitress. "Hello, Steph. How's the day going?"

"Busiest lunch in months," Stephanie said, stepping back and gesturing at the very casual environment. "We're going to end up needing extra help over the summer if business keeps growing."

"You and Brandon deserve it." She followed Stephanie Laramore into the back of the room near the kitchen door, where she had set up one of the tables as a work station to roll silverware into cloth napkins. Steph sat down, and Aria sat across from her.

The door to the kitchen opened, and a man with a shock of red hair and a red goatee stuck his head out. "Steph, I'm calling the produce guy. Can you think of anything you need to add to your list?" He looked from his wife to Aria and smiled, then came fully into the dining room. "Aria, hi there."

She returned his smile. "Hi, Brandon." She and Brandon met on the dock one day right after she moved to Portland. He'd flirted with her from the deck of his fishing boat while she leaned against the railing of the pier. They'd dated for months, and for about six weeks, they were engaged.

Once Aria started to launch into wedding plans, though, she felt more and more uneasy. It occurred to her one Saturday evening, sitting with him on deck chairs on his boat, that as much as she liked him and respected him and enjoyed his company, she didn't love him. When she told him that, he later admitted he'd felt relieved.

They stayed friends, though, and a few weeks later, he met Stephanie. Aria couldn't believe how beautiful the two of them were together, and in no time, they were married.

"What exciting plans do you have scheduled for today?" Brandon asked, grabbing a chair from another table and straddling it as he placed it next to Steph. He wore a white apron over his T-shirt and jeans and had a kitchen towel slung over his shoulder.

"I'm writing an article on jet propulsion analytics in a vacuum." She grabbed a fork and butter knife and tightly rolled them into a napkin.

"You rocket scientists and your need to get wild," Brandon observed.

"You know us; party, party, party." She tossed the flatware roll into the plastic bin and grabbed another set. "I guess I'm going with Peter to see a movie later."

Brandon frowned, looking skeptical. "You still seeing that guy?"

Aria shrugged. "I don't see it lasting much longer. He still won't go to church with me."

Steph rolled two sets of silverware to Aria's one. "I think you're hanging on for the kid," she said with a smile.

"I don't think so. She knows her dad uses me for a

buffer, so she resents it a little bit." Aria longed to tell them what was going on, but she couldn't. Maybe one day.

"Want some coffee?" Brandon offered. "It's pretty fresh."

Aria tossed another wrapped silverware packet on the pile and stood. "No, thanks, Brandon. I need to get back to my article. I just stepped out to clear my head."

Steph grinned. "Have fun on your hot date tonight."

Aria laughed. "You know I will." She lifted a hand in a wave. "I'll see you tomorrow at church."

"Bye, friend," Steph said, then turned to her husband. "Do you have the produce list? I'll look at it and make sure I didn't forget anything."

Aria walked through the restaurant, smiling. When she stepped back outside into the warm sun, she contemplated just strolling down the street and enjoying the Saturday afternoon. Except that her article beckoned and the deadline loomed, so she turned back toward home.

♫ ♫ ♫ ♫

The next morning, Aria dressed for the weather and walked to church in the rain. She wore pants, brown leather boots that had been waterproofed, and a rain jacket over a cream-colored sweater. Instead of an umbrella, she tucked up her blonde hair and threw on a rain hat.

She enjoyed her small groups class. She was in a group with eleven other single, professional women. One of the things she loved about the class was that they all had that in common. It made the issues that faced them in both the

Christian and professional worlds much easier to bear.

They often got together for dinners or weekend lunches and spent a good part of the morning planning the next gathering. All Aria could think about was the information she'd stolen from an intensely secure facility and the empty e-mail box this morning.

After small groups, she played the piano for the large worship service. This time spent playing with the other members of the musical ensemble was easily one of her favorite parts of the week. It thrilled her to have the talent and skill to make music for God that proclaimed her love and worship of Him.

She and a few friends from church typically spent the afternoon together after services, but today she begged off. Instead, she walked home and changed into running clothes.

After two months of suspecting, watching, essentially spying, she wanted it over. She wanted to hand everything over to some government spook in a black tie and cheap shoes and let him handle it from there. The idea that someone that she once trusted, someone she liked and admired, would use what she created with the intent of harming thousands and thousands of people just crushed a little part of her soul, and she no longer wanted it to be a part of her life.

She ran ten miles, letting the rain hit her face, wanting to cleanse herself from the inside out, wishing it could also wash away the fresh, sharp pain of betrayal. When she got home, she put a pot of tea on to steep then took a long hot shower. Once she had showered and dressed in a pair of sweat pants and a sweatshirt, she poured herself a cup of tea and sat down at her desk, booting up her laptop.

Her fake e-mail address showed she had incoming mail, and she closed her eyes and took a deep breath, then accessed the mail folder. The message was short and to the point.

5 PM Monday.

After she turned off her computer, she clenched her fist and pressed it against her rolling stomach.

Chapter 9

Nicholas "Nick" Williams woke with a start—eyes wide open and heart racing—fighting to keep calm despite the temporary panic of the nightmare that had roused him. He ascertained his surroundings, scanning every corner, and using all of his senses to get a handle on his racing thoughts. Within seconds, he'd gotten his bearings and forced his pulse back down.

He had awakened in his cousin Marcus Williams' apartment in New York City, thousands of miles away from the Middle East and the harsh desert of his nightmare. The dial on his watch gave a faint green glow as he pushed the button on the side and read the time. One o'clock. He'd managed to get three hours of straight sleep this time, which was pretty good for him. He usually didn't make it past two. The trip back to the States must have worn him out more than he realized.

He got up and took a shower, enjoying the luxury of hot clean water and a massaging showerhead. He'd learned the hard way that many things in life were taken for granted; clean sheets and hot showers with massaging showerheads sat at the top of that list.

He dressed quickly, impatient to drive to D. C. and check-in with the agency, debrief and, more importantly, start his vacation. He had in mind a hut on a beach and endless tall glasses of icy lemonade, maybe a fishing pole, definitely his Bible. He and God had to have a long-awaited conversation.

There was little packing to do since he'd only spent one night. He once again wrapped his worn Soldier's Bible in the linen handkerchief it came with and put it into the pocket of his slacks. He carefully checked the clothes he'd worn on the long journey home, ensuring that all the obvious and not so obvious pockets had been emptied. They went into a plastic laundry bag he would drop off down the street from the apartment at the one-hour cleaner's he had used a few times before. His cousin would pick them up and have them here for the next time he was in town.

When he came out of the bedroom, he was surprised to see Marcus awake and in the kitchen. Since it was barely one in the morning, he didn't expect to see him.

"Cuz," Marcus said, expertly using one hand to crack an egg into the hot skillet. "I have breakfast just about ready."

Marcus was the head pastry chef, or pâtissier, for the world-renowned Viscolli Hotel. When he wasn't managing and coordinating the desserts served by dozens of chefs around the world, he traveled the globe, designing and making cakes for presidents, celebrities, and kings.

Marcus was Nick's second cousin on his father's side

but had as much to do with his family as Nick did—which was basically nothing. Coincidentally, Marcus had attended Nick's basic training graduation to see his best friend graduate and recognized Nick's name. He approached him and introduced himself. Nick had nothing to do with his father or his side of the family. Regardless, Marcus pursued a friendship with Nick that Nick very cautiously accepted.

After Nick's "death," Nick was in Dubai *en route* to Libya and accidentally ran into Marcus while Marcus was participating in an international pastry competition in a hotel there. Marcus immediately recognized him, and Nick shared a meal with him, explaining his covert life and the need to keep his existence quiet.

Now he always came back into the country through New York and always spent at least one night with Marcus. The two forged a bond that only grew over time. Marcus kept Nick's existence a secret, and Nick had an ally outside of NISA who he could trust and rely upon.

"Thanks, man," Nick said, setting his bag near the door. "I'm heading back to D. C. as soon as I eat."

"After you debrief, where are you going?"

"Someplace with sand, warm water, and cold lemonade." He slid onto a barstool. "Care to join me?"

Marcus stopped artistically plating the corned beef hash and fried eggs to look his cousin in the eye. Nick felt like he'd been read thoroughly, and he tried not to shift under the gaze. "No. I think you need some alone time to decompress." He went back to the plate, added an orange slice that had been twisted to look like a seashell, and slid it across the bar to Nick. "Besides, I have a baby shower cake to do in Boston for a friend of Mrs. Viscolli."

Nick snorted. "Booties and bows?"

"Mrs. Viscolli always goes for simple, but definitely with chocolate and *ganache*. She's my favorite client."

Marcus paused while Nick bowed his head and said a prayer of thanksgiving for the meal. "I don't know how you bake cakes all day long without going crazy," Nick said, shoveling a forkful of corned beef into his mouth.

"God gave all of us different gifts. Mine just come with a master's degree in culinary arts." He pulled a bottle of water out of his refrigerator. "I personally prefer flour on my hands to Afghanistan sand." He took a drink of the water and grinned. "Of course, that's just me."

Nick laughed and took another bite of the perfectly prepared meal.

The drive to Washington, D. C., took him less than four hours. There was very little traffic this early on a Tuesday morning, and the streets showed the effects of the rain showers that had come through the area the night before. It was always weird to be back in the States. He'd been out of the country for so long that the lights, buildings, and surplus of material things would take some getting used to on his part.

He pulled into the Department of Treasury building and parked in the employees' parking garage below street level. In the elevator, he opened a stainless-steel access panel and punched a code into the keypad. The authorization light blinked green, and the elevator began its descent. Three stories down, the doors opened, and Nick stepped out of the elevator into a tastefully decorated lobby one hundred and six feet below ground.

Two stern-looking and armed U. S. Marines stood guard at the only door leading out of the lobby, and Nick nodded to them when he stopped in front of the door.

He accessed another computer panel within the door, and a screen slid out from the panel. He inserted his Common Access Card chip first and typed in a ten-digit PIN. Almost immediately, he heard the door unlatch, giving him authorization to enter. That meant that the armed guard directly inside might not shoot him dead the moment he stepped inside.

He stepped into the mantrap with a bulletproof window to his left and a guard station behind it. He passed his CAC and cell phone to the guard via the steel bank drawer. The guard waved him through without asking him to place his hand on the Plexiglas fingerprint scanner.

On the other side of the mantrap, Nick walked down a short hallway and entered a small room where, to his pleased surprise, a young woman named Jennifer Thorne sat at a table in front of the door. Nick felt his cheeks fight fatigue to form a sincere smile when he recognized her and took her in. He had not expected to see her back at the agency, and the sight of her made him unconsciously relax as he felt a wave of friendship flow through him.

He could count on one hand the people in the world that he trusted—much less liked—and Jennifer Thorne topped that list. A long while ago, he had figured out that Jen Thorne felt the same way about him, and more. He tried never to think about Jen's thoughts or feelings where he was concerned. Her thoughts about him—and feelings for him—always led to dangerous territory, a territory where feelings of mutual respect, trust, and admiration for sharply honed skills intersected with pain and loss in often confusing ways.

Jen Thorne had light brown hair pulled into a loose ponytail on the back of her head, wire-framed reading glasses perched atop her nose, and a prosthetic arm. Nick remembered the night she lost her arm very vividly. If he ever got fuzzy on the details, he knew that picturesque and relentless nightmares would soon refresh his memory.

She looked up from her computer screen as Nick came into the room. A returned smile lit up her face when she saw him standing there. "Well, if it isn't Nick Williams in the flesh! I didn't know Nighthawk was back in country!" she exclaimed as she stood up and began to walk around her desk to greet him.

"How's the 'one-winged' Dove?" Nick inquired in a teasing tone of voice.

"Just Dove!"   With a grin, Jen punched him in the shoulder, hard. Then she asked, "Did you just arrive?"

"I just got in yesterday, well... this morning early, you know," he explained, giving her a warm hug, always mindful of her prosthetic. It often surprised him how warm and gentle her plastic hand felt laid against the back of his neck. In her ear, he asked, "What are you doing here? Last I heard, you'd taken another medical leave."

She dismissed the remark with a wave of her human hand as they separated. "It wasn't a medical. Just a leave of absence. Did some consulting work in the private sector for some big bucks, but honestly, missed this place too much." With a grin that she only ever shared with Nick Williams, she said, "If you can imagine that."

The grin said that Jen Thorne had a lot more to say that she would not say. The grin said she didn't miss the place like some kind of cat. She missed the people, or one person in particular. The grin and the distant look in her eyes silently announced that an entirely different life path lay just within reach, just on the edge of possibility, if only either of them could ever confront it and work out the details.

All of that went unsaid, and Jen perched on the edge of her desk, swinging her denim-clad leg. "Where're you coming from? Can you say?"

Nick eased himself into the chair in front of her desk and leaned his head back, jet lag seeping through his system. There were too few moments in his life where he was given the opportunity to completely relax, and he decided to take advantage of this one. He absently rubbed the thin white scar that graced his temple. "Djibouti," he said, answering her question.

Jennifer frowned, knowing a few details about recent activities in the Horn of Africa. "Ooh. How did you manage to pull that duty?"

In other words, who at higher headquarters had a grudge against him to assign him that mission? He winked at her and leaned back in the chair, stretching his long legs in front of him. "Charlie thought that it might help purge some demons from my system," he acknowledged.

"Good old Charlie."

"Good old Charlie," Nick echoed.

"Did it work?" she asked, maybe not realizing that this now constituted the longest conversation she had held with another human being in months.

He gave a wry smile. "I purged a few of them." He looked at his watch. "Cable news will probably be reporting the details in about an hour."

She put her hand up, palm toward him. "Don't give me the details. I have a few demons myself when it comes to explosives." The telephone on her desk chirped twice. She walked back around and stabbed the speaker button with plastic fingertips. "Yes, sir?"

"Take me off speaker!" Charlie Zimmerman ordered.

Nick always wondered by it never occurred to Charlie that keeping the call on speaker left Jen's single working hand free. He had considered asking him, but never had, preferring to see how long it would take to occur to the man on his own.

Jen picked up the receiver with her remaining hand, then listened for a moment. She sat back down in her chair and said, "I'll have him come right down." She hung the phone up and opened the desk drawer, pulling out an orange identification badge and some keys. "Charlie said for us to quit yacking and for you to get yourself downstairs yesterday."

"Good old Charlie." Nick quipped, then accepted the ID badge and keys as he stood. He walked to the door behind the desk and waited. "Leave me word where to get up with you, Jen. We'll go shooting or something."

"Sure thing, Nick. Maybe we can get a game of croquet going if you have mallets. I'm sure I have some wickets somewhere." Her expression remained stoic, perfectly unreadable as she pressed the button beneath her desk that buzzed him through the magnetic lock of the inner door. Even without the visual clues, Nick knew without

Jen having to say another word that she wished he'd want more than time spent in target practice with her, but neither one of them ever said it. They both knew he didn't want more, never had, and likely never would.

"Check your SIPR mail later," she reminded as he walked through.

♫ ♫ ♫ ♫

"I'm tired, Charlie. No way do I want to go to China. The only way I want to go to China is on a tourist visa. Do you know I've never actually seen the Great Wall from ground level? Why don't you give me some cushy desk job here in the States for a couple of months and let me relax for a bit," Nick suggested. He'd just finished his debriefing about his trip to North Africa, and cut his boss off when he started to explain another mission. "After I come back from two weeks at the beach on Little Creek."

"Do this one job, and you got it," Charles "Charlie" Zimmerman agreed affably before leaning back in his chair. Being behind a desk for the last five years had done nothing to soften the rugged planes of Charlie's body. He was a few inches over six feet and kept his salt-and-pepper hair cut military short. He had a long scar down one side of his face, and when that wound had healed, he'd finally accepted the job as Director of NISA, the National Intelligence and Security Agency.

NISA is what personnel assigned to the Department of Defense, the Department of Justice, and the Department of Homeland Security called an O.G.A or "Other Government Agency" whose mandate was murky and whose objectives remained largely undocumented. The

National Security Administration, Central Intelligence Agency, and Department of Homeland Security all clandestinely called upon NISA to carry out tasks that they needed completed, but for which they required plausible deniability in terms of involvement. Like ghosts, agents assigned to NISA were all volunteers; unsung heroes whenever matters of national security ended favorably, and sometimes very public fall-guys whenever events ended badly. In short, NISA didn't exist. It was a "Black Operations" arm of the United States government.

Nick Williams was a spook.

"You told me the same thing right before you sent me to Djibouti," Nick said. "I'm through playing games here, Charlie. It's been ten years. I'm actually tired, and I won't be of any use to us out there if I burn out." He stretched out in his chair and propped his feet on the corner of Charlie's desk.

Charlie's face remained thoughtful for about thirty seconds before he nodded his head. "You're right. China isn't a place where we can afford any mistakes right now." He pulled a file out of the basket on his desk and opened it. "I need someone to take this job. It's smooth and easy, and you stay in CONUS."

In CONUS meant a domestic operation, specifically inside the "Continental United States." Charlie pulled out hard copies of an e-mail transmission that had been forwarded to him. "I need you to meet with this guy, find out what he has for us."

Nick shook his head. "I'll look at it later. I'm going to the beach." He started to push himself to his feet, but Charlie stopped him.

"Nick, this is personal."

Nick sat back down. He didn't owe Charlie Zimmerman a thing; quite the opposite, in fact. That meant the chain of obligation between them was about to undergo further strain, somehow.

Charlie folded his hands. "I've been pressing for a summit. A real one. A summit with the leaders of this country with a single agenda item. That is to discuss the ramifications to this great nation of bringing our soldiers up on charges for their efforts during the war," he said abruptly.

Nick felt a wave of sympathy. "Your son."

Charlie's lips tightened, and he cleared his throat. "You were a soldier. You know as well as I do that my son did everything right. He never violated the 'Rules of Engagement,' and he followed every legal order to the letter, yet faced felony charges like a common criminal."

He gestured at a stack of files on his desk. "You know what's up here at home. We've had two agents arrested in the last six months, and our agency barely breaches the security industry."

Nick slowly sat back down. Charlie continued. "In three weeks, and for the first time ever, we'll be speaking directly with the President, the Vice President, a good portion of the members of Congress, the Joint Chiefs, and even a few Supreme Court Justices... all together in one place to talk this out in person. No one phoning it in. I've been working on it for six months, and," he said as he lifted up the file and let it fall to the desk again, "this guy here is saying there's knowledge of the summit, and that there's a credible threat.

"You and I both know that it's probably nothing and will just be a big waste of your time, but we can't let something like this go. We can't afford any more delays. And now that I've told you, quite frankly, you're the only person, other than me and Jen, in this entire organization who knows about the summit. I can't trust anyone else."

Nick fought an internal war for about a millisecond. Then he took the file and scanned through the paper briefly. "Got any hard proof to support his allegations?"

"No. He refuses to transmit anything. Says if we want to see proof, we have to meet him to get it. I think he doesn't trust the electronic *communiqué.* Fair enough. After Petraeus and Clinton, who trusts classified e-mail? You have a strong sense of people when you first meet them, Nick. I trust your judgment with this guy. You'll probably be able to tell right away if he's for real."

"Have you traced the e-mail?" Nick asked.

Charlie laughed. "It's taken us a week to do it. This guy knows his way around a computer. We've been bounced from satellites to third world countries to Des Moines via every onion router in between. The e-mail originated from the Portland, Oregon area. Jen should have more info soon."

Realizing that Nick had accepted the mission, Charlie pulled a pack of cinnamon gum out of his desk drawer and offered a stick to Nick, who refused. Charlie popped a stick into his mouth and thoughtfully chewed. "Set everything up. Head on out to Portland today. Meet this guy, then take a couple of weeks off. Maybe head up to Vancouver or head south and hit San Francisco or Vegas. Not more than three weeks, Nick. I need you. Get your head on straight, and we can discuss China when you get back."

Nick took the file folder and walked to the door. "Better go ahead and line up somebody else. I'm not going to China in a few weeks, Charlie."

"We'll discuss it when you get back, Nick. Right now, we're spread too thin," Charlie said. As Nick left his office, he heard Charlie pick up the phone and say, "Jen? Take me off speaker. You know I hate that. Give Nick any details you have on the trace you made on those e-mails."

Chapter 10

Nick landed in Portland during a rainstorm. He knew weather like this was typical for the Pacific Northwest, but the deluge didn't make this little assignment any better. Airport construction forced the passengers to walk across about twenty feet of runway. During that short twenty-foot space, Nick got thoroughly soaked. The weather was cold, and his wet east coast clothes made him feel even colder.

He hated the cold. He'd take a tiger cage in Syria over snow skiing in Siberia any day of the week.

After waiting for nearly fifteen minutes for his luggage, then nearly forty minutes at the rental car counter, he enjoyed a nearly twenty-minute ride in a shuttle to the remote rental car parking lot. It took him eight more rain-soaked minutes before he found his agency approved and equipped rental car. All things considered, Military Space-Available flights seemed like models of efficiency in comparison.

The drive to the hotel did little to improve his mood.

The construction made the traffic worse than the streets of Bangkok. By the time Nick pulled out onto the interstate, he was gritting his teeth in annoyance. He'd memorized the map of Portland on the plane, and worked his way through the afternoon traffic to the hotel where he'd arranged to stay. He could hardly wait to get into a pair of warm, dry socks.

Once he checked in, he took a hot shower, forcing his body to relax, then he lay down atop the covers on the bed, wearing only the scratchy bath towel. He didn't intend to sleep, just shut his mind off for a while, but the jet lag finally caught up with him.

♫ ♫ ♫ ♫

The pain in his temple vibrated through his whole body. He wanted to open his eyes, but his body wasn't cooperating with him. His ears rang, and it made him feel isolated and trapped in darkness. Heat blasted his skin from his left. Acrid smoke burned his throat, and when he coughed, he inhaled more of it, causing him to actually gag.

As he turned his head to the side, coughing, he finally forced his eyes open. He lay on his back on the deck of the helicopter. The medic lay next to him, his eyes open and staring blankly, clearly not breathing.

Nick rolled over to his hands and knees, crawling to the medic. He couldn't find a pulse. Dead. Nick fought back the memory of the medic rushing out to him and pulling him to his feet, leading him back to the cover of the aircraft. If the medic hadn't saved Nick's life, the man would likely still be alive.

Shaking his head, Nick pushed himself to his feet and fought his way through the debris to the door. The pilot and copilot lay still and unmoving on the other side of the burning engine outside.

Stumbling, he worked his way back to his prisoner, who screamed and fought against the restraints. Nick ripped the hood off of his head and looked the man in the eye, putting a finger to his lips to silence him. Suddenly, the civilian on the other side of the prisoner reached up and grabbed Nick's wrist with a hand covered in blood.

♫ ♫ ♫ ♫

Nick awoke with a start, his pulse beating rapidly. He forced himself to take a deep breath and felt his body relax. This was the type of nothing job they gave new recruits, not seasoned veterans. He was in Portland, not Persia. He could dial down his vigilance about eight or nine notches. He glanced at the hotel clock, did the math for the Pacific time zone, and knew it was time to call in a report.

Jennifer answered on the first ring and told him she'd been waiting for his call. "I have a name and address for you. A.C. Suarez."

Nick could hear papers rustling in the background, but a feeling of dread started to work its way through his gut. How many people in this country had the initials A.C. with the last name Suarez? He gripped his cell phone a little tighter.

Jen continued, "We cross-checked the population within a hundred-mile radius of Portland and found a likely candidate in the greater metropolitan Portland area working for NWT. Matches the name except this subject is female." Jennifer paused to take a breath, but Nick didn't need to hear anymore. He almost said the name himself but stopped in time. "Her name is Aria Camila Suarez. Ready for the address?"

"One second." The lingering nightmare, coupled with the shock of hearing her name again after so many years, ramped his state of alertness all the way back up to eleven. Nick actually had to take a deep calming breath and center his thoughts. "Go ahead. I'm ready."

Nick committed the address to memory without having to write it down. In his business, he had learned never to write anything valuable down and never to write anything on stacked sheets of paper. "Thanks, Jen. I'll check in before Sunday. Usual times for station calls. Proof of life word is 'hacking' and I'll be using code blue protocol until further notice."

He hung up and reached into the pocket of his slacks to retrieve his Soldier's Bible, still wrapped in a linen handkerchief given to him as a token of the affection Aria Suarez felt for him a lifetime ago. To be honest, Nick had not connected the dots between the gift and the giver in nearly a decade.

He fired up the internet screen on the hotel television and pulled up an image search engine. Using the television remote control was cumbersome, but he eventually entered the name of his high school and the year he had graduated. In no time, he found himself reading an ancient news article from his senior year in high school when Aria had made the front page of the Leisure section. There she sat at the school's baby grand piano wearing a pink sweater, her hair pulled back with a matching pink headband.

Nick thought back past a decade to the last time he

had seen Miss A.C. Suarez. Could it really be her? What in the world was she doing in Portland of all places? And working for a government contractor of all things? If it really was her, she still had the last name of Suarez.

That didn't seem like her style. It was inconsistent with the Aria Suarez he had known all those years before. He always knew she planned on claiming her husband's last name. In Nick's mind and heart, Aria Suarez set every standard for female beauty and desirability. Someone as beautiful and desirable as her remaining single all this time simply did not compute.

Could she be divorced? No. No way. What kind of moron would marry her then divorce her? No moron Aria would ever marry in the first place, that's for sure.

Widowed? Maybe. She was an Army brat. She very well could have married a soldier or a man in a similarly dangerous line of work. That seemed consistent. She would require her husband to be physically and mentally tough. If that were the case, though, he assumed Aria would have kept her married name after losing her spouse.

It couldn't be her, he decided. This just had to be some kind of cosmic coincidence. With the shake of his head, he forced himself out of the past, turned off the television, and sat up. He had work that needed to be done. His top priority was to find out what kind of trouble surrounded this Miss A. C. Suarez and what she knew.

♫ ♫ ♫ ♫

When Nick first acquired his subject, it had taken him a good long while to recover from his shock upon seeing her again. Aria Suarez, his Aria Suarez, looked the same yet somehow different. Ten years had added confidence to her movements that had been largely absent throughout high school. It made him wonder how he had changed in the last ten years. Maturity or experience, he supposed, only accented and highlighted her already natural grace and beauty. In fact, each time he watched her, she looked more beautiful than the last.

He mentally noted—but filed away in the "to be dealt with later" category—the fact that each time he caught sight of her while performing his surveillance that his pulse began to race. Once, he even realized that he was holding his breath while watching her through a high-powered sniper scope from six hundred meters. He wrote it off to his sniper training but knew there was more to it.

Nick had observed Aria for three days now. So far, there didn't seem to be anything out of the ordinary in her life, other than the fact that she'd e-mailed the FBI with suspicions that someone whom she knew was planning a nuclear attack on the nation's leaders. In observing her, he noticed how she favored one hand, something he could not help noticing given Jen Thorne's circumstances. He also observed her genuine warmth toward her coworkers.

Mostly, he noticed her stress levels. Nick observed that she was still just as little as the last time he saw her, and he knew someone more powerful could break her in half with little effort. She was so small, so petite. He knew just how quickly he could disable her if tasked to do so. As he watched her, he noted that she felt anxious, maybe even scared. She continually darted furtive glances over her shoulder and checked reflections everywhere she went. This made her a difficult tail due to her vigilance.

Every morning, he watched her leave her little cottage—which sat in a small neighborhood within walking distance to a beautiful cove of the Willamette River—and go for a jog armed with earbuds and a can of pepper spray. Then she'd return and, within an hour, leave for work. During the day, he sat in his car near NWT to make sure Aria didn't leave for any reason. He stood ready to follow her wherever she went during the day, which was, so far, nowhere.

Saturday morning, she didn't leave her home. Nick kept waiting for her to go out for a jog, but she stayed put. Mid-afternoon, he heard the sounds of her piano playing come through the open windows, and he hit her with the parabolic microphone. He leaned back in his car and closed his eyes, listening.

Nick hadn't thought of her playing in years. Years ago, he had stumbled upon an old recording of Aria in recital during music school, but listening to her make music felt an awful lot like self-flagellation, and Nick really wasn't into self-torture. In fact, it was when he disposed of that recording that he also began to purposefully evict and eliminate any further thoughts or years-old feelings for the little girl from his former life.

Sitting in his car nearly half a mile away and well out of her sight with his stereo headphones connected to his powerful parabolic microphone, he couldn't keep the memories back—and didn't want to. Nothing beat listening to her play live. He closed his eyes and let it take him back to high school, to Georgia sunshine, to laughing brown eyes and shining blonde hair and soft, warm lips.

As the last of the chords of the piano faded in the air, he reached for his optics. He saw her come out of her house and start walking toward the river. He slipped on sunglasses and a baseball cap. As soon as she was out of sight around a curve, he started his car and drove down the same road on which she walked, passing her. He pulled into a convenience store parking lot and went inside. While thumbing through the Saturday Portland Tribune, he watched her cross the road, walk to a dock, and into a seafood restaurant.

He didn't expect her to emerge before ten minutes had even passed. If he hadn't been staring at the door of the restaurant, he would have missed her coming out. She stood at the curb and paused, looking down the street. Then she shook her head and headed back home without any more stops.

That evening, a man driving a silver Volvo and a pouty teenage girl arrived and picked her up. He memorized the license plate and took a picture of the man and teenager with his telephoto lens. So, there was a man in her life. Nick wondered who he was and what he might do for a living. Part of him was happy for her, but just a small part. As the man walked up to ring Aria's doorbell, Nick mentally killed him eight different ways.

They left, and Nick cautiously followed. He shadowed them to a strip mall about a twenty-minute drive away where they shared a pizza and some cheese bread before hitting a family movie. Nick waited until they left the theater and realized that the guy was taking Aria directly back to her home. This made the tail difficult in the thinning evening traffic.

Nick had no choice but to pass them and perform a "block" maneuver to avoid detection. After he passed them, he accelerated sharply to open up space, then turned left, sped for a block or so, and turned left again then rapidly accelerated. After his third left-hand turn, he ended up well behind them again. He slowly drove into her neighborhood and parked within binocular range to observe them. The man delivered Aria to her door with a chaste kiss then walked back to the car where the teenage girl patiently waited, playing with her smartphone.

Sunday morning, she walked to her church two blocks away in the pouring rain. Nick knew that he would have at least an hour, so he quickly and easily broke into her house. The tricky part was not leaving any obvious traces, like wet handprints or foot prints, that would serve as evidence of his presence.

A quick run through the house showed nothing out of the ordinary. He tried to get into her laptop but didn't waste any time attempting to break the password and decided to leave it alone. He went into the bedroom and searched through her dresser and nightstand drawers, and still couldn't find a single thing out of the ordinary. He performed a thorough check, looking under the drawers in case she had taped things to the undersides, and checking between and under every mattress and cushion.

Just as he made to leave her bedroom, something on her far wall caught his attention. He walked over and looked at it closely. A warmth that he wasn't used to and couldn't define spread through him when he realized that it was his Silver Star, Bronze Star, and Purple Heart. The medals were tastefully framed with a copy of a newspaper article that faithfully reported his official obituary.

He left the room, for the first time ever feeling like he had invaded something private. When he got back to his car, he called Jennifer Thorne.

"Dove, this is Nighthawk."

"How's life, Nighthawk?" Jen asked.

"I've had a hacking cough since yesterday, Dove," he replied. The phrase confirmed, with his proof of life safe word, that he was still on mission and not under any kind of duress.

"Task?"

"I have been observing the target, and I believe contact is needed to close the file."

"Roger. We'll arrange an in-person meeting with the principal. Code blue protocols are in order."

When Nick didn't respond, she asked, "Something else?"

Nick knew that if he informed Jen about his prior knowledge of this woman, he would be off to China on the next flight. Instead, he said, "Yeah. You still owe me a croquet match."

Jen simply hung up without another word.

♫ ♫ ♫ ♫

On Monday morning, Aria called in sick to work. She'd been with NWT for nearly four years and had used a total of two sick days in all that time. She shot Julie an e-mail and let her know she was taking a couple of personal days and asked her not to call her for any reason. While she felt nervous and apprehensive, she wouldn't stop now. She'd made her decision and planned to follow through.

She checked her e-mail all morning long, but by ten, there was no new message on where or when to meet whom, so she paced her house for a while, finally deciding to escape into music.

She sat at the piano and ran through a couple of warm-up exercises before she played the opening to the third movement of Prokofiev's Eighth Sonata, the piece she had very nearly perfected in high school. It didn't take long for her wrist to begin to ache under the strain of the piece, so she gradually eased into a simpler composition to give the muscles and tendons in her right hand a break.

She let her mind wander to Adam's new screenplay and thought about the plot, an action-oriented thriller set in San Francisco's Chinatown. As she thought about the complexity of the plot, the dark moments broken up by sheer action, she started thinking about music that would go with it. When her wrist couldn't take her playing anymore, she pulled out some staff paper and penciled in the notes she heard—the code she saw—in her mind.

It still sounded slightly imperfect, and the chords would have to be adjusted to match the mood and tone of specific scenes in the film, but she thought perhaps she'd stumbled upon the right melody to connect the entire plot to all of the characters' individual harmonious themes. It excited her that this one came so easily. The last soundtrack she wrote was the result of a week's vacation spent in twenty-hour days of sweat and tears with maybe even some blood mixed in.

Smiling, she looked up from her piano and realized it had been several hours since she last checked e-mail. She wondered if a location for the meeting had been arranged. She slid off the bench and went to her laptop, quickly typed in the security code, and accessed the program that allowed her to keep her identity somewhat of a secret.

While her computer worked with the program, she went to her kitchen and grabbed a container of yogurt. By the time she came back into the room, she had received another message. Taking a deep breath, she opened it. "Five o'clock today. Coffee shop on Macadam Avenue near Willamette Park. Far northeast corner table outside, male in a blue shirt. He'll wait for you there."

Chapter 11

Aria Suarez stood on the corner of the patio at the coffee shop on Macadam Avenue, observing the man wearing the dark blue shirt who occupied the corner table of the outdoor cafe. Sunlight glinted on his brown hair, revealing highlighted streaks that nearly glowed, lending his visage a halo-like appearance. He'd flirted with the waitress each time she'd come by, and had even grinned at a small child making a mess at a nearby table. He looked harmless enough, though she couldn't make out his face completely behind the sunglasses he wore and the Monday edition of the Portland Tribune he continuously ducked behind.

She clenched the purse strap in her hand a little tighter. She kept a sharp eye toward the crowd, scanning faces for anyone who looked either familiar or out of place. Finally, she mustered the courage to step forward.

Aria hesitantly began her approach, unsure of how this might work and trying very hard not to reveal even a hint of uncertainty. Then she remembered that she also didn't want to attract any undue attention to herself by appearing uncomfortable or out of place in any way, and she smoothed her stride.

When she reached his table, she stood still and waited for him to look up from his newspaper. When he failed to do so, she cleared her throat. When that didn't work, she said, "Excuse me."

He shifted the newspaper downward enough to peer over the top of it in her direction, staring at her through the dark lenses of his sunglasses, but she still couldn't see his eyes. All she could see was her own reflection in the tinted lenses. "Are you waiting for me?"

The man very purposefully glanced downward and very carefully folded the newspaper, which he set on the table at right angles to his silverware directly next to his cup. That accomplished, he gestured with his left hand in the direction of the chair across from him, silently inviting her to join him without raising his eyes. As she perched herself on the wrought iron chair, she thought to herself that this man looked familiar.

All those weeks when she had felt such apprehension, glancing over her shoulder in foreboding, she had checked all the shadows and every corner, always sure someone was following her. Had her trepidation been well-founded after all? Had this man been following her? Had she seen him somewhere before? Or was her nervousness and disquiet simply getting the best of her? Did this man just have one of those faces that you felt sure you recognized?

Aria started to feel some very deep, very real anxiety and did her best to quell it. She waited for him to speak, assuming if everything was on the up-and-up that he had done this kind of thing before, and would take the lead to get them to the next level, whatever that was.

The waitress came back to the table to refill the man's lemonade, and Aria ordered a cup of decaf with cream, no sugar, then folded her hands and waited. The man across from her sat up a bit straighter, then took a deep breath and finally spoke.

"Hello, Aria." His voice flowed over her like a warm baritone blanket. It was deep and comforting and frighteningly familiar. He removed his sunglasses. Ice blue eyes, almost silver in color, calmly met her glance. Already tense muscles contracted in her stomach and around her heart, stealing the breath from her body and sending a surge of adrenaline that made her palms sweat even though her fingers felt ice cold. Her throat let out a startled gasp as recognition dawned.

It can't be! her mind screamed. *It's not possible!*

"How've you been?" he asked. "You look even more beautiful than I remember."

Aria didn't know what to say, literally shocked speechless. She had never spoken to a ghost. Her mouth felt so dry that the air coursing in and out of her lungs scorched her throat. Finally, she made an attempt. "What?... How?..."

Nicholas "Nick" Williams leaned forward and spoke very quietly, but with great urgency, his low voice pitched for her ears alone. "It's okay, Aria. It's a long story, and I'll be happy to share it with you. But I have to call my superiors in less than twenty minutes, so right now, just show me what you have. We can stroll down memory lane later on, okay?"

Aria finally felt able to speak. She gripped the wrought iron chair handles beneath her fingers until her muscles ached. "You aren't Nick Williams," she announced as she stood. "Nice try, but I buried Nick ten years ago." So many emotions rushed at her: confusion, anger, shock, hurt. What was happening?

Nick crossed his arms and leaned forward. "I know this is a shock, but it's important that we focus on why I'm here. We can catch up later."

"F-f-focus?" She felt heat flood her cheeks. "Focus?"

He visibly sighed a heavy sigh. "I'm sorry to shock you like this, Aria. If I'd known it was you, I might not have even come out. But, we didn't know anything until I was already here. You did an outstanding job of covering your tracks."

An outstanding job? Was he complimenting her?

She closed her eyes and shook her head. This was unimportant in the scheme of what was happening. She opened her eyes and looked at him again. He obviously felt comfortable with the look on her face because he leaned back and gestured at her with his hand. "Please, talk to me."

"I..."

He reached around the table and laid a warm, firm hand over hers. "Aria, please. Listen to me." As he spoke, he rubbed the top of her hand with his thumb, soothing her, calming her racing mind. "Please tell me what you planned to say before you knew it was me."

Aria licked her lips, unsure of where to start. "I'm a nuclear engineer."

He released her hand and leaned back in his chair and

raised an eyebrow. "Far cry from your dreams of being a professional musician."

"Yeah, well, a broken wrist will halt a pianist's career quicker than almost anything."

He frowned and looked at the hands she had clutched together on the table. "Broken wrist?"

"Yes, Nick. Broken. So thoroughly that two surgeries couldn't fix it."

"When?"

"When what?"

"When did you break it?"

"I didn't break it."

"I don't understand."

Not knowing what could possibly be motivating her, other than a desire to maybe hurt him the way she had been hurt by him, she said, "*I* didn't break it. At *your* funeral, your father broke it."

He froze. There was no other way to describe it. He not only stopped moving, but a look of icy steel also crossed his face, and the arctic anger in his eyes took her breath away. Almost as soon as the anger appeared, it disappeared, and he looked absolutely void of any emotion.

Suddenly, she wanted to take back the words, but they couldn't be taken back. She felt sure he would have found out eventually, though she had no reason to tell him so heartlessly. He had nothing to do with his father's actions, then or now, but she certainly implied that she thought so by the way she'd worded it.

"Explain," he bit out.

"No. That isn't why you're here. You said it's important to focus on why you're here, right? We can catch up later, you said." She leaned back and crossed her arms in a purely defensive manner. "I changed my major. I bounced between math and computers for a while, and finally settled in on engineering. The nuclear part came with my Ph.D."

He still didn't move. She expected him to ask about her getting a Ph.D., maybe even be a little impressed, but he just sat, stony and frozen. She continued. "The company I work for is contracted with NWT. Do you know what that is?"

"Yes," he bit out.

"NWT has a contract with the government to design a nuclear-powered suit for astronauts. I head the project, but NWT has an administrative lead who handles all of the nuke side of it. He's our official liaison with DoE and NASA. His name is Peter Harrington."

She paused while the waitress slid a cup of coffee in front of her. She smiled her thanks and took a sip from the cup.

"Go on."

"I started dating Peter several months ago. We're not allowed to bring anything into our facility nor take anything out. They search bags, lunch boxes, purses— everything is open for inspection. Also, we're not allowed to talk about work outside of work. At some point in the last few months, Peter has been pressing me about details in my work. It's a highly competitive contract, and we're working for a highly sought-after patent. It was annoying that he wouldn't stop trying to get updates from me, and when I wouldn't tell him anything outside of official reports and meetings, he actually got angry."

Nick raised an eyebrow. "Angry, how?"

Aria waved a hand. "Not physically. Just emotionally. Impatient, angry, short-tempered. He cut a few dates short over it."

She took another sip of coffee, her mouth so dry she could hardly speak. "One day, he was arguing with me about giving him information, and he said, 'I just need to know if the shield will prevent detection!' When I asked him what he meant, he insisted he didn't say that. He said what he'd said was, 'prevent contamination.' As if to say it should shield the astronaut from radiation exposure."

Nick tilted his head as if to look at her from another angle. "What do you think he meant?"

"At the time, I had no idea. Then I started paying attention. I came to realize that what he meant was if a nuclear device was being transported in the container I was developing, could it go undetected."

"What kind of nuclear device?"

"I can only assume weaponized."

Nick propped his elbow on the arm of his wrought-iron chair and rested his chin on his thumb, conveying an ordinary relaxed conversation to any casual observer despite their subject matter. "You think Harrington is using your department to create a device to house an undetectable man-portable weaponized nuclear bomb?"

"I do. And if I had some way through security, I could prove it. Right now, everything I have is just circumstantial. But I *know* it."

Nick stayed in the relaxed pose and waved the approaching waitress away. "Circumstantial evidence on something this serious isn't a lot to go on. I need to see what you have so that I know what we're dealing with."

Aria looked at him, inspected his face. He'd aged. He looked tired. A scar ran across his forehead, right at the hairline. Another one ran the length of one side of his chin. He looked hard, unfriendly until he smiled at the waitress, and she acted like he was her best friend in the universe. Then he looked at Aria again, and for a split second, those icy blue eyes looked like they had seen the problems of a lifetime.

"I'd like to know you believe me when I say there's a very serious thing happening here, and that you're not going to blow me off."

He didn't move. It didn't even look like his facial expression changed. Only his voice sounded grave, and she couldn't help but pay attention to every single syllable. "There are exactly three people in this entire world I would trust implicitly. You happen to be one of them."

"That's nice, coming from a man who made me think he was dead for the last decade."

She saw a muscle twitch in his jaw. "Fair enough." He looked at his watch. "I need to call in. Let's go back to your place and finish."

"My place?" Aria waged an internal war with herself. She wanted to bring him back to her house. She wanted to hear about the last ten years, and tell him about hers. She wanted to pretend they were old high school classmates who just happened upon each other at a coffee shop and wanted to catch up.

Instead, she felt like he'd betrayed her. She had *mourned* him, truly and deeply, and yet here he sat, two feet away from her. Now she didn't know if she wanted him anywhere near her home.

"Yes. Your little cottage by the river about half a mile from here." He stood and tossed some money on the table. "Let's go."

Unwilling to argue with him about it, she sighed in resignation. He clearly knew where she lived. They might as well go there and enjoy a little more privacy than an outdoor cafe. "Lead the way," she said with a tight smile.

For the first time since she approached him, his smile appeared genuine. They walked from the riverfront into Aria's neighborhood. When they reached her cottage, she used her key to open the door and let him precede her inside.

In the main room, she gestured in the general direction of the fireplace. There, in a cozy circle around a low table, sat a couch the color of the Oregon evergreens accented with cranberry colored pillows and a wing-backed chair with wide stripes that matched the sofa and pillows. A large flat-screen television hung above the fireplace mantle. She gestured at the couch as she sat in the chair. "Please, have a seat."

"I need to call in first."

He stood there and didn't pull a phone out of a pocket, so she finally said, "Do you need to use a phone?"

"Yes, thanks." She gestured toward the end table next to the couch, where a cordless extension sat. He picked it up but did not turn it on. He stared at her, clearly waiting for her to leave before making his call.

Not knowing what else to do, she went into the kitchen to get them some drinks. She rested her forehead against the refrigerator door, trying desperately to comprehend the fact that Nick Williams, Special Agent for NISA, was in her living room using her phone. She finally composed herself, opened the refrigerator door, and grabbed two bottled waters. When she turned around, he was standing in the doorway to the kitchen. She jumped when she saw him, then squared her shoulders and walked past him. "Did you convince them that I'm not a fake?"

Nick sighed and rubbed the back of his neck, following her back to the front room. "Yeah. I still need to see your proof, but I believe you, which was what they wanted to hear."

"Did you let them know we went to high school together?" she asked, sitting on the chair and twisting open the lid to her bottle.

"No. I want to keep that to myself for now," Nick sat in the center of the couch.

"So, you have a little more time than you did back there?" Nick nodded. "Then, could you please tell me what is going on?" She could hear the anger in her own voice. "Can you please tell me why I've thought you were dead for a decade?"

Nick shook his head slowly. "Sergeant Nick Williams, United States Army, did die ten years ago in the Iraqi desert."

Aria folded her arms in a defensive gesture. "But he didn't. I'm looking at him."

"No, Aria. He's been dead a long time. I left him there."

Aria leaned back in her chair, her anger leaving her as quickly as it had come, feeling empty and defeated. "What happened?" she asked him in a whisper.

She saw a flash of emotion cross his face before his lips thinned in a tight line. "Our Chinook went down while we were transferring a high-level prisoner." He leaned his head back and closed his eyes. "I tried to rescue the pilot and copilot right after the crash and got winged in the forehead by a bullet." He ran his finger over the scar at his hairline. "When I regained consciousness, I thought the only survivors were me, the prisoner, and one very badly wounded government agent. I knew the people who shot us down were coming for us, so I took the prisoner and the agent, and we went over a rise and hid. As soon as they were gone, I got us back into the Chinook and gathered what provisions I could and headed back to the base at nightfall."

She had a feeling that he left out a lot of the story. He continued. "We walked at night and hid during the day. By the time we made it back to the base, I discovered the government agent worked for NISA, and he was telling me how I was the perfect candidate for them." He took a drink from his bottle of water. "The rest is history." He shrugged and smiled, "At least, secret history. The world typically never knows what we do."

Aria closed her eyes and rubbed her forehead. What would a twenty-year-old have to do with a wounded man and an enemy prisoner in the desert that so deeply impressed a secret government agency? "So what do we do now?" she asked, sensing the end of the conversation about Nick.

"Now I see what you have and what we can do with it," he said. "Show me your evidence."

Aria went to the end table by the couch and opened the drawer. In an envelope between two magazines, she recovered a micro-SD card. She opened the back of her phone, removed the micro-SD card already there, and replaced it with the new one.

"We went to an antique show on the coast one weekend about two months ago. During an auction, Peter left me and said he'd be right back. I gave him about a minute then followed him. I saw him in the atrium of the hotel talking to these two men." She accessed the picture and pulled it up. "I'm going to assume you know your most wanted. This one is Roj Singh. I never got a picture of the other man, but I did see his face, and I would recognize him."

Nick's eyes widened at the name, and he looked at the phone. "It's not a clear picture."

"You're right. It's not. But I saw them. This was clearly Roj Singh—one of the top nuclear physicists in the world, who, after writing some pretty scathing and almost threatening articles about the United States, was dismissed from his position at the University of New York and placed on the terror watch list."

"Not possible," Nick said, handing her the phone back. "Roj Singh is dead."

"I know those were the rumors, but I also know him personally. He did a special series of classes when I was in school, and I spent eight hours a week for a whole semester in a room with him and forty-nine other people. I'm telling you that's him."

With a frown, Nick shook his head. "I don't know how it's possible. I was there when he was killed in Syria."

"Nevertheless," she said. "That afternoon, I came around a corner, and Peter was on the phone. He said, '...that's right, the president, vice president, speaker, and a good portion of the House. The summit in May is the perfect time to strike.'"

"What did he mean, perfect time?"

"I don't know. I didn't hear any more of the conversation, and I certainly didn't ask him to elaborate."

"What else do you have? Surely you didn't contact the FBI because you saw a ghost and overheard half a sentence."

She stood and walked over to the desk and grabbed her laptop, bringing it back to the couch. She sat next to Nick and brought the machine out of hibernation. Very quickly, she pulled up the images of the files she'd scanned at her office.

"These are screenshots of my security program on my computer. Whenever someone accesses my files, a log is left telling me whom. My entire team works on the same network, so I had to really look for this, but this number is Peter Harrington's terminal ID, showing when he accessed my files."

Nick leaned closer to her to see the screen. "If he works with you, wouldn't he have access to your computer?"

Aria shook her head. "He doesn't work on the projects I do. He works in the administrative division."

"Meaning?"

"Meaning he makes sure we correctly turn in our time cards, that we stay in strict accordance with OSHA regulations, and he interfaces with DOE and NASA. There is no reason at all he would have a legitimate need to access these files, especially not over and over again." She clicked a few keys on her keyboard and pulled up the scanned documents. "I've highlighted the details of what he looked at and when he looked. He pays strict attention to the pack that the nuclear power will go into."

"Okay. This is still all rather circumstantial," he nodded.

Aria smiled. "Indeed. But, I'm not a government agent. I'm a pianist turned engineer."

Nick cleared his throat and leaned back on the couch. "Abraham Lincoln once said if you look for the bad in mankind and expect to find it, you will." He tilted his head as if to look at her from another angle. "I guess my question to you is, are you looking for something and finding it, or have you found something that's really there?"

Aria fought an immediate knee-jerk feeling of defensiveness and forced herself to analyze what he'd said. She felt her brows furrow together in a frown. "I think that's a good question. My best answer is, this is a terrifying idea, and I hope I'm wrong."

"Fair enough."

She closed the laptop and set it on the table in front of her, then turned her body to face him. "What do we do now, Nick?"

Nick lay his head back and closed his eyes, pressing the heels of his hands against them. She could see the fatigue on his face now that he started to relax. "Now, I take this stuff in, and we assign someone to watch Harrington, get more concrete stuff on him."

She looked at her watch and realized it was early evening. She stood and looked down at him. "Do you want me to make us something to eat?"

"That would be fantastic. Thank you." He didn't get up, but he rested his head on the back of the couch.

She glanced back at him as she left the room, but he hadn't moved.

♬ ♬ ♬ ♬

Nick could see them. There were three of them sitting around their vehicle, passing around a bottle of something, the guttural sound of their language filtering through the night. One of them laughed at something the other said and lit a cigarette.

The problem as he saw it, they were in his way. There was no cover for him to go around, and he still had six hours of darkness to move.

As a cloud shifted and covered the moon, Nick decided to try. He leaned in and whispered to Zimmerman, gesturing with his hand as much as possible.

Zimmerman, in turn, whispered in Arabic to the prisoner, warning him not to make a sound. Then the three, as quietly as possible, walked at a crouch. Until the prisoner shouted out.

The first bullet whizzed by Nick's head. He rolled to a kneeling position, one knee on the ground, one boot flat, and gestured at agent Zimmerman to keep his gun trained on their prisoner. He calmly lifted the gun to his shoulder and sighted it, picking the one furthest from him. Their Toyota HILUX sat between him and them. He gambled they would run to his side of the HILUX, thinking that it would offer them cover. He slowly squeezed the trigger and watched the first guy fall to the ground. His friends panicked and ran right where he wanted them. Now he needed to get the third shot fired before anyone *realized the second shot hit its target. Hit. Hit.*

Good shot, kid. You just won the state championship.

He kept his weapon at the ready and slowly headed their way. No one moved. The desert lay silent around them as he searched the HILUX, finding water and some food. He hadn't had anything to drink in over 24 hours. He took the water back to Zimmerman and helped him take a sip. They both knew he probably wouldn't make it back to base, but he spoke Arabic, Nick did not, and their prisoner didn't respond to English.

"Don't give him water unless he talks to me," Zimmerman said breathlessly. "Can we take the vehicle?"

Nick looked at it again. "Maybe. There's a bigger risk we'll be discovered in the HILUX, but we'd cover a lot more ground."

Zimmerman gestured at the piece of metal that had pierced his side. "I don't know how much longer I can make it without medical care. I'm losing too much blood."

Nick looked at the HILUX, weighed his options, and nodded. "Okay." He bent and helped Zimmerman to his feet. Zimmerman held the gun trained on the prisoner while Nick supported him, which was how they'd covered what little distance between them and the crash site they'd covered for the last two nights.

Three feet from the HILUX, Zimmerman lost consciousness, and the gun fell from his hand. The prisoner took off, hands bound behind his back, running. Nick let the government agent fall and sprinted after the prisoner, tackling him from behind.

As he hauled him to his feet, he pulled the hood out of his pocket. "You just earned yourself the hood back, buddy," he said, ignoring the prisoner spitting at him as he pulled the hood down over his face.

♫ ♫ ♫ ♫

Nick woke with a start, his pulse pounding. On the outside, he did nothing more than open his eyes, but inside he waged war with fear and panic. He forced his pulse back to normal and got his bearings. Aria's place. He looked at his watch. Six-thirty. He'd slept for about half an hour.

The room was filled with a soft orange glow from the setting sun coming through the window facing west, and the entire home was filled with the aroma of cooking meat. From the direction of the kitchen, he could hear Aria humming a hymn.

A wave of longing washed over him, leaving him feeling weak and scared. He clenched his hands as he fought it while he cursed himself. This was not for him. A normal life in a little bungalow on the Willamette River was something he could never have. After the things he'd done, it was something he didn't deserve. The dream had just left him feeling vulnerable.

He stood and stretched, then went to the phone. He started to engage the receiver but changed his mind. Tomorrow would be soon enough to return to the world. For now, he wanted to shut it off.

He walked toward the kitchen and leaned against the doorway, watching Aria while she was unaware of it. She moved around the kitchen, chopping vegetables, stirring something on the stove, moving around the room, but never looking behind her. She had to get a little stool out to stand on so she could reach something on a high shelf. Nick was reminded just how small she was. He thought of his old man and how he'd put his hands on her, had broken her wrist, and killed her future. Suddenly, Nick felt a white burn of righteous indignation re-ignite somewhere in his chest. He battled the desire to go to Columbus, Georgia, to reacquaint himself with his father as a grown man and discuss the variable forces involved in breaking the wrist of a petite blonde woman.

Shaking his head to rid himself of the darkness, of the pain of his past, he crossed his arms and leaned his hip against the bar. She stepped off the stool and turned, jumping a little when she saw him.

"You move very quietly," she said.

He raised an eyebrow. "One of the reasons I'm still alive."

She nervously shifted her feet. "Hungry?" she asked.

He was hungry. A raw, burning hunger that spread through his whole body. What he craved, he couldn't take. Time had done nothing to dim the want, and what had once been a boy's crush was now a man's longing. On the inside, he began a battle with himself that he hoped he would have the stamina to continue fighting. On the outside, he stayed leaning against the bar with his arms crossed, giving the appearance of total ease.

"Starving," he said smoothly.

"Good," Aria said, moving to the stove. She opened the oven door. "How do you like your steak?"

"Cooked."

Aria laughed and looked behind her. "Well, I can see you will be easy to please with food. Unlike my brother John, who almost requires a Cordon Blue chef to cook him a proper meal." She grabbed two potholders from the kitchen counter near the stove and reached in, pulling out a pan with two sizzling steaks on it. "You can go ahead and sit at the table, and I'll bring your plate."

Nick pulled out a chair and sat at the wooden table with a bowl of green apples in the center of it. The east wall of the kitchen was a window, looking out into the green Oregon trees. "Is John still a cop?"

Aria brought him a plate filled with steak, seasoned new potatoes, and green beans. "Yep, still in Atlanta. He's a detective now. Do you want water or some tea?"

"Tea's fine." He let her serve him, pouring him a glass before sitting at her own plate. He reached out, his palm up, almost surprised when she put her delicate hand into his. He watched as she bowed her head and closed her eyes. Absolute contentment washed over him at the thought of sitting in this little kitchen with this woman he had always loved, holding her hand, and blessing a meal with her.

He cleared his throat and prayed as he always prayed—simply and to the point. "Thank You, Father, for another day. And thank You for this food. Amen."

"Amen," Aria echoed before she picked up her knife and fork.

Nick took a bite of the steak and felt like he'd died and actually been transported to heaven. *Another one of the little luxuries that gets taken advantage of,* he thought, *is a perfectly cooked steak.* "What about your other brothers?"

"Henry is a doctor in Virginia, and Adam is making movies in California. Did you see *Leading the Way*?" Aria asked as she took a sip of her tea. Nick shook his head. "Anyway, that was the most recent one he wrote and directed. He's becoming pretty popular."

"The last movie I remember seeing was *Harry Potter*," Nick said, slicing off another piece of meat.

"Which one?"

"What do you mean, which one?"

"Which Harry Potter?"

"Didn't know they made more than one. Don't really know what you're talking about." Nick took a sip of tea.

"Where have you been?"

Nick shrugged. "Here and there. Mostly there, come to think of it." They ate in silence for several minutes. He wanted to ask her about his father and what happened, but he didn't know how to start the conversation. Instead, he enjoyed every single bite of this meal she had prepared for them.

He speared the last potato on his plate with his fork and popped it in his mouth. "Do you have a computer I can use? I need to pull up some information, do some research."

"Sure," she said. "Whatever you need."

I need you. The thought was there before he could control it and, angry with himself, he pushed back from the table and went to the other room.

Chapter 12

Aria rinsed the last dish and put it in the dishwasher. She added soap, shut the door, and turned it on. She could hear Nick a room away, occasionally hitting the computer keys. She wanted to go in there, but she was afraid to see what he was looking at. Buck up, kid, she thought to herself, you're the one who opened this can of worms. Now you need to see it through. She lifted her chin and went into the front room.

He'd switched on the lamp on the little desk in the corner, but the rest of the room remained in darkness. Aria suddenly felt the need for light, so she walked through, switching on lamps and flipping on the main switch.

"What are you looking for?" she asked, coming up behind him.

"Peter Harrington. Anything I can find, really," he said. "This is his employment record. I've already gone through banking and tax returns as well as his SF-86 on file in e-Quip." He clicked a few more keys. "You know, his daughter is a piece of work. One more demerit and she's out of that private school he has her in."

"How do you know that?" Aria moved a stack of books off a chair sitting against the wall, set them on the floor, then pulled the chair closer to his.

"I pulled up her records. Care to guess what the tuition cost is to send a kid to Saint Catherine's?"

"More than what I pay in mortgage," Aria declared. She watched his fingers move with ease over the keys. Nick was no stranger to computers.

"The annual tuition of that school is about a third of the claimed income on his tax return last year," Nick conveyed.

"Then how could she have gotten accepted?"

"Probably with the money he tried to hide in this offshore account. Didn't even take me long to find it." He clicked a few keys on the keyboard and said, "I need to get into his office."

Aria shook her head. "Impossible. The security is way too tight."

Nick turned so he was facing her but quickly held a finger up. She opened her mouth to ask what he was doing when he put the finger to his lips. When he did that, she listened more closely. She heard the sound of an engine shut off, and seconds later, a car door slam. Nick turned quickly and shut the lid to the laptop, then stood and picked up his duffel bag off the floor near the couch.

Nick moved through the room toward the hall. "If that's Harrington, let him in." He disappeared down the hall, and she heard the bathroom door shut.

When she heard the knock on her front door, she

almost jumped. Little butterflies of nerves danced in her stomach when she looked through the front window and saw Peter's car. Aria took a deep breath and slowly released it, then opened the door. "Peter. What are you doing here?"

"May I come in?" he asked. Aria stepped back and let him enter.

"Why weren't you at work today?"

"I had some unexpected personal business come up. Tom didn't seem to have a problem with it," she said, watching him pace. He always looked uncomfortable inside her home.

He finally sat down on the couch and began to tap his finger on the arm. "What kind of personal business would keep you from going to work in the middle of a major project?"

Aria felt her back straighten, and had to tamp down on her anger. "That is certainly my business, Peter."

"I've tried to call your cell phone a couple of times today."

"Oh," she said, pulling her phone out of her pocket. "I had it on silent. It's been kind of a crazy day."

"My daughter wanted to see you before leaving for spring break this weekend." He gave his watch a nearly dismissive glance.

"I'm not sure—"

The door to the bathroom opened, and Nick came out. Aria watched him come through the doorway of the room, noting that he was moving differently, and the look on his face made him almost unrecognizable. He looked as if he was startled to see Peter, then walked over with a welcoming smile and his hand outstretched. "Hey, man. Harvey Castle."

Peter stood and took Nick's hand a bit warily. "Peter Harrington."

"Nice to meet you." Nick shook Peter's hand then ran a hand through his suddenly longer and blonder hair. "You a friend of Aria's?"

"Yes." Peter sat back down. He looked over at Aria with obvious questions in his eyes. "Aria and I have worked together since she first began at NWT."

Nick nodded, "Cool, man. Cool. Oh, wait! You're *that* Peter. Dude, that's awesome."

"Ah, so Aria has mentioned me." Peter sounded relieved.

"Of course, man. Hit me up." Nick extended his fist and held it at Peter's eye level. "Go on, man. Don't leave me hangin' here. Pop the potato."

Looking completely uncomfortable, Peter bumped fists with Nick. Nick quickly snatched his hand back, simultaneously opening his fist and making an exploding sound. Then he shook his hand as if Peter's punch had hurt and let out a low whistle of admiration.

Peter recovered from his obvious shock and asked, "How is it that you know Aria, Harvey?"

Nick slouched in the chair near the couch, hooking his ankle on his knee, giving the appearance of relaxed nonchalance. Aria realized that he had also changed his clothes. He now wore a pair of khaki shorts and a T-shirt that had a drawing of someone surfing on the back. He was barefoot. He had tied canvas bracelets on his wrist and had small hoop earrings in both ears. His eyes looked bloodshot and puffy.

"What's with all the formality, man? Call me Harv. Or Rook. Get it? Like Castle is a rook in chess? Or Glow-stick, but dude, that's a long story. You kind of had to be there."

Barely moving his lips, Peter asked, "How do you know Aria, Harvey?"

"Oh, Aria and I go way back, man," Nick said, finally answering Peter's question. "I've been down in L. A. working with her brother. We're on a break, so I'm on my way to Hawaii to catch some serious waves at Laniakea in Oahu. Full moon, you know? Decided to pop in on her this morning, hoping she'd let me crash on her couch for a few days 'til my plane leaves." Nick pulled a worn pack of cigarettes out of his pocket. "Hey, man, got any flame? I left mine somewhere."

Peter sat very regally. "I don't smoke. And I can't imagine Aria would allow it in her home."

Nick shrugged and put the cigarette back, throwing the pack on the table in front of Peter. "It's all good, Petey. Those things'll kill me one day, anyway."

Aria was desperately trying not to gape. The change in Nick absolutely amazed her. If she had seen him like this the first time, she never would have recognized him.

"Hey, dude! I almost have Aria convinced to hit the town with me tonight. There's a reggae' band I want to see playing at the Silver Squirrel. It's gonna' be killer! Why don't you tag along, dude?" Nick asked.

"No." Peter stood and looked at Aria. "Thank you. Apparently, I've interrupted your reunion. Are you free tomorrow?"

Behind Peter's back, Nick gave a subtle shake of his

head. "I'm afraid not," Aria answered, "Harvey and I already have plans."

"Well, when you get done playing, give me a call." Peter went to the front door, and Aria followed. She opened the door for him, and while at this point, he would typically give her a small kiss, instead he looked behind her toward Harvey. Without a word, he pivoted on his heel and left the house, shutting the door behind him. Nick immediately appeared at her side. When they heard the sound of Peter's car start, he went to the window and watched him drive away.

Aria felt nervous laughter bubble up in her chest. Before she could control it, a giggle escaped. She slapped her hand over her mouth to try to contain any more, worried if she started laughing, she'd end up in some hysterical heap on the floor. Nick gave her a rare smile before going back to the sitting area. As he sat in the chair, he slid the wig from his head and pulled a contact lens case out of his pocket. In seconds, he'd popped the contacts out of his eyes, dropping them into fluid in the case.

"That's why you looked so different," Aria said.

"I have unusual eyes," he said, rubbing them. "Early in my career, I was told that I should always disguise them. People tend to remember eyes the color of mine."

Aria silently agreed. "Do you have to disguise yourself often?"

Nick shrugged. "Whenever it's necessary."

"You don't like to talk about yourself much, do you?"

"I've never really had anyone to talk to about that subject," Nick said. He looked at his watch. "I have an errand to run. Do you mind if I stay here, or would you rather I went back to the hotel?"

Aria stood and went to her desk. "I don't mind you staying here." She pulled open the top drawer and rummaged through it. "Here's a key. I'll leave the chain unhooked."

Nick took the key from her and went back to the bathroom again, coming out with his duffel bag. "I'll probably be gone for several hours. If Harrington decides to test us and comes back or calls, tell him Harvey went to see that band, but you didn't want to go with me." He put his hand on the doorknob. "Don't forget to refer to me as Harvey. Harvey Castle."

He left without another word. "Sure thing, Harvey," Aria acknowledged, locking the door behind him.

♫ ♫ ♫ ♫

Nick had seldom worked with a partner. One of the few times he had, her arm got blown off by a homemade improvised explosive device. Still, every once in a while, he needed one. Right now would have been a good time.

He sat in his car and watched. Security at NWT Incorporated was excellent, nearly perfect, in fact. But every chain had a weak link. It just took a little looking to find it.

There were cameras at all the right angles, and there were no trees anywhere near the perimeter of the fence. He put on his monocle night vision goggles and switched from starlight to infrared. They had infrared sensors crisscrossing the lawn between the fence and the building, which would make crossing the lawn an impossible task. He switched back to starlight and sat back to watch. On the outside, it all looked very hopeless and intimidating. Still, every chain had at least one weak link.

♫ ♫ ♫ ♫

Aria looked at the clock on the mantle for the third time in ten minutes. It was two o'clock. Where was Nick? The longer she sat there, the angrier she got. How dare he not tell her where he was going? Her job, and possibly her entire career, stood on the line right now. And he was off gallivanting around doing who knows what and leaving her sitting here without knowing what was going through his mind or where he was going. She looked at the clock again. Two oh three.

She got up off the couch and went to the kitchen, deciding to make a cup of tea. If nothing else, it would probably take ten minutes to make, and she would have something to do for that length of time.

She filled the kettle with water, then dragged her stool around the kitchen, using it to reach the tea bags and her cups. She'd quit waiting to grow about five years ago, and finally resigned herself to stand five feet two inches tall for the rest of her life.

When the kettle whistled, she poured the boiling water into a cup and added the tea bag, letting her mind wander while she waited for the tea to steep. She thought back to the last year of high school and the rifle team winning the state championship. It had been one of the rare times she'd seen Nick give a genuine smile.

She picked up her cup and turned to take it to the

living room. She gave a startled gasp and dropped the cup when she saw Nick standing in the doorway, watching her. To her absolute amazement, in the next second, he held the cup out to her. Nick had crossed the space between them and caught her cup in midair before it had hit the ground. Tea had sloshed out onto the floor and certainly had burned his hand, but he didn't flinch. Instead, he calmly extended the cup out to her as if offering a baseball to a pitcher. What kind of reflexes must he have to pull that off?

"I've got to get you a bell," she muttered as she accepted the cup then turned to grab a dishtowel to wipe up the spilled tea. She realized that her heart was racing and her anger with this man had vanished.

"I need you to draw me a map," Nick stated very matter-of-factly as he accepted the towel and dried his hand.

"To where?" she asked. She took the towel back and carried it to the sink, where she turned on the cold water to rinse it.

"Peter Harrington's office, and the entire floor of his building, if you can."

"What good would it do? You wouldn't be able to get in, anyway," she said, walking past him and through the door.

Nick sighed. "I need a map to Harrington's office, and I need to know as much as you can remember about where the security cameras are located in his building. Can you do that or not?" He followed her to the other room.

"You aren't seriously going to try to go in there, are

you?" she asked, realizing he really was serious.

"Even the best armor always has at least one chink in it, Aria. I found one in your precious security." He sat down on the chair. "Look, I could go to his house tonight, but if he catches me, it will put you at risk. He's already seen me with you. I'd rather go ahead and get his office out of the way, then I'll go to his house later."

Aria was shocked. "You're going back tonight? A few hours ago, you fell asleep in the middle of a conversation with me."

"Right. And I slept."

"For half an hour! No way, Nick. I'll draw you a map, and you can go tomorrow. You have to be too tired to be efficient tonight." She stood and headed for her bedroom.

"My mother left when I was five years old. I don't need another mom now. You can draw me a map, Aria, or I can go in without one," Nick said quietly from the chair.

Aria stopped and turned. "It's a nuclear weapons facility, Nick. What's the chink in the armor?"

Nick rubbed his face. "They don't patrol at random intervals, only at shift change. Between times, they rely on their technology."

"And you can get past the technology?" Nick just stared at her, his expression unreadable. Aria threw her hands up in the air and stomped to her desk. "All right. Go get yourself arrested or killed. I've already buried you once. I can do it again."

She ripped open her desk drawer and began to rummage through it, finding a pad of paper and a pencil. She carried it over to the couch and leaned back and closed her eyes, trying to picture the building in her head.

Nick came behind her and reached out, taking the pad from her trembling fingers. He ripped the top page off the pad and laid it on the coffee table. If Aria drew on the pad, it would leave an impression on the pages beneath, and Nick couldn't let her do that. Then he nodded to her to proceed. He rested his arms on the back of the couch, leaning over to watch her draw. He leaned even closer to see the details and began to question distances and cameras.

When Aria finished detailing everything she knew, Nick looked at his watch. "It's already too close to the start of the workday. I'm going to need at least four hours to do what I need to do," he said. "Let's sleep now, and I'll plan to go at midnight tonight."

Aria felt relief flow through her body. She wouldn't gloat, though. "You're the one who knows best," she said sweetly.

He obviously chose to ignore her sarcasm. Instead, he half-smiled, half-glared at her, kicked off his shoes, then lay down on the couch and appeared to instantly fall asleep.

Aria watched him for a few minutes, intrigued by this man for whom she'd once had such strong feelings. The feelings hadn't gone away, she knew, but she wondered if they were still those of an adolescent or those of a woman.

She got a blanket from her room and carefully draped it over him, not wanting to wake him up. Then with a yawn that nearly broke her jaw, she fell face down on her own bed and fell asleep in seconds.

♫ ♫ ♫ ♫

Special Agent Katherine "Kate" Royce, code-named Hecate, inspected NISA Director Charlie Zimmerman from where she sat in front of his desk, schooling her features into absolute blankness. Zimmerman looked positively exhausted. Deep dark circles ringed his eyes. His hair had a very unkempt appearance. He didn't look like a razor had touched his face in a couple of days. He did have on a fresh shirt, and a clean tie dangled loosely around his neck. Kate could only assume that he must have a high-level meeting later this morning.

She'd gotten the phone call at four that morning. Such calls weren't uncommon, and she never minded them much. She met Balder in the parking garage fifty minutes later, and the two of them sat in Zimmerman's office by five.

Despite Zimmerman's exhausted appearance, he sounded sharp, and his voice came out clear.

"Nighthawk is compromised," he said. Kate raised an eyebrow. Nick Williams? Compromised? Zimmerman continued. "He missed his last two check-ins. We must assume the worst and hope for the best." He tossed a folded file toward Balder. "Subject's name is Doctor Aria Suarez. She's a high-level nuclear physicist at NWT in Portland, suspected of nuclear espionage. She is an imminent threat. I'd like her brought in alive, but it isn't an absolute requirement."

Balder opened the file, and Kate looked over to see the photograph of the petite blonde standing next to a lecture podium at MIT. Aria Suarez didn't look the least bit dangerous, but then again, neither did Kate Royce.

"This is high priority," Zimmerman said. He looked at

his watch. "You both have seats on the seven-ten nonstop out of Dulles."

"Consider it taken care of," Balder said as he and Kate stood. She straightened her suit jacket and held her hand out for the file. She read the details, and she and Balder walked out of the offices below the Treasury Department to their waiting car.

Chapter 13

Nick left the HILUX with the empty gas tank sixty-two klicks from the steep ridgeline they gratefully hadn't had to cross on foot. Zimmerman lay on a canvas tarp Nick had found in the back of the HILUX, and he pulled it behind him like a pack mule having secured it to the bottom of his vest with parachute cord. The prisoner marched in front of him, weak from lack of water and lack of rest.

He knew an outpost lay just over the next rise. He prayed it was manned. The first time he had stumbled, he dropped any nonessential gear and left it for the desert to claim. He kept only his ammunition, his knife, his water, and his Soldier's Bible. The sun was starting to rise the second time he stumbled. On his knees, he prayed, "Please, God. Half a klick. I just need that much more strength."

Renewed, he rose back to his feet, picked up the parachute cord that connected him to Zimmerman's makeshift pallet, and started walking again. The prisoner went down next. Nick stopped and looked down at him, then removed the hood. He appeared to be unconscious, but he didn't trust that. He tied the man's hands at the wrist, then held onto the parachute cord and dragged him with his left hand and Zimmerman with his right hand, inch by inch up over the rise. The nylon parachute cord, or five-fifty cord, painfully cut into his chapped, dry palms and fingers so that his hands bled, making it hard to keep his grip.

From where he stood, what he saw definitely looked like American equipment, and was that an American flag? He raised his weapon in the air and fired three rapid shots, then three slow shots, then three rapid shots again. Nine shots in all signifying three short letters.

S. O. S.

Save Our Souls.

Then he fell, rolling down the hill, the parachute cords slipping from his bloody grip, cutting deep grooves into his baked skin. He felt the sun baking his face, but had no energy left to even shield his eyes. He lost the battle to get back up and, as he lost consciousness, he wondered if they'd find him, if they'd find Zimmerman, and if the prisoner had escaped or was really lying unconscious and bound at the top of the rise.

♫ ♫ ♫ ♫

Nick opened his eyes and raised his wrist to look at his watch, barely noticing the jagged scars across his palm and the back of his hand. It was seven-thirty. He couldn't remember the last time he'd been able to sleep for so long at one stretch. The place was quiet around him, and he knew that Aria was still asleep. He felt a brief tug of sympathy for what she was going through, then frowned at his emotions. The smart thing to do would be to get another agent in here to take care of this for him. He was too close to the source and knew his feelings could get in the way, cloud his judgment, but he couldn't conjure up enough trust to hand her over to someone else.

He'd been in love with Aria Suarez since he first saw her, and knew even then that the feelings he had were far more than some childish crush. He'd stopped being a child at age five, and by the time he'd turned fifteen, he'd gone through enough and seen enough to have no innocence left.

When she'd walked into that American History class two days before her fifteenth birthday, he knew he was looking at the only woman on the face of the earth he would ever love. He'd never have her, of course. She was a career soldier's kid; delicate, smart, and clean. That had been the first thing he thought about her. Very few things in his life had ever been clean. She not only looked clean, she even smelled clean. He was white trash from a family that had been white trash for generations.

In the last ten years, anytime he had thought of Aria Suarez, he had pushed that thought deep, deep down into the prison of memory. Perhaps a snatch of a piano tune or a woman in the grocery who smelled like soap and vanilla or a flash of blonde hair as church dismissed; whatever thing it was that reminded him of her, he had always forcefully suppressed the memories that threatened to flood his mind, and he had repressed the inevitable feelings that threatened to stop his heart. Seeing her again, smelling her, hearing her voice—all of it put Nick in a very dangerous and distracting place, because instead of doing his job, all he wanted to do, if he could admit it to himself, was pull her into his arms and start kissing her and never, ever stop.

Being this close to her for the next few days was going to put him through a test he wasn't sure he would pass, but he would do his best to keep from touching her. Every time she touched him, he felt his heart stop beating. Her touch, her gentle, light, burning hot touch was the one thing that could break him.

He rose from the couch and opened his bag, retrieving a pair of shorts and his running shoes. It was still okay to leave her alone right now, and it had been a few days since he'd given himself a good workout. He closed the door quietly and stepped out into the morning.

♫ ♫ ♫ ♫

Aria opened her eyes, rolled over, and offered the clock a look of pure hatred. She sat upright when she saw that it was noon, then collapsed back on the bed when she remembered what was happening. She lay there for a few minutes, trying to find the energy to get out of bed, then slowly sat up. She'd slept in her clothes, she realized, rubbing her hands over her face. What time had she gone to bed? Four?

With a groan, she pushed herself off the bed and stumbled to the bathroom through the door in her room. There was only one bathroom in the house, but it could be accessed from either the hall or her bedroom. Once inside, she realized she should have knocked first. At least he wasn't in there.

She locked both doors, stripped, and stepped into the shower; sticking her face under the spray, trying to erase the cobwebs. Getting up was the absolute worst, no matter if it was six in the morning or noon, she decided. As she stepped out of the shower, she realized that only coffee would get her going this morning. She didn't want to go running this late.

She pulled a pair of jeans and a sweatshirt out of her closet and dressed slowly, still feeling clumsy and fatigued. A cool hush had settled over the house like a blanket of snow. She thought maybe he wasn't even here, but when she stepped into the kitchen, she saw Nick sitting at her table, looking over the map she'd drawn early that morning. He looked far too alert for her taste.

"You slept a long time," he observed. "I made you coffee."

Aria chose to ignore him as she poured a cup of coffee from the full carafe. He offered, "I don't drink that stuff, so it may not be any good."

Aria glared at him while she rummaged through the cupboards, knowing she had a box of cereal somewhere. She found it in with the bowls and thought that it was a convenient place for it. "You should really spend some time organizing this room. Nothing's where you would look for it. I found the coffee filters in with the silverware."

Aria grabbed the carton of milk out of the refrigerator and stumbled to the table, her arms full. "Look, Williams, you want to stay here, you need to realize that mornings stink around here. You've done a good job up to this point of keeping our conversations to a minimum, so follow your normal pattern and save the small talk for someone else."

Nick smiled as he lifted his glass of water to his lips. "It's not morning. It's afternoon."

Aria ignored him and rested her head in her hands. When she lifted her head, he was gone. She was going to have to have a talk with him about making noise when he moved around, she thought. Then she put her head back down.

♫ ♫ ♫ ♫

Nick went to his car, opened the trunk, and grabbed up his other duffel bag. He carried it back inside and sat down in the middle of the floor, opening the bag. He was glad headquarters had provisioned his rental car with standard field gear in addition to the surveillance equipment. He hadn't thought he was going to need any of it, but he rarely went on assignment without it.

He pulled out a bundle of cable, some rope, a winch, and a converted grappling gun, then began to check his equipment. He re-bundled the cable, not knowing who had bundled it last and not trusting whoever that might have been. He would only get one shot at this. He pulled more gear out of the bag and spread it all around him on the floor in parade ground uniform lines.

Aria walked in about half an hour later, feeling more human and wanting to apologize for her outburst. She should have warned him, she thought. She stopped short when she saw her living room floor. "What are you doing?"

"Checking my equipment." Nick never looked up. He just kept opening and closing a snap link attached to a pulley.

"You're really going to try this tonight, aren't you?"

Nick didn't respond. "Tell me about the security on

the computers. I need to get into Harrington's e-mail."

Aria sat down on the couch and pulled her legs under her. "You don't need to break into his computer there. I'm pretty sure I can do that from here."

He stopped what he was doing and looked at her. "I thought you had a hard time getting the stuff off your computer there."

"I did. I'm on a different system because of the classified projects I work on. He's in administration on a different domain. He doesn't have half of the security I do."

"So, how will you be able to get in?"

Aria gestured with her hand toward her head. "Prodigy brain. Music, math, computers—it's all very similar. It's all patterns of code. Once I figure out how to assign a musical value to it, I'm able to do almost anything."

He stared at her as if inspecting her. Finally, he smiled and shook his head. "That's pretty incredible."

"I used to focus only on music. When I was a senior in high school, my brother taught me how to do it with chemistry. Once I realized it was all about the patterns and formulas, I started applying it to other disciplines."

Nick nodded toward her laptop. "Go ahead and get in. Let me know when you're there."

Aria went back to the kitchen, poured a fresh cup of coffee, then sat down at her computer. She could feel her neck tensing up and took a deep breath. She'd never broken into NWT's computer system before. Knowing how to hack in and actually doing it were two different things. It had been years; since college, really. She wondered if she could still do it.

While she worked, she caught herself muttering to herself a couple of times. She even caught herself humming out loud to the tuneless "tune" she created with her code. Twenty minutes later, she shifted in her chair, and her voice broke the quiet of the room. "I'm in," she announced.

"What was that song you were singing. Some kind of grunge thing?"

Aria shook her head. "It's nothing. I didn't mean to hum."

His expression didn't change, but he tilted his head a little to the right. She could tell Nick knew there was more to it and realized she wasn't ready to share. "Go ahead and go to Harrington's files and try to break in there," Nick directed.

"I'm already there."

Nick stood and came up behind her chair, looking over her shoulder. "You're pretty good at this."

Aria felt a little shiver run up her spine at his words, then stood and let him sit in her chair. "Go ahead and look around, but try not to stay on for more than fifteen minutes. I don't want them to be able to track us."

"If he logs on, will he be able to tell I'm here?" Nick asked her, accessing a file.

"Not unless he tries to get into the same file you're in. You'll get a little warning of a sharing violation, then all you do is close the file. He should think it was a glitch in the system. That happens occasionally. But the IDS will log it and security will be able to tell we're on. I hid this computer so they may not be able to trace it, but they'll definitely get a report of a remote access, so work fast."

Aria paced behind him for a while, then stepped over

the stuff on her floor and sat at the couch. She kept expecting a black sedan to come screeching up outside of her home, unloading men in dark suits to arrest her. She rubbed the back of her neck and picked up her dog-eared and highlighted Bible from the table in front of her. She opened it and started reading Psalm 59. "*Deliver me from my enemies, O my God; Defend me from those who rise up against me. Deliver me from the workers of iniquity, And save me from bloodthirsty men.*"

She couldn't help but think how fitting that verse was to her right now in this moment of her life and whispered a prayer of thanksgiving for God's provision in the gift of His Word.

Chapter 14

Nick could find nothing on Harrington's computer. He didn't think he would to begin with. The man was pretty good at covering his tracks from what Nick could tell so far, and to store something on his office system would be foolish. Nick didn't like to leave any stone unturned, and he knew that the most insignificant looking items sometimes revealed the key to malicious intent. Aria was no longer watching what he was doing, so he accessed her personnel file. He was reading her list of merits when the bottom of the screen he'd just switched to caught his attention. Under employment status, it read "terminated." The date was today.

He felt a cold chill run through his body, and his instincts told him to get her out of there. Immediately. Instead, he backed out of the NWT computer system. It was time to check-in.

He went to his duffle bag and rooted around until he found a small black box. He disconnected the cord from the base of the phone and connected it to the box, then ran a line from the box to the phone. Following the feeling in his gut, he engaged the scrambler, which would prevent anyone on the other end from determining his location, and dialed a fourteen-digit number from memory. When a recording asked for the extension he wanted, he dialed another twelve-digit number, then had to enter a passcode. He wasn't expecting Jennifer Thorne to answer the call. "Dove, this is Nighthawk hacking away."

Breaking protocol because she knew the connection was secure, Jen said, "Good heavens, Nick. Charlie's been asking every twenty minutes if you'd called in yet."

"I didn't know this was a priority task," Nick said. "Why are you answering?"

"He's on his extension, talking with the other agents in Portland."

"Oh? Who else is here?" He knew. The blood in his veins felt frozen, icy with fear.

"Balder and Hecate. Look, Nick, that Suarez is a real number. We've been researching her. Where are you calling from, anyway?"

"A payphone not far from her current location. I decided to scramble in case they have this booth tapped." He found a paper and pen in the top drawer of her desk. "When did Balder arrive?" He glanced at Aria, who was watching him with a confused look on her face.

"About ten minutes ago. Hang on a sec, Nick, I think Charlie just hung up." While Nick was put on hold, he scribbled a quick note for Aria:
Go pack 1 backpack with essentials and get ready to leave right now.

"Nick, where have you been?" Charlie asked.

"Enjoying the sites of beautiful Portland. Do you have any idea how many varieties of coffee they serve here?" Nick watched Aria move quickly to her bedroom, not questioning him. He knelt on the floor and began to very quickly and efficiently re-pack his bag.

"Don't play games with me. You don't drink coffee. You're supposed to check in every eight hours."

"I'm not some newbie, Charlie. When did this case elevate above code blue protocols?"

"We're dealing with something bigger than we first thought, and that Suarez girl is at the center of it all. She has a genius-level IQ, and she's the one doing the deal-making. It's pretty clear she decided to turn in a coworker to cover her tracks. I don't know what kind of evidence, and I use that term loosely, she's shown you, but you can bet your life it's all faked. Trust me, Nick. This girl is a puppet master."

"She hasn't shown me anything substantial yet. I've been working on researching the guy she's pointing the finger at."

"Find anything?"

"Nothing worth talking about." Aria walked into the room and gathered her laptop and power adapter. She put them into her backpack, then stood at the door watching him. "He looks pretty clean to me." Nick finished packing his bag and zipped it up.

"I dispatched Hecate and Balder. They just called in from the airport. I want the three of you to interview her vigorously. See what you can get out of her."

Nick stalled, "Want me to involve the locals or coordinate with any other agencies on this? The FBI field office..."

"No. Definitely not. Her target objective has to remain confidential." Nick guessed Charlie didn't want any other agencies to learn about the summit he had set up, though they likely already knew. Homeland and FBI would be all over it this close to the date. "Let's keep this in-house, for now, Nick."

"If they just arrived at the airport, they'll be here in about twenty minutes," Nick calculated.

"You guys call me as soon as you've taken her into custody. And remember, she's more dangerous than she appears."

"I don't need a baby-sitter, Charlie. And really, there was no need to bring Balder in." He stood and slung the strap of the bag over his shoulder and grabbed up the other one.

"We didn't know what had happened to you, kid. You didn't check-in, and like I said, she's a feisty one. I didn't want another Nigeria."

Nick closed his eyes and forced unpleasant memories back. "I'll call you when they get here." Nick hung up and disconnected the scrambler box from the landline. He turned toward Aria.

"Leave your phone. It's definitely compromised. Let's go," he ordered, grabbing her arm and propelling her out the door to his car, where he opened her door and practically pushed her inside. He threw his bags into the back-seat, not wanting to take the time to open the trunk, then started the car and backed out of the driveway.

"What happened?" Aria asked.

"The tables have turned on you. You're being set up

for this whole thing." Nick maneuvered his way through her neighborhood. After a few minutes of moderately light midmorning traffic, they approached the interstate, and at the last minute, Nick headed north.

"Can't we show them the evidence I have against Peter?"

"They dispatched Balder and Hecate. I've worked with them a few times before, and they have a reputation. Trust me. They're not at all concerned with your evidence." Nick merged with the traffic and kept the speed under the posted limits. He didn't want to risk a traffic stop.

"Who are Balder and Hecate?" Aria asked in a tight voice.

"Balder is an assassin. His second-best specialty is water-boarding. His first is long-range sniper tasks. Hecate's a tracker like nothing you've ever seen before. It doesn't matter where we go, now, or how we try to hide. She'll eventually find us. We need to dump this car."

♫ ♫ ♫ ♫

Just before they left the city, Nick got off the interstate and turned back toward town. "What bank do you use?" he asked.

She told him and directed him toward the main branch. "I don't want to run the risk of using my card. Balder might have already made it to your house. Do you have any money in the bank?"

"I still have most of the money you left me in a savings account." She leaned her head back on the seat and closed her eyes. Since meeting a dead man at a coffee shop yesterday, her life had become one more surreal event than the last. Could any of this actually be happening to her?

"What money?" Nick asked, pulling into the bank parking lot.

"You named me as your sole beneficiary, including your life insurance. I also got the money you had in your checking account."

Nick stared at her for a moment. "I'd forgotten about that. How much do you have?"

Aria shrugged. "I don't know. A little over two hundred thousand left, I think."

Nick blinked, twice, and realized that sometimes things actually did work out in his favor. He did a quick mental calculation. "Go ahead and get fifty thousand out if they'll let you. The main branch will have that much in small bills on hand. I'll wait out here for you."

Aria pulled her savings book out of her purse and went inside the bank. Twenty-six minutes later, she got back in the car carrying two rather full medium-sized rectangular faux leather bank bags with zippers on one of the long sides. "I got sixty thousand."

Nick nodded. "I don't want to get back on the interstate. They know we're gone by now. We'll drive east through town," Nick told her before starting the car.

"You're the boss," Aria asserted, then closed her eyes again.

Nick hardly spared her a glance, but he began to see the inside. How? Who? What had tipped Harrington off? It would take everything in his power to help Aria, and he thanked God Charlie had handed him this assignment.

About twenty miles outside the city, Nick spotted a

rest area and pulled in, parking way in the back near the dog walk. He turned and knelt in his seat, rummaging through his bag, finding the supplies he needed, then sat back down facing the front.

Aria rested her back against the door and watched him. He had a long flat box, and she snuck a peek when he opened it. Inside were dozens of little compartments, each containing a pair of contact lenses in every color imaginable. She watched as he selected a dark brown pair and popped them into his eyes, then tilted his head back with his eyes tightly closed. She saw a tear escape and run down the side of his face and resisted the urge to wipe it away.

"I hate these things." His almost absentminded admission surprised her. He wiped his eyes then restarted the car. "We're going to find a hotel and lay up, then I'm going to go back and break into NWT."

"Isn't that risky?" Aria asked. Her voice sounded a little bit panicky to her, and she tried to stifle it before she decided that she should be allowed to feel a little bit panicky.

"They won't expect me to go there. I'm supposed to be meeting up with Balder, and the security at NWT is pretty tight, so it seems risky for me to tackle it alone—even if that were the plan, which it never was. When I don't meet up with Balder or Hecate, they'll start looking for me. So tonight will probably be the only chance I'll get," he explained. "We'll need to leave immediately afterward, though. Once I'm out, they'll know it was me, and we'll have a hard time getting out of the city."

"Then, don't do it. Let's just go somewhere and hide,"

she suggested. Unexpected and unwanted tears filled her eyes, and she angrily wiped them away.

Nick put the car back in park and turned to her. "Listen to me, Aria. I don't know who's behind this, but someone wants to get at you so much they sent in Balder and Hecate. If they told him to, Balder would murder his own mother and sleep like a baby. He's like a machine. Hecate looks like an innocent schoolgirl, but she's more like a vampire. There's no telling how many men died with her face being the last thing they saw in life. You stumbled onto something big here, and I don't have anyone else I can trust right now. We need to find out what we can while we still have the chance."

Aria lifted her chin and fought back the emotions that threatened to consume her. When this was over, she promised herself she would find a dark room and have a good crying fit. "Some friends of my parents from when we were stationed here at Lewis-McChord retired a few years back. They bought a cabin near Mt. Hood not long ago. They gave me a key, hoping I would use it and check on their cabin a few times a year. No one else knows about it."

Nick looked at her for a few seconds, watching her keep a tight grip on her control. "Good girl. Where to?" Aria gave him directions, then leaned back in her seat and tried to relax.

♫ ♫ ♫ ♫

After several turns, each road becoming more rural and even narrower than the one before, they finally drove onto a climbing dirt road that twisted and turned through the Oregon woods. Nick had to navigate the car carefully over one particularly bad patch of road, then they rounded a curve and suddenly came upon the clearing and the cabin. Aria released a breath she hadn't been aware she was holding when she saw that it was empty. She dug around in her purse and found the key.

"I was almost afraid they'd be here," she acknowledged as she got out of the car and grabbed her backpack and her laptop. Nick accepted the offered key from her and opened the front door, then did a quick search inside with his pistol at the ready.

It was a relatively new, nicely built cedar log cabin with a kitchen, main room, and bedroom with a full bath. One wall in the main room was all glass and faced the view of the mountains rising up around them. The kitchen had obviously been designed for a cook and boasted state-of-the-art appliances. Aria inspected the kitchen and found a pantry filled with canned food and some dried goods. She gathered supplies and started putting together a light meal. It was already four, and the bowl of cereal she'd eaten at noon was long gone.

She started heating up a pot of water for some pasta and opened a jar of spaghetti sauce. It dawned on her as she stirred the sauce that she had started to feel relaxed. The shock of the events which had transpired over the last twenty-four hours and the situation in which she'd found herself for the last two months felt unreal right now. She realized that she completely trusted Nick to take care of this for her. He would find out who was behind this, she knew. He would stop the plan to detonate a nuclear device, and he would clear her name.

♫ ♫ ♫ ♫

Nick felt trapped by the almost overwhelming longing that swept over him as he stood in the doorway of the kitchen and watched Aria prepare the meal. He finally gathered up what strength he had and turned around, silently going back to the main room. Now was not the time.

No matter how cozy and intimate their surroundings felt, it was not the time to explore the feelings he had always had for her. Somehow his emotions were no longer manageable and insisted on coming to the forefront of his mind. He couldn't let his guard down now, and having that conversation with her would certainly require his complete attention. He paced the main room, shutting his eyes and forcing himself to think, desperately searching for his lost self-control. Finally, he turned and headed back to the kitchen, making as much noise as possible along the way.

Aria looked up from the sink where she was draining the pasta and gave him a small smile. "I figured you were hungry, too, and a can of soup just didn't sound very appealing," she said to him.

Nick lifted a lid from a pot on the stove and inhaled the fragrant spices coming up with the steam. "Spaghetti's fine."

"We're only about an hour outside the city," she said. "We kind of came in a roundabout way, so that's what took us so long to get here."

To break the relaxed and intimate mood, he said, "Aria, when I leave tonight, if I'm not back in six hours, I'm probably not coming back."

"If you're shooting for a way to make me wait up for you, you just hit the bullseye," Aria said. She pulled two plates out of the cupboard.

Nick ignored her attempt at lightness. "We need to plan what to do if that happens."

He watched her hands tremble and heard the plates clank together before she set them on the counter. "I don't want to think about that. Can't we just assume that nothing will happen?"

"You wouldn't last a day on your own, Aria. These people do this for a living. You need to have a plan if you want to survive." Nick sat at the table and watched her mechanically fill plates.

"I could go to my brother in Atlanta. He'll know what to do next," she said. Her brother, John Suarez, was a Detective with the Atlanta Police. Aria carried the plates to the table and sat down. "I forgot forks," she whispered as she turned to get them.

Nick rubbed his forehead. "Not Atlanta. Stay as far away from your family as you can. You've already been researched, and I'm sure your brothers and your parents are already under surveillance."

Aria sat back down and stuck her fork into the spaghetti, twirling it around. Without taking a bite, she set the fork down and put a shaking hand against her forehead. "I don't know what to do," she said. He could hear the tears in her voice.

Nick suddenly realized that, as of this moment, Aria had suffered more changes than she could emotionally handle. She wasn't trained for this. She was a civilian.

In the last twenty-four hours, Aria had realized that

the high school JROTC commander she buried was, in fact, alive. Then she abandoned her normal sleep pattern, then deserted her home, and had gone on the lam after withdrawing a ton of money from her bank. Now she sat here in unfamiliar surroundings discussing the very real possibility of him getting killed and her being completely alone with trained killers literally gunning for her within the next few hours, all over a plate of spaghetti.

By making this meal, she was trying to reestablish something normal in her life, and he had just increased her shock level to the point that he brought her to the edge of tears. He needed to back off and give her time to emotionally adjust. He decided to start by getting back to something normal.

"Mind if I ask God for a blessing over this meal you've made for us?" Nick asked as he folded his hands in front of him and watched her eyes widen a bit. Nick didn't offer to hold her hands while he asked the blessing. He knew he would not want to stop touching her if he did.

"Please do," she agreed, then bowed her head and folded her hands.

Nick said, "God, we thank you for Your gifts of provision. We trust that You have a plan, and we trust You will reveal to us the path you've set before us. We pray for the strength to walk that path. Please bless this food and let it strengthen our physical bodies as Your word strengthens our spirit. In Your holy name we pray. Amen."

Nick quickly began to put food into his mouth, forcing himself to chew and swallow. He needed the calories, though he didn't want the food. He thought hard, trying to come up with an alternate plan, and hitting dead ends every time.

Not counting Marcus, who was also a civilian, Nick had only one other person whom he could trust to keep Aria alive. He silently prayed he wasn't making a mistake. He hated himself for thinking it, but he had to admit, rationally, that she could very easily be part of this whole thing, too.

He swallowed and said, "Thanks for making this, Aria."

Aria grinned, thinking how oddly satisfying it felt to receive this simple expression of gratitude. "You're very welcome. Anytime." Indeed. Anytime at all, Nick Williams.

"Do you know if the Jeep in the garage runs?" he asked, all business again.

"I know the four-wheeler does. I don't know about the Jeep."

Nick nodded. "I'll check it out. Let's assume it runs. I know you can drive a stick. I remember your first car back in high school. At first light, get in the Jeep and drive east on 26 to the train station in Madras. Get to Washington, D. C., and take the Metro to the Treasury Building. In the lowest level of the parking garage, you'll find a late model white Chevy Impala SS in the handicap space. I'll give you a note to put on the windshield.

"Stay near it and wait. It may take several hours. A tall thin woman with brown hair and a prosthetic arm will come out. After she reads the note, walk toward her. She'll take care of you from there."

"What's her name?"

"Jen Thorne."

Chapter 15

Aria finished watching the evening news and turned off the television, then stood up and stretched. Though she didn't particularly care for the flavor, she decided to go into the kitchen to make some instant coffee, which was all the cabin offered. She knew she would not be able to sleep tonight until Nick got back. Because he would be back, she promised herself.

In some ways, Aria could already read a few of Nick's largely inscrutable body language signals, and she had picked up on his unvoiced concern. Having correctly interpreted those clues, Aria knew that sometime tonight or in the early morning hours, Nick would come back. He would come back so that she didn't have to take a train across the country and seek help from a one-armed woman who may or may not be in on this whole thing.

She turned the teapot on to heat the water and went to the back door where she'd seen Nick go out an hour ago. She found him sitting in a lounge chair facing the mountains, eyes closed, appearing to be asleep. She didn't want to disturb him, so she pulled another chair closer to him and sat down. She wanted to enjoy the view of the sun setting behind the mountains, but she was having a hard time concentrating on it. What would happen tonight? Would Nick come back, or was she going to be on her own?

She had just found him again. How many times had she let herself wallow in melancholy and allowed thoughts of what might have been to dominate her days? How many times had she wondered what their children might have looked like had they married and shared a life together after high school?

Now here he was, reappearing as if from the grave, resurrected in a very different form yet still oddly the same as she remembered. If she were to be completely honest, she didn't want him to leave. She never wanted him to leave again. She wanted to forever remain by his side as long as life endured.

She leaned back and closed her eyes, willing her mind to stop running in circles and willing her body to relax.

♫ ♫ ♫ ♫

*"**Hi**, kid. Welcome back to the real world. You did a good job out there—real survivor. I owe you my life, and your nation owes you a debt of gratitude." Charlie Zimmerman sat by Nick's hospital cot, wearing a blue terry cloth robe over sky blue scrubs.*

Nick took in his surroundings, letting his nose smell the sterile rubbery smell of pure oxygen being piped into his nostrils. He let his skin take in the scratchy, clean, cottony bleached warmth of the blanket that covered his body. He felt the floaty, disconnected feeling of pain killers bathing his bloodstream in artificial comfort. Mostly, he felt the pain in his head and shoulders. His head felt like it was going to explode, and his mouth felt like it had been stuffed with cotton.

"Thirsty," he managed to choke out, and a straw was placed between his lips. He greedily took a sip, then the straw was taken away.

"Not too fast, son. You need to take it slow, or you'll end up making yourself sick. I'm not sure you would enjoy vomiting right now."

Nick realized he lay in a CASH, probably at Striker but maybe some other installation or forward operating base. The rubberized walls and floors informed him that he was in a medical tent, and he wondered why there were no doctors or nurses attending him, only the guy he had dragged out of the desert on a tarp.

"Prisoner?" Nick whispered. Zimmerman grinned.

"Sang like a canary when a tall glass of water appeared in front of him. You did good, son. Saved about ten thousand lives."

Nick nodded. Zimmerman gave him another sip. Nick let the water fill his mouth and savored the feel of it on his tongue and chapped lips before he slowly swallowed, feeling the water trickle all the way down into his belly. He could not remember water ever tasting so good in his life.

At that moment, part of Nick's waking mind realized that he was dreaming, that he had experienced all of these events a lifetime ago, and that he would be waking up very soon.

Zimmerman said, "The pilot and copilot actually survived. They're calling it a miracle. You believe in miracles, son?"

Nick grinned, "I do now."

Zimmerman chuckled and held out his hand. "You survived, too. You're going to pull through and be as good as new, kid. Or, you know, you don't have to. You could die instead. Your choice."

Nick felt his eyebrows knot. What did that mean?

Zimmerman leaned in a bit and placed the straw between Nick's lips again as he said, "You've got skills, kid. And guts. Rare combination. I'd like to make you an offer you'd be wise not to refuse."

♫ ♫ ♫ ♫

When Nick opened his eyes, the sight that greeted him was breathtaking. The mountains spread out in front of him were framed with glorious streaks of red and orange, and dark clouds formed nearly solid shapes amid the backdrop. It was as if the sun waged a battle with the sky, fighting to the last second to keep from having to leave its realm. Then the darkness won the battle, pushing the sun further behind the mountains and, as if in sorrow, the sky around the mountains turned dark red, a final defiance against the darkness.

To be able to sit and enjoy a sunset this spectacular was a rare opportunity, one Nick wished he could take advantage of more often. He turned his head slightly to the left and saw Aria next to him, staring at the sky, lost in her own thoughts. He wanted to reach out and trace her profile, run his finger along the soft skin of her cheek, but kept his hand at his side, his fist clenched.

As if sensing his stare, she turned her head and looked at him with wide, scared eyes. "When do you have to leave?" she asked quietly.

Nick looked at his watch. Six-fifteen. It got dark quicker in the mountains. "In a couple of hours." He sat up and turned, sitting sideways in the chair and facing her. He almost didn't want to ask the next question, afraid to learn that Aria had intimate knowledge of Mr. Harrington's activities. "What kind of schedule does Harrington keep at night?"

Aria shrugged. "Not sure. When his daughter's here, they usually go out to eat. He doesn't cook, and so far hasn't asked me to make a meal for them."

Trying to keep his face impassive, he clarified. "That's not what I mean. What time does he usually go to bed?"

"I'm just sure I don't know." Aria turned her head back to the mountains. Only the tips were outlined in red now. Soon it would be completely dark. "I've never been at his house at bedtime."

Nick was once again staring at her profile. He didn't know if the sunset reflecting on her face caused the tinge of pink he saw, or if she was embarrassed about something. Why did he feel relief? What Aria Suarez did or did not do with her boyfriends had nothing to do with him. She didn't even know he was alive before they met at the coffee shop. "When's the latest time at night he's ever called you? Or sent a text?"

She closed her eyes, trying to think back. "Ten, I think. I'm usually up later than that, so I think it was about ten."

Nick nodded. "Good. I'll hit his house about eleven, then be at NWT by twelve, twelve-thirty at the latest."

"You're going to his house while he's there?" Aria asked, her voice shocked.

"No choice. This is the only time I'll get the chance. And, his security system may be turned off while he's home." Before he could even think better of it, he reached over and took her hand. The feel of her skin beneath his fingers startled him into realizing that touching her was a mistake. "I have to find a way to clear your name. I can't go back to D. C. without some sort of proof."

"I have proof."

"All you have could have been created by you or an accomplice just to frame him. Think about it. How hard would it have been for you, as skilled with computers as you are, to leave a log of his ID with timestamps on your files?"

Nick slowly ran his thumb over her knuckles. He should stop touching her now, but he couldn't bring himself to do so. Aria stared at their joined hands. When she looked back to meet his eyes, he felt his breath stop.

"I don't know," she whispered.

Suddenly, he released her hand and shot to his feet, needing to put space between them, needing to break the temptation of contact.

"Nick?"

Nick paused with his hand on the doorknob, his back to her. "If I get distracted, it could cost you your life." He opened the door and went inside.

♫ ♫ ♫ ♫

When Aria felt like she could face Nick again, she went back inside and found him sitting in the middle of the floor in front of the glass wall, the darkness of the night reflecting the room back to them on the glass. He was once again checking his equipment, opening and closing a pulley, oiling a grappling gun, checking the batteries in a pair of night-vision goggles. Some of the equipment was familiar to her. Since his retirement from the Army, her father had taken up mountain climbing as a hobby, and the tools were very similar. Some of the equipment, though, was very foreign to her, and she didn't want to know what it was all for.

"Do you want something to eat?" she asked, breaking the silence of the room. He didn't speak, just shook his head and kept fiddling with whatever it was he was fiddling with. "Is there anything I can do to help you?" She was going to lose her mind if she sat idle one more minute. She felt like she needed to do something.

"Still remember how to clean a weapon?" Nick asked. Aria shrugged, then nodded. Nick reached into his bag and pulled out a .45 caliber XD9525 GAP pistol, removed the magazine, checked to ensure there wasn't a round in the chamber, then passed it to her with the slide locked to the rear. Aria grabbed the cleaning kit she saw amid the stuff on the floor and studied the pistol.

"It's light," she observed. She sat on the couch and, when she felt confident she could do so successfully, disassembled the pistol to clean it.

"Peter has a standard house security system, no motion detectors, or anything inside that I ever saw," she confided a short while later. "He doesn't have a dog, and the house is a split-level, three-story. If you went in the front door, it seems like you're on the first floor, but actually, it's the second. His bedroom is the first door off the top of the stairs, here." She pointed to her tiny map.

"When you go in the front door of the house, his office is to the right. I've never been in there, only looked in through the open door a few times. The lower level has no windows facing the front but has a living area with a sliding door leading to the backyard. There's a little brick patio where he keeps his gas grill."

Nick turned to look at her and said, "Thank you."

"I brought my laptop with me. If you want, I can try to hack into his computer from here. That could save us some time."

"You can't do anything until after ten."

"Right," she agreed. "Neither can you."

Nick stopped what he was doing so he could direct his full attention to her. "Why didn't you hack his home computer before now?"

Aria finished putting the pistol together and set it on the couch next to her. "This is my first attempt at espionage. It only just occurred to me."

Nick smiled on one side of his mouth and went back to work. "You're proving that you're a natural. Maybe we'll recruit you when this is all over with."

"Ha. Ha. Ha. So funny." She stood and stretched. "I'm going to make some tea. Do you want anything?"

Nick shook his head and kept working.

Aria went into the kitchen, and the aroma reminded her that she'd already made instant coffee, so she poured herself a cup and sat at the table, then decided to write her mother a letter. She knew better than to try to call, as much as she needed to hear her mother's voice, so she opened the laptop and sat there, staring at the screen. How did she begin?

Hello, Mom. Remember Nick—the boy I always talked about in high school? The boy we buried who left me all that money? Well, turns out he's not dead. He's a secret agent, and he's helping me try to clear my name while simultaneously keeping trained killers from murdering me in my sleep and foiling a nuclear incident the size of Hiroshima.

She laughed at the thought, then felt tears come to her eyes. What would it be like to have no one? She couldn't imagine it, though when her brothers shielded her as if she were still ten years old, the thought had some appeal. She wondered what it might be like to claim the kind of anonymity only death could offer. What must the Nick of ten years ago have felt in his heart? Did he think maybe the only person in the world who cared about him was the girl with the locker next to his in high school? She turned her head and saw Nick standing in the doorway, watching her. She was starting to get used to the way he could sneak up on her and wasn't startled.

She stood up from the table and walked up to him until she had to crane her neck back to look up at him. They stood like that for several heartbeats. She wanted to touch him but was afraid he would push her away. Instead, she asked him a question that had been bothering her for years. "Why did you leave that money to me, Nick?" It came out in almost a whisper.

The look that crossed Nick's face was almost painful, and he lifted a hand to touch her hair. "I didn't have anyone else." His voice was as quiet as hers.

"That's no answer," she said, reading the look in his ice-blue eyes.

His jaw clenched three times, and he said, "Back in high school, I would have given you the moon if I thought it would make you happy." His deep voice carried through the still space and echoed quietly off the cedar walls.

Aria leaned her head forward until it rested on his chest. She felt his hand gently fall onto her hair. "You always rejected me," she said.

It seemed to Aria that they stood that way forever, when in fact it was just the span of a few seconds. He kept his hand on her hair and didn't pull her any closer. "I was always afraid I'd hurt you."

She thought about it. "You only hurt me when you rejected me."

He stepped back and ran a hand from her shoulder to her wrist, bringing her right hand up to inspect the small scars that crisscrossed the top of it. "Look what happened to you because of me."

"You didn't do that. Raymond did." She felt her eyelashes wet with tears. "And it changed him. He sobered up and found God. So, it became a good thing."

Nick's eyebrows drew together in a frown. "What?"

"It's an amazing story. But, to hear it, you need to come back tonight." She stepped back, wiping her eyes with both hands. "There. Now you have some incentive." Her voice sounded shrill, panicked, and she felt a bubble of hysteria trying to rise in her chest, but she pushed it back down. Suddenly, she noticed that he had changed clothes and was now dressed entirely in black. "Do you have to leave right now?"

He closed his eyes and gave a brief shake of his head as if to clear it. When he opened them again, all the depths of emotion she'd seen just seconds before had vanished. "Yes. Don't forget; give me only until about six-thirty. You won't be able to stay here by yourself, and the more of a head start you get, the better."

"What if you're on your way?"

"If I can't make it back in time, I'll head for the train station and meet you in D. C." They walked back toward the living room. Nick's duffel bags were packed and standing by the door. He pulled an envelope out of his pocket and handed it to her. "This is what you'll need to put on Jen's windshield. Don't open it, or she'll think it's been tampered with."

She looked at the envelope, recognizing his handwriting. She watched him pick up his bags, slinging one over his shoulder. Somehow, she felt calm, not panicky or scared at all. He put his hand on the doorknob, then turned back to her. "Aria—"

She moved closer to him, stood on her toes, and gave him a hard, quick kiss on the mouth. "God be with you, Nick."

He said nothing more. He opened the door and walked to his car. Aria watched him load the bags into the back seat, then she shut the door, locking both locks and latching the chain. She went back to the kitchen where she had set up her computer and sat down, typing out all the possible passwords Peter might use.

Opening up her compiler, she started constructing a script to automate her attack. She had a few password cracking programs from her college days back at her house, but she didn't have them with her. Instead, she was going to have to attempt to brute force her way through, and a script would speed things up. All the while, between humming and whistling nonsense music while she coded, she whispered prayers for Nick's protection and for her mental acuity.

Chapter 16

It took Nick an hour to reach Portland. He stopped on the outskirts to wash the car. In the event that he had to dump this car, he didn't want to leave any evidence of where Aria might be hiding. The soil from the dirt road leading to the cabin would shed light on her whereabouts like a neon sign pointing the way. It was nearly eight and completely dark now, with a light mist falling. He felt grateful for the mist, knowing how much more cover it would provide when he reached his objective.

He easily found Harrington's house and parked down the street, just close enough so that he could watch the place. He shifted in his seat until he felt comfortable and sat back, prepared to wait for two hours. There were still lights on in the downstairs windows. If Harrington wasn't in bed by ten-thirty, he wouldn't be able to take the time he needed to do a thorough enough search.

He took a quick look around, looking for movement or anyone observing him. His scan was as second nature to him as breathing. All the cars in sight of the house were empty and seemed to belong. If this house was being watched to see if Nick showed up, nothing he could see pointed to it. Good. That would just make it easier for him. He could break in under surveillance, and not be seen, but felt glad that he didn't have to worry about that this time.

With some time to spare, he pulled a penlight from his pocket and pulled his worn Soldier's Bible from the cargo pocket of his pants. It was falling apart, with loose pages and dust from countries all over the world, but he didn't have any desire to replace it. He just handled it with care and taped whatever needed to be taped.

Using the penlight, he opened the Bible and started reading. *Forgive your enemies...*

With a sigh, he closed the Bible and leaned his head back. Raymond Williams was sober and had found God? What was Nick supposed to do with that information? Could he actually pray for the man who had fathered him?

He looked at his watch. Ten-fifteen. The lights in the downstairs went off, and an upstairs light came on, then blinked off again. Nick waited ten more minutes, then started his car and drove around the block. An apartment building was on the other side, and he backed the car into a space, then got out, locked it, and put the keys behind the front tire. His black fatigue pants had several pockets, and he already had what he needed on him. He transferred his duffel bags to the trunk.

He cut through the back lawn of the apartment building and came to the fence surrounding Harrington's back yard. Alarm companies did not wire every window, and homeowners felt safe with the mistaken thought that second-floor windows provided a more difficult entry. A petty thief might be dissuaded by the signs in the lawn advertising the alarm company, but a professional would know how to get in, what windows were wired, and in the case of an empty house, how to disable the alarm in the ten seconds he had once the door was open. He climbed the fence and crouched on the top so as not to silhouette himself, balancing for the jump.

He landed perfectly and quietly on a low part of the roof, and ran silently across, up, and over to the other side. He crouched on a particularly steep part of the rooftop on the front side of the house facing the street and examined a window that led into the kitchen. The window was a steel frame vinyl clad double-hung double pane job. He checked the frame and the glass and saw no evidence of alarm wires. Using a titanium lock picking chisel that was almost paper-thin, he quietly and very quickly worked the latches open and then lifted the bottom sash. He counted to ten, and no alarm sounded. He went in, leaving the window slightly cracked behind him.

He moved through the house, and at the door to the office, he stopped and checked for wires. Just as he suspected—this room had added security. It was quick work to disable the door alarm, and he pulled his goggles out of his pocket and switched them to infrared just to be on the safe side. He could see no further evidence of security from where he stood. He stepped through the threshold and looked at his watch. Eleven—he had one hour.

♫ ♫ ♫ ♫

Another bleep sounded from her laptop sitting on the table, staring at her, announcing that Aria once again had input the wrong password. If it bleeped at her one more time, she was going to toss the stupid machine through the window.

Despite her frustration, an outside observer would be amazed she had gotten this far in this short amount of time. In moments of elegant activity and ingenious, if not inspired, hacking, she had already captured his hashes. Some programs could have cracked the password from those hashes in seconds flat. She was using a homemade script she had written a little over thirty minutes ago, coupled with her knowledge of the algorithm.

Aria took a deep breath and leaned back, trying to come up with another possible word. She'd tried everything she could think of. What could it be? She remembered Peter complaining about NWT's rule that passwords must be changed every thirty days. He said he always had a hard time coming up with something. His home computer was new. It would be something obvious. She'd helped him set it up, and had turned her back when he put in his password. Inspiration struck. She leaned forward and typed in "ariasuarez" as a possible password.

No bleep. She was in. She breathed a sigh of relief and looked at her watch. It was already eleven-thirty.

♫ ♫ ♫ ♫

Harrington obviously didn't think he needed to cover his tracks in his own home. He had copies of everything. Nick had struck gold. There was so much he didn't even have time to go through it all, so he started digitally recording everything without reading it first. They would enhance the images later, blow up the details of the papers, and maybe Aria would know what it all meant. It took him forty-five minutes to complete the film, and he looked at his watch. At NWT, they conducted a shift change at midnight, then again at two. He needed to be in by twelve-thirty to have the time to do everything he needed to do there.

Nick put the office back in order exactly as if he had never been there, then reconnected the alarm to the door. He made his way back through the house and out the window, carefully levering the locks back on the window sash. He couldn't close them all the way because he didn't have the angle from the outside. Still, the window was closed and locked. Unless Harrington was looking for signs of a home invasion, or until he opened or cleaned the window, he would never suspect.

He jumped from the roof to the ground and climbed back over the fence. A dog somewhere in the neighborhood began to bark, so Nick was careful to stay in the shadows of the trees cast by the streetlights as he cut back through the lawn of the apartment complex and got back to the car. Another glance at his watch told him he was right on time.

He started the car and pulled out of the parking lot with the headlights off. Once he turned on the street, he drove about fifty yards, then stopped, waiting to see if another vehicle followed him. Nothing moved, so he turned on the lights and drove on, turning in the direction of NWT.

♫ ♫ ♫ ♫

Peter obviously felt safe leaving things unsecured on his home computer. That was a common error. Simply disconnecting the computer from any outside internet and locking it down to a VPN only connection would be enough security for most people. All the better for her right now, she thought, and went to work.

He had another meeting arranged to hand over some more information. Aria wasn't able to trace where the message came from, but she copied the file and the headers and saved it on her computer to show Nick. He'd said they needed to see information actually change hands. She kept looking, finding copies of years' worth of correspondence stored in his old work folders.

Oh Peter, you foolish, foolish man. If nothing else, he should have encrypted the files or saved them onto a self-encrypting backup and erased his hard drive. The first thing the authorities would do if he were arrested would be to search his computer.

Aria looked at her watch. Twelve-fifteen. She felt comfortable staying on for another half-hour at the most. She didn't want to leave too many traces in the logs, in case Peter actually checked them.

♫ ♫ ♫ ♫

Nick aimed the grappling gun and fired, the hook traveling the distance and sinking into the wall exactly where he needed it to, burying itself eight inches into the steel-reinforced concrete wall. He waited for five minutes, making sure there wasn't an alarm on the outer walls, and when there was no movement around him, he secured the other end of the cable to the fence and pulled on it with all of his might. It didn't budge. He secured it to a turnbuckle and cranked the tension until the fence began to give.

Good enough.

He put on a backpack, hooked himself to a makeshift harness, and climbed onto the cable, wrapping his legs around it and hanging upside down. He hooked the harness to the cable and used a pulley to quickly propel himself along it like a reverse zip line. The problem with feeling secure about infrared sensors was that you could go above them or below them, and no one would be the wiser.

He reached the building, switched his goggles from infrared to starlight, and looked up. The ledge on the window a story above him was made out of concrete block and about six inches thick. He hoped that the block would retain its integrity after being speared with a steel hook, and aimed the grappling gun. It went through the block, about half of the hook coming out of the top. Nick pulled on the cable, then hung from it while still secured to the other cable. The block held, so he released from the first cable and climbed hand over fist to the ledge, then perched on the ledge and etched into the old glass.

He reached his hand in and had to break through the paint that had been coating the latch for who knew how long, finally able to unlock the window. He raised it up and waited another five minutes, his legs starting to cramp from his unnatural crouching position. No sirens sounded, and no lights flooded the yard, so he entered Peter Harrington's office. Information from Aria had saved him from having to search through any of the other buildings.

Nick needed to know how Harrington got the information out. Lighter security for administration or not, there had to be a place Harrington stored the data before he transported it, a kind of digital staging area. From what Nick could glean from the snatches of information he retained of the files in Harrington's home office, this had been going on for years. The fact that he had not been caught yet told Nick that everything was carefully plotted out and executed. That meant that there was a place where things were kept. Where else would he keep it but in his realm? Harrington struck Nick as the kind of guy who would only feel comfortable locating the stash somewhere he could check on it constantly, make sure it was still there and okay.

The glow of the security light was enough to enable his goggles to do their job, and he could see perfectly in the office. The desk revealed nothing; neither hidden compartments nor secret drawers. Next, Nick searched the filing cabinets, still coming up empty. Frustrated, he looked at his watch. He needed to move soon, needed to not be on the property during the next shift change. He went back to the desk and knelt to look under it. When he shifted his weight, he felt one of the tiles under his knee move.

Nick pulled a dark commando knife from the sheath at his ankle and pried the tile loose. *Got you*, he thought, and began to record the contents of the cache.

If Nick were a betting man, he would have bet that there was some sort of storage closet underneath him, and unless some major renovations were going to be done to the building, no one would be aware of the foot of space that was missing from the ceiling height. The shape of the hole in the floor was about that of a closet opening.

He finished recording and put the tiles back in place. As he stood, a bright flare blinded him, and he ripped the night vision goggles off to see Balder shining a flashlight in his direction. He stood in the corner of the room, near a closet opening. Nick cursed himself when he realized he should have checked the room with the infrared before he started searching to make sure no heat sources were in the vicinity.

Keeping an outward calm, he put the first strap of the backpack on one shoulder, and acted as if he were reaching behind him for the other strap, while he greeted the assassin standing in front of him. "Hey, Balder. Murder any innocents on your way over?"

The agent code-named Balder was a tall, thin man from Columbia. His real name was probably only known to some dead drug cartel members currently enjoying unmarked shallow graves in an anonymous South American jungle. He'd been sickened by the drug empires that sprang up around him in his lifetime and had moved to the United States, trading information for citizenship. Because of him, several drug lords were taken out of the picture, most of them by Balder's own hand, and he had proven himself capable of the job the government had in mind for him. He'd been with NISA for ten years and had never failed in a mission.

Nick couldn't stand the man, knowing how much pleasure he derived from every assignment he completed, and personally thought that he must have figured out how to cheat on the psychological evaluations they endured annually. No one who took that much pleasure in killing could qualify as sane.

He had always respected Balder's partner, Hecate. He didn't understand how someone who consistently remained on the up-and-up could partner with such a sociopathic killer. Over the years, Nick realized that Kate balanced Balder and, in a strange way, restrained him somewhat.

Balder ran his finger along the thin mustache gracing his upper lip and smiled a wicked smile. "Not as many as I should have, my friend." He flicked off his flashlight so Nick could see the pistol he held pointed in Nick's direction with a long suppresser attached to the end of the barrel. "Perhaps if not for your interference, I would be in a better mood this fine evening."

Nick had a grip on the handle of the knife that he wore strapped to his back and saw that Balder hadn't realized it yet. He also wondered why Balder hadn't just shot him already. It would be consistent with his style. Obviously, he did not have orders to take Nick out, only the girl. Nick searched his mind for a way to use that information. "Why don't you tell me where the girl is, Nighthawk? I'll make it quick and painless for her. Then perhaps I'll leave you for Charlie to deal with and not kill you myself."

The suppresser would nullify most of the explosive noise of the gunshot, but it would still be noisy. The main reason NISA used .45 caliber rounds instead of say, nine-millimeter, was that a .45 caliber slug traveled at less than the speed of sound. The noise of any supersonic round could not be suppressed despite the ridiculous gadgetry Hollywood paraded past popcorn-munching audiences.

"Leave me for Charlie to take care of? You mean the guy whose life I saved three times already? Better get your facts straight, *amigo*. You know I don't like you, but you also know me well enough by now to know—with certainty—that I wouldn't even be here without orders. When's the last time you checked in?" Nick asked. If he could get the suppressed pistol or use his knife, he could take care of Balder in a relatively quiet fashion.

Balder didn't like the question. Nick saw a shadow of doubt cross the man's face. "I communicated with HQ two hours ago."

Nick nodded. "So you know the girl took sixty grand out of her bank and fled. Did you also know the evidence against Harrington actually panned out? He's going to meet up with the girl and get his payout sometime tomorrow."

Balder took careful aim at Nick's face. "You're lying."

Nick shook his head. "Sorry to disappoint you, hero. They sent me here to retrieve the meeting time and place. It's all right here." He gestured at the hole in the floor using the long commando knife in his right hand.

Balder waved him backward with the barrel of the pistol. "If you're lying, I'll kill you slowly."

"In your dreams, hotshot." Nick taunted, then slowly laid his knife down with his right hand, making a big show of it while backing off two steps.

Balder took three steps forward. When he turned his flashlight back on to peer down into Harrington's cache, Nick struck. He simultaneously drew his backup knife from its sheath in the middle of his back with his left hand while he locked Balder's gun hand with his right hand.

With three downward tearing punches, Nick opened up Balder's neck and chest with the knife. He then very quickly blocked an incoming stab from Balder's left hand—in which a knife had replaced the flashlight—and pried the gun from his fingers.

Though mortally wounded, Balder was a trained agent. His training could very easily take Nick out of this world before he breathed his final breath. He came at Nick with the knife again, and the two of them began a struggle for life and death in the pitch-black room.

An expert might have picked out elements of both Jujitsu and Krav Maga during the exchange. Between the two of them, they exchanged sixteen successful blows and seven unsuccessful blows in the space of just eight seconds. Due to Balder's wounds, though, it was a rather one-sided contest. At the end, Balder had the grip of his own knife sticking out of the center of his chest.

As Balder slid to the floor, he gripped the knife handle in both hands, his breathing coming out in pants as he began to suffer from a tension pneumothorax. Nick leaned forward and grabbed the handle of the knife, his hands covering Balder's fingers. "Where is Kate? Is she here? Is she with you?" he demanded. Balder sneered. Nick asked another question. "What do you know about all this?"

Balder let out a laugh that ended in a cough, and blood flew from his mouth. "I know that I will never tell you...," he whispered, then his breathing stopped.

Nick checked his pulse but knew the man had died. He used the expensive silk of Balder's shirt to clean his own knife, then re-sheathed it. He checked Balder's pockets quickly and found car keys and a standard-issue field radio.

He turned to exit the building, leaving Balder's corpse along with his pistol and weaponry for security to find. He carefully closed Harrington's cache back up, leaving it looking as undiscovered as possible.

He departed just as he came in, not taking the time to cover his tracks, leaving his equipment behind. Likely, they would think it belonged to the dead man in Harrington's office. Besides, speed was the most important thing to him right now.

In the parking lot, he spotted Balder's rental almost immediately and pulled his car up to it. After transferring his remaining gear into Balder's vehicle, he got into his new car, then drove aimlessly around Portland.

Once he turned onto an empty and darkened street, he pounded the steering wheel with his fists and let out a wordless roar. Nick could not stop his brain from replaying the scene in Harrington's office over and over again. From past experience, he knew that this would persist until he could emotionally cope with what had taken place. To speed things up, he began clinically evaluating every word and every motion each time the little movie played out in his mind's eye.

Had there been any possible way he could have lived through the encounter and still ended the altercation without killing the man? Their training never focused on disabling or wounding. They were only taught lethal blows. Intellectually, Nick realized that from the second Balder had aimed his pistol at Nick's head, one of them was going to end up dead. The intellectual knowledge did nothing to assuage his overwhelming remorse at having taken another life.

He felt tempted to report in, to call Charlie, but he knew that doing so would lead Kate directly to him, and then to Aria. He had to protect Aria. He struggled to collect his lost control once more and started breathing deep, slow breaths.

He roared again, adrenaline pumping through his veins. He slammed his scarred palms into the steering wheel over and over with tremendous force. It was the only pointless act of aggression he could allow. It was a natural human instinct to seek some kind of relief from the inevitable remorse he felt. Nick also knew from past experience that the kind of self-destructive behavior he instinctively wanted to engage in at that moment would only make things worse.

Suddenly, he remembered the only way he had ever been able to cope with the violence that seemed to follow him like a shadow all his life. "God, please help me," he prayed. "Help me, God."

He drove randomly for another hour with the standard-issue radio set to receive. At three o'clock, when he was sure he wasn't being followed and wouldn't lead anyone to Aria, he turned back toward Mt. Hood.

Aria Suarez was a five-foot-tall, bookish, piano playing, female civilian with no history of violence; the sister of a cop, and the daughter of a Sergeant Major. With that profile, NISA had sent three of their best agents to interrogate and kill her.

By contrast, in about an hour, NISA would start dealing with the Nick Williams problem. They would be coming after their rogue agent like the four horsemen of the apocalypse. As good as he knew he was, Nick knew in his heart that Hecate was better. In addition to orders, Nick had just gift-wrapped a whole lot of personal motivation for Kate by killing her partner. There would be no hiding from Kate. It would take all of his skill just to stay one step ahead of her.

Chapter 17

Aria paced the front room, watching her reflection in the glass wall. Where in the world was he? It was already four-fifteen. All the things that could have gone wrong on this mission of his replayed over and over in her mind. He acted so confident, but nothing was easy about breaking into a nuclear weapons facility. Nothing.

Taking a deep breath, she looked at her watch again. Before he'd left, she had known that this would be a hard wait, but that hadn't prepared her for it. Since she'd gotten off her computer, the last three hours had dragged by. She promised herself she wouldn't start panicking again for another hour.

Deciding that she would be more comfortable if she changed clothes, she went to the bedroom. She still wore the same jeans and sweatshirt she had tossed on after her shower the day before. There had been so little time for her to pack that she wasn't even sure what she had with her, but at the bottom of the backpack, she found a T-shirt and a pair of sweat pants.

After a quick shower and a change of clothes, she felt a little better. What she wanted was her piano. She could lose herself for hours in music if she could just sit at a piano.

As she turned to pace the room again, she heard the sound of a car's tires crunching on the gravel. She started to run to the door when she realized that it might not be Nick, so she went back to get the pistol and waited in the doorway of the kitchen. Suddenly, the glass wall of the living room made her feel very exposed, so she moved further back into the kitchen.

"Were you planning on shooting me for being late?" Nick asked from behind her.

Aria jumped and whirled around. When she saw Nick, she set the pistol down on the counter and launched herself into his arms. He didn't have any choice but to catch her, so he dropped the bags he held in his hands and put his arms around her. "Nick, I was so scared," she admitted, her lips brushing against the well of his neck as she spoke.

She felt his arms tense like he was about to push her away, but suddenly everything about the way he felt shifted. Instead of bracing her, his arms felt like they cradled her. He moved a hand to the back of her head and turned her face upward, crushing her mouth with his. Aria kissed him back with a decade's worth of love and grief.

As soon as their lips met, it was as if an explosion ripped through her. She'd never felt like this before. The two kisses they'd shared so many years before had been the kisses of children. Now her entire body felt consumed with him. She didn't feel like she could get close enough. She felt him groan as he pulled her nearer. She wrapped her arms tighter around his neck and stood on her toes to get as close to him as possible while he buried his hands in her hair.

Before she knew what happened, he put his hands on her hips, pushed her backward, and ripped his mouth away. He didn't completely break contact, though. Instead, he rested his forehead against hers and closed his eyes. She could see his chest move as he drew in ragged breaths.

"We have to stop," he said hoarsely.

For some reason, Aria felt the sting of tears. "I know."

"I don't want to stop."

"I don't want you to."

He raised his head and cupped her face in his palms. A smile of pure joy flickered momentarily then vanished. Her heart skipped a beat at the intensity of emotion swirling in his ice-blue eyes. He stared down at her for an eternity before finally speaking. "Get some rest," he said, releasing her and taking a step back. "I'm going to go outside."

Aria touched her bottom lip with shaking fingers. She could still feel his mouth. "Nick?"

He picked up her hand and brought it to his lips, kissing one of the scars at her wrist. "Yes?"

"When I thought you'd died, I cannot explain what that did to me. Everyone was so concerned about me. I mourned you like we actually had a relationship. The pain of your death, the loss I felt, it ripped me apart."

She could see the pain and regret in his eyes. And

something more. "I'm just asking you, please don't shut me out anymore."

His hands holding her hand squeezed almost reflexively. "I'm afraid I don't know how to keep from doing that."

"Then I suppose you have to learn." She reached up and gently laid her free hand against his cheek. "Trust me. Start there. Trust your thoughts and feelings with me. Because I feel incredibly alone right now, and you're all I have."

He closed his eyes and leaned into her hand. "Aria—"

"But you're all I've ever really wanted, so it's okay. Just don't shut me out."

He opened his eyes and stepped back, breaking contact with her. "Go to bed. I'll be out here on the couch." The look in his eyes clearly said he would be wishing he weren't out here on the couch, but he didn't say it.

♫ ♫ ♫ ♫

Nick pulled on a pair of sweat pants and left the bathroom, ice-cold water glistening on his scarred skin. The bedroom door stood partially open, and he was surprised that Aria was still awake. She sat on the bed with her laptop on her lap and reading glasses perched on her nose. She glanced at him as he paused in the doorway.

"Peter has a meeting arranged with Roj Singh in three days. On Friday."

"Where?"

"Panama City, Florida." She took off her glasses and rubbed her eyes. "He actually invited me to go with him and his daughter for spring break."

Nick nodded. "Did you find any other pertinent information on his home computer?"

"I'm deciphering."

She slipped her glasses back on and looked at the laptop screen. He clenched the clothes in his hand and left the room, shutting the door behind him. He needed to unwind, but his body was fatigued, so a good workout wouldn't do. Maybe he needed to feed his soul. He found his Bible in the pocket of the pants he'd worn that night. As he pulled out the Bible, he also pulled out the square of linen cloth that he always carried with him.

The cloth showed twelve years of war. He washed it as often as he dared, but he didn't want to wear out the linen. By now, it was soft, worn, almost transparent. It had bloodstains on it, smears of black that he couldn't source, and a rip in one corner that he'd clumsily sewn back together. He ran it through his fingers and stared at the closed bedroom door.

Many years before, when Nick had asked his one-time mentor Staff Sergeant Ahearne how he had met his wife, he had asked Nick, "Ever see a girl and know—just know—that God made her especially for you?"

His chest tightened. How many times over the last ten years had he wished he could just leave his job behind him, find Aria Suarez, and beg her to forgive him for the deceit of his death. What would she have done if he'd just shown up at her door, and she didn't need him like she needed him now?

He had to stop thinking about that. Distraction would mean death. Her death—or his, which would ultimately mean hers. He needed to focus on the current mission.

An hour later, Nick laced his hands behind his head and leaned back against the couch. His Bible lay open on his lap, but he couldn't focus on the words right now. He knew he had to sleep, but he was still really hyped up from the activity of the night.

His mind wouldn't stop running. How deep did this go? Where would his investigation lead?

He needed to stop his thoughts. He needed to sleep so that he could be sharp and protect Aria. To try to still the ruminations, he started praying. Pushing his mind toward God rather than man.

He jumped, startled, when he felt the couch cushion move. He opened his eyes and watched Aria settle onto the couch next to him. Before he knew what she was doing, she pressed up against his bare side. He hesitated before bringing his arm down around her. Her hair tickled his chest, and he lowered his head just enough so that he could breathe in the smell of her shampoo.

"Where were you?" Aria asked.

"The throne room of God," he said quietly. He took a deep breath and slowly let it out. "Look, Aria—" he started to say, but she cut him off.

"Where did you get that scar?" she asked him, running a thin finger down the jagged line at the top of his chest.

"Nigeria. Listen—"

"What about this one?" she asked him, tracing the one on his ribs. He felt his nerves jump under her touch.

"Libya. Aria—"

"And this one?" she asked, reaching to trace the deep mark on his hairline.

Nick closed his eyes at her touch, taking the hint that she clearly didn't want to talk about anything now. "Iraq."

She leaned forward and kissed the scar at his hairline. Nick closed his eyes and felt himself relax under the soothing brush of her lips. He felt his mind still, and his exhausted body finally succumb to sleep.

♬ ♬ ♬ ♬

Kate Royce did not key her radio when Balder didn't check-in. In eight years, Balder had never failed to check-in, so she assumed the radio was compromised.

She began her backtrack and arrived in the parking lot adjacent to NWT shortly before two in the morning. Balder's car wasn't there, but another agency rental was.

Kate casually strolled up to the vehicle and circled it twice, checking for anything suspicious inside or outside the vehicle. After checking her surroundings, she got down on all fours and shined her flashlight beneath it, giving it a thorough check for explosives or traps.

Satisfied, she walked up to the car and shined her light inside. She tried the rear passenger door with her weak hand, her strong hand gripping her pistol, and did not feel a great deal of surprise when the door opened, unlocked.

Within a very short amount of time, she ascertained that this was Nighthawk's issued vehicle as she had suspected and that it had been stripped clean, just as she suspected. Dozens of possible scenarios played out in her imagination, and she quickly narrowed them down to the three most likely.

First scenario, Nighthawk had been somehow turned,

had avoided Balder, and was now fleeing with the principal. She judged that scenario as very unlikely.

Second scenario, Nighthawk had somehow been turned, had taken Balder out, and was now fleeing with the principal. She judged that scenario as very, very unlikely.

Third scenario, Balder had finally fulfilled his ten-year dream of terminating Nighthawk after a brief but effective interrogation and was now disposing of his body in several small pieces all over the Pacific northwest while simultaneously running the principal to ground. Kate judged that much more likely, and the thought made her sigh.

Then Kate saw and heard the sirens racing toward the NWT facility—a lot of sirens—and decided she needed more information. More important than that, she urgently required the location of Balder's issued rental car.

Chapter 18

"Don't worry, Charlie. We'll get you out of here," Nick said. He wouldn't look at Charlie's face, wouldn't see the skin hanging down, or else the rage would consume him, and he wouldn't be able to concentrate. The wound in his side hurt like mad, and the way he was having trouble breathing, he was sure that a lung had been punctured. He concentrated on that instead.

"Leave me here, kid. I'll just slow you down," Charlie panted. He was obviously going into hypovolemic shock. He'd lost an awful lot of blood.

"Charlie, I've seen the ending to the Dirty Dozen. I know what happens when I go on without you. And I'm nothing like Lee Marvin."

Charlie chuckled despite his near mortal wounds. "Always with the jokes, son."

"Two minutes until the drop, then we're out of here. You have to see your boy graduate from Basic Training, remember?"

"Yeah. My boy."

Nick stepped over the corpse of the Libyan guard and

brought the laser designator to his shoulder, sighting on the chemical weapons plant, and depressed the trigger, painting the bullseye for the incoming laser-guided missile. Once the target lit up, time always felt like it slowed to a crawl, and everything around Nick moved in slow motion.

He only had so much time before he wouldn't be able to move Charlie, and it seemed as if two minutes had expired. Finally, the laser began to beep, signaling that the fighter pilot thirty thousand feet up had locked onto the target and fired. Nick started counting down the time. Ten seconds before it struck, he prepared himself for the force of the detonation.

Before the sound of the explosion had finished reverberating through the desert, Nick had Charlie on his shoulders as he ran through the chaos. He had five minutes to get to the pickup point, or else they would be left behind. As he topped the last rise, he saw the Blackhawk settling quietly in the sand. Twenty more yards and they were home free.

♫ ♫ ♫ ♫

Nick knocked on the door of the bedroom but heard no response. He waited for about ten seconds and knocked again. "Aria?"

Nothing. Worried, he threw open the door. On the bed, he could see the lump of a figure buried under a mound of pillows and blankets. He could only see part of one arm.

"Aria?" he called, rushing to the bed. She didn't move. He reached through the mound and found a shoulder to shake. "Aria, you have to get up. We need to go." Nothing happened. Had Kate found them? He felt an empty sinking feeling in his gut. Had she suffocated Aria with all the covers?

He ripped the covers off her and checked her wrist for a pulse. Her pulse was steady. He shook her again. She opened her eyes and glared at him, then sat up and brushed her hair out of her eyes. Nick suddenly felt like he wanted to leap into the air like a prima ballerina. Where was all this coming from inside him? All he could think the second he knew she was okay was that she looked positively appealing like that.

"Nick, I hate waking up." She closed her eyes like she was going to fall asleep just sitting there.

Briefly, Nick fantasized about wrapping his arms around her and the two of them sleeping side by side until they woke. The real world and life or death priorities impatiently but insistently intruded on his flight of fancy. Nick laughed and turned to leave the bedroom. "We leave in thirty minutes, Suarez." He didn't hear her entire response, but the tail end didn't seem like she'd said anything flattering.

♫ ♫ ♫ ♫

"Where are we going?" Aria asked from the passenger's seat of the Jeep. They had left the cabin, and Nick had driven in near silence for twenty-five minutes. He had pulled off the dirt road and turned onto the highway heading to Portland but then stayed on Interstate 5 headed south toward Salem.

Nick didn't even glance in her direction when she asked the question. "Does your brother Adam have his own equipment?"

"You didn't answer my question," she observed,

unconsciously crossing her arms. She wasn't in the mood for him to start evading her questions this morning.

After a few seconds, he nodded, just once, a bit sharply, then said, "My answer is dependent upon your answer."

Aria sighed and asked, "What do you need to do?"

"Enhance some videos. I can't risk sending them to our labs."

"Yeah. He has his own equipment." When he didn't speak again, she cleared her throat rather pointedly. When that didn't prompt a response, she insisted, "Well?"

Finally, he glanced at her, taking his eyes from the road and the mirrors for the first time since they left the cabin. She wondered if he was continually checking to see if they were being followed. "We'll dump this car at a train station, either in Salem or maybe in Eugene. Eugene is better. The more ground we can cover by car, the better. Trains move fast, but they make a lot of stops, so driving on the interstate is actually faster on the West Coast. Either way, we'll hop a train south."

His eyes immediately went back to scanning the road and each of his mirrors. Aria leaned back in the seat and closed her eyes, then opened them with a start and sat up straight again. She'd gotten so distracted last night that she hadn't thought to ask the obvious questions. "How did it go last night?"

Nick's mind flashed back to the sound of the knife as it entered Balder's chest. "I found a lot of stuff we can use. I didn't take anything with me, just got it all on video."

"Did you have any problems at NWT?"

Nick passed a caravan of recreational vehicles bound for the coast. He refused to let his mind review the events of the previous evening. "Nothing I couldn't handle."

Her patience was at an end. She could take all the information he'd given her over the last three days and put it on the back of a postcard. "What does that mean? 'Nothing I couldn't handle.' What were you able to handle?"

Nick's eyes flashed to hers, ice blue clashing with dark brown. She was able to see impatience reflected in their depths before he pulled the shutter back down. "Balder was waiting for me. I had to take care of him."

Aria knew what he meant. She didn't have to have the details, but it scared her that NISA had been able to predict Nick's plans. "What about the other agent? Hecate?"

"She wasn't there." By the tiny change in his expression, Aria knew Nick was grateful Hecate hadn't been there. He said, "We can't stay anywhere for very long. She'll be right on our tail if she isn't already one step ahead of us. If she finds us, we'll never see it coming."

Aria felt her mouth suddenly go dry. She asked, "So you have contacts further south?"

Nick answered, "The less fake ID we generate, the lower under NISA's radar we'll stay. I need to see a contact in L.A. He might be able to get us to Florida without having to dig up a birth certificate to create a whole new identity for you. And I *need* to see what I filmed last night."

Aria realized what he meant and the reason for his earlier questions about Adam's equipment. "Are we really going to L. A.?" Nick only nodded. "I thought we had to stay away from my family."

"While I'm certain Adam is being watched, we'll just have to be careful. You need a safe place to stay while I talk to my contact. I'd prefer he not see you because he might just sell us out."

"Will this put my brother in danger?" Aria asked, her voice oddly steady.

Annoyed, Nick said, "What? No. He's not in danger. He's just a means to an end."

Aria realized she may never have been described as an end before. The end Nick referred to was the end of her life, yet he said it so clinically. Was he really so detached? She pulled her laptop from the back-seat and opened it, accessing Peter's mail files that she'd saved the night before. "I found Peter's hotel confirmation, so we know where he's staying."

"I've been thinking about that. I left Balder in Harrington's office. But I didn't remove anything and left no indication that I'd found Harrington's stash of information, so I'm going to hope that whoever's running this operation will assume Balder stopped me before I found anything."

"Are we going to try to apprehend Roj Singh?"

"No. We need to gather intel. We need to know who's building a nuclear device and what their target is. Apprehending Singh will only make anyone else more cautious."

Aria nodded. "It's scary to think about someone planning something like this."

"Planning happens all the time. What's scary is how they successfully infiltrated NWT and gathered so much information. This thing goes deep, and the people behind it are totally committed."

She felt her lips thin. "Either way. The devastation from what I assume they're building cannot be worth all the political power in the world."

"You only say that because you don't desire all the political power in the world. You'd be surprised what people are capable of doing when money or power is their primary motivation." He gestured at her laptop. "Take Harrington. He's doing this for nothing more than money. The Bible's clear in telling us that the love of money is the root of all kinds of evil. I think Harrington could be a poster child for that if you consider what he's done and what he's planning."

Feeling cold from the inside out, Aria rubbed her arms. "I just pray we're able to stop them."

♫ ♫ ♫ ♫

Kate Royce slid out of the car and drew her weapon from her shoulder holster. The cabin appeared deserted. It didn't feel like anyone was within a few hundred yards, but she kept the comfortable weight of the pistol in her grip just in case. No need for a silencer way out here. To her never-ending frustration, the weight of a suppresser always messed with her aim anyway.

The shock at discovering Balder's death had worn off. From the stolen glances of his body she had managed to obtain while pretending to be a member of the CSI team, the fight had been a match of skill. She couldn't fathom how Nighthawk had done it. Despite his sociopathic tendencies, Balder had truly been one of the best agents among the rank and file of NISA. Then again, so was Nighthawk.

Nighthawk never liked working with anyone else, not even Jen Thorne, who was so obviously and disgustingly in love with the man. Kate didn't mind working alone, either. Off and on during the course of her career, she'd been a solitary agent. Throughout her partnership with Balder, she recognized that it was often helpful to have someone else with whom to bounce ideas around. For now, though, it was just her. She, alone, had to find Nighthawk and the principal.

She cautiously stepped around the perimeter of the cabin and the garage. Seeing no visible signs of human life, she went to the back door of the cabin. She pulled a small kit out of her jacket pocket and quickly picked the lock. Entering through the kitchen, she could smell the remnants of a meal, of coffee, of dishwashing detergent. She found the garbage, but the bag had been removed.

As she moved through the cabin, she found little tidbits here and there. Someone slept on the couch and someone on the bed. The shower had recently been used. She observed no evidence of blood in any of the sinks or basins. Two towels tumbled in the dryer.

She moved outside and found the issued rental car in the garage. When she inspected the tire tracks leading out of the garage, she determined that they'd left in a utility vehicle, likely a Jeep. Looking at the clear morning sky, she dialed the Washington number, entered a 10-digit code, and accessed the information line. "I need specifics on all DMV records for the owners of the cabin at this location," she said after identifying herself. "Be prepared to issue a BOLO to state and local as well as federal agencies with a 'notify but do not approach' order. Suspects considered armed and very dangerous."

Chapter 19

The fugitives drove two hours south of Portland into Eugene. Nick parked the Jeep in the parking lot of a twenty-four-hour grocery store, knowing it would be just a matter of time before Hecate found it. In the strip mall by the grocery store, they went into a wig shop next to a beauty supply store and fitted Aria for a long, straight, black wig. She left the store wearing it, and he led her to a cheap discount clothing store. She bought a tight button-up turquoise shirt she tied up under her breasts, tight yellow jeans, and three-inch wedge shoes. Dressed like that, with the wig and big sunglasses covering her face, she was absolutely unrecognizable.

Nick dressed in a white linen suit with a coral-colored silk shirt. When he came out of the dressing room, she didn't realize it was him at first. He'd put in dark brown contacts, added a black mustache and thin goatee, and wore a dark wig. He had a thick gold necklace on his neck and a matching bracelet.

"How fluent is your Spanish?" he asked quietly.

"*Hablo español con fluidez y Puerto Rico el acento de mi abuela.*" She assured him that she spoke Spanish fluently with her grandmother's Puerto Rican accent.

"*Brillante,*" brilliant, he said in Spanish with a wink, tapping her on her temple. Then, louder, he said with a Castilian Spanish accent, "*Vamose a salir de aquí.*" Let's get out of here.

Aria gathered her bags, and the two of them walked the three blocks to the train station. Nick moved and talked differently, and it took her a while to reconcile him with the man she knew.

"*Dónde está* Harvey Castle?" Where's Harvey Castle, she asked in Spanish while they waited at a traffic light to cross a four-lane highway.

In perfect Spanish, Nick replied, "Harrington met Harvey. He has to die for now. Meet Carlos García. Not as nice of a guy as Harvey. You probably don't want to know what he does for a living."

Aria raised an eyebrow and nodded. "And where did you learn to speak Spanish so fluently?"

"Columbia. Well, and Nicaragua, too, I guess." He tapped her on the chin. "And you are Annalisse Rivera."

"Annalisse," she said, testing it on her tongue. "Good name."

When they got to the train station, they went to separate windows and bought tickets for Oakland, California. As they boarded the overnight train, Nick nodded to two rows of seats that both had free window seats. He sat behind her and reached up and squeezed her shoulder after she sat down. Not long after the train began the long journey, Aria put a pillow between her head and the window and closed her eyes.

Thirteen hours later, they left the train, and Nick used a different ID to rent a car. "I secured the Blankenship identity on my own. NISA doesn't know about it," he said quietly as they walked to the rental counter. "Go to the restroom and dally a bit. I'll meet you out front."

She fretted that he separated her from him because there was going to be an issue with his ID or renting the car. After spending fifteen minutes in the restroom, reapplying the heavy makeup, brushing the wig, brushing her teeth, and freshening up, she left the restroom. She walked through the busy lobby out into the bright California sunshine.

As she stepped toward the curb, a dark blue sedan pulled up. She glanced inside the open passenger window and saw Nick at the wheel. She smoothly slipped into the car and buckled her seat belt.

"I want you to know that I hope one day to burn these shoes," she announced, peeling the wedge sandals from her feet. She wondered if her arches would ever be the same again.

Nick smiled. "I remember the high heels you used to wear to your piano recitals."

Aria leaned back against the seat and said, "Recitals? Plural?"

He stole a quick glance at her before looking back at the heavy traffic. "I, uh, went to a few of them."

A rush of warm love shot through her, spreading from her heart and rapidly moving through her whole body. "Did you, really?"

"Do me a favor. Get me a bottle of water out of my

bag?"

"Changing the subject isn't going to save you, Carlos," Aria said with a smile. She turned and got on her knees in her seat and reached into the back. She opened a side pocket of his duffle bag and reached in, but didn't find his water.

Instead, she found the Soldier's Bible and handkerchief she'd given him at their high school graduation. She'd seen them in his lap the night before last, but she hadn't looked at them closely enough to realize they were the same ones. Overwhelmed, her breath caught in her throat. Why did he deny them a future together when he so clearly had feelings for her, too?

Shoving them back into the pocket, she opened the one next to it and pulled out the bottle of water he'd asked for. She handed it to him as she straightened in the seat and rebuckled her seat belt.

"How long is the drive?"

"Maybe five hours."

"Okay." She looked out at the city as they worked their way out of town. After a few quiet minutes, she asked, "Nick?"

"Carlos," he corrected.

Unperturbed, she asked, "Why did you write to me when you were first gone? You wrote me so many letters."

She turned her head to look at his profile and could see his hands clench on the steering wheel before he relaxed them again. He finally admitted, "I couldn't stop thinking about you."

"Then, why die? Why not just come home and be with me?"

"I didn't want to hurt you." He said it with such a deep voice that she almost felt the words inside her chest instead of hearing them with her ears. "I still don't."

It took her a minute to process his meaning behind them. "Well, you did. You hurt me by rejecting me, then you crushed me by dying. I've been in pain for more than ten years. It felt like my heart had been ripped out of my chest." She pressed the heel of her hand against her temple and willed herself not to cry.

"That isn't what I meant. I didn't know what kind of person I'd become. They talk about cycles of abuse, and how the abused becomes the abuser. What kind of husband would I be? What kind of father? Like him? The thought of any part of Raymond Williams concealed inside me that may one day come to life terrified me like nothing else, and made me incapable of loving you or being with you. I left you to live your life without me to protect you from me, from the worst part of me. The part of me that scares me. The violent man that I really am by nature."

Aria nearly whispered, "I know that's a lie. I know you aren't a violent man by nature, only by choice. You're lying to yourself if you think otherwise."

He glanced at her quickly then put his eyes back on the road, as if to ascertain that she actually believed her own words. "Do you remember Deller? Big. Dumb. Mean. Racist. Harold Deller from the football team?"

"He owns a hot tub business in Phoenix City now."

"No kidding? Huh." Nick tried to reconcile that information for a few seconds then continued, "Did you know that I nearly killed him because he called you a name one time?"

Aria searched her memory then gasped. "Is that what happened to him? I thought he was in a car wreck!"

Nick cut a glance at her, but with the contacts changing the color of his eyes, she found it hard to read his face. "And now," he said, looking back at the road, "with all the other things I've done..."

Aria snorted. "I would put money on the fact that you've never done a dishonorable thing in your entire life."

Nick startled her by holding up one finger. His jaw clenched several times, and he finally nodded and said, "I don't know if that's true. The truth is that I've done... questionable things."

"But you question them. You are not a man without a conscience. Without remorse."

There was a long silence. Then, instead of answering, he just nodded, slowly, once.

"So now that you know that you're capable of controlling yourself and your reactions, you find another excuse? That's wrong, Nick." She took the water bottle from him, opened the lid, and took a long pull. "You're just making excuses now. I don't know why you think you can't have a future and be happy, but you can. I've watched you these last few days, and I've seen you praying, reading a Bible that's so worn out you have it taped together, and making good decisions for this nation and for me. If that doesn't make you a good, honest man, then I don't know what does."

Nick's jaw clenched and unclenched before he said, "You realize that since I came back into your life just a few short days ago, I have already killed a man."

She didn't know what to say about that. She could tell he regretted the necessity of taking that man's life. She knew without the subject having to be discussed any further that Nick had killed the man who had been assigned to take her life. Balder would have hunted her to ground like a helpless animal then killed her without remorse. Nick had taken a jaded life to save an innocent life. Did he think that was questionable? Aria had no questions.

His reaction led her to silently wonder about the darkness in his eyes, and the darkness that continually haunted Nick Williams in his sleep. How much remorse could one man with a conscience handle? Was there any way she could help him cope?

He finally finished maneuvering through the city and pulled onto the interstate. Nick gradually accelerated up to one mile per hour below the posted speed limit then set the cruise control. "I don't know what you want from me, Aria. Right now isn't a good time."

"You're right," she whispered, reaching into the back and pulling out her laptop. "It's a very bad time. But eventually, this will be over. And I'll be right here waiting for you. So, you think on that and be prepared to make some decisions."

Surprising her, he reached over and took her hand. He brought it to his lips and brushed his lips over her fingers, then lowered their joined hands but did not let her go. "Tell me about what happened to your wrist."

Aria started the story with the morning she found out about his supposed death. She admitted to always leaving a ticket for him for her recitals. He interrupted her and said, "I never missed a performance in high school."

A pleased glow flushed her cheeks, and she smiled as she told him the story. "After my dad tackled him, they arrested him. Two days later, Daddy and John went to visit him in jail."

Nick had so many impressions as Aria spoke, as she referred to her father as her daddy, a term of both adoration and respect. He had never felt either for his own father.

Aria continued, "Raymond was utterly broken, going through horrible DT's, really needing a drink, but refusing treatment because he'd hurt me. Daddy and John went every day after that, praying for him and with him. He accepted Christ, started reading his Bible, and has never had another drink."

He raised his eyebrows. "You still keep in contact with my father?"

With a shrug, Aria answered, "Yes. He is a dear friend, and I pray for him every night."

She prayed for the man who broke her wrist and stole her future. He let go of her hand and ran his fingers over his fake goatee. "I'm having a hard time figuring out how to feel about that."

"He works in a boys' home south of Columbus now, teaching the boys how to work on cars and whatever. He's so good with them. He said every boy he helps, he hopes will make up for the way he treated you, but it never resolves for him. It's like he's trying to fill the Grand Canyon with a water dropper, he says, and he'll never be able to do enough."

Nick's lips thinned. "I can see that."

"In a way, what happened to me is good. It took me a long while to see it. I felt so sorry for myself and how my dreams were completely crushed. But if you could see the boys his life touches, and how much he helps them, then I guess it's okay that there's one less concert pianist in the world. And as for me, I never would have had the challenges I faced getting my degrees or working with so many brilliant men and women every day."

"I'm glad you can see it that way because, to be honest, my initial instinct was to go hurt him back."

Aria reached out and put a hand on his thigh. "I know. That's because you have feelings for me that you deny and suppress."

His head whipped around, and he looked at her with such shock that she laughed. "I was just teasing. Trying to lighten the mood." She ran her tongue over her teeth. "Still, it's true."

A hesitant smile formed on his face. "You're probably right." With a gesture at a blue highway sign advertising amenities, he said, "Hungry, Annalisse?"

"*Sí. Sambriento.*" Starving, she admitted.

After a late lunch at a fast-food chicken place, they hit Los Angeles just at rush hour and the traffic was stop-and-go. She leaned her head back on the seat, closing her eyes.

Aria was grateful for the last few minutes of alone time with Nick before they included her brother, Adam. She felt Nick's fingertips as he gently squeezed and massaged the back of her neck and was surprised at how much comfort passed into her through his touch. She semi-relaxed for the rest of the ride.

♫ ♫ ♫ ♫

Aria ran through Adam's back yard to the kitchen door. Adam had a large sprawling house just outside of Beverly Hills that he bought after directing his third blockbuster. The back yard was fenced with eight-foot-tall hedges. No one from the street could see her approach his back door. The only staff he had was a housekeeper who came three times a week, so if her brother wasn't home, they would at least have the house to themselves.

She reached the door and knocked just as Nick appeared at her side. He had already taken off his wig and facial hair and removed the contacts. Aria slipped her wig off and nervously waited for Adam to open the door.

She lifted her hand to knock one more time but stopped when Adam opened the door, wearing a swimsuit and rubbing his thick black hair with a towel. His years in the southern California sun had darkened his already tan skin to a deep cocoa color. He stood nearly the same height as Nick. His eyes widened when he saw Aria, but Nick put a hand to the small of her back and propelled her forward and into the house before Adam could say anything.

As soon as the door shut, Aria put her bags down and threw herself into her older brother's arms. "I cannot tell you how happy I am to see you," she announced.

"Aria, what is going on?" Adam demanded. "John called me not two minutes ago and said an APB had been put out on you by the FBI."

Aria pulled away from Adam and put her hands on her cheeks. "Good heavens," she whispered. "What a mess." She felt her eyes fill with tears and picked up her backpack and laptop, deciding that they couldn't have this conversation in the kitchen doorway. "We need your help for a little while. Can we go sit down to talk about this?"

Adam looked at Nick. Aria felt something she couldn't define traveling the space between the two of them and took a step closer to Nick. "Adam, this is Nick Williams."

Adam raised an eyebrow in question, "Last time I saw you, you looked considerably more ashy."

His tone even and low, Nick explained, "Well, I died. But I got better."

Aria's youngest older brother held his hand out and took a step forward. "I see. Well, nice to finally meet you in the flesh, Nick Williams."

Nick shook Adam's hand. "You probably won't feel that way in about ten minutes," he said, then followed Aria through the house to a large sunken room. She threw her stuff on the floor by the couch and sat down.

"I'm going to go get dressed," Adam said and left the room.

Nick said, "Hey, Adam? Don't make any calls until we've talked, okay? Not even to family."

Adam nodded and left the two of them alone in the room. Nick took the chair across from the couch, so Aria got up from where she was sitting, and climbed into Nick's lap, putting her head on his shoulder. He froze for a moment before finally putting his arms around her.

"Why am I suddenly so scared?" she asked. "I wasn't really scared before."

Nick kissed the top of her head and started rubbing her back. "Contact with the outside world tends to make it more real," he said, and watched Adam come back into the room, "coupled with the fact that someone you love and trust may not believe you."

"I have no reason to doubt anything she says," Adam said. He'd changed into a pair of shorts and a sleeveless shirt. Aria jumped at his voice and slid down off Nick's lap to pace the room. "Why don't you start at the beginning, sis?"

Nervously, she picked up a carved onyx figurine of a film director sitting in a director's chair that she'd bought Adam for Christmas the year before and put it back down. Sticking her hands in the pockets of the ridiculous yellow jeans, she walked to the window and looked out at the manicured lawn. "This would probably make a good movie for you, Adam. Maybe I'll sell you the rights." She wandered back to the couch and sat down. "By coming here, we're probably putting your life in danger, so I'll begin by apologizing for that." She stopped for a minute and played with the fabric on the knee of her pants.

"Oh, for Pete's sake, Aria, get on with it."

♫ ♫ ♫ ♫

Aria took a deep breath and told as much of the story as she could without going too deeply into the technical details. When she was done, Adam stared at her for a long time. "Is there anything John can do to help?"

"He's probably already under surveillance. My superiors know how much I hate working with anyone, and they probably think I'm getting ready to dump Aria with someone."

Adam lifted his head to stare at him. Nick noticed that the brother and sister had the same eyes. "Is that your plan?"

"No." Nick looked at his watch and decided not to tell Adam that if he left Aria here, odds were good that he and his sister would just enjoy an inconvenient yet fatal accident within a few days. "Look, we can only be here for about three more hours. Aria said you have your own equipment here. I'd like to use your equipment to enhance some night vision film I took. The second they trace us to L. A., they'll know we're here with you."

Adam stood. "Come this way. I'll show you where my equipment room is." The two men started to leave the room when Adam turned back to look at Aria. "Aren't you coming, Aria?"

She shook her head and kicked off her shoes. "No. I'm going to relax." She walked to the piano at the end of the room and ran her fingers along the keys. As the two men left the room, Nick heard the sound of Aria playing the James Bond theme song, which segued nicely into Mission Impossible.

Chapter 20

Nick whistled in appreciation as he stood at the entrance of the equipment room. It was all state-of-the-art, wall-to-wall electronics, with monitors, consoles, computers, and screens. Other pieces of equipment were set up in the middle of the room, and on the walls above it all, shelves overflowed with everything from old videotapes to microscopes.

"Quite a setup," Nick observed, running his hand over the console of an editing machine. Nick had always loved the equipment he occasionally used on his job. Machines were easy for him to understand, much more so than people.

"My brother John has a good connection with the M and L electronics firm. I just get a lot of this stuff below cost. What do you need to do?"

Nick handed over two flash drives. "I recorded some paperwork. I need to enhance the images on these so I can print a good enough hard copy of each that I can read what's on them."

Adam walked over to the far corner of the room and turned on a large computer. He inserted one of the flash drives into it and held the chair out for Nick. "Do you know how to work this?"

Nick walked over and sat down, immediately turning to the keyboard where he began typing. He looked up at Adam for a second, offering in a quiet voice, "I got this from here. Thank you."

Adam nodded, clearly taking the hint. "Let me know if you need anything else. I'll be in the kitchen."

"One other thing," Nick said, turning to look at him. "I need to borrow a car. Preferably one with tinted windows, maybe with garage access. I have a dark wig I can use to pass as you."

With a nod, Adam gestured toward the door. "I'll get you the keys."

Nick turned and nodded. "I appreciate it. If it has any kind of GPS system, go ahead and remove it if you can."

♫ ♫ ♫ ♫

Nick didn't take the time he wanted to read what he had collected. He got a few brief snatches at the beginning and decided to make a hard copy of everything for Aria to look over later. The longer they stood still, the closer Hecate got. Then he saved the enhanced images onto a flash drive and made a copy. When he was done, he checked the time and realized that two hours had passed. He rolled his head on his shoulders and stretched neck muscles that had cramped from being in the same position for so long.

Back in the living room, Nick secured the hard copies and the original micro-SD cards in one of his bags, then followed the smell of spices and meat until he found the kitchen. Adam was at the stove, flipping a tortilla in a pan, and Aria was sitting at the table, sipping on a cup of coffee, reading from a stack of papers.

Nick watched them from the doorway, and another unexpected wave of longing went through him. He suddenly longed for the scene in front of him, for the closeness of a family, and for normal.

"The changes really work, Adam. When are you supposed to start filming?" Aria asked, taking a sip from her cup and turning to look at her brother, putting her back to Nick. She hadn't seen him yet.

"We already have. It's just chance that you caught me home today. We had a tie-up with the permits to shoot a scene at the beach, or I wouldn't have been."

"We would have been in and out of here, and you never would have known it," Aria said in a teasing tone.

"I know. I'm worried about you, Aria. What's going to happen now? Where are you going to go?" He still stood at the stove with his back to Aria and Nick. Nick stepped back from the doorway into the shadows of the hall and waited and listened.

Aria got up from the table and went to the refrigerator, rummaging around. "Not sure. We have to have enough evidence so we can prove I had nothing to do with any of this. Then, somehow, we have to take it to someone who'll believe us who also has the authority to do something about it and put a stop to whatever nefarious plan I've stumbled upon."

She stepped back from the refrigerator and shut the door with her foot, her arms filled with vegetables and cheese. She set everything down on the table where she had been sitting, then began to rummage through drawers.

Adam stopped what he was doing and grabbed Aria by her upper arms. "Wouldn't it be better to put you somewhere safe and let him do all the work?"

"Where do I go, Adam? What's safe?" She had a large knife in one hand, so she set it on the counter and framed Adam's face with her hands. "Do I stay here and let them come kill you, too? Do I go to Johnny or Henry and let them do the same? The safest place I can be is by Nick's side, and it's the only place I want to be."

"I'm worried about you, Aria."

"You probably should be," she said, "but you should also trust Nick to keep me safe." She gave her brother a quick kiss, then stepped back from him. "I can't reach your cutting board."

Adam reached above her head and grabbed the cutting board off its hook, then handed it to her. She picked the knife back up and went back to the table, where she sat down and began to slice vegetables.

Nick waited several minutes before he walked into the kitchen. Aria looked up from her vegetables and gave him a quick smile, then went back to what she was doing.

Adam glanced at him as he set a steaming platter of meat and tortillas on the table, but didn't grab him by the shirtfront and start beating on him like his expression clearly indicated that he wanted to. Nick knew it wasn't anything personal, just some protective primal instinct Adam fought—and won, as he merely handed Nick a plate, and calmly asked, "Did I have everything you needed?"

Nick began to fill his plate and nodded affirmatively. He put the copies of the discs on the counter. "Lose those wherever you store your data," he said, then handed Adam another disc. "You need to mail that to your brother John and tell him to keep it on him. Tell him if we disappear, this is evidence that can be used against Harrington."

Fear sliced through Adam's gut. "What else needs to happen if you disappear?" he asked Nick.

Nick shrugged. "Nothing can really be done. We'll either be dead, or I'll have us in deep cover somewhere out of country."

"She hasn't done anything. Why would you have to take her out of the country and hide her like some criminal?" Adam set his plate down and began to pace the kitchen.

"If it comes down to it, that's exactly what I'll do. It may be that's the only option to keep her alive." On the surface, Nick seemed extraordinarily calm and unattached, but deep within, he felt the same fear Adam was showing with his clenched fists and angry movements.

Adam whirled around. "So, I'm supposed to sit back and wait to see what happens? Then if you two disappear, I'm supposed to hope that your bodies aren't at the bottom of some lake?" He kicked a chair that was in his path. "Whose fault is this?"

"That's what we're trying to find out," Nick said.

"You're the trained professional. Why can't you put her somewhere safe while you go do that?" Adam demanded.

Nick sat down and folded his hands, giving a quick prayer of thanksgiving for the food, then began to eat. "She's safe wherever I am," he said.

Nick watched Adam's temper snap. He grabbed Nick's plate and threw it across the room, where it hit a wall and shattered. Before the pieces even hit the ground, Nick had Adam pushed up against the wall in an armbar hold and started applying very moderate pressure to the slightly shorter man's Adam's apple. The two men stood nearly eye to eye.

"She's my sister," Adam hissed, visibly struggling to regain the control he'd lost a moment before.

"I can predict their moves. I know all the cards up their sleeves. They have to get through me," Nick calmly explained. Something in his eyes told Adam that they would never get through him as long as he had breath in his body. "Understand?"

An unspoken understanding passed between the two men, an acknowledgment, before Adam said, "Okay." Nick let go of him slowly, and Adam turned and got another plate down, refilled it, set it in front of Nick, and sat back down, clearly embarrassed that he had lost his temper.

"We leave in thirty minutes," Nick said to Aria after glancing at his watch, then he started to eat again. Between bites he said, "I have a—friend—who runs a low-key charter company from a private airstrip just the other side of the Nevada border. Aria, get ten thousand dollars out of the money and band it together for me."

♫ ♫ ♫ ♫

Kate stood next to the Jeep and turned in a full circle, scanning the name of every business she could see. When she spotted the wig store, she walked directly to it with an economy of motion born of instinct and experience.

She pushed the door open with her hip and walked inside. "Hello," Kate said with a smile for the clerk. "I was wondering if you've seen this woman in the last couple of days."

The twenty-something woman with the blonde Marilyn Monroe wig looked at the photo of Aria Suarez. "Maybe. I think she might have been in here yesterday."

"Yesterday? Wow, that's great. Can you tell me what she bought?"

The woman lifted a heavily lined eyebrow. "Why do you want to know?"

Kate pulled her badge out of her jacket's inner pocket. As she predicted, the girl was extremely impressed with the badge and suddenly gave Kate her full attention. She smiled as she held it up and said, "Because the information is of the utmost importance. It's a matter of life and death."

♫ ♫ ♫ ♫

"As far as I can tell," Aria said, turning off the interior car light and taking off her glasses, "most of this stuff is my work. Some of it is from the last week, new research, but most of it is from the last year."

She propped her feet up on the dashboard and cracked her window, letting the cool night air blow her hair. She'd been looking through the copies of the paperwork from Peter's office at NWT. She hadn't even begun to delve into the stuff from his home office. There were hundreds of pieces of paper, and even more data stored on a flash drive.

They seemed to have the road to themselves this late in the evening, seeing a stray car only every so often as they drove the desert highway through California, heading to the Nevada border.

"We knew he'd been stealing your work. Why do you sound perplexed that this is yours?"

"This is recent stuff."

"How recent?"

"We ran a test last week. It had beautiful results. Look at this," she said, holding a picture of a blueprint up so he could see what she was talking about. "You see these notations here?" He nodded. "That's my writing. I made those notations right after the test, which was less than a week ago."

"Which means—?"

"Which means Peter almost has final plans, and he can give his clients a working container that will shield an active and armed nuclear device from detection."

Nick paused and processed that before asking, "Where did you keep those plans?"

"In my office, in the safe. The only thing I can think of is that he went in there with a security team to clean out my office when they, quote-unquote, terminated me." The words tasted bitter in her mouth. Four years of her life had been spent at that company. She decided to leave the subject alone for now. She looked out the window and saw a sign advertising a restaurant in two miles. "Are you hungry?" she asked.

Nick shook his head. "Me, either." They passed a diner sitting next to the lonely desert road. The lights inside revealed just a few scattered customers.

Aria got tired of watching nothing out the window, so she turned the light back on, put her glasses on, and picked up the stack of papers. She steadily worked through the stack, making notes on some of the papers and occasionally in her notebook. An hour later, Nick interrupted her concentration. "You said there was other work there that wasn't yours. Can you tell whose work that is?"

"I can tell you whose computer it came off of, then I can tell you the names of the team members that person works with," she said, distracted. She made another note in the corner of a page, reminding herself to go back to that one later. "Do you need to know that?"

"I might. Any information is helpful. Most of the time, you gather ten times more information than you end up needing. That's just part of it. Go ahead and label everything. Tell me whose computer and the team members, then create a cross-reference identifying the team members you worked with on anything Harrington stole from your computer. Maybe we'll find a match somewhere."

Aria's eyes crossed at the thought. "You realize we're talking about over sixty people here."

Nick shrugged. "Once you have matches, it will be narrowed down some."

She took off her glasses and looked at him for a long time before saying, "A good bit of your job is incredibly boring, isn't it?"

"Long periods of intense boredom punctuated by intense seconds of real excitement. Those seconds make up for the boredom, I can assure you," Nick said dryly.

She twirled her glasses around in her hand, her mind wandering. "Do you ever stop to think about 'what if?'"

"What do you mean?" he asked. They passed a sign informing them that they would arrive in Nipton in forty miles.

"I don't know, just to speculate what might have been." She adjusted her seat belt so she could sit with her back to the door, facing him. "What would have happened to your life if that helicopter hadn't gone down?"

Nick knew it would be hard on him to spend this time with Aria. He'd thought, though, that the problem would be this nearly overwhelming physical attraction he felt toward her. He never imagined the emotional turmoil she would put him through. Thoughts about what might have been sent him back more than twenty years.

He remembered the day his mother left him alone with the man who had fathered him. If she had taken Nick with her, would his life had been better or the same? For there was no worse.

Then, like pressing fast-forward on a recording, his memory reviewed his life through high school, to all the times he could have asked Aria out on a date. Would she have gone out with him, or would she have laughed in his face?

Then through the years when he served in the armed forces. Life was a series of endless, hard days. Every waking minute was taken up with orders, rapid reactions to ever-changing requirements, harsh conditions, bad food, and loneliness. Every free moment he stared at an old picture of Aria and wondered what she was doing with her life or hopelessly filled pages and pages in the form of heartfelt letters to her even though he knew he could never have her. That was his life up until the day he died.

In an instant, Nick's mind raced through the last ten years. All the time he had spent in one stinking third world country or another where the air always smelled like stale corn chips and dirty feet. He was either killing people or running for his life from people intent on killing him. Any time thoughts of Aria or thoughts of 'what if' surfaced, he plunged them back down. He'd had access to technology that would have given him all the information about her he could have ever wanted, but he chose to never delve into it. That would have been no better than asking 'what if.'

"There is no 'what if,' Aria. For me, there is only 'what is.'"

Out of the corner of his eye, he watched her jaw tighten in frustration. "Are you married?" she asked out of the blue.

He whipped his head around to stare at her. "What? Married? No. No, I'm not married."

"Just thought I'd ask. You're so closed-mouthed about yourself, I figured you must be hiding something." She examined the nails on her left hand. "Ever been married?"

"No." He sighed. "No, I've never been married."

"Keep your eyes on the road. If we end up in the hospital, they'll definitely find us." She took a sip of her water. "Have any kids?"

Incredulous, he bit out, "What in the world's wrong with you, Aria?"

"Annalisse," Aria corrected. "Just trying to have a conversation with you, Carlos. I'm searching for a subject you'd be willing to talk about." Nick opened his mouth then shut it again because he honestly didn't know what to say. "Where's Harvey? He looked like the kind of guy who could sit back and have a normal conversation."

Nick suddenly braked and whipped the car to the side of the road then put it in park, leaving the engine running. He put his arm along the back of the seat and turned to face her, effectively blocking her in the position where she sat in the passenger seat. "You want to play games? Okay, I'm not married, never been married, and have no children. What else do you want to know? Let's see, I don't do drugs, I rarely drink, and I'm not gay. The weather's usually great wherever I am unless it's Serbia, then the weather sucks. I enjoy traveling, shooting guns, and working on computers. What else do you want to know?"

She licked her lips nervously. "I'm sorry. You can consider the subject closed."

"No, you wanted to know, so ask away."

She looked at her lap and played with the cuff of her shorts. "What's your favorite country?"

"Any of them that offer hot showers in the hotel rooms. If the water isn't brown, I consider that a bonus."

"What's your favorite food?"

"Whatever I didn't cook."

"What do you do in your spare time?"

"I don't."

Her breath hitched, and he saw tears well in her eyes. "Never mind," she said quietly. "Can we go now?"

Nick turned back in his seat and put the car back in drive. "You need to put on Annalisse's wig," he said, pointing to the back seat and pulling back on the road.

Aria pulled the bag from the back-seat and looked through it, finding her wig and the makeup bag. She put the long, black wig on, and used the mirror on her visor to adjust it. Then she found the eyebrow pencil that matched the wig and darkened her eyebrows. He stole a glance at her while she applied the heavy makeup. She entirely transformed into Annalisse Rivera.

"When we get to the airstrip, let me do the talking. Don't ask any questions. Don't act like you're looking around," Nick commanded.

"Why not?"

In Spanish, Nick answered, "Because I don't want anyone with an itchy, nervous trigger finger to think you're something you're not and shoot you in the face." He spared her another glance and caught her staring at him, her mouth partially open. "Understand?"

She closed her eyes and gave a quick shake of her head as if to clear it. "Uh, sure. I understand."

He gestured with his head to the back seat. "I bought three kinds of cell phones. Look through them and see which one will work for you to use as a wireless connection for your laptop and make sure it's plugged in and charged."

♫ ♫ ♫ ♫

"You have some serious brass coming here, Garcia. Last time I saw you, I almost got arrested." A short, thin man with a pencil-thin mustache came out from behind a Cessna. "No way am I going back to Columbia. No way, man. I don't care how much money you got."

Nick smiled at the man. With confidence and the ease of familiarity, he slipped his arm over Aria's shoulders. "I don't want to go to Columbia, *amigo*." His accent was thick. "Just to Florida." He squeezed Aria to him. "Someone wants to party for spring break."

"Florida?" The man paused then looked around like he expected someone to jump out from behind an oil can and yell, "April Fools!"

"*Sí*. Florida." Nick reached into his inside jacket pocket and pulled out a stack of money.

"Not Miami," the man stated.

Nick whistled with his teeth. "Not Miami. Too hot, in more ways than one. How about the panhandle?" He ran his finger over the bills. "What will it be, Ricardo?"

The man looked behind him to the office door and shook his head, then shot Nick a thumb's up. Aria wondered if he had signaled someone to shoot them or to let them live.

"When, ah, do you want to leave?" he asked, taking the stack of money from Nick and eyeballing Aria.

"Now's good." He turned to Aria. "*Listo, mi amor*?"

Aria smiled and twirled her black hair with her finger. "*Preparado*."

Nick gestured to the plane. "Let's be off, then."

♫ ♫ ♫ ♫

Nick put his head close to Aria's. "When we land, I need to you try to get into the hotel's system and get us a reservation."

"I've never done something like that before," she said. "The security is going to be different. I don't know if I can."

"It's worth trying. Once we're there and in a room, you need to hack into Harrington's hotel and assign him a room." He looked out the window at the desert around them, lit by the runway lights, then leaned in close again. "You look like you're about to be sick."

She shrugged. "I'm just concerned about my family. What's going to happen to Adam?"

With a raised eyebrow, Nick said, "Nothing. You don't need to worry about that. They aren't going to go busting in with guns, Aria. They'll watch them, see if anything's up."

He squeezed her hand and pulled her as close to him as their seat belts would allow. He could feel the engines of the plane as it accelerated down the runway. "You don't need to spend energy worrying about your brothers. You have enough to worry about here."

"We left his car back at the airstrip. They'll find it."

"Assuming Ricardo's buddies don't chop it and shop it, we'll be long gone by then."

"I didn't realize that was a possibility."

"Can't blame them, really. Your brother has good taste in cars."

"I don't know if I'm cut out for this," she whispered to him.

"You're holding up fine," he said, then, because Ricardo turned in the pilot's seat to look at them, gave her a lingering kiss on the mouth as the plane left the ground and head east toward Florida.

Chapter 21

"Welcome to Panama City's Beachcomber, Ms. Rivera. If you and your companion will just follow Leroy over there, we'll get you settled in," the desk clerk said to Aria with a forced smile as she handed over the key. Aria felt a quick wave of guilt for hacking the system and forcing a reservation on one of the busiest weeks for the hotel but knew there hadn't been a whole lot of choice.

Nick had been set on staying in this hotel. When they pulled into the parking lot half an hour ago, Aria saw that the Sandpiper Hotel, where Peter had a reservation, sat directly across from it and realized why.

Nick had also been particular about the room she was to get them. The balcony faced the Sandpiper next door. They followed Leroy as he led them to the elevator and up four stories to their room. Leroy went through all of the motions, adjusting the air conditioner, showing the room to them, then Nick handed him a tip and he left them alone.

Aria left Nick as he went out on to the balcony, and

pulled the wig off her head on her way to the bathroom, where she stripped and practically stumbled into the shower. She washed the makeup off her face and ran her hands through her hair, feeling freer without the tight wig. When she got out of the shower, she wrapped herself in the thick white terry cloth robe provided by the hotel and went back to the room.

Nick was still on the balcony, and Aria was too tired to go out there with him. With a yawn, she fell onto one of the two beds and was instantly asleep.

♫ ♫ ♫ ♫

Nick sat on a chair on the balcony, watching the hotel across from them and the beach to the side of him. He could hear Aria's movements in the room but remained where he was. She needed to sleep now. The morning traffic sounded like it was coming from far away, and did nothing to disturb the peace of his spot. He stretched his long legs out in front of him and felt his body relax. He hoped they had a day or two of breathing room.

♫ ♫ ♫ ♫

"You want me to be her what?" Nick yelled in outrage, pacing Charlie's office. The walls were still bare, and there were boxes in the corner. Charlie had only been in his new position as director for a week, and there was so much involved in his new job that he hadn't had the time to put things up yet.

"Her partner, son. I want you to be her partner."

"Since when do I need a partner? I don't like working with anyone, not even you, much less some girl fresh out of some academy."

"She's not just some girl, Nick, she's the best explosives expert I've ever seen and a better wheel man than I ever was. She needs your help with this one, and you're going to give it to her." Charlie leaned his chair back and propped his feet on his desk. He'd fought this new administrative position, but as far as Nick could tell, he'd adjusted to it rather quickly.

The door opened, and Jennifer Thorne came storming into the room. "For your information, Williams, I can hear every word you're saying." She stood with her hands on her hips in front of him, almost eye to eye with him.

"Good. That'll save me from having to repeat myself." Nick didn't like her and didn't care that she knew it. He wasn't here to make friends. "Girl power and political correctness aside, I'm not going out in the field with some newbie skirt who's going to get me killed."

"Look, Williams, I don't want to be paired up with you any more than you want to be paired up with me, but I need your skills. No one can get in and out of a country the way you can, and I need an expert shot."

"Nick," Charlie said. "This isn't a debate. It's an order."

He was going to get killed. He knew he was. "How long you been doing this, Thorne?" Nick asked.

"Three years."

"Good. I have seniority. You do what I say when I say it, and when it's time to play with your bombs, I'll stay out of your way."

"Fine. We leave in ten hours," she announced.

"No. We leave in five." Nick corrected. "Grab your 'go bag' and maybe touch up your lipstick, honey."

Jennifer Thorne stormed out of the office and slammed the door behind her.

Nick studied the disapproval on Charlie's face and asked innocently, "What?"

"Was that really necessary, Nick?"

Nick shrugged. "I like lipstick."

♫ ♫ ♫ ♫

Nick opened his eyes and saw the tropical Florida sun high overhead shining nearly directly down on him. He stood and stretched then went into their room.

Aria lay face down on one of the beds wearing, as far as he could tell, nothing more than a bathrobe and sleeping very deeply. It took actual effort to keep from looking at her for what he would consider one second too long. He went to the phone and called room service, ordering a breakfast big enough to feed four, then went to take a shower.

As he locked the bathroom door, he gritted his teeth and said to himself, "I hate cold."

♫ ♫ ♫ ♫

Adam heard the pounding on his door before he saw the blue lights reflecting from every surface in his driveway. He checked the clock and saw that it was not yet five in the morning. He took a deep breath and got out of bed.

When he answered the door, the uniformed police officers shined their very bright flashlights directly in his eyes, dazzling him. Adam closed the door in their faces.

"Mr. Suarez. Open up! Open the door, Mr. Suarez!"

He opened the door, and they began to raise their flashlights again. "Don't do it," Adam warned.

Ignoring his warning, they shone their lights in his

eyes again. Adam slammed the door. "Now, you'll have to wait for my attorney to get here. He should be here soon, maybe three or four hours tops."

He heard sounds outside, low voices, and a calm female voice. Then he heard the uniformed police officers stepping down off his porch. A light tapping on the door preceded a female voice, "Mr. Suarez? I'm Special Agent Kate Royce with the Department of Homeland Security? I'm very sorry about all this, but it is vital that we find your sister. It's a matter of national security. Mr. Suarez? Is that your rental car in your garage? Where is your white sedan?"

Smiling, Adam opened the door again. "Oh, you searched my garage? I wasn't aware you had a search warrant."

The woman in front of him held up a badge and a set of credentials for his inspection. "I'm very sorry, Mr. Suarez. I know it seems like a terrible invasion of privacy. I'm afraid that where certain matters of national security are concerned, the document known as the Constitution is seen as more of a formality these days. Are you familiar with the Patriot Act, Mr. Suarez?"

Adam grinned and decided he would not challenge this woman to an arm-wrestling contest. "I'm pretty familiar with how DHS interprets the Patriot Act, Agent Royce."

"Special Agent Royce, Mr. Suarez." Hecate corrected with a smile that may as well have appeared on a mannequin for all the feeling it conveyed. "Sir, have you seen your sister recently?" She had to raise her voice to be heard above the sounds of a helicopter flying by overhead.

Adam looked from her face to the six uniformed police officers and eight police vehicles crowded into his driveway. When the helicopter suddenly dropped to within a hundred feet of his swimming pool and hit his backyard with a blinding spotlight, it genuinely surprised him. Despite all the action movies he had ever seen and the two he had made, he could not have imagined a more surreal scene.

He looked back at Kate Royce, who—Adam knew with a certainty he could never explain—was definitely *not* an agent assigned to the Department of Homeland Security. He looked into her eyes and realized that there was absolutely no emotion contained within them; neither love nor hate, neither passion nor apathy. Her eyes were simply cold, reptilian, and he felt a chill deep in his soul when he kept eye contact with that baleful gaze.

He said, "You know what? Talk to my lawyer."

Adam shut the door again and started praying for his sister, praying that Nick Williams was better or smarter or faster or tougher than the woman whose cold, cold eyes he had just stared into.

"We're not going anywhere, Mr. Suarez," Kate said. "Please don't make me take you into custody."

Chapter 22

"**I** cannot believe how hungry I was," Aria said, biting into a piece of melon.

"It's just a side effect of the constant stress coupled with the constant stress," Nick explained with a smile. "Eventually, you start burning through some serious calories."

Aria laughed and poured herself a glass of juice. She'd eaten until she could eat no more, and was now relaxed and tired. It was only noon, though, and Nick convinced her she didn't want to sleep all day so that she would be able to sleep tonight.

"Do we need to worry about Hecate finding us any time soon?"

Nick shrugged and rubbed the scar on his forehead. "She'll find us eventually, but I don't think we have anything to worry about for a day or two."

Feeling a little band of tension release on the back of her neck, she asked, "Do you want to go down to the beach?"

"Why?"

Aria stared at him. "To go splash in the water, lay on a towel under the sun, catch some rays." He still looked confused. "To play, Nick."

"I guess we can. I thought you wanted to run."

"I need to let this food settle first. I figure I'll go running toward evening when it's a little cooler." She set her glass down and stood up. "Come on. We have to go shopping first."

Nick watched her put her hair up in pins then put her wig on. "Shopping for what?" he asked.

"Everything we need." She grabbed the eyebrow pencil and went into the bathroom, emerging a few minutes later as Annalisse Rivera. "Come on, Carlos, we're lovers enjoying spring break. Let's go live it up before they get here tomorrow, and we have to get back to business."

Nick felt defeated as he stood up from the table and went to the bathroom to put in his contacts. His idea of living it up did not include shopping along a beachfront, then intentionally lying in the sun to let it bake him. He frowned at his reflection in the mirror, then leaned his head back, popping the contacts first in one eye then the other. He closed his eyes and waited for the burning to pass, and when he opened them, he felt only mild discomfort, the kind that could easily be ignored. He pulled on a pair of worn khaki shorts, a surfing T-shirt, and a pair of sandals then went back to the room. Aria was waiting for him by the door, holding her purse.

"Let's get this over with," he said and grabbed his two bags and her laptop. He put them in the closet and locked the closet doors with a chain and padlock, then put the key in his pocket.

"You aren't on your way to an executioner, Nick," Aria laughed at him as she held the door open for him. "We're just going out to have some fun."

"People have different definitions of fun, Aria. Take me to a shooting range, and I'll show you mine." He led the way down the hall and passed a maid pushing a housekeeping cart. "It's a good thing you won at that roulette table, *mi amor*, or we'd have had to stay next door at the Sandpiper." The maid smiled at him, and he winked at her, then held his hand out for Aria to grab, and pulled her into the elevator.

♫ ♫ ♫ ♫

"Just buy a suit, Aria, and let's get out of here," Nick said through gritted teeth.

"I'll be done in a minute," Aria bit out. Shopping was one of her favorite things to do, but Nick could bring even her down. In an hour's time, she'd managed to find almost all the necessities she'd missed in packing. She'd had no idea that she would end up thousands of miles from home with only two pair of underwear, not to mention the lack of toiletries. Now all she was doing was trying to find a bathing suit that she liked, and Nick picked this moment to breathe down her neck. She should have done the fun stuff first, she thought.

She finally settled on a bronze-colored bikini, grabbed some tanning oil that was on display at the counter, and paid for her purchases, throwing a pair of cheap sunglasses on the stack. "Are you sure you don't need anything?" Aria asked. He grabbed her arm and steered her out of the store.

"No, I came prepared," Nick said under his breath.

"You also had more than thirty seconds to pack," Aria retorted. Her temper nearly matched his.

Nick realized she was right, and purposefully let go of his annoyance. They stopped at the car rather than going up to their room and put the packages in the trunk. Aria kept the one that held her new suit, and they walked around the back of the hotel to the beach patio, where there were restrooms, umbrella-covered tables, and a bar. Aria went to the restroom to change into her suit while Nick got them some iced tea at the bar. He sat at a table in the shade and waited for Aria to come out, watching the people around him.

Because it was spring break week for several major universities around the country, the area was packed with college students, and as Nick watched, he thought back to the first few weeks he was at the 101st, before being shipped off to Afghanistan. These kids were acting no different than he and his friends in that unit had, though at the 101st they'd had a lack of coeds in bikinis, and he realized for the first time that he missed the freedom he'd had back then.

Shaking off the mood that seemed to have descended upon him, he picked up his drink and took a sip, almost choking when he saw Aria emerge from the restroom. The bikini covered way too little of her, and the bronze color attracted way too much attention. The muscles in her legs were well defined from years of running and, despite her short stature, they appeared to go on for miles. She had on a wrap that came to her knees, but it was unbuttoned and sheer and didn't offer much cover.

Aria saw the expression on Nick's face before she got to him. His pout, because she had to buy a few things, was not going to ruin her afternoon. She pulled a chair out and sat down, glaring back at him.

"Do you think you could have bought a suit that covered a little more of you?" Nick asked in a quiet voice.

Aria stared at him in shock, then felt a warm glow. "What? Are you my dad? This is a very modest suit. Look around you."

"I don't care what's around me, I care about what's in front of me, which right now is way too much-exposed skin."

"You are not going to ruin my afternoon. You can sit up here and glare at me all you want, but you'll have to look down at the beach to do it," she said, standing and taking off her wrap. She walked past him and down the steps to the beach. It was a beautiful day, just on the right side of hot, and the sun shined in the blue sky. The sand was warm but not hot on her bare feet, and she walked to the water's edge, letting a wave wash over her feet to test the temperature. Even the water was perfect. She started strolling down the water's edge, staying where the waves could hit her.

A college student chased a volleyball to where she stood, then snatched it up and ran back to the game. Aria smiled, remembering the spring break of her senior year at college when she and several of her friends had come down here for a few days. They'd had fun, almost too much fun, as if denying the fact that in two months they all had to transform into responsible adults. When she got back to school, she dove into finals feeling relaxed enough so that the pressures of the exams almost felt like a mere annoyance.

She thought of Nick and thought that he hadn't had that opportunity—those four years between adolescence and adulthood. He'd never been given a chance to even *be* irresponsible. If he was too serious, it was because he had to be, and just because she wanted to spend a few hours playing, pretending that she wasn't on the run trying to find evidence that would save her life, didn't mean that he had that luxury. She was here now, and not lying dead in her home due to an assassin's bullet, because Nick didn't relax and play.

She suddenly felt guilty for getting upset with him, and turned to go back and apologize to him, and ran right into his chest. She almost fell backward, but he caught her and helped her steady herself. "One day, I'm going to hear you," she said.

"No, you won't," Nick declared before brushing a strand of hair that had blown into her eyes, tucking it behind her ear. "What do you want to do?" he asked.

She smiled and hooked her arms around his waist. "I wanted to swim, but I remembered this wig. The waves would probably knock it off."

"You might be right." He put his hands behind him, covering hers. "You could splash around here in the shallow water."

"Where's the fun in that?" she asked, having to crane her neck back to look at him. His expression gave nothing away. One minute he was lowering his head to kiss her, and the next, he kicked her feet out from under her just as a wave came. She landed on her rear end in three inches of water, and before her shock turned to outrage, she started laughing. She stood up and ineffectively tried to wipe the sand off the back of her legs, then started walking toward him. "You'll have to pay for that one, W-w-w-Garcia," she said, almost calling him by his real surname.

He crossed his arms over his chest and stood his ground. He outweighed her by nearly eighty pounds and stood over a foot taller, so when she approached him, he didn't even try to ward her off. When he landed in the water in the same fashion she did, he just sat there staring at her. "Where'd you learn that?" he asked.

"Are you kidding? My dad was in the Army my whole life, and I have a brother who's a cop." She brushed her hands off and stood over him. "Come on, tough guy. See if you can get me down when you're not distracting me."

He stood and began to take his shirt off but then pulled it back down. He crouched and started stalking her. In Spanish, he said, "This is war, Rivera."

Thirty minutes later, they were both wet and sandy, and Aria was laughing so hard she had to sit down before she could get towels out of the bag. "I'm never going to get all of this sand off of me," she said, brushing at her legs.

Nick smiled at her and stood, offering his hand. "Looks like what you need is a shower," he observed.

Aria took his hand and let him pull her up into his arms. She looped an arm around his neck. "I think you may be right." She stepped back and shoved the bag stuffed with their wet towels into his arms. "Race you to the room," she said with a laugh, already ten feet in front of him.

♫ ♫ ♫ ♫

They sat at a table in a little restaurant, eating fried grouper and coleslaw. A candle in a round glass holder desperately trying to stay lit gave the table a sense of intimacy even with all of the noise around them. Aria rested her chin in her hands and watched Nick talk, thinking that the evening would be so much more romantic if they weren't discussing shielding nuclear energy technology.

"What are the specifications of your device?" Nick asked.

"Well, it's about the size of a briefcase. We tried to keep it compact because the astronaut would wear it on his back and because every ounce of weight that we have to launch into orbit costs about a gajillion dollars to get up there, so lighter is always better."

"And the size of the device it could contain?"

"Roj Singh developed a nuclear warhead about the size of a 155-millimeter artillery shell if that gives you any idea."

Nick nodded and lowered his voice further. "And how big of an explosion or reaction would that create?"

Aria pursed her lips. "Five kilotons, easy."

"Which means—"

She felt a cold chill run up her spine that seemed to come from nowhere. "That it would take out about the entire mall area of Washington, D. C. from the White

House to the Capitol Building before accounting for fallout." She sat up and pulled a notebook and her glasses out of her bag and started to make some notes. "The fallout would be catastrophic from a ground-level detonation of that size. It would hurl radioactive material as high as fifteen miles, and that would contaminate major water supplies and poison the earth for thousands of miles downwind."

"What would the device look like?" Nick asked.

"Hmm?" Aria looked up. "Oh, like an armored case, really. But the thing is that it's really heavy."

"Heavy?"

"Yes. Well, here on earth it is. It's designed for use in zero gravity. I didn't worry about the weight at all during design until we had to consider the cost of putting it into orbit. Then I started cutting the weight down pretty seriously. But, it's still heavy for planet earth because nuclear material is really, really heavy. Once you add the weight of the bomb, you're looking at hundreds of pounds. Basically, it's a suitcase-sized engine block."

Nick pulled his wallet out of his pocket and laid some bills on the table, then stood up. The later it got, the more crowded the restaurant became, and he didn't want to chance someone overhearing their conversation. "Let's finish this back at the room."

Aria stood up and groaned, putting her hand on the top of her thigh. "Taking you down came at a price," she said with a laugh. "I'm feeling muscles I'd forgotten I had."

"Want to call a ride?" Nick asked, putting a hand on the small of her back as they walked through the restaurant.

"No. The walk will probably help loosen them up." They stepped out into the warm night and turned in the direction of their hotel. The street was crowded with kids partying, and the traffic was pretty much at a dead stop. Some revelers were in convertibles with their tops down, sitting on the back of their seats. Some were hanging out the windows of their cars. Those who were serious about the party had their cars pulled off in the middle of the road and sat on the hoods, talking to the people in the cars next to them. Hundreds of car stereos were competing with each other, no longer creating music, just noise.

Aria looked out at the street in front of her, and turned to Nick, picking her voice up to be heard over the din. "I've changed my mind. I think I do want a cab," she said with a smile.

Nick laughed, knowing she was joking because no cab would be able to make it through the throng, and they kept walking in the direction of their hotel. Aria saw the awning of the Beachcomber ahead of them and happened to glance at the two men standing next to the awning pole. The light from the building shone directly on the face of one of them, and she stopped suddenly.

"Nick!" she exclaimed as quietly as she could manage overall the street noise. She couldn't understand how he heard her above the hubbub coming from the street, but when he turned in her direction, she could see the change in him. Gone was the relaxation of the day, and in its place, Agent Williams stood ready.

He stopped directly in front of her and leaned his head down so he could hear what she was going to say. "What's wrong?"

"The men leaning against the pole in front of the hotel are Roj Singh and the other man that met Peter at that antique show." The shock of seeing them was wearing off, and Aria felt her control come back. How could she have forgotten why they were there?

"Are you positive?" Aria nodded. "Okay. Turn around. We'll go down one block and come into the hotel from the back."

They entered the hotel through the staff entrance, following a bellhop. Nick took her up the maintenance elevator to their floor and stopped her in front of their door. He reached behind him and unsnapped the holster at the small of his back, freeing the compact .45 caliber pistol he kept there. There was no sign that someone had forced themselves into the room, but Nick went in first, anyway, and did a quick scan. Nothing was disturbed, and the hidden indicators he'd left behind showed no one had been looking through their things.

Aria watched him do the scan then sat on the bed while he put on a pair of glasses and a baseball cap over his black wig. "Be right back," he said.

"Where are you going?" she asked.

He took the pistol out of its holster and handed it to her. "I'm going to get a good look at our friend. Stay here, and don't let anyone in."

Nick closed the door behind him and went back down via the maintenance elevator, out the back door, and around to the front of the building. He walked in the direction of the main entrance, where he let himself blend in with a group piling out of an airport shuttle and heading into the hotel. The men were still standing next to the awning pole where they had first spotted them. Nick couldn't get a clear view of either face at first. When the man with the lighter complexion pulled out his cell phone and turned his head slightly to read a text, Nick saw his entire face clearly.

He reentered the hotel without being seen, and rather than wait for an elevator, he went up the four flights using the stairs. Anger coursed through his veins, and he was too close to losing control of it. He slammed into the hotel room, where Aria stood by the window looking out.

"Are you absolutely positive that man with Roj Singh is the same man who met with Harrington?" he demanded.

Aria nodded, and Nick felt the control he held onto by a very thin thread snap. He punched the wall next to him, sending his fist through the drywall. "Who is he, Nick?"

"Jerry Simmons." He ran his hand through his hair and paced the hotel room with harsh movements. Finally, he stopped and stared out the window next to Aria, though his eyes looked far away. "Supervisory Special Agent Jerry Simmons, Assistant Director of NISA."

Chapter 23

Jen *was holding them off, but there were just too many of them.*
Five against one was a hard battle to wage. If things got any
further out of hand, he was going to have to blow his cover. She
already had two bodies at her feet, and her shirt was nearly
ripped in half.

"What's going on here?" Nick questioned, his voice heavy
with an Irish brogue

"Petie found her inside looking through our things,"
Daniel O'Reilly said, "Looks like she was here trying to find a
good time." The men standing around all laughed.

"Let her be, O'Reilly," Nick said, "the lass obviously isn't in
the mood."

"Stay out of this, Callahan. We've been hiding up here too
long, and it's time we had a bit of fun," O'Reilly declared, and
his companions grunted their agreement.

They'd quit trying to take Jen down one on one, and were
circling her. Jen tried to keep everyone in her line of sight, but
it was becoming impossible.

"That's the whiskey talking, O'Reilly. Our cause doesn't

have room for filthy rapists. Are you a buncha' Limeys now, is it?" Nick taunted, referring to allegations that British soldiers had raped many Irish girls when they had occupied Belfast during "the Troubles."

O'Reilly turned on Nick, his eyes blazing, and not for the first time Nick reminded himself that this man wasn't sane. "Don't you be preachin' to me about what my cause is, Callahan. My men and me have worked hard for tomorrow. Everything's in place, and there isn't a t'ing that can be done to stop it. The world will finally pay attention to us when that American Embassy goes up, and all the credit will be ours for the takin'. So if it's a bit of drink and a wee spot o' sport with a lass we want, then it's a bit of drink and a spot o' sport we'll have."

Nick heard a grunt and looked back at Jen, where another man was lying at her feet, his knife in her hands. O'Reilly roared with fury and pulled a small pistol out of his pocket, aiming it at Jen. The men stopped circling, and a couple of them started to smile. O'Reilly nodded to one of them, who went behind Jen and grabbed her, forced the knife from her hands, and pulled her hands behind her back. She eyed the gun warily but didn't look particularly concerned yet.

Nick sighed and pulled his own pistol from the small of his back, stepping up behind O'Reilly and placing the barrel behind his ear. "Drop the gun," Nick said, ridding himself of his accent. He'd really wanted to wait a couple more hours before dropping his cover. There were more bombs out there, and he still needed their locations. Now he would have to interview a crazy man to get the information.

O'Reilly slowly lowered the gun to the ground then put his hands up over his head. "What's this, Callahan?"

"This, O'Reilly, is what happens when you try to pull the Americans into your little conflict," Nick said. He lifted his gun and brought it crashing down on the back of O'Reilly's head, then, as O'Reilly slid to the ground, pointed it at the three remaining men, who stood in shock, forgetting that Jen still stood behind them.

They lifted their hands at the sight of his gun, and Jen pulled a phone out of her pocket and dialed, while she bent down to pick up the forgotten knife. She spoke quickly and quietly, then hung up and walked to stand beside Nick, where she casually picked up O'Reilly's pistol.

"What are you doing here, Thorne?" Nick asked, keeping his weapon trained on the men.

"We found the bomb at the embassy. It goes off in ten hours, but it's so full of booby traps I thought if I could find the specs, maybe I could diffuse it without an accident. That guy Petie, or whatever his name is, came back ahead of the rest of the group. Where've you been?"

"Calling my London contact to let them know the locations of the other devices." He could hear the sound of approaching vehicles. "The specs for all twenty of the bombs set to go off tomorrow are under O'Reilly's bed."

"Do you know where all twenty are?" One of the men started to step to the side, but Jen lifted the gun and pointed it at him.

"All but four."

"You know, Nick, I had it under control. You didn't have to blow your cover."

"At what point did you have it under control, Jen?"

She laughed as six British MI-5 officers suddenly filled the clearing in front of the small house set ten miles outside of

London. They went to work taking the terrorists into custody, while Nick and Jen looked through the stack of bomb specifications that were hidden in the house. They found what they needed and headed back to London to diffuse the bomb at the American Embassy.

♫ ♫ ♫ ♫

Nick jerked awake and fought the dream back. The room was dark and quiet, and he could see the form of Aria's body on the other bed, lying still. Exhaustion had finally overcome her from the exertions of the day before, and she'd fallen asleep about midnight. Nick had followed not long after, giving in at long last to his body's demand for sleep. He looked at his watch and saw that he'd managed to get about three hours of downtime.

He was still angry, though now the anger burned deep inside him, no longer trying to push its way to the surface. He could control it because he had to. If he lost control of it again, he could lose control of the situation, which meant he would be putting Aria in jeopardy. It was time for him to get some answers.

If Simmons was there for Aria, he wouldn't have been out in the open like that. Nick felt comfortable with the theory that Simmons was there for the drop, and that meant he could leave Aria alone. He wanted to wake her and let her know he would be right back, but she had been so tired when she finally fell asleep that he figured he wouldn't be able to wake her up enough to understand him without throwing her in the shower. So he left her a note and weighted it down on the nightstand with his pistol.

He grabbed a few supplies from his bag and left the hotel room quietly. As he made his way out through the back door, he noticed how quiet the night was compared to a few hours before. The revelers had apparently succumbed to too much sun during the day, followed by too much drink during the night. He walked about three blocks before he came to another hotel, and stepped into the large lobby, heading straight for the phone booths in the darkened corner.

Keeping an eye out for the desk clerk, Nick quickly disassembled the phone, attaching two scramblers just to be on the safe side. Then he dialed the long series of numbers to connect him to Charlie, who answered on the first ring.

"This is Krait," said Zimmerman.

"Nighthawk," Nick replied as he looked all around the hotel lobby, checking his perimeter.

"It's about time. You have a lot of explaining to do, son. You are so far off the reservation I'm not even sure you were ever a tribesman."

"I can explain. But understand you get nothing from me until you give me your word the girl stays safe."

"I never thought you'd fall for some little girl's story, Nick. Always thought you were smarter than that." Nick could hear Charlie's chair squeak and could picture him as he leaned back and put his feet on the desk.

"I know her."

"You think that's news? You think I don't know that by now? Listen, just because you two were high school sweethearts, I'm supposed to turn my back on a truckload of evidence that links her to years of nuclear espionage?

Nuclear, Nick! We're talking everyone's worst nightmare, here."

"You're supposed to trust the judgment of someone you've worked closely with for over ten years and who has saved your life on more than one occasion. You're not supposed to send in Balder before you even know for sure what's going on." Nick was really close to losing his temper, and he struggled to get it back.

"I'm glad you brought that up, Williams. Where do you get off killing one of my best field agents, then leaving his body there like a birthday gift?"

"He was going to kill me, then kill the girl. Better him than me."

"Easy for you to say. I guess we'll never hear Balder's side of it, will we." It wasn't a question.

"You sent that bloodthirsty maniac in when, five days before, you didn't even know her name. To me, Charlie, that stinks of something. Something really bad."

Nick heard Charlie breathe a heavy sigh. "Look, Nick, bring the girl in, and we'll take it from there. You're obviously too close to this situation."

"Bring her in? Why? So you can eliminate her before you even hear what she has to say?"

"She doesn't have anything to say I don't already know."

"She's been on the inside gathering evidence for over two months."

"You mean she's been planting evidence for over two months. Is that what you meant to say?"

Nick clenched the receiver tighter, wishing he could crawl through the telephone lines and beat some sense into the man on the other end. "If that's the way we have to play this game, so be it," he said in a quiet voice. He struggled and finally felt the control slip back into place.

"You're good, Nick, but I think you're forgetting who trained you. You're not going to be able to stay hidden forever. Sixty thousand only goes so far. What's your burn rate? And Nick? Kate will find you. It's what she does best, and you killed her partner. She's, ah, motivated."

"I won't need to hide forever, Charlie. I just need to hide long enough."

There was a long pause on the other end. Nick began to wonder if Charlie had hung up on him. "You're on the wrong side of this one, son. Tell me something. This girl, is she worth it? You'll end up destroying your life and everything you've worked for up until now."

"My life ended over ten years ago, Charlie. You took it from me."

"Wrong. I gave you a life, son. And now I'm giving you a chance. Maybe your last chance. You bring that girl in. Wherever you are, you find the nearest field office, and you bring her in. Get it done by tomorrow, and all is forgiven. And I'll give you that time off you've been whining about."

Nick bristled, "Don't make me do this, Charlie. A lot of good people will get hurt. Not like Balder. People I actually respect will be in the way if you make me go toe to toe with you."

He could hear Charlie taking a deep breath and letting it out. "Son, you and I have some history. Here's my final offer. You sleep on it. If you don't turn the girl in by noon tomorrow, don't bother to call back in."

Nick ran a hand through his hair and saw the desk clerk come back into the lobby. "I'll be in touch, Charlie. Count on it. And don't forget to check your six from time to time. You understand?" In other words, look behind you every once in a while, Charlie.

He hung up the phone, then carefully put it back together. Because the desk clerk was back at his post, Nick nodded to him, then went to the bank of elevators as if he were a hotel guest. He went to the third floor, then back down again using the staircase, and exited the building through the back.

He walked back toward his own hotel, staying in the shadows. The Sandpiper next door to his hotel, where Peter Harrington had a reservation, was closer. When Nick reached the Sandpiper, he stopped at the front entrance and ran his hands through his hair to muss it, then entered, walking with an unsteady, drunken lumber. He saluted the desk clerk, who looked like she was going to fall asleep at her post and pushed the button for the elevator every few seconds until the doors opened, leaning against the wall for support the entire time. He took the elevator to the fourth floor. When the doors opened, he checked left and right locating the security cameras, then made his way down the hallway to the room located across the alley from his. He checked the ceilings and corners, and adjusting his stance for the cameras, he pulled a small tool kit out of his pocket and quickly gained access to the room.

It was empty, the people who had been there having left just hours before, and Nick headed straight for the telephone. It took him seconds to take the phone apart, place his device in it, and put it back together. On his way out of the room, he installed a small sensor just above the door frame.

He took the stairs then exited directly to the parking lot from the side door in the stairwell so the desk clerk wouldn't see him leaving again. He crossed the two parking lots, then using his access key, he reentered his hotel through the back door. Rather than wait for the elevator, he took the stairs back up to the room. He rubbed the back of his neck while he pulled his key out of his pocket.

♫ ♫ ♫ ♫

Aria wanted to sleep, but her mind ran in so many circles that rest eluded her. She had made a living out of solving puzzles, and the one she had stumbled upon required her to solve more mysteries than any she'd ever encountered. She must have dozed, because when she opened her eyes, Nick was asleep in his bed. Then when she opened her eyes again, he was moving around their hotel room. She rolled over and sat up, but he was already gone.

Aria turned on the lamp next to the bed and saw Nick's note beneath the pistol. It was to the point if nothing else, and she hoped it meant he would be back.

Stay here.

Roused, she sat in the middle of the bed with her head in her hands, imagining the impact a nuclear device that size would have on any city in the United States.

Unable to just sit there any longer, she got out of the

bed and pulled out the copies of the data from Peter's office. Her laptop was already on the table, along with the evidence collected from Peter's house. She dug through the stack and found her glasses at the bottom of the pile. As she put them on, she powered up the computer.

She accessed the file she'd had open and picked up where she left off, writing out every detail she could remember about Peter and her suspicions of him. She'd been using her datebook to go back and remember specific outings, specific meetings, specific conversations.

It was important to her that she be as detailed as possible. Right now, she worked on identifying all the files he'd accessed on her computer and what that meant to someone looking at it from the outside. While doing this, she tried to see if there was a way to determine if someone else had also accessed her computer.

She sat back and pulled her reading glasses off, rubbing her eyes. When she lowered her hand, Nick was back in the room.

"How do you do that?" she insisted.

"Do what?"

"Never mind." She put her glasses back on and turned back to the computer. "Where did you go?"

"Had to make a phone call. I thought you were sleeping." Nick lay down on his bed and put his hands behind his head, staring at the ceiling.

"My mind's too busy. I keep thinking there's something I'm not seeing, something important." She checked the time. It was just after three o'clock.

"Last night was a full moon. There's still good light outside." Nick sat up. "I need to burn off some energy.

Want to join me?"

Aria took her glasses off, sat back in the chair, and raised an eyebrow at him. "Doing what?" she asked him with a small smile.

♫ ♫ ♫ ♫

The only sounds in the early morning were the waves crashing against the shore and their shoes as they hit the wet sand. Even the birds were asleep. They kept a steady, smooth pace down the beach, and after about four miles, turned and headed back.

Neither spoke, knowing the effort would take the energy they would need to finish the eight-mile run, but both appreciated the beauty of the moonlight on the ocean and the peace around them. In a few hours, the place would slowly fill with people in one continuous stream of humanity until someone would be lucky to find a spot to lay their towel. The peace would be interrupted by the sound of ten thousand conversations and high-powered stereos competing with each other. For now, though, for this time in this place, it was just the surf and the moonlight and the two of them.

An hour later, lethargic from the long run and lack of sleep, their bodies relaxed after hot showers, and as the sun battled the darkness away, they gave in to their tired bodies' demands, and lay down on their separate beds and slept.

Chapter 24

"It would probably be a good idea for you to leave, Mr. Ambassador. You never know how unstable these homemade things can be," Jen said, putting on her body armor.

"Agent Thorne, this package was addressed to my wife. I would like to wait here and see if it actually contains explosives or not," the Ambassador to Great Britain said.

"Sir, one of the ways we'll find out is if it goes off. Agent Williams heard them reference this package, and after the five devices we diffused yesterday, the chances are excellent that it contains explosives."

"I don't think..."

"These people were serious, sir. Please leave with Mr. Reynolds over there, and as soon as Agent Thorne is done, we'll let you know," Nick said. As the door closed behind the Ambassador, Jen tossed Nick a helmet and opened her tool kit.

"How many times have you seen me do this, Nick?"

"Once was too many. Why do you ask?"

"Ever heard me say I'm scared before?" Jen crouched down to eye level with the package, staring at it.

♫ ♫ ♫ ♫

Nick sat on the balcony staring at the hotel across the way when Aria woke up. She called room service and ordered a pot of coffee and a fruit and cheese platter, then went out and sat in the chair beside him. He didn't acknowledge her presence, so she remained quiet, leaving him to his thoughts.

It was just past noon, but she felt rested and clear-headed even without her normal sleep. Who knew how long Nick had been awake?

She remembered her wig just before the room service waiter knocked on the door, but she didn't have time to darken her eyebrows. She hoped he would be bored enough not to notice. She took the tray, signed the check, and took her cup back out to where she had been sitting.

"I need to get another digital camera," Nick said, finally breaking the silence.

"I thought you might make a video of the drop," Aria said.

"I am. You're going to take pictures." Nick took sunglasses out of his pocket and put them on, blocking the light that was suddenly reflected off the window across from him.

"What are we going to do after this happens today?" Aria asked.

"It depends on what I see. I haven't made up my mind yet," Nick said. He reached down and snatched up the nearly empty bottle of water from the ground next to his chair and took a long swallow.

Aria was tired of his evasiveness. "When you decide, be sure to let me know," she said through gritted teeth, then stood and started to go back inside. Before she even saw him move, Nick's hand was gripping her arm, halting her progress.

"Don't get angry again, Aria. I'm not used to discussing things with anyone." Nick sounded tired. Aria looked at him closely, but with the glasses on his face, she couldn't see enough details to tell if he was rested or not.

"How much sleep did you get this morning?" she asked him.

Nick rubbed the back of his neck. "Enough," he said.

She sat back down and turned the chair so that she faced him. "How much does 'enough' mean?"

"A couple of hours."

"You've only slept a couple of hours at a time since this thing started." Nick only shrugged at her statement, and she wanted to shake him and scream at him. Instead, she turned her chair back around, resuming her earlier conversation. "What are the scenarios you're expecting today?"

Nick stretched his legs out in front of him and crossed them at his ankles. "What I hope to see is Simmons keeping tabs on Harrington and Harrington giving information to someone else. That would ease my mind. What my gut is telling me I'll see is Harrington giving information to Simmons. That will worry me because I won't know who to trust within my own organization, and it would mean that you're in more danger than I anticipated."

"Why does your gut tell you that?" Aria asked.

"Because Simmons would have no reason to be in the field. He had any number of agents at his disposal to send out. I've known him for eight years and never known him to get his hands dirty."

Her coffee had cooled, but she took a sip anyway to help relieve her suddenly dry mouth. "And why would it put me in more danger?"

"Because you know. And, again, he has any number of agents at his disposal. Not all of them are in it for the right reasons." Nick stretched his long body and stood. "You need to put makeup on and go down to that computer store and buy a camera. I would, but I don't want to run the risk of bumping into Simmons." He looked at his watch. "What time was Harrington's flight due in?"

Aria pursed her lips, trying to remember the details of the confirmation. "Two thirty-five, I think."

"Okay. There's time. We need to be prepared for Harrington to arrive around three o'clock. I need you to hack into the Sandpiper and make sure Harrington gets assigned to that room right there," he said, pointing.

With a nod, she said, "I can try."

Aria stood and went into the hotel room and connected to a remote proxy using the hotel's wireless internet connection. Having once hacked into the Beachcomber's reservation system, hacking into the Sandpiper took little time. Once she moved Harrington's reservation to the correct room number, she backed all the way back out, covering her digital tracks as she went.

She hibernated her laptop and informed Nick that the deed was done. She grabbed her makeup kit and headed back out onto the balcony. She opened a compact and took out the eyebrow pencil, going to work on transforming Aria Suarez into Annalisse Rivera.

"What if I see Simmons?" she asked as she finished putting the makeup on and closed up the case.

"Don't make eye contact or look nervous. Just buy the camera and come back upstairs."

She left him on the balcony and went back inside, threw on some clothes, then grabbed her platform shoes and went back outside to put them on. "How do I look?"

Nick briefly looked her way, then looked back at the hotel. "Like a drug cartel henchman's girlfriend." She started to leave, but his hand stopped her again. "If you don't come back in fifteen minutes, I'll come down and look for you."

"Are you reassuring me or warning me?"

He stared at her for several heartbeats. "Reassuring you." He let go of her hand, and she put her hand on the door. "Aria, get me a paper while you're down there."

♫ ♫ ♫ ♫

Curse Charlie for making him doubt her, even for a second. He had spent the last three hours reminding himself that he believed her and trusted her, now he'd spent the last ten minutes worried about what she was doing. Even all of the evidence supported her. Nothing told him that she wasn't telling the truth, except Charlie. His mentor and friend.

Nick paced the hotel room, looking at his watch every ten seconds. She would be fine down there. The dark hair and clothing, the way the shoes changed the way she moved, all completely changed her look, making her unrecognizable. If Simmons had even paid attention to her when she saw him before, he wouldn't be able to recognize her now in a lobby filled with college students. Even if he was looking for her.

The idea caused Nick to grind his teeth in frustration as he started to leave the room. Just as his hand touched the doorknob, he heard Aria's key in the lock. He flung the door open, and she stood there in the hallway, looking shocked.

"Hey, Nick. Everything okay?" she asked.

He nodded and stepped back, letting her enter the room. She handed him a small bag that held a palm-sized camera, then took a newspaper out from under her arm and gave it to him.

"Let me have the want ads when you're done. I need to start looking for a new job soon," she said dryly, then walked past him, throwing her purse on the bed.

Nick took the paper and sat down at the table, spreading it open in front of him. He looked through every page, looking for any kind of news article about Aria. If they thought she was in the area, they might make her out to be a wanted fugitive and have her picture everywhere. It had worked the last several times for people they had wanted to bring in for one reason or another, especially when a reward was offered for information leading to an arrest. People were always ready to make a quick buck.

While he looked, Aria opened her computer and started punching keys. She sat across from him with her glasses perched on her nose, and immersed herself in the papers in front of her and the information on her computer screen. He finished looking through the paper, finding nothing about himself or Aria, then sat back in his chair and watched her.

She hadn't removed her wig or the makeup, and he thought to himself that he preferred her as a blonde. The black was too striking for someone as basic as she was. He didn't realize it had been possible for his love for her to grow, and it scared him how overwhelming the feelings were. He tried very hard to set those feelings aside for the time being.

She stopped what she was doing and took her glasses off, meeting his eyes. "Do you want me to order a pizza or something?" she asked.

He had to clear his throat before he could speak, and he felt himself returning to the real world. "Sure," he said.

"I suppose you don't really care what's on it?" she asked as she pulled the phone book out of the drawer in the nightstand.

"I don't like a lot of pork or fruit on them."

"Good, because I like it loaded with every vegetable on the planet." She found a local organic pizzeria and dialed the number, turning her back to him. He wanted to go to her and hug her and tell her that everything would be all right. He didn't move. He couldn't lie to her. He wasn't certain what the next twenty-four hours would bring, and they had absolutely no guarantee that everything would turn out fine.

Nick went back out on the balcony and tried to relax. He needed to sleep, needed to let his mind rest for a while. This assignment had come too soon after a mission that had been both physically and emotionally draining, and he was worn out. He'd been worn out long before he even went to Portland. He'd only taken this job because he thought it would be something easily handled in a few days and allow him to take some time off afterward to recuperate from the last ten years.

If only there were someplace he could take her where he knew she would be safe, he could relax for a while. Maybe then he could get a grip on the emotions that ran rampant through his mind and heart. The constant contact with Aria was draining him, and he felt more exposed than usual today.

"Are you okay, Nick?" Aria asked, sitting on the chair next to him. Her voice was soft, gentle, loving—like he remembered from all those years ago. "You've been acting strange since last night."

He took hold of her hand and pulled her to him, making her fall onto his lap. "I'm fine, Aria. I'm just not used to worrying about anyone but myself."

She laid her head on his shoulder and put her arms around his neck. "Is there something I need to worry about?"

He thought about it for a long time. It would be best if she knew what the situation was and what the consequences may be. "I called my boss last night. He didn't believe you. They're sticking fast to the fact that you're the culprit." His hands were making lazy circles on her back, soothing while he spoke the words. "From the way he was talking, I don't know if there's anything I can bring him that will clear you in their eyes. If I can't, we have to go on the run."

"I'm sorry you're in trouble because of me," she said against his neck.

"If I weren't here, Balder would have killed you by now."

"I'm still sorry you're in trouble. I should have minded my own business and ignored Peter."

"You did the right thing, Aria. Don't ever doubt that. This is the type of thing I believe in fighting for." He pushed her up and cupped her face in his hands. "We aren't wrong. They are. Don't let them bring you down."

She was overwhelmed by the intensity in his eyes, and her eyes filled with tears. "I know you don't want to hear it, Nick, but I'm really scared."

Nick felt a tightening in his gut. The only other time a woman had uttered those words to him had been about three minutes before an improvised explosive device blew her apart in front of his very eyes.

"You're doing just fine, Aria." He softly kissed her lips, then pulled her back into his chest. "We'll know our direction soon."

She looked up, her breathing deep and fast. His lips touched hers again, and as he possessed her mouth, he heard the door open onto the balcony across from him and heard Harrington's daughter yell to her dad that they had a grill.

Chapter 25

"No, no, no, no," Nick said under his breath, trying to get a grip on the desk with blood slick fingers. His ears rang so badly that he couldn't hear anything but a long, solid tone, and he still couldn't see through the smoke. His fingers and his face felt numb, and he couldn't seem to catch his breath. He was finally able to grab the desk and heaved it off into the corner, off of Jen Thorne's shattered body.

She didn't move.

Nick knelt down beside her and searched for a pulse. His fingers found her wrist, but he could detect no pulse whatsoever. He closed his eyes, took one deep, slow breath, and felt for her pulse again. Nothing.

He looked down as blood slowly began to pool beneath her arm. He was about to start coming to terms with her death when Jen's eyes fluttered, and she stared up at him, a look of confusion and shock in her eyes. His fingers still gripped her wrist, and she still had no pulse. Those diametrically opposed facts did not compute in Nick's mind.

She opened her mouth, which had filled with blood, but

Nick couldn't hear her words. He reached up and checked her carotid and felt a weak pulse there. He didn't think he had much time.

"Hang in there, Jen. Hang in there," he said as he rolled her over. He screamed, but he could not hear his own voice though he could feel himself screaming. His throat felt raw as he roared. When he rolled her, the arm he had been checking her pulse against did not move with her body. Instead, it remained motionless on the floor, severed, the upper part of the arm completely crushed. Nick tasted bitter bile in the back of his throat.

Keep it together, *he scolded himself.* She needs you.

Jen Thorne lay there in a pool of her own blood. He cracked open her armor vest to survey the extent of her injuries. When he saw her torso, Nick forced his emotions way into the background and became a machine. His only objective was to keep her alive until someone came.

He reached for the field tourniquet he always kept next to his zip-tie handcuffs, the one clipped to his gear, but it wasn't there. Nothing was there. The explosion had ripped everything from his vest, and he had no idea where anything ended up. Maybe across the street for all he knew.

He removed his belt and made a makeshift tourniquet. He ignored her blood that mixed with his own. He ignored the pale face and the look of agony before him.

Jen's hand reached up weakly and grabbed at him as if she were sinking, and he could somehow pull her up, pull her out of the flooding river of pain slowly drowning her. Her mouth moved, repeating the same word over and over. He couldn't hear her, but he knew she was saying, "Hurts! Hurts!"

The tourniquet mostly stopped the bleeding from the

jagged stump of her arm. Now, all he could do was apply direct pressure to the mortal looking wound in her side.

Jennifer Thorne needed a miracle. Nick had witnessed miracles before. He knew Who handed miracles out. He started to pray, though he didn't let Jen see the desperation of his prayer.

Save her, God. God, please save her. Keep her alive, God.

The ringing in his ears kept him from hearing the door being broken down. It wasn't until a hand touched his shoulder that he realized help had finally arrived.

♫ ♫ ♫ ♫

Nick put the finishing touches on his makeup, then washed his hands and left the bathroom. He had darkened his skin around the black hair, dark mustache, and dark brown goatee. Harrington had gotten a really good look at him in Aria's apartment, and he wanted nothing about his current appearance to connect him with her.

Aria was already dressed to go out, sticking to the Annalisse Rivera look. She had dressed in a tight dress that hit her mid-thigh and incredibly tall high-heeled silver shoes. Nick had overheard Harrington telling his daughter, Becky, to get ready to go out, and he planned to follow them until they went back to the hotel. Nick hoped Simmons decided to go out as well so he could keep an eye on both of them.

"You ready?" he asked. When she nodded, they left the room. They left the hotel via the front entrance rather than the back, hoping to get a glance at Simmons. He was nowhere to be seen, though, and they walked out through the lobby. The street party was even bigger than the night before now that the weekend had arrived, and the atmosphere was that of joy and celebration. Inside the lobby was a sitting area sectioned off with couches and chairs, and Aria sat down while Nick stood next to her, looking at his watch. To the most casual observer, they were waiting on friends for an evening out.

Ten minutes later, Harrington came out of an elevator with his daughter and left the hotel, glancing around him nervously. The teenager appeared oblivious to her father's movements and gaped in awe when she witnessed the party on the street. Nick and Aria followed behind arm in arm, keeping pace with them, not speaking.

They went to dinner at a seafood restaurant, dining on grilled flounder. Nick managed to secure a table in the corner for them, where he sat with his back to the wall so he could see everyone who entered and exited. Harrington glanced around him a few times, and at one point looked right at Nick, but there was no recognition in his eyes, and he kept scanning the room. Nick watched for signs of Simmons and for signs that Harrington was under surveillance, but he saw nothing. If he was being watched, Nick couldn't see it.

An hour later, they strolled back down the parkway, heading back to the hotels. They reached the Sandpiper first, and Harrington and his daughter turned to go into the building. Nick steered Aria around so that her back was against a light pole in front of the hotel, and he faced the entrance. He lowered his head as if he were going to kiss her, watching to see if anyone would follow them in. When he was sure nothing would happen, they made their way back to their hotel.

As soon as they returned to the sanctum of their room, Nick quickly checked the indicators he'd left around to make sure no one else had been there. Only when he felt sure all was clear did he speak.

"We need to watch their room round the clock," he said as he opened the closet door and pulled out one of his bags. "We'll do it in shifts." He pulled a case out of his bag and opened it, revealing two pairs of earphones, a small box, a small dish, and a microphone with an antenna attached to it.

"I hate to say this, but I really need to sleep right now," he conceded, hooking the blue earphones to a small black box that contained a recording device, then he ran wires from both earphones to the recorder.

Aria threw her purse onto her bed and sat down, taking her shoes off. "I don't mind going first. What do you want me to do?"

Nick went to the bathroom and began to remove his makeup and facial hair. Aria followed and leaned against the doorjamb. "Wear the green earphones and keep the microphone pointed in the direction of their hotel room. If the phone rings, hit record on the box, put on the blue earphones, and keep the microphone pointing that way. You'll hear the person calling in your right ear and Harrington in your left," Nick said.

As soon as he was done and out of the way, she went to the sink and removed her wig and makeup. When she came out of the bathroom, Nick was already stretched out on his bed. "Turn out the lights and sit near the glass door. You'll be able to hear better there. If the light on the box turns red, that means their door opened." Aria looked at the box and saw a green light.

"Do you want me to wake you if I hear anything?"

"Only if the light turns red, or if you hear a call that tells you they're meeting right then. Otherwise, let me sleep. I'll wake up in about two or three hours." His eyes were already closed, and Aria turned out the lights, pulled a chair near the door leading to the deck, and sat down.

It was weird, she thought after an hour, how easily you could eavesdrop on someone when they thought they were safe in their seclusion. It was actually kind of eerie, and it made her wonder if anyone had ever done this to her. Anyone with this simple piece of equipment could hear anything they wanted.

She heard Peter's daughter, Becky, call her mother, she heard Peter and Becky argue about what they would do the next day, she heard the shower running. One time when the microphone slipped, she heard the couple in the room next to Peter's discussing the poor service at the hotel restaurant.

Peter and Becky got ready for bed, arguing the entire time about anything they could argue about, then the light went off in their room. Aria moved the black box closer to her so that she could see the light if it switched to red, and settled in her chair, preparing herself to sit for another couple of hours.

♫ ♫ ♫ ♫

The agent code-named Hecate, called Kate, stared down at the sleeping man. His round body lay curled around a pillow, and he regularly mumbled in his sleep. She reached over and slapped at his shoulder. "Wakey, wakey, Ricardo."

The small man jerked awake and gave a startled cry. When he saw Kate standing over his bed holding a gun on him, he sat up and scooted quickly back against the headboard.

"Wha—?"

"Shh," Kate explained, smiling as she put a booted foot up on the bed and leaned forward. She had to keep herself from gagging at the stink of the breath panting in and out of his open mouth. "I'll do the asking."

For her own health and wellbeing, she straightened some and put a little bit of distance between them. "Now, a man and a woman came to you a couple of days ago. She had long dark hair, and they probably didn't speak much English. Know who I'm talking about?"

"I don't know nothing," Ricardo said defiantly.

"It's *anything*," Kate corrected. "As in, 'I don't know anything.' But it's a common misuse. Now, tell me, what names did they give you, this couple? Carlos Garcia? And what was the girl calling herself?"

Ricardo crossed his arms and stared down the barrel of the pistol. "I... don't... know... *anything*. *Comprende?*"

Kate reached into the boot she wore on her foot she currently had propped up on Ricardo's mattress and slowly withdrew a long knife. "Oh, my. How very impressively *macho*," she observed, clucking her tongue. "I see I'm going to need to jog your memory. I bet if I surgically removed the source of some of that *machismo*, it might just help you to recollect some details."

Ricardo looked into her eyes and realized that he did

not want to proceed further down this conversational path, not with this woman. He held both hands up and whispered, "Florida. I took them to Florida."

"Better," she said gently as she resheathed the knife. "Now, I bet you remember where you took them in Florida, don't you?"

♫ ♫ ♫ ♫

Aria sat quietly in the dark. She sat so still Nick thought she might have fallen asleep until she lifted her hand to rub her eyes. He rolled over and stood next to the bed, raising his hands above his head to stretch the tense muscles. He shook off the feelings left behind from the dream, and walked over to Aria, kneeling beside her chair. She jumped a little when he touched her leg, then gave him a small smile.

"You look much more rested," she declared.

Nick hadn't realized he'd looked tired before and merely raised an eyebrow at her remark. "You don't," he asserted.

She laughed and quickly leaned over, planting a quick kiss on his lips that both surprised and pleased him.

"Anything exciting happen?" he asked as he pulled another chair over to sit next to her.

"Not unless you count that I learned Peter snores," she answered, then added, "loudly." She lifted the earphones off her ears for a second, then put them back in place. "I couldn't have fallen asleep sitting here if I'd have wanted to. It sounded like two rhinoceroses fighting."

Nick reached over and unhooked the wire that ran from the earphones to the recorder, then hit a button on the box. The sound of Peter's snoring filled the room, and Aria gratefully removed the headset from her ears. She had propped the microphone up with some pillows from the bed.

"I always thought that secret agents lived exciting, action-filled lives. If this is the norm, you can have it."

Nick smiled. "I told you before, Aria, the times that there is some 'action,' as you call it, more than make up for these long hours of inactivity." He took a drink from the cup sitting next to her chair then made a face. It was coffee. Cold coffee.

He forced himself to swallow, then asked, "How do you even drink this stuff?"

"It requires an adult palate," she acknowledged, enjoying how he narrowed his eyes at her teasing. "Do you like your job, Nick?" she asked.

Nick shrugged. "It's what I do."

"Sure, but do you like it?"

Nick thought about it for a moment, never really allowing himself to have the internal debate before. The truth was that there were things about his work that he loved. There were amazing people who he completely respected. But there were a lot of things he had done in the line of duty that didn't leave room for enjoyment unless he was willing to become like Balder was in life. He would never allow himself to get to that point. If it meant living with the nightmares that came every time he allowed himself to fall into a deep sleep, then he would live with them. He would rather the past haunt him than celebrate some of the more questionable things he had done in the name of duty.

"I believe in what I do, but I don't always enjoy what I have to do."

Aria jumped a little with the sound of the telephone ringing. Nick put a hand out to stop her from answering theirs and leaned over to press the record button on the box. Harrington's snoring stopped, and his voice filled the room as he answered his room phone.

"Hello?" Harrington's voice still sounded foggy.

"Enjoy your dinner?" the caller asked. Nick immediately recognized the voice of Assistant Director Simmons.

"Yeah. Sure. What's up?"

"The little shop in your hotel has a nice arrangement of beach bags. I especially like the blue straw one."

"I can understand that."

"Good. I should hit the beach around eleven-thirty tomorrow. Perhaps I'll see you there."

"Perhaps."

"I should send my condolences to you at the end of such a wonderful relationship." Nick heard Aria take a deep breath, holding it.

"She had mostly served her purpose. I would have had to do something soon, anyway." Nick's jaw felt like it might break, he clenched it so tightly. He consciously relaxed his jaw muscles but clenched his fist.

"From what I hear, you need to keep a tighter grip on your boys," Harrington said.

"We're taking care of that. No need to concern yourself with it."

"How do you know he's not after me?"

"Because he's not stupid. From what I've learned, she's his priority. He has her in tow as precious cargo. He won't risk bringing her within a hundred miles of you."

"Good. We're almost to the end. Another few weeks, and what they know won't mean a thing."

"Enjoy the beach tomorrow."

They heard the sound of a click followed by the sound of a bed squeaking. Nick's vision was close to red. He spared a glance at Aria, who looked nearly white. He stopped the recorder and reached over to grab her hand. She jerked away and stood so fast that the chair fell behind her.

"Don't," she said. She stepped backward, looking like she wanted to flee, and her breath started coming rapidly.

"Aria," Nick said, but she held her hand up to stop him. The firmness of her stance was belied by the tears that filled her eyes, though, and he didn't care whether she wanted his compassion or not. He wanted to give it, so he went to her and grabbed her by her upper arms, giving her a little shake. "Get over it, Aria. You knew what he was. You've known for months."

She shook her head. "Not that. I didn't think he was that." Her voice cracked at the end of her statement. She put a hand over her mouth as if to stop the distress.

Nick folded her into his arms, and for a moment, she was stiff and unyielding. Then she collapsed against him. Sobs tore from her so violently they practically wracked her body.

He picked her up and carried her to his bed, where he sat against the headboard and held her in his arms. He didn't know the words to give her, so he just let her cry, knowing this had been building for days. She'd been stronger than he would have given her credit for, and he knew her well enough by now to know that she would be even stronger when this night was over. He hated that any part of this whole situation had caused her to harden in any way. He wished there was a way he could turn back the clock and hand her innocence back to her.

She eventually stopped crying, but neither moved. Only when his arms began to tire did he realize she had fallen asleep, so he slowly moved her away from him and pulled the covers over her. He plugged the earphones back into the box and prepared his body for several hours of keeping vigil.

♫ ♫ ♫ ♫

Aria was going to rip her hair out by the roots in another second. "Nick, be reasonable. I would stand out more on the beach if I didn't wear a suit." They stood in the middle of the hotel room, almost nose to nose. If his eyes narrowed any further, she thought, he wasn't going to be able to see.

"I didn't say you couldn't wear a suit. I said you weren't going to wear that one."

"Watch me," she ground out. If Nick thought he was intimidating her, he was way off base. All he was doing was making her angry.

"He'll recognize you."

"He's never seen me in a swimsuit."

"You're going to draw too much attention in that thing."

"No, I won't, Nick. Get over it."

"You know, I've been in countries where they beat women who show just an inch of skin."

"You're welcome to try it."

She watched as the shutter came over his eyes, and he closed himself off. The look on his face took the satisfaction out of the argument she was sure she just won. "Fine. You blow this, it's your funeral. And I mean that literally."

The light on the black box switched from green to red, and Nick gave Aria one last long stare, then left the hotel room. She mumbled insults at him behind his back while she gathered their things and ran after him. He wasn't at the elevators, and she wasn't going to chase him down four flights of stairs, so she pressed the button on the panel, and the elevator doors slid open instantly. She entered with a smug smile and accessed the lobby knowing she would be waiting for him when he came out of the stairwell if she didn't have to stop at any floors on the way down.

She forgot for a moment that they were already in full makeup and was looking for Nick, not her drug cartel boyfriend, so when she came out of the elevator, and he grabbed her arm, she jumped and nearly screamed before recognition dawned. "What did you do, slide down the banister?" she asked.

"What are you talking about?" he asked, steering her through the crowded lobby to the door leading to the deck.

"How did you get down here so fast?"

"I came down the stairs." He pushed open the door, and they exited into a crowd twice the size of the one they'd seen two days earlier. Now the place was full of tourists and local kids. She saw Nick scan the crowd on the deck next door, and spotted Peter and Becky come out of their hotel and walk down the steps leading to the beach.

Nick kept an eye on them and said to Aria, "Go get us some sort of tropical-looking drink with fruit and umbrellas and stuff. No alcohol, but make sure they look alcoholic."

Nick secured a table at the far corner of the deck closest to the other hotel. Aria worked her way through the crowd at the bar, and ordered virgin *pina coladas*, then waited the nearly fifteen minutes it took the harried bartender to serve them. She carried them over to where Nick sat and set them down on the table, then she pulled her sunglasses out of her bag and put them on as she took her seat.

"You might be more comfortable if you took your shirt off," she said, noticing the sweat beading on his brow in the ninety-degree heat.

"I can't," he said, taking a sip of the drink then grimacing.

"Why?"

"My scars would give me away." How could she have forgotten that already? He turned his back on her and looked down at the beach. "Do you see them?" he asked her.

She pulled her mind away from his scars and looked in the direction of his gaze. "No."

"Look at my shoulder, then go about two degrees to the right," he directed.

She spotted them almost instantly. "I see them."

Peter sat on a towel, taking his shirt off, and Becky stood with her hands on her hips, arguing with him about something. She probably wanted to take her top off, Aria thought. Her mouth almost dropped when she saw the glint of metal flash off Becky's stomach.

Aria looked at her watch and saw that it was eleven-fifteen. Something in her told her that the drop would be exactly at eleven-thirty, so she raised the camera that Nick had given her and pretended to shoot several pictures, trying to appear professional about it.

"Look, love. Remember when we used to be that young?" Nick said with a Spanish accent, pointing his video camera at a volleyball game going on not far from Peter's towel. As she watched him, Jerry Simmons passed her, glancing down at them.

She tipped her glasses down her nose, gave him a slow, seductive wink, and responded to Nick. "I'm still that young, Carlos. You wouldn't be here with me if I weren't." Simmons almost tripped going down the stairs, and Aria belatedly noticed his companion, who was glaring at her in fury. She grabbed his arm and steered him down to the beach.

"Good girl, Aria," Nick complimented under his breath.

"Who's that with him?" she inquired.

Nick trained the video camera on her and took several seconds to answer. "That, Aria, is none other than Special Agent Nancy Warren, whose specialties happen to lie in the field of nuclear weapons technologies. She and Jerry Simmons have also been an item for about two years now."

"Did you know she was here?" Aria whispered. She raised her camera and took several shots, both of the couple and the people around them.

"Nope, and I wouldn't have recognized her with all of that blonde hair if it weren't for the tattoo on her hip. The wings of the butterfly are showing." He kept the video camera on them and didn't see Aria look at him.

"Exactly how do you know she has a tattoo of a butterfly on her hip?" she demanded.

"Aria, some things are better left to the imagination."

"No, Nick, really. If you had a relationship with her, you run the risk of exposing both of us."

"Keep taking pictures, Aria. I know she has a butterfly on her hip because we were undercover together one time, and she played the role of a stripper. I don't get involved with women I work with."

"Why not?" Nancy Warren and Jerry Simmons made it down to the beach and stopped next to Becky and Peter.

"Because emotional entanglements risk lives," Nick said distractedly. The two agents on the beach spread their beach towels on the sand next to Peter and Becky, and Aria started snapping pictures of Nancy Warren as she set her blue straw bag next to the one that Peter brought.

"Am I an emotional entanglement?" she quizzed while still taking pictures,

Nick kept sweeping the area with his camera. "Aria, this isn't really the time for this conversation."

Aria stopped taking pictures long enough to look at him. She had just started to raise the camera back up when she bit out, "Are there no emotions involved? Is that why you feel safe with me?"

Nick lowered the camera from his eye but kept it

trained on the beach. "Three things, Suarez. First, this video camera is recording sound, too. Second, this is neither the time nor the place for this discussion. Third, you've been an emotional entanglement to me since I fell in love with you when I was fifteen years old." He put the camera back up to his eye. "You better start taking pictures, or we'll have nothing that will help you."

Aria's heart leaped at his admission of love, but she lifted the camera and started snapping pictures again. She took pictures as Nancy Warren sat on her towel and grabbed the blue straw bag that had been Peter's and looked through it, pulling out a bottle of sunscreen. Simmons was on the towel next to her, pretending to be asleep on his back with sunglasses perched on his nose. Then she took pictures of Nancy Warren as the woman put that bag next to her hip and slowly pushed it against the one she had brought until the bags had switched places. Becky lay on her stomach with her head turned the other way and didn't see any of it take place.

Nick stood with the camera. "We need to get shots of what's inside the bags. Go down to the beach and flirt openly with a couple of guys, then at my sign, back into her bag, and try to knock it over."

Aria snapped a few pictures as she walked down, then turned to see Nick following her, filming her. She was now in sight of Nancy, so she blew a kiss at the camera, and caught the eye of a young, muscular college student. She winked at him and waved, and his jaw dropped.

"Sexy," Nick said with a Spanish accent.

Aria waved again, then caught the eye of a guy that was walking in her direction. She was nearly in front of

Nancy now and boldly threw him a kiss.

Nick cursed loudly and aggressively in Spanish, then said, "Do you think I can't see you through this thing?" He stormed toward her. The glare in his eyes looked real, and she almost thought he was serious as she backed away from him. "Can't you at least wait until my back is turned?" he yelled.

Aria made herself trip and fall backward, landing almost on top of Nancy and rolling over again very quickly. Her hand knocked the bag, sending papers flying out of it.

"Oh, I'm so sorry," she said, making to help her pick them up.

"I got it," Nancy said harshly, snatching papers right out of her hand. Simmons sat up and tried to help gather papers, running after one that was blowing in the wind. "Leave it alone. I'll take care of it." Peter and Becky sat up, staring in shock. Aria would not look at Peter in the face, afraid he would recognize her.

Nick reached the woman and grabbed Aria by her arm. "Now look what you've done. *Mujer estúpida*!" He hauled her up and kept a hand on her arm as they went back up the stairs to the deck.

Aria reacted in character. "*Mujer estúpida*?" She jerked her arm out of his. "Stupid? I'm stupid?" Then she let out a long line of Spanish so fast it surprised her she didn't trip over any of the words. As soon as they were out of earshot of the party below them on the beach, she stopped and took a deep breath.

"Good job, Aria. Now, get angry at me and go to our room ahead of me," he commanded. She had started to shake and thought if she didn't get to a bathroom soon, she would disgrace herself by throwing up all over Nick.

Aria jerked her arm from his and slapped at his hands, then she ran into the lobby. She glanced behind her one time while she waited for an elevator, and saw Nick at the bar, watching the beach. She entered the elevator and accessed her floor, pacing nervously inside it.

Did any of them recognize me? she wondered. Had she known that she would have to get that close to them, she never would have agreed. Which, she told herself, was precisely why Nick didn't tell her.

The hallway on her floor was empty, and Aria was eternally thankful because she dropped her key three times before she was able to get the door open. She rushed inside and slammed it shut behind her, ripping the hated wig from her head as she went. She turned on the shower, wanting to wash the sand off, along with the makeup that made her Annalisse Rivera. If she could just get the makeup off, she would be okay, she thought, and she stepped into the shower before the water was even warm.

The shock of the cold water calmed her down some, and by the time steam filled the room, she felt better. She wrapped herself in a hotel robe, and when she came out of the bathroom, she saw Nick was already in the room, and hanging up the phone.

"Did they seem to know who I was?" Aria asked him.

"No." He stared at her for a long time, then said, "We've been here too long already. I ordered us something to eat. Go ahead and pack, and we'll leave after we finish the meal." He sat down in a chair and opened the little screen on the camera, playing back the recording.

"Did you get what you needed?" Aria inquired, coming up behind him.

"Yes. You did a great job, Aria. I have enough here that they can't deny what we saw."

"Will it be enough to clear me?"

"I don't know for sure, which is why we're going to drop you somewhere safe, and I'm going to take it in." He set the camera down and rubbed his face.

Aria stepped back from him. "Where's safe?"

"I'm trying to come up with that myself," he said.

"You told Adam there was no place safe for me except with you," she said. "I don't want to be away from you. If something happened to you, I'd never know it." She stood there, wringing her hands, trying to keep herself from grabbing him or throwing something at him.

Nick stood and paced the room a few times. Stopping in front of her, he stuck his hands in his pockets. "You can't go with me to Washington, Aria. And I can't bring them to you. The only other option is to put you somewhere else."

Without a word, Aria grabbed clothes and rushed to the bathroom to get dressed. She thought about it as she threw off the robe and started pulling on her clothes. He was right. Think, she told herself. Think about where to go. Her family was off-limits. She had no real friends outside work or church, and Peter would know them all anyway. There had to be someplace no one else would know about. She started to pull a shirt over her head then stopped. Of course. No one would even think of it.

"I know a place," she said as she came out of the

bathroom.

Nick met her eyes. "Good. Where?"

"Virginia. Near Richmond, not too far from Fort Lee."

He nodded. She watched Nick set up the parabolic microphone then carefully aim it toward Peter's hotel room. He hit the button to turn it on and left it on speaker. Once finished, he said, "Checkout's in an hour. Go ahead and put Annalisse back on, and we'll get ready to leave."

While Aria put on the wig and darkened her eyebrows, Nick packed his equipment, all but the microphone. As soon as Aria had successfully transformed, she packed up her computer. They listened to Peter and Becky come back into the hotel room.

"What do you want to do for lunch?" they heard Peter ask.

"I wish we could find a place to get cheese bread like at home," Becky mused.

Peter chuckled. "You sound like Aria."

"That reminds me," Becky said. "I saw a woman on the beach today who looked exactly like Aria, but with dark hair. It was kind of weird."

"On the beach?" Peter inquired.

Aria gasped, and Nick's gut tightened so hard that it became painful. He had heard one time that the only people you couldn't fool were kids. No matter how old a fifteen-year-old thought she was, she was still just a kid.

"Yeah. The one who almost stepped on me. Remember?" Becky clarified.

Peter cleared his throat. "They say everyone has a twin somewhere, Beck. Don't worry about it. Go take your shower, then we'll go get something to eat."

Nick picked up every bag within his reach. "Okay, Aria, we are moving our timetable up by about fifty minutes. We need to leave right now. In thirty seconds, we need to be out the door."

As he reached to unplug the mic, he heard Becky's shower start and heard Peter say very quietly into what Nick assumed to be his cell phone, "We might have a problem."

Aria was ready in twenty seconds, and the two of them left the room, heading out the back way, down the service elevator, and out the back door. Nick wanted to run to the car, but he kept their pace normal, and as they loaded the bags into the car, he looked around to ensure no one watched them. It had been one minute since Becky spoke, and he knew there had been time for Simmons to call in the proverbial cavalry.

Nick hopped into the car, started the engine, and put it in drive before either of them even had their doors shut. As they left the hotel parking lot, he fastened his seat belt. Aria had to try more than once to buckle hers because her hands shook so badly.

"We were so careful. How did that happen?" she whispered to Nick.

"Kids are hard to fool." Nick put on sunglasses and headed in the direction that would take them north and out of Florida. He slowly peeled the mustache and goatee off with one hand and handed them over to Aria. "Put those in my bag, and find me something to wipe this spirit gum off my face. There should be cold cream and wipes in there." She looked through his bag and found some wet wipes in his makeup kit, handing one over to him.

"Who do you know in Richmond?"

"My best friend from high school. We haven't really been close since your funeral, but she left me a message before all this started. I didn't call her back." She leaned her head back against her headrest and took some deep breaths. Her adrenaline was still pumping full force.

"Carol Mabry?" Nick asked.

Aria nodded and, despite her tension, felt her heart ache a little with the knowledge that Nick remembered the name of her best friend from high school. He had remembered so many details, from the names of everyone in her immediate family to her first car, that it shouldn't have surprised her, but it touched her even so.

"She never liked me," he remarked.

"That isn't true," Aria defended Carol as if they were still sixteen years old. If she had to be honest, Carol, the musician, simply moved in different circles from Nick, the JROTC cadet back then. Carol also never put Nick and Aria together despite Aria's feelings for him.

Nick shook his head. "It's okay. I wasn't very likable in high school."

Aria had more than liked Nick in high school. She decided to change the subject. "They'll know the drug cartel leader and his girlfriend by now. What will we do?"

"I swiped this from a coed at the bar. She, in turn, stole it from her older sister," Nick said, pulling a Vermont driver's license from his pocket. At a glance, Aria could pass for the fuzzy blonde in the picture.

"You are now Emily Stafford. I am Gregory Thomas. There was a family emergency while we were down in Florida that requires us to cut our trip short. We kept our driver's licenses and some cash in the hotel safe, but our credit cards were stolen by pickpockets, so we'll just have to pay for our return tickets in cash."

"So, we're going to fly?"

"Yes, but we need to make a stop first."

Chapter 26

Nick stood next to Aria on the little porch of the estate's cottage and looked around. The grass was healthy and lush, the front porch swept clean. Suspended from the porch was a hanging basket of spring flowers. It didn't look like any place he'd ever lived as a child.

The main house, run by the Montgomery-Lawson Trust, stood several hundred yards away. It had once been a plantation house and now held thirty boys ranging in age from six to eighteen and ten full-time staff. Raymond took care of the grounds and the vehicles, and acquired old vehicles, refurbished them with the boys, and sold them for a profit that then supported the estate.

When the door opened, Nick had to stop himself from running away. A part of him didn't want to have this scene. Some very human side of him needed to hang on to the past, cling to resentment for the way he was raised. He didn't have room in his heart for forgiveness and acceptance.

Right?

Then he remembered the words of his Savior Christ Jesus, the Son of God. *"If you don't forgive, then I can't forgive you."*

His heart twisted in his chest, he felt a cold sweat break out all over his body, and nausea swirled in his stomach. He remained outwardly calm and collected, and as the figure of the man who raised him stepped out onto the porch with wide, disbelieving eyes, he stepped forward and said, "Hi, Raymond."

Raymond Williams had aged. Nick remembered a tall, lean man with strength in his arms and a brawny back. This man was older, more frail, tall and thin with graying blond hair and a well-wrinkled face. Who knew the kind of damage that had been done to his body after decades of serious alcoholism? Clearly, even after ten years of sobriety, his body still showed the effects.

"Nick?" Raymond whispered. His pale blue eyes filled with tears and disbelief as he looked from Nick to Aria. "Aria, what in the world?"

Nick watched Aria step forward and hug his father, but had to fight to keep from snatching her away from him. Instead, he watched his father's face, saw a genuine emotion of love wash over his expression as she hugged him. She turned, her arm around his waist, and smiled at Nick. "Surprise, Raymond!"

Raymond looked down at Aria and back at Nick, tears falling unashamedly down his face. "My son."

No. No. Not his son. Nick's mind screamed at him, but he shushed the voice and simply did not respond.

"Come in. Come in," Raymond said, opening the screen door. "I am so shocked, I can't even think."

Aria grinned further and stepped closer to Nick. Nick did not step into the house. He raised a hand in a halting gesture and announced, "We can't stay, Raymond."

Raymond's face fell, a confused look entering his eyes. "Why not?"

With a sour taste in the back of his throat, he admitted, "We need your help."

The hesitation was very brief as Raymond processed the sentence. Then he looked at his son intently. "Of course. Anything."

"We need a car. And we need to get rid of this car."

"Is everything all right?"

With a deep sigh, Nick said, "No. Nothing is all right. Aria's life is in danger, and I'm trying to help her. If you care as much about her as she says you do, you'll help us, no questions asked."

The old man nodded. "Okay, then. No problem." Raymond momentarily disappeared inside then reappeared, holding a set of keys. "Follow me."

They walked across the grounds of the estate to a large building with several closed garage doors. He used a remote control to open the closest one. Inside, a dark blue Mercedes gleamed back at them. "Take her. Tires are new. Tank's full. We just finished rebuilding it and were about to sell it."

Nick walked around the car, then nodded. "Any kind of GPS?"

"Not yet. This model is two years before they came standard."

"Thanks. We'll take it." He gestured at his rental car. "I've disabled the GPS on it as well as the LoJack. Get it as far away from here as possible, then re-engage it. I'll leave this in Atlanta's long-term parking lot. I'll get a message to you where to find it."

They swapped keys. Nick opened the passenger door, but Aria went to Raymond and hugged him tight. "Thank you," she said.

"Anything for you or him," Raymond said, patting her on the shoulder. "You get in touch with me when you can." He looked at Nick. "I owe you years of apology, son, but that can wait until your business is handled. Just know that I love you and I'm so very sorry... for everything."

Nick stared into eyes identical to his own. His heart gave a painful tug, and he realized he wanted to sit down with this man who fathered him, this man whom he had never called Daddy. "I hope we can spend some time together soon," he said, holding his hand out.

Raymond took his hand but pulled Nick to him for a hug, openly sobbing. "My boy," he said, pounding him on the back.

♫ ♫ ♫ ♫

"Hello? Grandma?" A small girl's voice inquired.

For a moment, Aria wondered if she had dialed the correct number. "Hello. May I speak to Carol Mabry, please?" Aria asked. She jiggled the extra coins in her pocket nervously and bit the corner of her lip.

She heard an exaggerated sigh. "Hang on." There was a long pause. Aria could hear an echoing "Mooommmyy," and she smiled in reaction.

"Hello?"

"Carol?"

"Yes?"

"This is Aria Suarez." She paused for a moment, waiting for Carol to respond.

"Oh, my goodness," Carol said. "When you didn't return my call, I was sure I would never hear from you."

"I, uh, I've been pretty busy since then." She licked her lips nervously and decided that a payphone at a gas station wasn't the place to delve into a decade of separation. "Listen, I'm in town for a few days. Can I come over to your house? We could catch up."

There was another long pause while she heard Carol mumble something to someone about seeing her later, and Aria's stomach muscles started doing somersaults. Then Carol came back on the line. "Sure. Tell me where you are, and I'll give you directions."

A few minutes later, Aria hung up the phone and got back into the rental car. Nick sat patiently waiting on her. "How did it go?" he asked.

"We're about five minutes from her house. She said to come over," she said. She gave Nick the directions Carol had given to her, and they pulled out of the gas station. "Are you going to come in with me?"

"I've been trying to decide that myself, and I think I will. She may think you've gone off the deep end if you go in with your story without me." He pulled his portable contact case out of his pocket, and handed it over to Aria, then popped the contacts out of his eyes. She held the case steady while he put his contacts in fluid, then handed the case back.

"Nick, she has a kid. I didn't know," she said. "Let's find somewhere else to go. Take me back to your dad's."

"Aria, you'll be okay here. There's nothing connecting you to her for the last ten years." Nick reached over and grabbed her hand, giving it a reassuring squeeze.

"There's a call from her to my cell in the last week. Won't they check that when they try to figure out where I've gone?" Aria asked.

"Doubtful." Nick pursed his lips. "Maybe you can hack into the phone company's system and remove the call. That might make you feel better."

They pulled in front of a large brick house with a manicured lawn. They were in a nice neighborhood with large oak trees gracing the front of most of the houses. A dark green sports utility vehicle sat in the driveway under a basketball hoop. Aria stood at the end of the driveway and stared at the house, searching for the courage to walk up the long walk to the door. Nick finally took her hand and led her up.

Before Aria could lift her finger to ring the bell, the door was thrown open, and she was enveloped in a warm hug. She had to fight back the tears at the tug of emotions the embrace created, and she hugged Carol back with the same enthusiasm, realizing how much she'd missed her.

"I'm so glad you're here," Carol said, stepping back from Aria and wiping her eyes.

Aria smiled at her. "I'll tell you the same thing we told Adam a few days ago," she said as she grabbed Nick's hand and pulled him closer, "you probably won't be in ten minutes."

While Aria had cursed the mirror as each year passed, hating that she still looked like a teenager, Carol had changed almost to the point of not being recognizable. In high school, she had worn her auburn hair permed and bobbed to her chin, had holes cut in almost every pair of jeans she'd owned, and had worn nothing but baggy shirts usually "borrowed" from her dad's closet. Carol believed the shirts made her look shorter than her nearly six-foot frame.

Now she looked nothing less than elegant. Her hair was longer, stopping at her shoulders, and straight. Her frame could no longer be described as skinny, but still thin, and she was dressed rather stylishly, considering all she had on was a pair of shorts and a shirt. Aria felt wrinkled and travel-worn next to her, not to mention short.

Carol looked confused for a moment, but the minute she made eye contact with Nick, her eyes widened in recognition. "You remember Nick, don't you, Carol?"

"Of course, I..." she began, clearly shocked and confused. Then she smiled again. "I'm really looking forward to this one." She stepped back into the house and gave them room to enter. "Come in, please," she said.

She led them through the spacious house into her living room and waved her hand in the general direction of the couch and chairs. "Have a seat. You two want something to drink?"

Aria and Nick sat on the couch, close but not touching. "No. Sit down, Carol. We need to talk to you," Nick said.

♫ ♫ ♫ ♫

Nick watched Carol's reactions throughout Aria's recitation. At first, her eyes reflected amusement and disbelief, but the more Aria told, and the more Carol looked to Nick for reassurance, the more her eyes reflected sympathy and a bit of fear. Nick couldn't help wondering if the fear was for herself because the two of them were there, or for Aria.

Aria left nothing out for Carol. She explained everything in full detail, and the telling took forty-five minutes. When she was done, the three sat silent, Aria and Nick waiting to see what Carol would say, and Carol taking it all in. Finally, she spoke. "What are you going to do now?" She directed the question to Nick.

He leaned forward and rested his elbows on his knees, lacing his fingers. "Now we need a place to tuck Aria away for a few days where she'll be safe. Her family is pretty much out of the question, and she has no friends outside of her work or church that Harrington doesn't know about." He let that hang in the air for a while. "Then, I'll go to D. C., take the extensive collection of evidence I now have to my superiors, and see where they take it from there."

Carol sat back, carefully composed, and looked at them for a long time. "Can they trace you to me?" she asked.

Nick answered, "Not after Aria fixes the phone company's records."

"She won't need to fix the records. I called her from my office, which is the District Attorney's office. Thousands of phone calls are made from there a week." She finally gave in to nervous energy and got up to pace the room, sticking her hands in her pockets. She made one pass, then another, finally stopping near them. "Aria is welcome to stay here as long as she needs to," she agreed.

Nick watched her and could see that a part of her was

holding back. "You have to be certain. I know you have children."

Carol ran her hands through her hair in a habit that Nick remembered from high school. "I have a daughter who's almost six. Her name is Lisa. If you think Aria will be safe here, then I trust that my daughter will be safe here, too." She tilted her head to one side and looked at him closely. "I don't think you would leave her if you didn't think she would be safe."

Nick gave her a faint nod and looked at Aria. She looked like she was going to fall asleep sitting there. "I'll go get your bags, Aria," he said and left the two women in the house while he went outside. He glanced at his watch while he opened the car door and saw that it was only three. He felt safe staying for a few hours. He grabbed her bag and laptop.

He walked back up the drive and reentered the house. Aria and Carol weren't in the living room, so he stopped and listened, hearing a sound coming from upstairs. He headed in that direction, and at the top of the stairs, heard the sound of feminine laughter to his right. They were in a room just down the hall, sitting on the bed, and he went in, putting everything down near Carol's feet. She jumped when she saw him and put a hand to her heart as he straightened up.

Aria laughed. Nick just stared at them, wondering what the joke was. "He does that to me all the time, Carol. You eventually get used to it."

"What?" Nick asked.

Aria stood and took his face in her hands, giving him a hard kiss. "You sneak," she said, then grabbed her backpack. "I'm going to take a shower."

"I'll show you where the bathroom is. I think I have some shorts that might even fit you. Might be a little long on you," Carol said and led the way out of the room.

Nick went back down the stairs and stood at a large window in the living room, looking out into the backyard where a swing set and a sandbox sat under an oak tree so large that it had to be at least a hundred years old. The early evening light made the yard almost glow, giving it a welcoming look. He couldn't believe that they'd been on the beach in Florida just that morning. He thought back to his childhood and realized that he'd never had a swing set. Or a sandbox for that matter, unless you counted the dirt yard in the last trailer park. More things that should be added to his list under the category of normal.

He heard Carol come into the room but didn't turn around. He wasn't really in the mood for polite conversation and hoped that she would take the hint. Apparently, she didn't because she spoke after a few minutes of silence.

"Do you still think she's too good for you?" she asked in a low voice.

Nick turned and looked at her. She'd always been extremely astute, and if she were a lawyer as she had earlier hinted, she was probably a good one. "I'm not sure what you're talking about," he replied evasively. He wasn't in the mood to delve into the intricacies of his feelings for Aria with Carol Mabry.

"Sure, you do. She did everything in her power in high school to place herself in your path, and you never gave her the time of day. Not because you didn't like her, but because you thought she was too good for you." Carol sat in the chair she had vacated earlier.

"Why worry about something that happened twelve years ago?" Nick asked. He stuck his hands in his pockets and remained standing.

She didn't answer his question but asked her own. "Do you know what it did to her when she found out you were supposed to be dead?" Nick said nothing, just continued to stare. He was sure there was going to be a point made soon. "She cried so hard she made herself sick, literally. She went home to Georgia, and two days later, her mom called Henry to come stay the weekend, worried something was wrong with her. She laid in her bed and wouldn't move unless it was to go to the bathroom and throw up. She wouldn't talk to anyone, wouldn't eat, and every couple of hours she would cry so hard it hurt your heart to hear."

"Is there a point to this tale, Carol?" Sorrow washed through him at the picture she painted.

"My point, Nick, is that you hurt her terribly. You didn't do it intentionally, and there probably wasn't a whole lot you could do to prevent it, but it happened anyway. I couldn't understand it, because you'd never given her the time of day, and I didn't see how her feelings for you could be so strong." She looked wistful for a moment, then continued. "I understand now, and I wonder how much worse it will be this time."

"I'm not planning to die again, Carol."

"No, but you're not coming back, either, are you?" She stood and walked up to him, putting a hand on his cheek. He fought the instinct to back away and waited. "Nope.

That is not in your plans."

He felt his cheeks grow hot beneath her fingertips. She said, "If you had been planning on coming back for her, you would have left her in some hotel room in some obscure city and told her to wait for you. Instead, you're leaving her somewhere where you won't need to come back."

He wanted to deny it, but couldn't. He wished he could, but Carol's gaze was too strong and saw too much. "She'll survive."

"Yes, but she'll hate you when it's over, and since I have to pick up the pieces again, I'll probably hate you, too." She kissed his cheek and started to step away, but he caught her hand.

"You started the fight with her intentionally." Aria had told him the story on the way there, to help him understand that Carol may not let her stay there.

"Yes. I figured anger was better than grief. I suggested that she never had any real feelings for you and was just seeking attention. It broke my heart to do it, but it worked." She shrugged, and when she walked away, he didn't stop her this time. "She went back to school that weekend, and started living again, learned how to live without playing piano twelve hours a day, figured out what she could do with her life. It destroyed our friendship, but I wasn't worried about her any longer," she said over her shoulder.

She left Nick alone in the room, and he went back to stare at the swing set again. His heart ached, and he desperately wanted something that was out of his reach. The word normal whispered around his head until the sound of Carol coming back in the room interrupted his thoughts.

"I'm having dinner out with some friends, then I need to go pick up Lisa. Her grandmother picked her up while I was on the phone with Aria," she said. "I'll be gone a couple of hours."

"I'll keep her safe until you get back," he promised.

"When can I tell her you're gone for good this time, Nick? A week? A month? Or will a different detail arrive at my door with a folded flag and some medals?"

He turned his head to catch her eyes, her very frank eyes. "You'll know."

He turned his face back to the world outside the glass doors, keeping his back to the room and listening to her leave, understanding and appreciating the opportunity she had given him to say goodbye to Aria in private.

♫ ♫ ♫ ♫

Aria walked down the stairs dressed in a comfortable pair of yoga pants and a sweatshirt so big it hit her knees. She felt better than she had in days, glad she was safe for a little while, and sure Nick would straighten everything out. She frowned when she thought of him leaving her to go to Washington. She had no idea what awaited him there and worried a little about what they would do to him.

In her imagination, his organization was a group of faceless killers with sniper rifles who were known as "they," as if anyone would instantly know to whom "they" referred. When she realized that was how she had just mentally referred to NISA too, she laughed a little at herself.

When she walked into the main room, she found Nick standing at the glass doors, looking out into the backyard. He turned to look at her, and her breath caught in her throat. His eyes were more intense than usual, and his stare made the pulse pound furiously in her neck. She cleared her throat. "When are you leaving?"

He didn't speak, but before she saw him move, his lips were on hers, and her back was against the wall. She didn't hesitate before she wrapped her arms around his neck and kissed him back. He raised his head and looked into her eyes, and she felt a wave of love so strong that it startled her. As his head lowered a second time, she wondered when she had fallen in love with him again. Then, as his lips moved from her mouth to her neck, she wondered if she had ever stopped loving him.

Chapter 27

The Special Agent code-named Hecate strolled into the Florida hotel just as a group of ten young men and women in various stages of sobriety and attire stumbled out into the street. She stepped aside and let them pass then marched to the hotel registration desk.

She held out a set of credentials identifying her as one Special Agent Katherine Royce of the Florida Department of Law Enforcement and announced, "I'd like to speak with the manager on duty, please."

The hotel manager and part-owner, Adriano Gonzolez, came to the front and shook hands with her saying, "Welcome, welcome! Spring break, huh? How can I help you, ma'am?"

Kate placed her sketches, and a few indistinct surveillance photos snipped from closed-circuit traffic cameras, onto the desk and stated, "This couple checked into your hotel recently. I need to know the names they used for the reservation, and I need to see the room they stayed in as soon as possible."

Adriano waved his hands, all smiles and nods. "Of course. Of course. No problem. We always cooperate with FDLE in any way we can. Of course, I only need to inspect your search warrant in order to safeguard the confidentiality of all of our guests."

Kate kept her expression blank. It wasn't difficult. Without moving, she said, "You know what Mr. Gonzolez? It appears I have misplaced that search warrant today. But it isn't a problem. What I will do is make a quick call and obtain a search warrant for your scrutiny. And of course, since I am obtaining one, I may as well bring in every member of the Florida Highway Patrol, as well as FLDE, and bring in the Panama City Police Force, as well as the County Sheriff and all of his deputies to this precise location to conduct our very thorough search."

She paused just long enough to let the implications of that sink in. "Now, tell me something, Mr. Gonzolez, before I make that call. Do you suppose while we are conducting our search, and performing our due diligence, that we might find any kind of underage drinking or use of illegal or controlled substances taking place inside the walls of this establishment? Because, you know, that might not go so well for you.

"In fact, we will probably have to cordon off each and every single area where we observe any malfeasance—or possible wrongdoing—as a crime scene and perform an extensive and lengthy investigation."

She reached into her pocket and pulled out her cell phone. She met his eyes and emphasized, "Extensive. And lengthy."

Adriano Gonzolez smiled like the dawn breaking over

a new day. "You know something? I don't need to see your warrant today. Like I told you, we cooperate with the FDLE in every possible way. Will you give me just a moment to collect the room key for you?"

"Of course, I don't mind waiting," Kate answered. "I just need you to hand me that room key before I finish dialing this phone number for the clerk of courts." She glanced down at the cell phone in her hand and slowly began to dial. Adriano Gonzolez moved faster than he had in the previous three years.

♫ ♫ ♫ ♫

Nick *felt disoriented and fought off the panic that came with that feeling while he tried to open his eyes. He remembered the fight in the bar and the knife that was pulled on him. He remembered the pain as the knife sliced his chest, and the fury as he took his own knife from the hands of the attacker and returned the favor. Then the frantic trip to the pickup point, worrying the entire time that he would pass out before he got there and be left behind in this forsaken country. Did he make it to the rendezvous point, or was he in an Iranian prison, awaiting execution for the murder of one of their military leaders?*

His whole body ached, but he heard a sound to his left and forced his head to turn in that direction, finally able to pry his eyelids up. Jen Thorne sat next to his hospital bed in a wheelchair, lightly dozing. The scars on her face were barely visible now after many cosmetic surgeries, but the right sleeve of her robe hung loose and empty. Plastic surgery couldn't fix that.

"Jen," he said. His voice came out very hoarsely, and he

desperately wanted a drink of water.

She jerked awake at the sound of her name, then gave a hesitant smile. "Hey, big guy. How you feeling?" She wheeled her chair closer, her hand stroking the wheels one at a time like paddling a canoe, her knees hitting the side of the bed.

"Seriously? I feel like worm food. Is there any water here?"

She poured him a cup of water from the pitcher by the bed and held the straw to his lips. His mind went back to the last time someone had done that for him. "Where am I?"

"Bethesda. You were transported straight here once they found out you were going to live. Apparently, they lost you a few times en route."

"I made it to the pickup point, then?"

"Yeah, you ended up rolling halfway down a rocky hill and landing in a puddle of your own blood, but you made it."

"How are you feeling, Jen?" he asked.

"Better. I still think it's there sometimes, but four weeks is a long time. I'm getting better." She reached through the bars on the bed and grabbed his hand. "I've wanted to see you since the explosion, but Charlie told me he sent you right back out. They told me what you did, with the doctoring in the field, then the blood you gave me at the hospital."

Nick was uncomfortable with the conversation, so he just squeezed Jen's hand and closed his eyes, letting his body drift back to unconsciousness.

"Thanks for saving my life, Nick. I... Thank you, Nick."

♫ ♫ ♫ ♫

Nick cradled Aria to his chest then rolled over, untangling himself from her. They had first sat down on the couch right after the sun went down. Eventually, they laid down on the couch together, and she had snuggled her head into the crook of his arm and his chest. Within seconds, she had fallen asleep. He had watched her sleep, intending to remain awake until it came time for him to go, but he felt so relaxed that he had apparently fallen asleep as well. The dream had roused him.

He checked the time. Aria had been asleep for nearly an hour now, and he was sure that his movements wouldn't wake her. Hopefully, without him there to disturb her, she would sleep through the rest of the night and into tomorrow. She needed to catch up.

Briefly, he considered carrying her up to her room and putting her to bed, but he didn't want to disturb her. Instead, he shifted her body so that he could cover her with the crocheted afghan draped over the back of the couch.

He started to leave the living room, stopping at the entryway and looking back. For the first time in his life, he didn't want to leave, and it was ripping his insides out to do it. He would never see her again, he knew, and he wanted to wake her up and hold her. He wanted to express all the love he had held inside for years, the love that now threatened to consume him.

Instead, he walked to the front door, opened it, and walked out of the house into the twilight. He didn't look back at the house as he got into the car and drove away.

♫ ♫ ♫ ♫

Kate stood on the balcony squinting against the glare of the Florida sunshine and doing her level best to ignore the revelry in the streets below. She had searched the hotel room and, as expected, had come up with nothing useful. There was a fist-sized hole in the wall that revealed nothing. There were traces of makeup on some of the linens she found before the maids sent them to the laundry. Nothing else.

She had interviewed witnesses, including a maid who had seen them and spoken with them twice. She had even verified that Nighthawk had used the phone in the lobby of the hotel down the block. And that is the fact that she kept circling back to over and over again. What had Nighthawk been doing here? He wasn't trying to dump the principal. By all accounts, they were pretending to be a couple. He wasn't getting a night's worth of sleep, then moving on like a man on the run should. For that matter, Ricardo could have flown them just about anywhere from Vancouver to Bogota. Why Panama City, Florida during Spring Break?

Why stay here for so long and risk getting caught? Why this room? Why use the phone in the other hotel?

Standing on the balcony of Nick's former hotel room, Kate had a sniper perfect view of the room across the street. Following a hunch, she counted floors and counted windows, then she spun on her heel and left.

Kate walked into the lobby of the Sandpiper for the second time that day, and the hotel clerk suddenly stood up rigid and tall. "You again?"

Kate ignored it and demanded, "Tell me who was in room 420 two days ago. Pull up the reservation. I want to know the name, when they checked in, when they checked out, what they ordered from room service. Understand?"

♫ ♫ ♫ ♫

Before Aria opened her eyes, she knew Nick was gone. She hadn't yet woken up with him next to her, but it wasn't the lack of his body on the couch that told her he wasn't there. It was the lack of his presence around her.

It was bright daylight outside. As she rolled off the couch and stumbled upstairs to the bathroom, she realized she must have slept for at least fifteen hours. She was sore, and her head was full of cotton, but she had caught up on some much-needed sleep. After her shower, she threw on a pair of shorts and a shirt and went downstairs. She made her way to the kitchen, hoping to catch up on some much-needed food.

The house was quiet, but she found the kitchen, and as she pushed open the door, the eye-opening aroma of coffee filled the air. Taped to the coffee maker was a note in Carol's handwriting.

> Aria - gone to church - didn't want to wake you - coffee was made at nine, so if it's too old, everything is in the cupboard above your head - see you around twelve - C.

Aria looked at the clock on the coffee maker, and seeing that it was already twelve, almost dropped the coffee cup she had grabbed off the counter. She'd slept eighteen hours. No wonder she was so sore.

She grabbed an apple out of the big bowl on the table and nursed her cup of coffee, slowly eating the apple to the core. As soon as the food hit her stomach, she realized that she was famished and dug through the refrigerator until she found sandwich makings.

She was putting the top piece of bread onto the stack of meat and cheese when a little girl who could have passed for Carol's twin came flying into the room. She was dressed in a yellow dress with matching ribbons in her hair, and she had a bright pink cast on one arm. When she saw Aria, she stopped short and stood there, gauging her.

"You're Aria," she finally announced, then headed for the refrigerator, where she pulled out a juice box.

"And you're Lisa," Aria returned with a smile.

"Mommy said you two are friends like me and Amy Bradford and that you're visiting for a while with us," she said, expertly popping the straw into the hole on the top of the box.

"Is Amy Bradford your very best friend?" Aria asked, sitting at the table with her sandwich.

"Yep. Where do you live?"

"Oregon."

Lisa's brow wrinkled in concentration, then she said, "That's the state that's below Washington and above California." She took a long drink of her juice. "On the left side."

Aria was duly impressed. Apparently, Lisa got more than her looks from her mother. "You're right. Where's your mom?"

"Right here," Carol said, coming through the kitchen door. She carried a sack of groceries that she set on the table next to Aria's elbow.

"Need any help?" Aria asked around a mouthful of

sandwich.

"No, that's it." She took her purse off her shoulder and set it next to the groceries, then sat down in her chair with a sigh. "Lisa, go change out of your good clothes, then come back down here, and I'll fix you some lunch," she said.

Lisa set her drink box on the table, then left the kitchen in the same manner as she had arrived, at a dead run. Aria smiled after her fleeing back, then looked back at Carol, who was taking off her shoes. "She looks just like you, Carol."

Carol smiled and put her chin in her hands. "She has her father's eyes. Bright blue."

Aria waited for her to say more, but she remained silent. "Is the father subject off-limits?"

Carol shrugged. "There isn't a whole lot to the story. Girl meets boy, girl falls in love and loses her virginity one reckless night, girl finds out she's pregnant two weeks after boy goes off to realize his dreams, leaving girl behind to struggle through law school with a baby."

Aria felt a twinge of sympathy for Carol. "Does he know about her?"

She shrugged. "I couldn't find him, but I was able to get a hold of his parents. They said they told him, but I've not heard from him at all. He sends me money through them, which is why I can raise Lisa in this neighborhood on an assistant DA's salary. It's starting to get rough, though, because she's starting to ask questions."

"Where is he?"

Carol stood and went to the refrigerator. "I don't want to give you too many details about him, because you'd probably know who he is. Honestly, I can't figure out why the whole town can look at her and not see him." She pulled out what she needed to make sandwiches, and started putting together a lunch for Lisa. "He really threw me for a loop. I'd never have thought that he'd be like this, and I'm usually not wrong about that type of thing. Before him, I always considered myself a pretty good judge of character... in men anyway."

"When do you take her back to Henry?" Aria asked.

Carol shrugged. "I'm not supposed to see Henry. I'm supposed to take her to her own pediatrician to get the cast removed next week. But I can come up with some excuse to go by the hospital, give Henry a message for you."

"I'm not sure you should do that. Nick said they're probably going to be watching my family, and I know Henry would come running over here as soon as he knew." She finished her sandwich and took another apple out of the bowl.

"Maybe I can tell him I heard from you, and that you asked me to give him a message. That would at least alleviate his mind."

"I'll think about it. I may just wait to see if Nick can take care of things on his end." Carol stared at Aria for a long time. Finally, Aria held her hand up.

"I know, Carol. I'm not stupid. He's probably not coming back to get me. But he'll get a message to me somehow, how ever things work out. Until then, I'll probably just hide here and wait. If you give Henry a message, he'll call my folks, and I've learned this week that no conversation is necessarily sacred. I don't want to put you or Lisa in jeopardy."

"What makes you think he won't be back?" Carol asked. She cut the sandwich she'd made in two, added a few potato chips to the plate, then started slicing an apple.

"His line of work doesn't exactly call for a wife and kids, and he won't want to make me one of the women at a port, waiting for her sailor to come passing through. I could tell last night that he was telling me goodbye."

"I'm really sorry, Aria," Carol said, reaching out to grip Aria's hand.

"So am I. But right now, I have to think about working on finding out who was in on this with Peter. This isn't the time to fall into a heartsick depression. I'd prefer to do that when this is all over and done with." She squeezed Carol's hand and pushed her chair back from the table, carrying her plate to the sink.

Lisa came running back into the room and sat in her chair, where her mother set her lunch in front of her. "My birthday is next week, and my grandma Kent is having a big gigantic party for me at her farm. Are you going to be here so that you can come to my party?" she asked Aria in between mouthfuls of food.

"I should hope so," Aria said. "How old will you be?"

"Six. Grandpa Mabry said that six is the magic age, where little girls can make their dreams come true." She looked thoughtful for a moment. "I don't believe him, of course, but mama says that he's taken to flights of fancy." She waved an apple slice in the air. "That means he has a huge imagination."

Aria sat back at the table. "He told me the same thing

when I turned sixteen."

Lisa's eyes widened. "You know my grandpa Mabry? Did you know he was a drill something in the army?"

"Yep. That's when I knew him. I saw him in his uniform and everything."

Carol laughed at Lisa's awed expression and started to unpack the groceries. "You just struck pay dirt, Aria." She kissed Lisa on the top of the head. "Grandpa Mabry walks on water around here."

"I remember that he walked on water at your house, too," Aria teased.

"Not any more than your father did," Carol teased right back.

They started talking about their high school days. They riddled Lisa with stories for hours, and as the sun set and the night grew, Carol and Aria found what they had lost so many years before. When Aria lay in bed that night, half of her heart rejoiced in the rekindled friendship, and the other half of her heart wept for the lost love.

Chapter 28

The drive took Nick twelve hours, but it would help cover the tracks to Aria all the more, so it was of small consequence. If he flew out of Jacksonville, they'd think she was somewhere in Florida or Georgia.

The airport was busy and crowded with people coming and going on this Sunday morning, but he wove his way through the throng without a problem. When Nick was undisguised, and in this kind of mood, people tended to subconsciously clear a path for him, which suited him just fine right now.

Nick found a locker and put one of his bags inside, transferring what he needed to the other bag. Carrying just one bag, he found a newsstand that offered overnight mail service. He purchased two overnight express envelopes and a notepad, then went to a bank of payphones where he called information to get the addresses he needed.

He addressed two envelopes, wrote quick notes, stuffed them, and sealed them. Then he handed the envelopes back to the clerk at the newsstand. One envelope contained the location of Raymond's car so that he could find it. The other contained the key to the locker containing all of the evidence clearing Aria that he had gathered to date. He addressed it to Henry Suarez's medical practice, along with a brief letter of explanation.

He was curious as to whether his company card still worked, and was almost surprised when authorization to purchase a first-class ticket came through. Apparently, he still had a job. By now, NISA had been made aware that he was in the airport, they knew his flight, seat reservation, in-flight meal, and they knew what time he would arrive. If things went in the usual pattern, there would be at least two agents waiting for him at the airport in D. C. to escort him to Charlie, which was all the better to Nick. It saved him the hassle of paying cab fare.

He boarded late, not wanting to sit idle while other passengers came on after him, and once he was seated, he declined a beverage. The flight attendant in charge of the first-class passengers seemed to sense that Nick wanted to be left alone, and didn't approach him after that.

Nick knew that he would have escorts once he arrived. Other than that, he didn't know what was waiting for him at the other end. Once the aircraft cleared the airport below, he used the phone in the back of the seat in front of him and a credit card he had secured under Harvey Castle's name to dial a number that had been given to him just two weeks earlier.

The person on the other end picked up the call on the first ring, and Nick fought the doubt about her integrity. "It's Nick," he said.

There was a long pause, and he worried she would hang up on him before he was given a chance to explain anything. "I'm listening," she finally answered.

"I need to know if you believe in me," he said. He wasn't being fair, and he knew it. It would take a blind man not to see what Jennifer Thorne's feelings were for him. Perhaps if Sergeant Major Suarez had been stationed somewhere other than Fort Benning, Georgia, fifteen years ago, Nick might have found a spot in his heart that reciprocated her feelings.

He never had.

Though Nick wished for years that there was some way it could work out between them, he always reached the same inevitable conclusion. There wasn't room in his heart for anyone other than Aria. That didn't change the fact that he liked and trusted Jennifer Thorne and deeply respected her. It also didn't change the fact that he really needed a friend on the inside right now.

"You know I do, Nick. You're in a lot of trouble right now." Her voice held none of its usual warmth and hinted a bit at caution.

"I'm on my way in. If something happens, I need you to do a couple of things for me," he said, then began to layout a shortened version of the story and what he needed done.

"I'll take care of it," she said when he had finished. She asked no questions, and he felt a little touched by her trust.

"It's a big risk I'm asking you to take," he said.

"You've taken a few risks for me in the past," she returned. "Watch your back, Nick."

He hung up and leaned back in the seat, closing his

eyes. He needed to prepare himself for the upcoming ordeal.

♫ ♫ ♫ ♫

Kate stood next to the Mercedes in the Atlanta airport remote parking lot. She dialed the number, entered the long digits at the prompt, and waited.

Less than twenty seconds later, the hold music abruptly stopped. "This is Krait," Charlie Zimmerman answered.

"This is Hecate. I'm checking in to let you know that I've hit a cold trail. I need to go back to Columbus and question the dad."

"No need. Nighthawk's boarded a flight to D. C. from Jacksonville. No word on the girl. Get up here, but try to get the manifest of his flight as well."

Kate squinted up at the hot Georgia sun. She tried to pretend that she didn't feel like she'd just lost a week of her life and her partner for no reason. "Yes, sir."

♫ ♫ ♫ ♫

Nick showed no outward reaction when he saw just who waited there to escort him to headquarters. He refused to give them the satisfaction of seeing anything other than mild boredom. He wanted to scream and punch and ask if Charlie had sent them on purpose. Instead, he raised an eyebrow at Jerry Simmons' pleased expression and Nancy Warren's curled lip as he stepped away from the gate.

"Well, well," Nancy said, "if it isn't Charlie's little golden boy."

"Hello, Nancy. Strip in any clubs lately?" He had told

Aria the truth. He'd never slept with Nancy Warren, and she'd never forgiven him for it. They'd been undercover in Bangkok together, looking for a Senator's teenage daughter who had been abducted. They'd been there together for five straight weeks, and Nancy had tried everything she could to get Nick to lose his religion, as she called it, even going so far as to tell him how much she liked stripping when he was there watching.

That resulted in having the opposite of the intended effect, and Nick had never been able to look at her since without feeling his skin crawl. She had reminded him too much of some of the women in his father's family.

"A bit tardy, Nick?" Simmons quipped.

Nick shrugged, and his eyes narrowed. "I don't *feel* tardy."

"You need to surrender your weapon to us, Williams," Simmons said with a smile. "We're supposed to place you under arrest."

"You're welcome to try," Nick said quietly.

"Come on, Williams. Don't make this any harder than it has to be," Simmons said.

"I'll ride with you as my little baby-sitters, but I won't surrender to you, and I certainly won't surrender my weapon to either one of you. I will surrender only to Zimmerman. Just to be clear, I don't think I'll let either of you arrest me today. Charlie can arrest me if he still wants to after he hears me out."

Simmons and Nancy stared at Nick for several seconds, then Simmons finally consented. "Come with us peacefully. We're parked in the front."

♫ ♫ ♫ ♫

They were silent during the drive to the Treasury Building. Nick sat perfectly still in the back-seat during the drive, hoping that Jen came through. He felt an impending sense of doom and fought every instinct in his body to get out of the car and meet with Charlie on neutral ground.

They pulled into the parking garage, and Nick walked between them to the elevator. Still, no one spoke during the brief ride down, and Nick stepped out of the elevator in front of them. He nodded to the guards in the mantrap. Their faces remained impassive, and they insisted that he place his hand on the security plate.

After he received clearance, he stepped through the threshold into the outer office. He didn't recognize the agent at the desk, but the agent handed Nick a Day-Glo orange badge without asking for his name or ID. Simmons and Nancy were given their ID badges and keys, and Nancy led the way through the door, followed by Nick, then Simmons.

The door led to another small foyer with an elevator, and the three stepped in. The offices of NISA were actually one more floor down, and when the elevator doors opened to a hallway that had several offices off of it, Nancy stepped out first. Nick followed her, and they moved down the corridor toward Charlie's office. As she put her hand on Charlie's door handle, Nick felt a movement behind him but didn't turn around in time as a searing pain swept through his head, and he lost consciousness.

♫ ♫ ♫ ♫

Nick didn't know how long he'd been in there, but he recognized the room. He'd used it himself the few times in the past when he'd had to bring someone in for interrogation, which NISA euphemistically referred to as vigorous interviewing or tactical debriefing. It was a plain room, with a table and two chairs, and only one door leading out. There wasn't a two-way mirror to give the obvious clue that someone was watching an interview, but Nick knew that there were several fiber-optic cameras and microphones scattered around the room, hidden in the walls, ceiling, and light fixtures.

He'd woken up hours before on the floor, with a headache that made his stomach roll. As soon as he opened his eyes, he remembered what had happened and knew where he was, so he'd lain still, not wanting to give anyone watching the satisfaction of knowing how much he hurt. He kept his eyes closed for a while until the pain became manageable, then stood up and moved to a chair, where he sat. He didn't look at his watch. He knew it had been set to the wrong time anyway. He didn't feel the bump on the back of his head, nor did he fidget. He just sat.

He knew they were just playing mind games at this point, wanting to make him desperate, wanting to soften him up, but he also knew how to play those very games. It would drive them a little crazy to see that he wasn't in distress, and he could last longer than they could. He'd been in much worse situations without breaking.

♫ ♫ ♫ ♫

Aria spent Monday morning with her computer and the paperwork that Nick had left for her. He took the original micro-SD cards, leaving the hard copies behind. The house was quiet as she worked, with Carol at work and Lisa at school, and four hours passed before she even realized it. Her cross-referencing had helped her eliminate another twenty names, and when her eyes began to blur, she decided to give it a rest for a while.

She lay on the couch with her eyes closed, battling a headache that tried to take over when she suddenly realized what she hadn't been seeing. She ran up the stairs to her room and started going through the papers, trying to find the anomaly.

She finally found it at the bottom of the pile. It was a page of the specifications that had her notations on it after the most recent test. She dug a little further and found a copy of the same page that had been recovered from Peter's home office. She compared the two, going down each item line for line. They were identical. However, on top of the page taken from Peter's home was the date showing when it had been printed, the day before her own personal specification book had been printed. He didn't copy the specifications, he actually printed them before she had them printed, and incorporated changes she made the day before printing.

She had to search for a while, but she found a printout of the pictures she'd made of her security program from her workstation at NWT. She had two months worth of logs to search through to identify the terminal ID of the person who had accessed her workstation. It was tedious work because there were hundreds of entries in the two-month time frame before the specifications were printed, and she had to pull out her appointment book to cross-check the times she might have been in someone else's office on their computer accessing her own files. The teams worked together so tightly that it was almost impossible to determine all the hits in that time frame that might or might not have been her. Finally, she found a terminal ID that didn't make sense. She wouldn't have had a reason to use that computer. She felt tears come to her eyes as she recognized the ID number, feeling betrayal that was almost as bad as when she overheard Peter discussing killing her as if she were a pesky fly.

To make sure she wasn't jumping to conclusions that could be wrong, she thought back through conversations, then hacked into the appropriate bank. It took several hours because she had to write a program that would bypass security codes. After some time, she accessed the right account.

Digging through the system, Aria stared in disbelief at what she saw. Throughout an eight-month period, more than two hundred thousand dollars had been transferred into her secretary Julie Wilson's bank account.

That gave her a little more information to uncover. Not only was she looking for the times that Peter accessed her files, but she also checked to see the times Julie did, and if the times Julie did were for work or espionage.

She typed away at her report, detailing everything she knew and everything she figured that Peter knew. It was late in the afternoon when she finally finished. She secured it, packaged it, and e-mailed it to the address Nick had given her. Now he could give it to his superiors, and they couldn't possibly deny the evidence.

♫ ♫ ♫ ♫

Nick heard the electronic locks unseal and focused his eyes in that direction. Though he was surprised to see Charlie, he didn't show it.

"Wow, Nick, you look like dog food," Charlie said, coming into the room with a takeout bag from a fast-food restaurant. "I told them to bring you here when you came in and have you wait for me, but I had no idea what they did." He set the sack of food and a bottle of water on the table in front of Nick and pulled out the other chair. "I brought that in for my breakfast this morning but, if you've been here as long as they say, you need it more than me."

Nick glared at him. He had not yet convinced himself of Charlie's sincerity. "What day is it?"

"Monday." Charlie always took Sundays off. Nick knew that. That tradition began the very first Sunday after Zimmerman assumed the post of Director, and only on a few rare occasions did he ever violate it. Nick had never had anything but respect for, and a shared camaraderie with Charlie. He had no reason to doubt him now. Did he?

Deciding to withhold judgment and see what happened next, Nick ignored the little nagging doubt inside his gut and pulled the bag toward him and reached in, bringing out one of the three chicken biscuits he saw in there. "I got here yesterday morning."

Charlie's eyes widened, then he said, "I'm sorry, son. I've already contained Simmons and Warren for knocking you out the way they did. I'll go ahead and start disciplinary procedures for this."

Nick finished the first biscuit and reached in the bag for another one. "Take me to your office, and I'll give you information that will help in those proceedings."

Charlie nodded and stood, going to the door. Nick picked up the bag of food and the bottle of water and followed him, continuing to eat. When they reached Charlie's office, he held the door open for Nick to enter first, and as he sat down, Charlie slammed the door. "Do you care to start explaining and tell me what the blue-blazes is happening around here?" he bellowed as he walked around his desk and sat in his chair, now in the sanctity of his office, away from the cameras and the microphones.

Nick shrugged and continued to devour the last of the biscuits. "Charlie, you'd be the first I'd explain things to if I had it all figured out. I know most of the what and when, but the why still has me puzzled."

"You have some of your own whys to go into, Nick. I've never seen anything like what you did in my entire career, and I have to tell you, son, I don't like it one bit," he said, slamming his fist on the desk for emphasis.

Nick let Charlie blow off steam while he finished eating, then wadded up the paper and threw it in the trash can behind Charlie's desk. He leaned forward with his elbows on his knees and said, "Save your energy until I finish telling you what's been going on."

He leaned back in his chair, drained the bottle of water, and began his report. Although, for now, he left a few pertinent details out of it, like where Aria hid and where he'd stored the evidence.

Chapter 29

Nick sat in Charlie's office, his feet propped up on the desk. He felt confident that Charlie believed him when he informed him about Balder holding him at gunpoint. Even though Charlie was clearly not happy about Nick killing the man instead of disabling or otherwise getting around him while leaving him alive, he appeared to accept the facts. Nick could tell that there was still some anger lurking toward him for not reporting in more regularly, but he felt it would eventually blow over.

Because it was his summit, this case was personal for Charlie, and his inability to personally run the operation from the field obviously frustrated the man. Nick had just spent the last two hours relaying an abbreviated and filtered version of what he'd learned over the last week to Charlie and silently waited to gauge his reaction.

"Why did you hide out the way you did, son?" Charlie demanded.

"I didn't know how far this thing went. Now I'm glad I hid because Simmons is as deep into this thing as he can get."

"I know. He's the one who brought me everything I had on Suarez. He had me convinced she was some black widow type, and you were probably already dead. As much evidence as he had, I felt comfortable sending in Balder." Charlie looked tired, and Nick realized how draining this week must have been on him. "You know, you expect betrayal from the enemy, but you don't expect it from someone you've worked with so closely, and even been partners with, for over eighteen years."

"I have enough hard evidence to counteract anything he may have given you," Nick said.

"I know you do, son, and even if you didn't, the way they treated you the past couple of days would definitely make me doubt their motives." Charlie pulled a stick of cinnamon gum out of his pocket and smelled it like it was an expensive cigar before he opened the foil and popped it into his mouth. "Where is the evidence? If you had it on you, it's probably gone."

Nick raised an eyebrow at him. "It's safe. When it's needed, I'll bring it forward."

"What about the girl?"

"As soon as I know the danger is completely gone, I'll bring her forward as well. She's safe for now."

Charlie nodded. "Good, good. I'm sure you have her in a good place. Now, you and I need to discuss China."

Nick started laughing. "No. You and I need to discuss which desk I get for the next three or four months."

"Come on, Nick. You're probably the only agent I have that can handle this assignment. But you know I can't order you to go. You have to volunteer."

"No way, Charlie. I am not volunteering. I'm not leaving the city for a while. I'm going to go upstairs and have an apartment assigned to me, and I'm going to come here every day and report to my desk." He put his legs down and sat forward. "I'm burned out, man. I need a break."

Charlie nodded. "Okay, son. Go see Clemmy at the desk upstairs, and he'll assign you a car and an apartment." He stood and reached across the desk to shake Nick's hand, dismissing him.

♫ ♫ ♫ ♫

"What are you going to do?" Carol asked her as she drained pasta at the sink.

Aria propped her chin in her hands and stared into space. "I'm not sure. I guess all I can do is wait until Nick calls. I'm sure she wasn't an integral player in this. Probably all she did was enter my computer and print out the specifications whenever I changed them."

"How long has she been working for you?"

Aria thought back. "I think about two years. She started before this project began, and we started that about eighteen months ago."

Lisa came tearing into the room. "Mama, can I go over to Amy's house?"

"May I," Carol corrected.

Lisa almost rolled her eyes but didn't. "May I go to Amy's house?"

"No, Lisa. Go wash your hands, dinner is almost ready," Carol said.

Lisa turned around and slowly walked out of the

room, her head bowed as if following a funeral wake. Carol smiled after her, and when she was sure that Lisa couldn't hear her, she said, "That girl is going to be on the stage one day."

"That was a pretty impressive show of the blues," Aria acknowledged. She turned back to the salad she'd been making, and finished slicing tomatoes. "I guess her motive was money. It's insane to think about the destruction that is possible over money."

"I prosecute people all the time who just throw their lives away because of the love of money." Carol dished up plates and walked to the kitchen door. "Lisa, dinner's ready! Are your hands clean?" she called.

♫ ♫ ♫ ♫

Nisa kept the apartments for the agents pretty well stocked with generic stuff, but Nick stopped at a twenty-four-hour grocery store on his way to his new place anyway, to pick up a few items they always forgot. Steaks were one of those things, and toothpaste. Whoever did the shopping for the NISA agents always forgot to get toothpaste.

As he drove to his new place, he decided that what he needed more than anything was a hot shower, a hot meal, and to sleep for six straight hours. It was closer to midnight than he wanted. He'd spent all day and night with Charlie composing his reports from the mission. He wasn't sure if he could actually make it through a meal and a hot shower before the bed claimed him.

He found the address easily and thought Charlie couldn't be too angry with him if he got a townhouse instead of an apartment. He walked around to the back of the car to open the trunk to get out his groceries. He yawned as he tried to insert the key into the lock, and the force of the yawn was so strong that he dropped the key. If the house key hadn't been on the same ring, he would have left the groceries in the car and just gone to bed, but it was so he bent down to get it.

As soon as his fingers touched the keyring, he heard the ding of metal hitting metal, and immediately dropped into a prone position. He looked up and spotted a jagged hole that could only be made by a bullet in the trunk of the car.

Adrenaline had effectively knocked back the fatigue, and his mind was instantly alert.

They must have been using a suppresser because he still hadn't heard the shot. That meant they had to be close because they could only silence subsonic ammunition. Using his forearms as leverage, he low-crawled to the car door.

There were so many buildings around him that the shooter could be almost anywhere. His head was near the rear tire when he heard the sound again. He looked up and saw that the bullet had hit just a few inches above his head, missing the tire by just a few millimeters. It took a split second for him to decide to keep going in the direction he was headed rather than turn around and go to the other side of the car. Half a second later, the window next to him exploded as a bullet forced its way through the glass.

He opened the door and lunged inside, staying low, and put the key in the ignition. He really hoped they didn't shoot out his tires. It wouldn't stop him, but it would slow him down and make him even angrier than he already felt.

He started the car and put it in drive, keeping his head below the dash. After several yards, he sat up. As soon as his head came over the seat level, his rear window exploded behind him. The bullet exited through the front window just to the right of his head. He ducked back down.

He turned onto the first street he came to and waited until he was several yards down the street before he sat back up again. As he did, a sharp pain ripped through the left side of his body, causing his vision to gray. He gritted his teeth to keep from crying out from the intensity of the pain and looked down. Blood covered his shirt. He started praying in every language he knew as he kept his left hand on the wheel and drove, using his right hand to ascertain the entry and exit wounds of the bullet.

The seat was already soaked with his blood, and he knew if he didn't get help soon, he was going to pass out. He drove around the city for about ten minutes, turning as often as he could, and made sure he wasn't being followed. Finally, he couldn't risk taking any more time, and since he didn't know where Jen lived, he found a payphone. There was no way he was even going to turn on the cell phone Clemmy had issued him.

He slowly got out of the car and wobbled a bit as he stood, but he was able to stand without falling, so he walked to the phone. His hands shook as he inserted the change, and it was work not to drop the coins. A wave of weakness washed over him. He felt his knees start to give, so he gripped the side of the phone booth with one hand to support himself while he both held onto the receiver and stabbed in the number with the other hand. He finally punched in the last number and held the phone to his ear. It rang three times before it was picked up, and he worried that she wasn't home. She hadn't been on duty when he was there.

"It's Nick," he said when she answered.

"What's wrong?" Jen asked.

"I need help. I'm shot. It really hurts, Jen."

♫ ♫ ♫ ♫

He stumbled on his way back to the car and got in on the passenger's side, pulling his pistol out of the holster in the small of his back and putting it in his lap. If they had followed him, he wouldn't be able to see straight enough to shoot anyone, but he felt comforted by the weight in his lap. Then he started praying. For strength, courage, strength, wisdom. Eventually, he couldn't even keep the words of his prayer straight. Five minutes later, the driver's door opened, and he tried to raise the gun but didn't have the strength.

"Oh, Nick," Jen said as she slid into the car. She leaned forward and lifted his shirt, and he could hear her gasp at the sight. "You need a doctor," she told him, and he could feel her cool fingers as they probed his skin.

"You... know... Bett—tter... than... that," he said. His words came out in pants, and his teeth chattered as if he were freezing cold.

"There isn't anything I can do, Nick. You need a doctor, or you're going to die."

"Then, I'll die. But I won't do it in a hospital room

where I'm defenseless." He was about to pass out and had to win this argument before he did. He heard the engine start and felt the pull of his body as the car started to move. "Where are we going?" he asked her. He prayed he passed out before he started throwing up.

"To a doctor."

He was going to kill her when he came out of this, and if he didn't come out of it, he would make absolutely certain to come back and haunt her.

♫ ♫ ♫ ♫

Henry Suarez walked through the corridors of the hospital. It was two o'clock in the morning, and he'd been at the hospital for twenty hours now. The bus accident that happened in the afternoon rush hour on the interstate had caused an eight-car pileup. Every doctor on the hospital staff that had been there or on-call had spent the last several hours up to their eyeballs in crash victims, and he was well past the point of tired. There wasn't even any sense in going home, because his next shift started in four hours, so he decided he would sleep on the couch in his office.

He entered his darkened office for the first time in ten hours and turned lights on. His secretary had left his messages and his correspondence on the center of his desk for him to see. He sat down and looked through the messages, seeing one from every member of his family telling him that there was still no news. He'd known that there was still no news because his phone hadn't gone off to alert him. It had been exactly a week since it all began, and five days since Adam saw her. He was going to have to start handing out sedatives to his family if something didn't change soon.

He began to go through the stack of correspondence and came upon an overnight envelope with no return address. It was marked "personal and confidential," so his secretary hadn't opened it. He ripped it open, and a key fell out. Henry's hands shook a little as he picked it up and looked at it, instinctively knowing it was a key to a locker. Then he pulled out the single piece of paper that had come with the key.

"She is safe. She is no longer with me, and if she stays smart, she'll stay safe. If I disappear, someone will come to you. Trust her. If I don't disappear, hopefully, Aria will be with you in a few days. The original plan I discussed with your brother cannot happen. This goes too deep for it to work. I have an alternate plan that will go into effect either by my hands or my friend's. This is why you'll have to trust her. You'll recognize my friend. She has one very obvious distinguishing physical feature."

It wasn't signed, but Henry knew who sent it. He put the key in his pocket and leaned back in his chair, contemplating the message.

When his phone rang, his stomach turned a little, worried about whether the call would be good news or bad news.

"Yes?" he said when he answered.

"Is this Doctor Henry Suarez?" the woman asked.

"It is."

"This line is secure, I've checked, but your office isn't, so watch what you say."

"Go on."

"Nick needs your help."

His mind was instantly alert. "Where are you?"

"The hospital and your apartment are being watched. I can't come to you. Do you remember the surprise you had when you set a broken bone a few weeks ago?"

His mind flipped through all the broken bones he'd set in the last few weeks when what she said hit him. "I do."

"Go there. Make sure you're not followed."

"How do I do that?"

"Call for a cab to pick you up at the emergency entrance. Don't wait outside."

"It will take me about half an hour to get there." He was already standing and taking his lab coat off.

"Doctor, bring supplies. It's very serious."

"I need to know what to prepare for." He needed specific information. She didn't disappoint him.

"Gunshot in the lower left abdomen. There's an exit wound, and he's lost a lot of blood. We have the same blood type, so I can help there. Just get there as fast as you can. I stopped the bleeding, but it's already been two hours."

"I'm on my way."

♫ ♫ ♫ ♫

What was that constant ringing? She rolled over and tried to get away from it, but it persisted. Finally, it dawned on her that it was the telephone, and she reached for it, her eyes still shut.

"Hello?" she croaked out.

"Is this Carol Mabry?" asked a woman.

Carol's heart immediately began to beat faster.

Nothing good was going to come out of the phone call. "Speaking."

"Nick needs your help."

She knew it. She sat up and turned on the light, looking at the clock. It was two-ten. "What do you want me to do?"

"Do you have a garage?"

"Yes."

"Go open the door and make room for a mid-sized car. Don't turn on any lights. I'll be there in three minutes."

"Okay." She started to hang up the phone but heard the woman's voice again.

"We'll probably need Miss Suarez's help, too. I don't think you and I can lift him on our own. I kind of have a leverage problem."

The caller hung up, and Carol jumped out of bed, running down the hall to Aria's room. She threw open the door and hoped that Aria woke up easier than she had when she was a teenager. "Aria, Aria, wake up," she said as she shook the form on the bed. Aria groaned out loud, rolled over, and buried herself deeper under the covers. "Nick's in trouble. Get up."

Aria immediately sat up and brushed her hair out of her eyes. Carol didn't have time to explain, so as soon as she saw Aria sit up, she ran out of the room to move her car out of the garage.

Chapter 30

Aria turned the lights out in the garage at Carol's signal and hit the button for the automatic garage door opener. Carol ran in ahead of the car that was pulling into the garage, and as soon as it cleared the doorway, Aria hit the button to bring the door back down. She left the door leading inside the house open so that some light would shine into the room, and when the garage door shut completely, she turned the lights to the garage back on.

Strangely, she wasn't a hysterical mass of jelly but actually felt quite calm. She wasn't sure if her mind was still asleep, or if she was just learning to deal with hysterical situations. She was sure that as soon as they took care of Nick, it would all catch up with her.

She ran up to the car just as a woman was getting out of the driver's seat. Aria recognized her from the description that Nick gave her. "You're Jen, right?" she asked. The woman nodded and rubbed the back of her neck. Aria went over to the passenger's side and started to open the door.

"Don't," Jen said. Aria stopped and looked at her in question. "He's leaning against the door. Wait until we can help you."

"What happened?" Carol asked.

"He was shot," Jen replied. "Do you have a bedroom on the first floor?" Carol nodded. "Good. Go strip the bed, then put your shower curtain on it and cover that with blankets you don't care about."

"We need to call my brother," Aria said, "he's a doctor."

Jen turned to Aria. "I already called Henry. He's on his way." Aria went around to the driver's side and crawled in. "You're going to get covered in blood," Jen said to her, but Aria didn't care.

Nick had his back to the door, and he appeared to be asleep. For the first time in her life, she was thankful for her small frame as she maneuvered herself so that she was crouched on the floorboard on his side of the car. She reached for his hand. She felt how cold his skin was and began to pray.

In hindsight, she couldn't figure out how the three of them got him out of the car and into the house. She held him up while they opened the door, and somehow, they lifted him and carried him through. They took him to the small spare room behind the staircase and laid him on the bed.

"What happened?" she asked Jen.

"He was shot," Jen repeated with a sneer. Unspoken but understood were the words... and it's your fault! Aria gritted her teeth and stared at the other woman, waiting. Jen finally shrugged her shoulders and said, "I don't know. He passed out before he could tell me. From the shape of the car, I assume someone was sniping him."

Carol came into the room with a pair of scissors, and Aria took them from her and began to cut his shirt away. "Has he talked to his boss yet?" she asked Jen while she worked.

"Yeah, all day today. I thought everything was under control." She sat on the foot of the bed and watched Aria work. "Someone needs to watch for Dr. Suarez," she said tiredly.

Carol left the room as Aria finished and put the scissors down. "I don't want to move him to take this off until Henry gets here."

"It's probably a good idea. Carrying him in here caused the bleeding to start again. We need some towels to make a compress and get the bleeding under control."

Aria looked at the woman in front of her and decided that there wasn't a whole lot left keeping her upright. She couldn't imagine the drive she must have just had, coupled with the thought that he might die on the way. "I'll take care of it. You stay sitting. I'll also get Carol to start some coffee."

She moved through the house as quickly as she could, not wanting to be away from Nick for a second longer than necessary. She found some dark blue towels in the linen closet, then searched out Carol, who was standing at the front door looking out of the window.

"Can you put on some coffee?" she asked her.

Carol nodded, then as Aria was turning away, said, "Do you think they'll find him here?"

"I hope not. Do you want us to leave?" she asked. She

prayed the answer was no. She didn't want to have to try to move him.

Carol shook her head. "No, but I think I'll take Lisa to her grandparents' house in the morning. I don't want anything to happen to her."

Aria felt tears come to her eyes for the first time that night. She went back to Carol and wrapped her arms around her. "Thank you. Thank you for everything for the past couple of days."

Carol pushed Aria away and wiped her own eyes. "Hey. Go take care of him. I'll bring the coffee in as soon as it's ready."

Aria ran back to the room and saw that Jen had pulled a chair next to the bed. She was sitting straight and holding onto Nick's hand, but Aria could see that she was barely hanging on. "Here are some towels," she said. "You have to show me what to do."

Jen rubbed her hand over her face, then said in a tired voice, "Put one under him covering the entrance wound, then one on top of the exit wound and press down. You have to apply good pressure." She stood and looked out the window while Aria began to apply towels, but she was looking into the back yard instead of the driveway. "Where is your brother?" she murmured almost to herself.

Aria wondered the same thing as she followed Jen's instructions and looked into Nick's face. She was hoping for some reaction, even a grimace of pain, but there was nothing.

Ten minutes later, Jen sat up in her chair and went to the door just as Aria heard murmured voices coming their direction. Suddenly, Henry filled the doorway, and she thought he might be the most welcome sight she'd ever seen.

"Aria," he said as he came into the room and set his bag down by the bed, "you doing okay?" He started to unpack his bag, taking out the different tools of his trade, then took her by the shoulders and gently moved her out of the way.

"I have to keep the pressure on to stop the bleeding," she said, feeling hysteria trying to fight its way to the surface.

"I'll take care of it." He looked around the room while he opened a pack to start an IV, his eyes finally resting on Jen. "Did you call me?"

"Yes."

"You're positive his blood type is the same as yours?"

"He gave me blood a couple of years ago," she said. "Besides, I'm type O neg."

Henry nodded as he looked back down at Nick and started the IV. "I'm going to have to run a direct line. I didn't have room to pack a bag for your blood. You need to get Carol to find you something to lie down on," he said as he pulled some metal wire out of his pocket and wrapped it around the headboard, then hooked a bag of saline to it.

When Jen left the room, Aria went to look over his shoulder. "Is he going to be all right, Henry?"

Henry lifted the towel covering Nick's wound. "I don't know yet, Aria. He's in pretty bad shape." He cleaned the wound while Carol and Jen brought a cot in and set it up next to the bed. Aria had to move out of the way and felt helpless as she watched Henry's competent hands while he worked. Finally, she stepped forward to help, no longer able to stand in the corner and watch. She got him towels, handed him gauze, even held a flashlight that he'd sent Carol to get while he sewed Nick's skin back together. Then she helped turn him and do the process over again. Then he showed her how to change the bed, and helped lift Nick while she did it.

Carol came back in the room with coffee, and Aria gratefully took a sip as Henry ran a line from Jen to Nick, and her blood began to give him his life back.

When she had given all that her body could take, Carol helped Jen from the room, taking her to a bed where she could lie down while her body replenished itself. Finally, Henry sat back and took his gloves off, then rubbed the back of his neck. "I wish there was a way I could get him to the hospital, but gunshot wounds have to be reported to the police."

"He needs more help?" Aria asked.

"He needs more blood for one," Henry said. He began to clean up the mess that had been created the last hour, putting everything in the garbage can that Carol had brought in earlier.

"Is he going to be okay?"

"Yes. I'll try to bring another banana bag of antibiotics to run intravenously this afternoon sometime." He pulled a bottle of pills out of his bag and handed them to Aria. "Those are pain pills. He's going to need them when he wakes up."

"When will that be?"

"Soon. I wasn't able to bring any to give him through

the IV, and as soon as the shock wears off from his system, the pain will bring him around if nothing else."

"Will you be able to get him some blood?"

"I took a sample to test the type. If she has type O Negative and he's given her blood, then he has to be O Neg as well, and it's the only type he can take. I'll be able to get a little more from her tonight, but I can't bring any from the hospital. We had a massive trauma yesterday that cleaned us out."

Her tears could no longer be held back. Now that there was nothing else to do, she felt them from deep inside her, and her first sob nearly broke her in half. Henry put everything down and pulled her in his arms, then simply held her. The eruption ended as quickly as it began, and she suddenly felt better, knowing that Henry had done what he could and that Nick would live. She hugged him tight then pulled away, wiping her eyes as she did. "Thank you, Henry. I don't know what we would have done without you."

He put his finger under her chin and tilted her face up, looking at her for several seconds before he spoke. "What's going on, Aria?"

She took his hand and squeezed it, then stepped away from him and began to pace the room.

"It's a long story, Henry. And I'm sure you've heard a good chunk of it from Adam."

"I heard the abbreviated version you gave him. Now, I have about two hours before I have to be back at the hospital, so you have time to start talking."

She let out a deep sigh. As she sat down in the chair by the bed, she started talking. She told Henry more than she'd told Adam because he was the most easy-going of all her brothers, and she thought he would hassle her less. She was wrong, of course, because he began to drill her with questions before she even began to get into the meat of the story.

She ended with the discovery she'd made the day before, then rubbed her face tiredly. It had been such a long week, and while she'd been able to let her body rest for the last couple of days, her mind was still exhausted.

"Is that the whole story?" he asked.

Aria nodded, and when she moved her hands from her face, she jumped a little when she saw Jen in the doorway. "You move like Nick," she said.

The other woman didn't acknowledge her but spoke to Henry. "Is he going to make it?"

Henry nodded. "I gave Aria some pain pills to give him when he wakes up. I might need to get a little more blood from you tonight."

"You can't come back here. Once it's been discovered that you've disappeared, you'll be watched more closely." She stepped further into the room, but with Aria in the only chair, she was only able to stand. She'd changed out of her bloody clothes and looked like she had taken a shower, but her eyes still showed signs of fatigue.

"I'll find a way. No one will follow me here." He put the last of his supplies back in the bag and closed it with a snap. "You need to rest now. I took a little more blood than I probably should have, and you need to give your body time to restore itself."

"I'm not going to rest until I see him wake up and know he's going to be okay," Jen said.

"Look, you did the right thing, bringing him here and calling me. He really needs to be in the hospital, but I can handle it from here."

"How do you know for sure he's out of the woods?" Jen challenged. Aria moved out of the chair and walked to the window, and Jen immediately sat in her place.

"I stitched the wounds, pumped him full of antibiotics, and we've replaced his blood. He'll hurt, but he'll recover, and from the look at the scars on his torso, he knows how to hurt and live through it."

Henry didn't miss the way she squeezed Nick's hand then immediately let go. "Aria, find me a towel and some sort of razor. I need to get ready for work." As soon as she left the room, he turned back to Jen. "I can tell it took a lot for you to come here and ask for help."

Jen put her elbow on her knee and rested her head in her hand. "I didn't know what else to do."

"You did the right thing. Don't fight these women. Let them care for Nick while you rest, or you won't be much good to him when he does wake up." He paused for a moment, but when she didn't speak, he continued. "You can trust them."

Jen started to speak, but Aria came back in the room with a towel over her arm, carrying a disposable razor and some shaving cream. "This says it's for legs, but it will probably work on your face," she said.

Henry groaned and took everything from her. "Thanks, Aria. I guess I'll smell pretty today." He started to leave the room but stopped at the doorway. "If it takes all three of you sitting on his chest, don't let him up. I don't want to run the risk of him tearing his stitches." He left the room and worked his way through the house, finding Carol in the kitchen. She looked up when he came in, gave him a small smile, and went back to turning the thin steaks she had on the stove.

"How's Lisa's arm?" Henry asked her, collapsing in a chair at the table. As soon as he'd left the room, he felt the lack of sleep and the physically draining twenty-four hours he'd had.

"I think the novelty's worn off. She's starting to get tired of her cast." She took the steak out of the pan and began to crack eggs into the sizzling grease. "Why don't you call in to work today and rest for a few hours, Henry. You look like you'll collapse at any time."

"That's tempting, but I have patients I need to check on." She poured a fresh cup of coffee and set it on the table in front of him, then filled a plate, bringing that to him as well. "Watch those two in there. They glare at each other like they're about to duke it out," he said as he started shoveling food into his mouth.

Carol sat next to Henry and took a sip of coffee. "They're both in love with him," she said.

Henry rubbed his eyes again, no longer dreading going to work that day. "That's great. Well, then, you have fun today." Carol laughed and patted his hand.

♫ ♫ ♫ ♫

Aria stepped around the chair where Jen had finally fallen asleep and reached over to feel Nick's forehead. She was so worried that he would start running a high temperature and felt some control when she constantly checked. As soon as her hand touched his skin, his hand came out of nowhere and grabbed her wrist. She gasped in surprise at the contact, then looked down and saw his eyes were open.

She knelt down by the bed. "I'm so glad you're awake, Nick. I've been so worried," she said as she kissed his forehead.

"Where am I?" he asked in a hoarse voice.

"You're at Carol's house. Jen brought you here early this morning." He started to shift his body, but the movement brought an involuntary moan from him, and she saw the sweat bead on his forehead. "Henry said not to move," she said as she put her hands on his shoulders to keep him still. "Do you want some pain pills?" Nick nodded and leaned his head back with his eyes tightly closed, obviously fighting the pain his movement caused.

As Aria reached behind her for the bottle of pain medicine, she saw Jen jerk awake. Her eyes immediately sought out Nick, and a flash of concern crossed her face when she saw him awake. Aria ignored her and opened the bottle, pouring out two pills. She turned back to Nick and put a pill against his lips until he opened his mouth, then she gave him some water through a straw. He seemed to gain some control back and opened his eyes again.

"Where's Jen?" he asked.

Aria felt pain slice through her heart at the question, then slowly stood and moved out of the way. "She's right here. I'll leave you two alone." Her whole body ached as she walked to the door, and when she turned back to look at him, she saw Jen leaning forward and reaching for his hand. She opened the door very gingerly as if it would break if she wasn't extra careful, and walked out of the room, turning for the stairs. She obviously wasn't needed in there, and a shower and bed were what she needed now, she thought.

♫ ♫ ♫ ♫

Nick watched Aria leave and fought off the impulse to call her back to sit beside him and hold his hand. Instead, he turned his head toward Jen. "Are you completely out of your mind?" he asked in a weak voice.

"I made sure I wasn't followed, Nick. You needed medical care, and I couldn't take you to a hospital, so I was kind of out of options. Who shot you, Nick?"

"Who do you think?" he spat.

"Did you see the shooter?"

Nick shook his head. "Close range silenced subsonic. Not too good adjusting for depth perception with night vision yet."

"Looks like he was good enough to nick you, Nick."

"It was at least his fifth shot."

Jen sat back a bit, "Well, that's just sloppy."

He closed his eyes for a moment and fought off another wave of pain, then opened them back up. "Carol has a kid. A little girl. You put them at risk."

"How?"

"Did you change cars?"

"No." When his eyes narrowed, she swallowed and said, "I didn't want to move you. Actually, I didn't think I could have moved you. I'm kind of half the girl I once was in terms of upper body strength." She squeezed his hand, but when he didn't return the gesture, she let go and sat back in the chair. "I disabled the tracker then drove for two hours. I would have known if I'd been followed."

Nick could feel his consciousness slipping away, but there was more he needed to say, so he shifted a little, and as the pain attacked, his fatigue was pushed into the background. As soon as he had his breath back, he opened his eyes again. "That was a NISA car, Jen. They didn't need to follow you. They probably already know where we are." He saw tears fill her eyes and cursed quietly to himself. He needed her to shift her focus from herself to the situation.

"What reason could they have for tracing you?" she asked him.

"To find Aria. She knows what they're up to, and she knows who they are." He could feel himself slipping away again, but he didn't have the strength to fight more pain, so he let himself drift as helplessness claimed him. "You need to protect them, Jen. I can't do it. You need to follow my original plan."

♫ ♫ ♫ ♫

Aria was sitting at the table in the kitchen, staring at her laptop screen, not really seeing what was on it when Carol walked in. "Did you get Lisa settled in?' she asked.

"She was excited. What six-year-old doesn't want to play with horses for a week?" she said as she opened the refrigerator and started to dig around in it. "I told her I'd be back for her birthday party." She grabbed a ginger-ale and pulled out a chair next to Aria.

"Where did you tell them you were going?"

"I said I would be unavailable due to an attempted murder case that's recently come to light." She popped the top on her ginger-ale and took a swallow. "So that I wouldn't get caught in a lie, every time they asked me a question, I told them that I really couldn't discuss it."

Aria shut the top to her computer and pushed it away from her. "Do you have to do that often?"

"Leave her?" Carol asked. When Aria nodded, she shook her head. "I've only had to do it once or twice in the past two years." She took another sip of her drink and asked, "How's Nick?"

"He woke up a couple hours ago," Aria said, rubbing her temples.

"What did he say?"

"First he said, 'where am I,' then he said, 'where's Jen'." Aria crossed her arms on the table and rested her head there.

"Then, he fell back asleep?"

"No, then I left the room so that the two of them could have some privacy."

Carol paused for a few heartbeats. "Aria, from what I can gather about Nick, he is going to think about the situation before he thinks about letting you sit there and hold his hand. Of course, he would want to see Jen first, unless you've suddenly developed mad ninja skills and connections at NISA." She looked at Aria more closely. "Have you been sitting in here pouting this whole time?"

"No. I took a shower first." Though she'd prefer a little sympathy right then, she knew Carol was right and started to feel a little foolish.

"Why don't you go sleep, then go back in there and tell Jen to get some rest."

Aria nodded and stood slowly. "Thanks, Carol. I'm sorry I came barging in here like this. We kind of disrupted your life a little."

"Maybe it needed a little disrupting," she said, then waved her hand at the door. "Go sleep. I'll wake you at two. That will give you a good three hours."

The thought of that made Aria's whole body long for the bed, so she nodded. "I'll see you in a couple of hours." She turned and headed for the stairs, ignoring the door underneath them as she made her way up.

Chapter 31

"My friends assure me that there are girls in your establishment that are truly virgins. I must say what a relief it is to find a place that doesn't try to cheat their customers," Nick said with a leer as he addressed the woman sitting in front of him. Human traffickers disgusted him. If the place wasn't an impenetrable fortress full of armed men, he would have simply slit her throat and been done with it, but since he had no reliable backup nearby, he decided to play it safe. He hoped that the contacts he'd established over the past five weeks were reliable.

"You must know how hard it is to come by true virgins in Thailand. If that is what you want, you must be prepared to pay, Mr. Vincent," she said, taking a sip of her tea.

"I can assure you, madam, that I am prepared to pay handsomely."

"Very good then. It will be three thousand dollars. American, of course."

Nick pulled a money clip out of the pocket of his tailored Italian suit and counted out four thousand dollars. "How much *more if I say I prefer an American girl? Preferably blonde."*

"What makes you think there are American girls here?"

"My friends would not lie to me, would they?"

She stared at the money, and he was sure that she had to keep from licking her lips. "Two thousand more dollars." She took the money and made it disappear with almost mystical speed. "I assume you want a young woman?"

"The younger, the better, madam." Nick stood to follow her and slung his duffel bag over his shoulder.

"What is in the bag, Mr. Vincent?"

"Just some toys." He opened the bag revealing ropes, handcuffs, and whips, among other things. "I prefer that my women remember me."

"You must not leave any permanent marks on her body."

Nick looked visibly shocked. "I am well aware of the investment you have, madam. Do not insult me again."

"I do apologize. Please, follow me." She led the way up a winding staircase, down a hallway that had several closed doors. Nick could hear nothing as they passed the rooms, and he was sure they were soundproofed. She opened a door near the end of the hallway and stepped back so he could enter. "You have one hour, sir. A thousand dollars an hour after that."

"An hour is all I need, madam." He stepped into the room, and she shut the door behind him. At first, he couldn't see anyone in the room, but as he opened his bag and knelt down, he could see her huddled in the corner, almost behind the bed. She was watching him with wide, terrified eyes, and he cursed to himself when he thought about the evil this thirteen-year-old girl must have witnessed in the last several weeks.

He moved to stand with his back to the bed and looked up, seeing a vent directly in his line of vision. There was a chair in the corner of the room, and he pulled that over so that he could stand on it and reach the vent. He quickly unscrewed it and removed the cover, seeing the camera there. He shook his head and waved his finger as if to say, "tsk, tsk," and disabled the camera.

A thorough check of the room showed no more cameras or microphones. He emptied his bag then walked around the bed until he was in front of the girl, then he knelt down to eye level with her. A petite girl with blonde hair and brown eyes—it was impossible not to make a connection to Aria Suarez in his mind.

His heart ached a little as he recognized her from the picture he had stared at hundreds of times in the past five weeks. "Hi, Mary. My name is Nick, and I'm friends with your daddy. He sent me here to get you out."

Her eyes filled up with tears, and she nodded her head. "I need you to do something that's probably going to be pretty scary, but it's the safest way to get you out of here."

She nodded again, and he ran a hand over her head to comfort her. "For now, though, we'll just sit here for a few minutes. Don't worry, Mary, you'll be safe in just a little while."

She nodded.

He said, "I need to ask you some questions, okay?" She nodded again. "Who is Sawback? Who's Sawback, Mary?"

She whispered, "My horse."

Nick nodded. "That's right. Sawback is your horse. That's good. What did you do in Fredericksburg last June, Mary? Do you remember?"

"I was in my aunt's wedding."

Nick smiled. "That's good, Mary. Very good. Last question.

What is a mocha frappe milkshake, Mary? What is that?"

Mary sat up, "That's my favorite milkshake at Dave and Busters."

Nick nodded and kept eye contact. "Your daddy told me to ask you all those questions to make sure it was you, Mary. Now I really believe you're the girl your daddy wants me to help. For this to work, you have to believe that I am here to help you. Do you believe me, Mary?"

She nodded quickly, a tear streaming down her face.

He waited and watched the time go by while he spoke to her about everything he could think of, and when it had been forty-five minutes, he said, "Okay, Mary. You have to trust me more than anyone you've ever met, okay?"

She nodded again, and he wished she would speak to him again. He held his hand out, and when she took it, he saw the burn marks on her wrist from the ropes that had bound her. Combat had given him similar scars on the palms and backs of his hands. He walked her over to the bag and knelt down again. "Make yourself as small as you can and climb into the bag. You have to be very still. Don't move even a muscle, don't make a sound, and in five minutes, we'll be out of here."

♫ ♫ ♫ ♫

Carol intended to persuade Jen to take a break, so she carried a cup of coffee and a plate with a sandwich and some chips on it to the room. She already missed Lisa, but Carol knew her daughter was in good hands at her grandparents' house.

She opened the door without knocking and stepped in before she realized Jen wasn't there. She set the plate and cup down then did a quick walk-through of the house, looking for her. When she opened the garage door and saw that the car was gone, little fingers of fear began to work their way up her spine. She wanted to wake Aria, but couldn't figure out what good that would do, so she went back to the bedroom to sit with Nick until it was time to wake her up. Maybe Jen would be back by then.

As soon as she sat down, she looked at Nick and saw that his eyes were open, staring at her. She'd always thought that he had the most powerful eyes. "Hey, Nick. Pushing the limits of my hospitality, aren't you?"

He almost smiled, and she felt pretty confident that he would live. "Carol. What day is it?"

"Tuesday. It's only about noon." She wished she knew how to check a pulse or something, thinking that she should probably be doing nursely things.

"Where's Jen?"

"I don't know. The car's gone."

Nick nodded. "Good. How long ago did she leave?"

"I've been gone all morning, so I'm not sure. You don't want her here?"

"I don't want the car here. Where's your little girl, Carol?"

The little fingers of fear slowly grew into full-blown fists. "Do I need to worry about something, Nick? I've never been really good with surprises."

"Not if she got the car out of here in time. Where's your kid?"

"Gone. Safe. Grandparents' house."

"Good." He closed his eyes, then opened them again. "Can you get me another one of those pills?" She nodded and opened the bottle, pouring out two. "I only want one.

I don't want to be knocked out."

"Henry should be here in a few hours. He said you might need more blood."

"I probably lost a lot." He opened his mouth for the pill, then let her raise his head to sip from the straw. Then he leaned his head back on the pillow, and she watched sweat bead his brow from the exertion of that small movement. He said, "I hate being weak."

"Oh, Nick, you're about the most un-weak man I've ever met. Even when you were a kid sporting all those cuts and black eyes."

The smile that he fought back earlier actually showed up that time, and she felt like maybe she'd accomplished something. "I had on a holster yesterday. I don't remember, but see if I put my pistol back in it," he directed. Carol found the pile of clothes, but the holster was empty. "It must still be in the car," he said. "Do you own a firearm?"

"Yes. I have a revolver. Do you want it?"

"Yes." She started to leave the room, but he stopped her. "Wait, Carol. Where's Aria?"

"She's sleeping," she said. He hid his reaction carefully, but she was still able to see the faintest flicker of disappointment cross his face. "I never would have been able to get her to lie down if she'd known Jen was gone." She opened the door. "I'll go get my gun. Do you need anything else?"

"Ammo," Nick answered, and she shut the door behind her.

When she came back downstairs a few minutes later, she opened the door and saw that he was already asleep again. She lifted the sheet and put the .38 Special Remington revolver against his leg on the far side of his body, letting it touch his leg so that he would know it was there, then sat back down in the chair and opened the book she'd grabbed off her nightstand when she got the gun and settled in.

♫ ♫ ♫ ♫

Someone was touching his arm, and he grabbed the hand and opened his eyes. For an instant, he thought it was Adam. Then he remembered where he was and something about his circumstances and decided this must be Henry.

"I think with reflexes that quick, I can safely say you're going to pull through," Henry said with a smile.

"That's nothing. You should see me on a trapeze," Nick tried to joke, but he hurt too much to be convincing. Henry finished hooking up the IV line to the needle that was still in his arm and attached it to a bag hanging over his head.

"How would you appreciate your pain, Nick?" Henry asked.

"Well, gosh, Henry, I don't like it very much," Nick admitted.

Henry grinned. "Scale of one to ten?"

Nick relented, "Probably worse than giving birth from what I gather but so much better than a kidney stone."

"I hear that," Henry agreed. "So, would you rate your discomfort at about a six or as a seven?"

Nick nodded, his eyes closed. "Honestly, it hurts almost as if I've been shot."

Henry studied him, happy he was in such good spirits,

then he also nodded. "We'll call it at least an eight. It's easy to see you've had your fair share of comparisons. Have you considered retiring, giving your body a break?"

More and more every day, he thought. "What is that?" he asked, indicating the banana bag.

"Amoxicillin. A common antibiotic. And a whole bunch of vitamins. Don't worry. I won't knock you out. You seem to be managing the pain pretty well," Henry said as he sat in the chair.

"That's easy to say on your end."

"Want another pill?"

"No. Do you have any aspirin?"

"I have naproxen and acetaminophen. I'd rather you alternate doses of each every 3 hours. Aspirin might make you bleed a bit more than you'd like and doesn't mix well with ibuprofen," he explained as he dug through his bag.

"Where's Aria, doc?" Nick asked, no longer willing to deny his need for her to be there.

"I think my sister's in the kitchen with Carol. Do you want me to get her for you?" He handed Nick the pills, and Nick surprised himself by being able to lift his arm to put them in his mouth without unbearable pain. Henry held a straw to his lips so he could wash the pills down, then he leaned his head back and closed his eyes, nodding.

He must have drifted off, because when he opened his eyes again, Aria sat in the chair by the bed. She had her elbows propped on her knees and her face in her hands. He felt a tug at the sight of her. "You don't know how many times I've woken up like this and wished you were next to me." He didn't realize he'd spoken out loud until she jerked and raised her head up to look at him. He narrowed his eyes at her when he saw her face. "You've been crying," he said accusingly.

She smiled at him. "Off and on for about two hours now. I guess this whole week is finally hitting me."

"I thought I'd taken care of everything. I guess I overlooked something," he said.

"Jen told me they had Simmons and Nancy in custody."

"They do."

"Then who shot you?" she asked him.

"Probably Hecate. She never could shoot straight with a silencer."

Aria gasped. "What? But you debriefed them and gave them enough information to arrest Simmons and Nancy. She is an honorable agent, you said. She wouldn't have just tried to kill you because she could. Who would have told her to shoot you?"

"Only one person it could be, and I don't want to think about that right now." He held his hand out so she would take it, and, when she did, her touch eased some of the pain, both in his heart and in his body.

"Jen took the car and left."

"I know."

"Do you know where she went?"

"Away. That's all that matters right now. She'll be back." He closed his eyes and willed his body to heal faster than it should, and gripped her hand tight. "Will you pray with me?"

"What? Of course." Aria sandwiched his hand with hers and bowed her head. "God, we need You now more than ever before. We need Your wisdom, and we need

Your healing power. And God, we also need Your protection, as much for this nation as for ourselves. Please protect us. Help us do the right thing here. Amen."

She kissed his hand and raised her head. He opened his eyes, squeezed her hand, and fell asleep.

♫ ♫ ♫ ♫

Charlie Zimmerman sat back in his desk chair and stared at Kate. "How could you miss?"

"I had a bead on him even with the suppresser messing with my aim. When I fired, he moved unexpectedly. As soon as he realized he had come under fire, his *training* kicked in. You and I both know once I lost the element of surprise, I had nothing."

"So you didn't miss on purpose? You didn't let any feelings get in the way of your abilities?"

"What feelings? I don't know Nighthawk socially. I only know him on a professional level." She stood. "I missed. Balder missed. Simmons missed. Clearly, either Williams is just the better agent, or else maybe God wants him alive and sent some guardian angels to watch over him."

Charlie let out a deep sigh. "You're right. My apologies." He waved a hand. "Go type your report and get Simmons to debrief you. We still need to find him."

Chapter 32

By Tuesday night, Jen hadn't returned to the house. Nick didn't seem concerned, so the rest of the household tried to follow his lead. Henry spent an hour with him in the bedroom that night with the door shut, and when Henry came out, he called the hospital and informed them that he had a family emergency that couldn't be ignored, and he would come in again at the end of the week. Since Henry was off for the next two days anyway, all that did was take him off call and allow him to stay at the house without having to come and go, worrying about being followed.

When the women questioned him about the discussion he and Nick had, he told them nothing about Nick's concerns that the car could be traced to the house. The two looked like they would shatter at any moment, and he didn't want any more patients on his hands.

Nick woke up more and more regularly, partly because he wasn't taking the pain pills anymore, and partly because his body was healing quicker than Henry had thought it would. He was able to walk a short distance that night, with Henry's support. Though he fell back to sleep as soon as he laid back down, and though he was in more pain when he woke up again, Henry was amazed at the pace of his recovery.

Aria's eldest brother, John, had enlisted the help of a friend in the computer business and had set up a secure, encrypted, private blog on the Internet, allowing his family to leave messages there that could not be traced. Henry checked messages that night in his room and discovered that Adam was with John in Atlanta, waiting to hear from Henry. Henry left a message telling them as much as he could, then answered the deluge of questions that appeared within the hour.

When Henry came down to the room Wednesday morning after a mere two hours of sleep, he found Nick sitting up in the chair and Aria asleep on the bed. He stopped short in the doorway when his tired mind registered the sight of the two of them.

Exhaustion must have finally set in because he started laughing so hard that he left the room to keep from waking her up. It took several minutes to rein in the hysterical laughter. Finally, he decided he could go back into the room.

"What happened here?" he asked Nick, putting a blood pressure cuff on his arm.

"She was about to topple over, so I told her to sit on the bed for just a minute while I sat in the chair. I think it took her about thirty seconds to fall asleep," Nick answered.

"How long ago was that?"

"About an hour."

"Do you want me to help you upstairs to another bed?" Henry asked.

Nick shook his head. "I'm fine, as long as I sit. I'll let you know when I need to move."

"Do you always heal this quickly?"

He shrugged. "A lot of it is mental, Doc. You know that. Most people lie around expecting to feel bad and be in pain, so their bodies comply."

"And you, what?"

"I tell myself I don't have time to feel puny and fight the pain back."

"People like you could put me out of business. You took a bullet in the gut and swallowed a total of three pain pills, now thirty hours later, you're sitting in a chair." He removed the cuff. "Your blood pressure's good in case you were wondering. Want me to check your cholesterol?" he joked.

"When can I take a shower?"

"Tomorrow. I want to keep the wound dry for a little bit longer." He put the blood pressure cuff back in his bag. "I can help you to the bathroom if you want to shave. I have an extra razor with me."

"Oh, man. That sounds like a great idea."

"I'll just add it to my bill."

Nick wanted to laugh, but though he was putting up a good front, the pain was still making a strong presence, so he stood very slowly and started the long walk to the bathroom. "I have some things I need you to do, Henry," he said.

♫ ♫ ♫ ♫

Aria woke up stiff and disoriented. She lay still and let her mind come into focus. As soon as she remembered what was going on, she sat up in a panic, wondering where Nick was. She found him in the living room, asleep on the couch, the television muted on a news channel.

His eyes opened as soon as she walked into the room, and he held his hand out for her to take. She sat on the floor next to him, holding his hand, and rested her head on the edge of the couch. "How long did I sleep?" she asked.

"About four hours. Do you feel any better?" He gently ran his fingers through her hair.

"Let me get a shower and some coffee, then ask me that." She raised her head and looked at him closely. "You feel better." He nodded. "Good. Where is everyone?"

"Henry had to run an errand. I think Carol's in the kitchen."

"What about Jen? I'm starting to get worried about her, Nick."

"She won't be back for at least another day." He squeezed her hand and let it go, then slowly sat up. "Listen to me. God is our refuge and strength, a very present help in times of trouble."

Aria nodded. "Psalm 46."

"That's right. Quit worrying. It adds stress, and stress causes mistakes. When you feel like your worry is overwhelming you, I want you to quote that Bible verse out loud. Say it as often as you need to in order to steady yourself."

Already feeling the worry dissipate, Aria smiled.

"Thank you."

"You're welcome. Now, go take your shower and get your coffee, then you can come back, and we can watch some silly action movie. I'll tell you all the technical mistakes they make with the firearms," he offered. Aria laughed and kissed him, then left the room.

♫ ♫ ♫ ♫

Nick convinced Aria to go up to her room to sleep that night. She wanted to protest, but she was too tired, so she complied as soon as she saw him settled back asleep in his bed. It took her a while to fall asleep, because she laid there worrying about Jen and where she was, and then about Henry. He hadn't returned yet from whatever errand occupied him, and though Nick didn't seem concerned, she couldn't help wondering if something had happened to him.

Eventually, her mind gave in to her body's demands, and she fell into a fitful sleep that was filled with confusing dreams. She dreamed about armed nuclear devices in small cases that would keep them from being detected. They were planted in every city she could find her family.

She finally jerked herself awake and lay there in the bed, afraid to go back to sleep. She didn't know how long she'd slept, but she knew she didn't want to be alone in the dark, so she put some clothes on and left the room. When she was putting on her watch, she saw that it was four o'clock and realized she'd slept longer than she thought.

The door to Nick's room was shut, and the light was

off, so she decided to make some coffee before she disturbed him, knowing as soon as she opened his door, he would wake up. As she neared the kitchen, she saw the light was on in there and thought perhaps Nick was already up. As soon as she pushed open the door, she saw who was there and stopped dead in her tracks, her mouth falling open.

John, Adam, Henry, and Nick were all seated at the table, papers and laptops strewn around between them. All four men stopped speaking and stared at her until Adam finally broke the silence. "Good morning, Aria. Sleep well?"

John said, "Don't tease her, man. You know she's not exactly a morning person."

It took a while for her brain to acknowledge that her brothers really were standing there. The second it did, she squealed and launched herself one after the other into her brothers' arms. For a small moment, the exhaustion, the worry, and the fear seemed to fade away as she allowed herself to be passed around. When she'd hugged and kissed all of them at least once, she pulled out a chair next to Nick and sat down, squeezing his hand in her excitement.

"When did you guys get here?" she asked.

"An hour ago," John said.

"How?" She was suddenly worried that the *them* out there would learn her brothers were here.

"John asked James Montgomery if we could use his jet. Nick needed us to run a couple of errands for him," Adam said.

John had worked a case in Atlanta at the first of the

year that had become very personal for him and ended up becoming friends with the people who had been involved. Billionaire James Montgomery, the Montgomery in Montgomery-Lawson Incorporated, was one of those people. His continuing generosity toward John and their family seemed inexhaustible.

The kitchen door opened again, and a very tired looking Jennifer Thorne came into the room. John stood and held out his chair. She practically collapsed into it without even looking at him. Aria took one look at the other woman and got up to fix her a cup of coffee.

"How'd it go?" Nick asked.

Jen glared at him. "The next time you ask me to do the European tour in forty-eight hours, remind me of this moment in time, will you?" She accepted the cup from Aria with a nod and took a sip. "They're all shocked and appalled and will do anything in their power to help us out. Meanwhile, 'stiff upper lip and all that sort what-what' was their best advice," she said. "Nick, please reassure me that you're absolutely certain about this, because I just opened a huge can of worms, and I want to make sure that it wasn't for nothing."

"I'm absolutely sure."

"It's hard to believe, then it's not hard to believe. How horrible is that?"

Aria looked at Nick then Jen then back at Nick. "What are you two talking about?"

"I needed some help from the powers that be and had to call in a few favors to get that help. Don't worry, Aria. This is all almost over," Nick said.

Jen suddenly looked up at John, who stood dutifully

behind the chair he had abandoned for her with a half-grin plastered on his face. "Of course," she said, almost to herself. With a surprised and curious look between John and Aria, she gasped. "Suarez."

"Small world, Thorne," John smirked. "Almost like God was orchestrating something with us."

"Indeed." She held out her hand, and he took it. "Good to see you again, Detective."

"Likewise," John said, releasing her hand. "I take it you are no longer in the private consulting business?"

Jen shook her head. "Too dangerous. People get shot."

"You don't say?" John grinned. "Well, sorry it didn't work out."

Jen shrugged. "No big deal. Sorry things didn't work out with your girlfriend. I heard the breakup was a real trial."

John barked a laugh and, with an appreciative smile of chagrin, said, "Now you're just being mean."

Adam, who had been watching the private interplay between them since Jen first sat down, demanded, "Okay, you guys have got to tell me what's behind all this."

"Long story," John hedged with a secretive grin.

With a half-grin on her own face, Jen took a cellular phone out of her pocket and slid it across the table to Nick. "Everyone has this number. I'd give it about twelve hours before the music starts."

"Thanks, Jen." Nick turned back to the papers in front of him. "We need to compile all of this into a simple report, with backups and attachments. I need at least five copies of everything. Adam, there's a printer in Carol's office. Did your friend Montgomery have what we needed to convert this video I took?" Adam nodded, so Nick slid the camera across the table to him. "Go ahead and transfer it, and print as many clear pictures as you can from what's there." Adam took the camera and left the room. John took the chair that he'd vacated.

"Nick, what's going on?" Aria asked.

"I'm calling in some favors." He gave her a very, very quick summary, then said, "I need you to try to summarize that report you e-mailed to me, giving as many details and names as you can, then make five copies of it. Start at the beginning, from the day you started the project for the shielding, and try to be as specific as possible. Don't worry about getting too technical or about classified information, but you do need to watch the clock. I need it done by this afternoon."

"Who is this going to?" she asked.

"Whoever shows up. Start now. The longer you sit here and ask questions, the fewer details you can give." He dismissed her by turning back to his computer and speaking to Jen while he started typing. "Go sleep, Jen. We don't know what kind of backup we're going to need, and I need you on your toes." Aria watched while Jen merely nodded and left the room.

"What kind of detail do you want out of this?" John asked, holding up a sheaf of papers.

Nick glanced quickly at what he was holding then handed it back to John. "I need to know the dates and times of each flight, where they went, and where and when their paths crossed. I need to get an estimated amount of money spent on this on the government's side if you can possibly figure that out, and the amount of money that was transferred into everyone's accounts."

Aria went back to her bedroom, where she found her reading glasses and her laptop. Not wanting to be away from Nick any more than necessary, she went back to the kitchen to work on her report.

They worked in silence for several hours, stopping only to fill coffee cups and to make more coffee. Aria worked hard at remembering the timing of everything. Thankfully, she had so many records on her computer that it was just a matter of transferring information.

When her stomach growled, she grabbed an apple out of the bowl on the table and munched on that, not wanting to break her pace. At one point, Carol came into the room and made a breakfast that no one ate. She was in and out, giving Nick printouts of things, taking flash drives to her office to print, and binding things already printed into folders.

Nick came and went, going to his room and lying down, returning to work for an hour, then lying down again. Around noon, he received the first call on his cellular phone. Aria couldn't hear the other end of the conversation, but she stopped what she was doing while she listened to Nick's end, hearing respect in his voice she had never heard him use when addressing someone before.

"Yes, sir," he said, then paused to listen to the other end. "I appreciate all of the inconvenience you're going through." Pause. "Well, sir, that was part of my job. This isn't part of yours." Nick sat perfectly still while he listened. "Yes, sir. If you just arrive at the time that Special Agent Thorne instructed, I will have any information you feel you may need. We are working on compiling it right now." Another pause, this one longer. "I appreciate your concern, Mr. Ambassador, but I can assure you I am on the mend, so to speak." Pause. "Thank you, sir. I look forward to seeing you again, as well."

She watched him hang up the phone and set it down. Without even breaking stride, he went back to work. She looked at John and Henry, who were also staring at him, and then they all shrugged and went back to their reports. Ten minutes later, he received a call nearly identical to the first, referring to the caller as senator rather than ambassador, and once again hung the phone up and went back to work. Two more came through within the hour, both ambassadors.

Jen came into the kitchen right after the last call and sat in a chair next to Nick, holding her hand out. He typed with one hand while he handed her the phone with the other, not even looking at her.

"Krait, this is Dove." Pause. "I don't care if you told me you didn't want me on this case yesterday. I located Nighthawk. He's closer than we realized." She listened to Charlie while she took a stack of papers near Nick's elbow and started reading them. "I don't think he's going to go anywhere anytime soon. Someone shot him. Whoever sniped him hit him. That was his blood in the car."

Aria could hear the man's voice as he started yelling. Jen cut him off. "No, I don't mean he's dead. I mean, he's laid up. The girl's brother's a doctor. He must have gone back to her for help after ditching the car." She tapped her toes while she listened to the man bellow. "Just come to me. I don't know if he's going to trust me or not. I'll meet you at five-thirty at the restaurant of the hotel where I'm at." She rattled off the address, then ended the call before tossing the phone back to Nick.

"I wish I didn't know. It makes me want to hate things," she said, then she took the stack of papers and left the room.

About three minutes later, John Suarez picked up his work along with two cups of coffee and followed her, making his brothers both raise their eyebrows and share a knowing look.

♫ ♫ ♫ ♫

Aria finished late that afternoon. She left her brothers at the table and went to find Nick, who'd been gone for about an hour. She found him in the living room, standing at the window that faced the backyard. She stood next to him and took his hand, wanting to wrap her arms around him, but worried she would hurt him.

"Adam just left," she said.

Nick looked at his watch. "Good."

"Who's Krait?" she asked him softly after a few minutes of quiet.

"Charlie Zimmerman, my boss." He let go of her hand and started to pace, but sat down instead. She could see the strain of the day on his face. "No, he's more than that. He and Jen are about the only friends I have. Charlie was like the dad that I wanted when I was growing up." Nick slowly walked to the couch and painfully sat down.

She sat down at his feet and put her head on his knee. "Is he involved in this?"

"Yes. There's no other explanation."

"Do you know why?"

"No, but I'll find out before the night's over." He put his hand on her hair and began to run the strands through his fingers.

"Do you think this plan will work?" she asked him.

Nick shrugged, and she could feel him wince at the movement. "I have a plan that relies on too many people playing their parts to perfection. The timing is going to matter. It probably won't work, but there wasn't anything else I could do. Five days ago, Simmons said in a few weeks it wouldn't matter anymore. I need to take care of this before it's too late."

Chapter 33

Taxis arrived throughout the afternoon and carried her brothers and Jen away. At five, Aria helped Carol load her truck with the binders they had compiled, then helped Nick get settled into the front seat. No one spoke on the drive to the meeting place, each of them dealing with his or her own worries and fears. They moved through the evening traffic to the outskirts of town and stopped at an abandoned railroad yard. Several empty warehouses lined the yard. They pulled in and parked in front of one of them.

Carol carried the cot she'd brought from her house into the warehouse and set it up in the warehouse's office. Nick slowly walked into the building and looked around him. "This is perfect, Carol. How did you know about it?" he asked her as she brought in an armload of linen.

"There was a murder here about three or four months ago. I had to come check out the crime scene," she said as she handed Aria the linen and went back outside.

Aria went into the office and made up the cot, and

when she was done, Nick stretched his long body out on it with a sigh. "Are you hurting?" she asked him, finding a questionable looking chair in the corner of the room.

"I was fine until we hit the yard. The potholes and railroad tracks I could have done without," he offered dryly. He shifted and reached behind him, pulling Carol's little .38 pistol out from behind his back and laying it next to him.

She dusted the chair off and carried it over to the cot then sat down. "As soon as this is all over with, you can lay in a bed and not move for as long as you want to. I know I plan to," she said.

Nick started to say something, but Carol came back into the office. "You know, I don't see a sign of anyone. Are you sure that everyone is in place?"

Nick nodded. "Jen and John know what they're doing. They would have directed everyone else." He closed his eyes. "What time is it?"

Aria looked at her watch. "Just after five-thirty."

"We have about thirty minutes," he said, and Aria felt her stomach tighten with nerves. "I need to see Adam."

♫ ♫ ♫ ♫

Nick got a grip on the pain just as he heard the sound of gravel being shifted by car tires. He took a deep breath and sat back up, ignoring the sweat that broke out on his body from the effort. He stood and fought his legs when they tried to shake, then put the gun back in its holster and walked out of the office into the warehouse.

Plenty of light still streamed in through the broken windows. If everyone played their part, this would all be over before they lost the light. He glanced up toward the rafters, hoping there was enough light for Adam to do his job. Aria and Carol were in a room in the back of the building, hopefully helping Henry entertain their guests.

Nick heard a car door slam and walked to the center of the large room as the door opened. A figure entered the building, silhouetted by the sun shining behind him, but Nick knew who it was.

"I was willing to overlook it the first time, son, but I don't think that I'm going to be able to do it the second time," Charlie said as he stepped into the warehouse. "You can't just decide to run things the way you want to see them run and expect your superiors to sit back and let it happen."

"I'm sorry I didn't cooperate with the sniper, Charlie. Perhaps if you had spelled it out for me, I would have known what was expected of me," Nick quipped. He stood where he was and crossed his arms over his chest. Anger was boiling through him, and while he wanted to let it vent, he needed to control it for now.

"Look here, Nick. What makes you think that I had anything to do with that?" Charlie asked. Simmons and Nancy entered the building and flanked him.

"I often judge men by the company they keep," Nick sneered.

Charlie ran his hands through his hair, and while he attempted to look innocent, his eyes flashed with impatience. "You don't know what you've gotten into the middle of here, son."

"I think I've come pretty close to figuring it out."

"I never would have sent you there if I'd known you

knew her. I thought you were going to help me take care of that little problem, then we could have gone on with our business without you being any the wiser."

"You planned to eliminate her from the beginning?"

"Sure, but I had to make it look like we investigated her first. She sent the original message to another agency, so she just couldn't show up dead. I figured you'd take her as a dumb blonde, knowing your attitude about women, and would blow her off as a joke."

Nick felt the betrayal slice through him as if it were a knife. He was close to losing control and struggled to get it back. "Why are you doing this?" Nick asked as calmly as possible. "I thought you had integrity. I thought you believed in what we do."

"This whole country has gone down the drain, and you know it," Charlie said, stepping closer to him. "War, Nick. You love it, I know. But some soldiers are just a few years from retirement and have known nothing but war. They come back broken and abandoned."

He raised his fist in the air. "My boy." He slammed his hand into his chest. "My only son went off to fight for freedom and democracy, and came back a shell of a man, facing criminal charges for following orders. He took his own life." Tears streamed down his face. "How do you tell a mother that her only son couldn't live with the things he'd done, with the way his country treated him?"

"What was the plan?" Nick asked. "Nothing you do is going to bring your son back."

"No. But this country needs to be purged. We need a fresh start. Create a summit. Use your ranking and expertise and the respect you've earned from people all over the nation, and create an environment where all of the people in charge of our nation's defense are together in one place." He quickly raised both hands in the air. "Then, BOOM! A nuclear bomb, hidden under the tight, tight security, will take them all out, and we'll be forced to begin anew."

"Oh. You're insane." Nick could see it in his eyes and wondered why he hadn't been able to see it before.

Charlie turned to Simmons. "You see why I didn't bring him in on this in the first place? He thinks we're fighting for truth, justice, and the American way. There is no more glory in that." Simmons chuckled, and Charlie looked back at Nick. "You're the best agent I've ever worked with Nick. It isn't too late to bring you in. You can be part of my administration."

"Who's involved, Charlie?" He needed him to talk, to confess as much as possible.

Charlie shrugged. "You spend enough time abroad, you make friends, even if they are the enemy. We have counterparts who are now driving taxis in Moscow or working in fast-food in Hong Kong. They want to see the destruction of the great red, white, and blue beast as much as I do."

Though it didn't show, Nick felt a wave of weakness wash over him. He needed to sit soon, or he was going to fall down. "Your son is gone, Charlie."

"You don't understand," Charlie began, but Nick cut him off.

"I don't need to understand, Charlie. Plain and simple, this doesn't happen this way."

"It took us two years to get to this point, Nick," Charlie said, stepping closer to him and waving a finger at him, "and you and your little self-righteous girlfriend aren't going to do a single thing to stop us."

"You wanna bet?" Nick asked. Charlie pulled out a gun, and Nancy and Simmons followed his lead. Nick suddenly had three guns trained on him by three people he knew wouldn't hesitate to kill him, but he didn't even flinch. "You think you can kill me, and it's over? Free pass to kill hundreds of leaders of this country along with thousands of civilians?"

"All we have to do is kill you and your little girlfriend, and our tracks will be covered. No one else knows about it," Nancy said.

"Her family knows."

"That's easily taken care of. Even if we didn't get to all of them, there isn't enough time for them to be taken seriously. In two more weeks, the project will be complete," Simmons said.

Nick felt his vision start to gray and knew he had to end this. He looked up and nodded, then looked back at Charlie, who was watching him closely. Nancy and Simmons both looked up but didn't see anything, then the door at the end of the warehouse opened. "Are you going to kill everyone who knows about this, Charlie?"

He could hear footsteps echoing through the empty warehouse. "How about Sidney Franklin, Ambassador to Great Britain?"

Charlie's eyes bugged out of his head as he turned to see who was coming his way. "Or Senator Lawrence Macon, who's daughter was, as you called it, stupid enough to get herself kidnapped and shipped to Bangkok? Oh, here's a good one for you. Mitchell Lewis, Ambassador to Iraq.

Wait, how about Michael Daugherty, Ambassador to Russia?"

Charlie shook his head to deny what he was seeing and stepped backward as the men came forward, surrounded by bodyguards and Secret Service agents. "Are you going to kill every one of these men, their staff, and their families?"

"You... you don't understand, Nick," Charlie whispered. "You have to understand what we need to do."

"Sorry, Charlie. You have to understand what *I* need to do," Nick corrected. Charlie started to lower his gun, then Nick watched as the realization of his situation fully dawned on him. Charlie stared into Nick's eyes as he slowly began to raise the muzzle of his pistol again, this time in the direction of his own ear. Nick heard himself scream a denial as he lunged, tackling his boss, the man he had once called a friend. The shot from Charlie's handgun echoed around the warehouse.

♫ ♫ ♫ ♫

It had been nearly an hour since it all began, and the warehouse was still in chaos. Jerry Simmons and Nancy Warren were detained by none other than Special Agent Kate Royce.

Hecate had been assigned to cover point during this excursion, but as soon as she realized her orders came from the wrong side, she had no problem arresting the perpetrators. When the FBI arrived to arrest everyone involved and to take the statements of the ambassadors and the senator, she gave a full report to the Special Agent in charge.

Henry examined the unconscious Charlie Zimmerman. Thanks to Nick, he had not been able to take his own life, but the fall onto the concrete floor had earned him a concussion. Henry treated him until the paramedics arrived, and three Homeland Security Agents escorted him to the hospital.

The paramedics tried to persuade Nick to go with them as well, but he wouldn't leave. Henry wasn't able to sway him either and had to be talked out of trying to force Nick onto the ambulance. He settled for helping him to the cot in the office where Nick refused to lie down, choosing to sit on the cot instead.

"Everybody knows you're tough and stubborn, Nick, but I thought you were supposed to be smart. Who are you trying to impress right now?" Henry asked.

"Stuff it, Henry," Aria explained.

Aria sat next to Nick, clinging tightly to his hand. She hadn't let go of his fingers since she heard the shot. She'd been in the back watching a monitor streaming one of the three video recording feeds Adam had set up. From the angle of the camera, she couldn't tell if Charlie had shot himself or Nick. When she heard the shot ring out, neither Jen, who had snuck into the backroom after being ordered by Charlie to keep watch outside nor Carol had been strong enough or fast enough to keep her in the room.

A Special Agent of the FBI sat in the office with them, questioning both of them over and over again, until Aria wanted to rip her hair out and scream at her to quit asking the same questions. Adam pulled the video feed up on his tablet. With the evidence compiled in the notebooks and the confession that had been caught on video, the federal agents finally decided they had enough information for the night, but asked Jen and Nick to be in Washington by Monday.

Adam and Henry helped Nick to Carol's vehicle, then stayed behind with the agents to pack up the equipment. Aria and Jen got in the back, Nick leaned the passenger seat back, and Carol drove. The four of them stayed quiet during the long drive back to Carol's house.

When they arrived, Nick wouldn't get into the bed he had occupied downstairs, but instead sat on the couch in the living room. It took an hour of persuasion, but Aria convinced him to lie down, and exhaustion finally overtook him. Aria called her parents as soon as she saw that Nick was snoring, and spent an hour on the phone with them, dividing her time between laughing and crying. As soon as she hung up the phone, Adam and Henry arrived, and they all ate a light meal that Carol prepared, then the household went to bed, each one exhausted from the ordeal they had been through.

Fully clothed, Aria carefully settled in on the couch beside Nick and slept deeply next to him. When she woke up the next morning and saw he was gone, she didn't even have to look in the garage to know he was completely gone. Jen Thorne, too, had disappeared without so much as a note.

Though Carol and her brothers knew Aria was heartbroken inside, she kept a good face on the outside. Tears and hysterics would do nothing to change Nick or the situation. She knew that. So she tried to convince herself to let him go while she tried to convince everyone around her that it didn't matter.

During the weeks of interviews and depositions, while she traveled between Richmond, Washington D. C., and her parents' home in West Virginia, she never saw Nick and wondered if that was intentional. If so, he must have gone to great lengths to ensure they were never scheduled to appear to testify at the same time. She would have loved to see him again, if for no other reason than to force him to say goodbye to her face.

Within three months, despite Charlie Zimmerman refusing to speak, Nancy Warren, Jerry Simmons, Peter Harrington, and Julie Wilson had confessed all they knew and given up the names of their coconspirators in other countries who had been involved in the plot. Aria watched it all unfold on the television in her old room at her parents' house. They were being taken from the courthouse to federal prison as she packed her bags to fly back to Portland and pick her life back up where she'd left it.

NWT, Inc., had offered her job back with back pay and a bonus, and the idea of the challenge of work was more than she could turn down. It had been too long since she'd worked a puzzle or sat in on a meeting in a room filled with brilliant minds, and she looked forward to resuming normalcy. If she was going to recover from losing Nick for the second time in her life, she needed to reestablish her normal life and all of her usual routines.

♫ ♫ ♫ ♫

Nick woke up with a start, his body tangled in clean sheets. He visually cleared the room for threats and quickly ascertained his surroundings, scanning every corner, and using all of his senses to get a handle on his racing thoughts. Within seconds, he'd gotten his bearings and forced his racing pulse back down to normal. Once again, he had awakened in his cousin Marcus Williams' apartment in New York City, thousands of miles away from where he had started nineteen hours earlier.

He checked the time and realized he had managed to get five straight hours of sleep. His skin tingled, and his mind felt cleared of cobwebs. This last trip back to America had obviously completely worn him out.

He got up and took a long, hot shower, enjoying the luxury of his cousin's massaging shower head as always. He no longer longed for a hut on a beach and endless tall glasses of icy lemonade, but he very much craved his Bible and a quiet place. He and God still had to have a talk. It would be a long talk. He was reading his Soldier's Bible when Marcus returned to the apartment.

"Hey, Cuz. I was hoping you were back. You hungry?"

Nick nodded. "The last thing I ate was some halal thing in Dubai."

"At the airport?"

"Yeah. The food court was closed."

Marcus nodded. "That stinks. I'm gonna' make you an omelet."

To his surprise, Nick heard his stomach growl. Marcus barked a laugh. "And some waffles and corned beef hash, too, I guess."

They didn't really talk until Marcus sat across from him, and they started eating. Instead of shoveling his food in, Nick actually savored every bite. "I could get used to a famous White House chef making breakfast for me."

Marcus looked up, surprised. "How'd you hear about

that?"

Nick raised his eyebrow. "Try to remember where I work."

Marcus grinned. "It was just a cake. But I got to ride in Air Force One. That was, oh, you know, fantastic and amazing."

"I'm really proud of you, man. And just to be clear, any cake you've ever made was never 'just' a cake." Marcus made pastry into art, pure and simple.

Humbled, Marcus asked, "You like your omelet?"

"It's amazing." It was.

Marcus nodded. "I tried something different this time. I'm part of this televised cooking competition for breakfasts next month. This is what me and the chefs at the Viscolli came up with for the eggs."

"I'd vote for you." They made small talk, and Marcus told Nick all about making cakes for the Presidential party at Camp David as well as on Air Force One. He also briefed him about events that had taken place at the children's camp for which he volunteered each year. The camp was especially designed for children who had lost a parent in combat.

Nick filled his mouth with fresh-squeezed orange juice and sighed with contentment. "This was really good. Thank you."

"You want any more? I can make more waffles."

Nick shook his head. "No, thanks. It was perfect. I'm stuffed."

Marcus sat back. "I heard from my father that your dad knows you're alive."

Nick nodded. "Guess so. But I thought your dad was

estranged from the rest of the family."

"Apparently, the two brothers have been tentatively talking for about six months now. I'm not sure who contacted whom, but I heard about it last week." He leaned forward again. "They gonna' take back your life insurance then? Seeing as how you aren't dead and all."

Nick felt his eyes widen. "Oh, man. I hope not."

"Well, if they do, you should make me your beneficiary for at least half next time. I've just been sitting here adding up all the breakfast and hot water and laundry service you've helped yourself to over the last ten years."

He saw his cousin's eyes twinkle, and Nick grinned. "Marcus, it would be impossible to repay you for your hospitality over the years. I really mean that." In that very moment, Nick started to think about how he might repay his cousin.

"Start by doing the dishes. I'm taking a shower, assuming you didn't use all my hot water—again."

By the time Marcus got out of the shower, Nick had cleaned the dishes and relocated to the living room. His packed bag sat on the floor in front of the couch, and Nick had his long legs stretched out with his feet propped up on the bag like an ottoman. Using the morning sun for light, he quietly read from the book of Psalms.

"What's next for you? More windmills to tilt? Back in the saddle?" Marcus asked.

Nick shook his head. "Actually, I've been praying a lot and... I think it might be time to return to the land of the living and hang up my spurs."

Marcus' eyes widened. Without a hint of teasing in his voice, he asked, "No kidding?"

"Not even a little bit."

"Well, don't get me wrong or anything, Nicholas, but I just don't know if I could feel safe at night knowing you weren't out there somewhere defending liberty on the frontiers of freedom. What will you do with yourself?"

Nick closed his Soldier's Bible and tossed it on top of his bag. "I have some ideas."

"No more international travel to destinations unknown? No more months-long trips to 'Europe' you can't tell me much about even though you have Saudi Riyals and Yemini Dinars stuffed in your pockets? No more risking your life and getting shot and stabbed and burned? No more guns and knives and kung fu for you? No kidding?"

Nick sat up straight. "Here's the thing. I used to really love parts of my job. I used to really, really love parts of it. And the people I work with. I still love most of them. They're an amazing group of individuals. But the fact is I have always hated other parts of my job. Lately, there's way more I hate. I'm tired, Marcus. I've been tired for a while." He looked out at the New York City skyline as the morning sun painted the buildings and skyscrapers gold and yellow. "My soul is tired."

"How you planning to pay the bills? You aren't even thirty, yet, are you?"

Nick grinned. "I've got some savings tucked away. I've been making a salary for ten years that I haven't touched on any real level."

Marcus snorted. "When that runs out, then what? You got a job offer?"

Nick shook his head. "Not exactly."

"The Viscolli's looking for a sous chef. You want to be my sous chef? You have mad knife skills."

Nick grinned, "It's tempting, but I have something else in mind if it works out. If it doesn't, I'll be sure to let you know."

Marcus tilted his head. "There's a girl, isn't there?"

Nick let out a long sigh. "There's always been a girl. I just don't know if I'm the right boy for that girl."

"Hogwash."

Nick raised an eyebrow. "Hogwash?"

"You heard me."

"You of all people know where I came from."

"Past tense, Cuz. Came from. Where are you going? Where will you be? Your childhood isn't an issue here." Marcus held up a finger to forestall Nick from objecting. "It simply is not. Look at my dad. He pulled himself out of the same trailer park you grew up in. Look at all he's accomplished and all the doors he's opened for me and my sister."

Nick contemplated that. "You're right. I've never even thought of it that way."

"I know I'm right." Marcus smiled.

"How's *your* love life, Marcus?"

"Oh, you have to go there, do you? That hurts, man. It does." He laughed then innocently inquired, "What's her name?"

Nick didn't know what kind of look he gave his cousin or what exactly Marcus saw in his eyes, but Marcus relented with his hands raised in a calming gesture. "Okay, man. Forget I asked."

"No. It's okay. I'm just not used to sharing. Aria. Her

name is Aria."

"You going to go see that girl now? Aria?"

Nick shook his head.

"See, I always knew you were stupid. All this time," Marcus nodded. "I could probably get the President to order you to go see her. I could use cupcakes as a bribe. Oh, I have the First Lady's ear, let me tell you."

"I might have a slightly bigger bargaining chip with POTUS than a cupcake." Nick hinted, thinking of the nuclear device he had recently helped to secure, and that the President of the United States had already personally signed his commendation.

"Maybe so," Marcus agreed affably. "But not with the First Lady. She loved my icing, Cuz."

"I think I may need to do something first. But," Nick hesitated then went for broke, "I have a favor to ask."

"Anything, man. What's up?"

"Pray with me. I need someone to pray with me right now."

Marcus clapped. "You got it, Cuz. Let's do this!"

Chapter 34

Nick stood in the yard and stared at the little cottage. The sweltering summer sun beat down on the back of his neck while he breathed in the humid air, sending him back to his childhood, bringing with it a flood of unwanted memories. After they had prayed together, Marcus had convinced him that coming here was the best idea.

So, Nick caught the next flight. Now here he stood, wondering why he had listened to his cousin. In his heart, he wanted to walk up the steps and knock on the door, but uncertainty paralyzed him, so he stood and stared.

What was he doing here? What did he hope to accomplish?

As he contemplated leaving—making as if he'd never come in the first place—he heard his father call his name from behind him. "Nick?" He turned and saw his father walking up the path from the garage. As soon as Raymond realized it really was him, he ran the last few yards. "Nick!"

"Raymond," he greeted coolly, stepping back when

Raymond drew closer and reached out as if to hug him. Instead, Nick stiffly held his right hand out and offered a handshake.

"I wasn't expecting you," Raymond said, gesturing to the cottage. "Please... please come in this time." He looked around. "Is Aria with you?"

"No," Nick answered, following his father into the cool air-conditioned interior of Raymond's home. "She's with her parents."

Out of long habit, Nick mentally cleared the room for possible threats as he stepped inside. The main room was simple, a couch and recliner behind a low coffee table faced a small flat-screened television. A cut-out bar with a Formica countertop separated the living room from the small kitchen, which had a narrow refrigerator and a two-burner stove.

Four photographs hung on the wall. The largest had a little plaque that said, "Ribbon Cutting with James & Melody Montgomery," and depicted a man in a suit that likely cost the equivalent of Nick's monthly salary and a woman wearing the most outrageous pair of boots Nick had ever seen along with a matching cowboy hat. Together with Raymond, they held a gigantic pair of golden scissors to cut the ribbon opening this facility. The woman looked really familiar to Nick, like maybe some kind of celebrity. Three smaller pictures below the larger one depicted Raymond with different groups of boys wearing different colored T-shirts emblazoned with a year, all with enormous smiles on their faces. They looked so... happy.

"I don't ever have any kids in here," Raymond said, "so unless one of the Suarez's comes by, I don't ever really have any company. The Montgomerys usually pop in some time after Christmas to see if the boys liked their presents. I'm not really set up for company, but I might have some water."

"Water would be great," Nick uttered, his eyes on the pictures of the boys with their arms around his father.

"Take a seat," Raymond offered, gesturing toward the couch.

As Nick sat, he saw that the coffee table was a type of shadow box filled with coins. Nick knew military coins signifying units, but he didn't recognize these until he looked closer and realized they were Alcoholics Anonymous coins.

"I just got my ten-year coin in May," Raymond conveyed as he came into the room. He tapped the top of the table over a coin with a large X in the middle of it. "That one."

"Congratulations." Nick's mouth felt dry, so he took a drink of water out of the bottle Raymond handed him. "Quite an achievement."

Raymond sat in the recliner and nodded, but his face was heavy. "I didn't achieve anything, son. All the credit for that goes to a higher power. Besides, it was about twenty years too late and came at a great cost." He cleared his throat. "I'll never be able to make up for it."

There was a long pause before Nick replied. "No. No, you can't."

He started to get up to go, but Raymond spoke again. "I fell in love with your mother when we were in high school. I drank then, ever since I was 14, but she asked me not to drink, and I quit. I was her act of rebellion. Stick it to her rich daddy and marry the grease monkey. Then we were married and robbing Peter to pay Paul. Apparently, the reality of life with a poor Georgia boy wasn't as glamorous as she imagined." He took a drink of his own water. "When she left, I lost it, and I never could seem to ever get it back again."

Nick felt his jaw clench as he thought of his mother and the scars she placed on his heart. "I was five."

A tear slipped down Raymond's cheek, and he swiped at it, looking annoyed. "Yes. And I was a horrifying human being. If I had the power to change that time, I would."

"You don't know what you did to me."

Raymond raised an eyebrow. "You don't think I know? I know all too well. My father and his brother used to pass me between the two of them, using me as a drunken punching bag. Why do you think I started drinking so young? I ain't saying I'm right. I'm just saying I know."

He leaned forward and ran his hand over the table. "I been trying to make it up to you. I help these boys, and some of them have been through things even you wouldn't believe—I'm talking the worst of the worst. They survived, but they're completely broken. They come here and learn how to heal and how to live, and I work with them and love them unconditionally so I can make up for the way I never loved you proper."

"Raymond—"

Raymond held up a hand. "God saved me. He came to me in the form of Jose and John Suarez, and He saved me not because I deserved it, but just because He wanted to. I can't go back and change time, and I can't allow myself to be destroyed by the past. All I can do is take one day at a time and serve God with all of my heart, love Him, and help these boys. So that's what I do."

He put his hand to his heart. "I don't expect you to forgive me or love me. But I pray that you will someday, for your own soul's sake. Not for me. God knows I don't deserve your love or your forgiveness. But know this. Know that I do love you, son, and I'm proud of you."

Nick stared into the face that looked so much like his own. He could see the pain of deep regret in those ice-blue eyes, and he could see the sincerity and the love. "You pray for me?"

Raymond hurried to Nick's side. "I pray for you every day, Nick, ever since I found out you were alive. Not one single day goes by. I pray that you'll have a closer walk with our Savior. I pray for your safety in this life. I pray that you'll let yourself be loved. You deserve it. I pray that you'll find your wife, and I even pray for her, even though maybe I haven't met her yet, and maybe I never will. I want you to be just as happy in this life as you can, son. I pray you'll find joy. But mostly, I pray you'll step up to God's purpose for you and be strong enough to take it on when it comes. I pray you'll be a much better man than I ever was."

Nick had extensive training in interrogation techniques. He could tell within a few seconds when someone was lying. In everything Raymond had just said, he had spoken only the truth. Nick tried to reconcile this gentle man, this Raymond, with the brutal man he remembered and could not manage it. He finally asked, "Why?"

Raymond's eyebrows knitted. "Because you're my son, and I love you."

Words spilled out of Nick. It was as if he had held his breath for hours and had no choice but to release this sentence that burst forth from his lungs in an explosion of sound. "I don't love you, Raymond."

Calmly, his father nodded. "How could you?"

How could he?

The truth is that Nick never wanted to see this man again. When he walked off the football field of his high school graduation ceremony and got into the car with his Army Recruiter all those years ago, he intentionally left his old life behind. For years he didn't care if his father was even still living. All he had ever offered in his heart for the man he had lived with until he left high school was rejection and denial. Raymond knew that, and despite that, or perhaps because of that, all he offered Nick today was his unconditional love.

Maybe that's how God felt all those years of Nick's childhood. Whenever God would speak to Nick through the words of others like Aria and Carol—and the Ahearnes—and Nick rejected God. No matter what Nick did, God never stopped loving him. Was Nick in a position to reject even that love?

Why was he holding onto the past? Nick suddenly realized that he was nursing his resentment and unforgiveness like an old wound he never wanted to heal. It was as if he kept part of his soul broken, and bound up in a cast, as if Nick walked through life on spiritual and emotional crutches.

Nick suddenly remembered the story of the blind man

at Bethesda from the fifth chapter of the book of John. The man had so much faith that he had cast off the cloak that informed the world he was blind and sought the Savior; the equivalent of a modern blind man tossing away his red and white striped cane. The blind man knew he wouldn't need the cloak once he met the Savior, so he simply left it behind, discarded and forgotten. Did Nick have that kind of faith?

He suddenly realized that he didn't *want* to forgive his father. He *needed* to forgive him. He needed to forgive his father and just let go of their dark past. Mostly, he needed to stop being afraid of himself: afraid of the man he *might* become and just become the man he ought to be.

If Raymond could be a foster father to so many hurting kids, certainly Nick could be a loving father to children of his own and a loving husband to the woman who loved him. He cleared his throat. "I'd like to stay here for a couple of days if you don't mind. I think maybe we have some catching up to do."

He paused then asked, almost in a whisper, "Is that okay, Dad?"

"Nothin' could make me happier, son."

♫ ♫ ♫ ♫

Aria sat at her piano, reading glasses perched on her nose, pencil clenched between her teeth, staff paper spread out all around her while she fine-tuned the soundtrack for a really intense action scene in Adam's new movie. She keyed a few notes, wrote them down, erased half of them, keyed a few more, and continued on as she had for several hours.

Music in a movie was just as important an element as the set. Good music could make a mediocre movie better, and bad music could break a great one. She wanted to take a great movie and make it fantastic.

She'd read the scene and had watched the digital sequence designed by the CGI team so many times that she could see the action in her head. While she played, the action ran through her mind, the timing of it, the perfect choreography. Finally, she was satisfied with the end result.

Starting over all the way back from the beginning, she played the whole thing, feeling goosebumps at the perfection of the piece. Adam was going to love this. Maybe she'd take a weekend and fly down so she could play it for him in person.

Giddy, grinning from ear to ear, she slid down from the bench. As she went through the house toward the kitchen, she rubbed her aching wrist. Too many hours at the piano had put a strain on the weakened muscles. She opened the cupboard but belatedly remembered that she'd run out of coffee. She briefly considered making a pot of tea but really wanted coffee instead.

As she left the kitchen, she gripped and massaged her right wrist with her left hand and decided she should probably wear her brace for the rest of the day. She went to put it on before she made her trip to the store for coffee.

In her room, Aria opened the top dresser drawer then retrieved her wrist brace. When she strapped it on, it almost instantly alleviated her pain. Despite the early September date on the calendar, the air outside her warm little cottage had a bit of a bite to it as the shivery wind blew in from the river. Aria grabbed a light jacket and turned to leave her room. As she turned, her eyes caught sight of the framed display on the wall.

She walked toward it slowly. It had been weeks since she looked at Nick's medals and his obituary. Most days, she tried not to think about him but failed miserably. Lately, whenever she thought of him, she prayed for him. She tried very hard not to pray selfish prayers where he was concerned, but she had to be honest with herself and admit that sometimes she failed in that regard, too.

Carol once projected that Nick put her on a very high pedestal; that he thought the Sergeant Major's baby girl was too good for the kid from the trailer park. Aria was beginning to believe, after being so thoroughly rejected by him twice in her lifetime, that maybe she just wasn't good enough for him. Maybe there was something wrong with her that kept him from being able to be with her despite his feelings.

Her feelings for him, she discovered, only grew. That frustrated Aria. The more she thought of one Nicholas Williams, the more she respected and desired him. Knowing the weight of the scars on both his body and his heart only made it worse. She wanted to soothe his heart and troubled mind. Having witnessed how those scars pained him and plagued his dreams only made her heart ache to love him even more.

Shaking her head at her romantic fantasies, she took her car keys down from the hook by the back door. On impulse, Aria decided to stop in on Brandon and Steph and see what dinner specials they had before she headed to the store to get some coffee. She chose her thin wallet, the one she could stick into the front pocket of her blue jeans, and walked through her house. Lastly, she grabbed her cell phone and slipped it into her jacket pocket before she walked out the front door. As she turned to lock it, the voice startled her.

"Hello, Aria."

With a gasp, she spun around. Nick Williams sat on her porch swing. He pointed at the window. "I knocked, but you were so wrapped up in what you were playing I don't think you heard me, so I waited."

Aria put a hand to her racing heart. "What are you doing here?" The words came out in a pant as she struggled to catch her breath.

He looked rested. For the first time in recent memory, he looked rested and refreshed. "I needed to see you."

Not willing to feel the pain of his rejection again, she started to build a wall up around her heart. "Yeah. Well, here I am. Now you've seen me. Box checked. Now you can leave again without a goodbye." She shoved her hands into her jacket pockets and rushed down the steps.

"Aria, wait!" Nick said, running after her. He grabbed her arm, and she pulled her hand out of her pocket and whirled around.

"What?" she bit out.

He stared at her braced hand. "What happened?"

"With what?"

He let go of her hand as if it had burned him. "What happened to your hand?"

Aria looked at her wrist brace then back at him. The look of anger on his face made her take a step back. "Nothing. I just... I overused it this morning. It's the reason I don't play piano for a living."

She watched the anger drain from his face. "I thought maybe someone hurt you again."

Putting her chin up, she said, "Just you." She pivoted on her heel to leave, but halfway down her walkway, he stopped her again.

"Please don't go." His voice was barely a whisper. Though he spoke quietly, the sound resonated around her yard.

"Why shouldn't I? Isn't that what you did to me?" she asked, her back still to him.

Even though she couldn't see the gesture with her back to him, Nick nodded in a quiet agreement. He put his hands into the pockets of his jeans. "I quit NISA. They promoted Jen Thorne to Director."

"I know," she said, finally turning to face him. "John told me. They've been seeing each other."

"Really?" He frowned. "I didn't know that."

His eyes squinted for a few minutes as if reviewing some memories, then he nodded as he processed the new information. "I had actually turned it down before they offered it to Jen, and I resigned before she accepted the post. She tried to talk me out of it, but I wasn't going to bite. Just finished up the last of the paperwork I had to do for final debriefing yesterday."

Aria merely raised an eyebrow and waited. He didn't say anything else. She stepped closer to him. "And?"

Nick ran a hand through his hair, then stuck his hand back in his pocket. "I've been talking a lot with Adam lately." He waited a beat to see if she was also aware of this. When she remained silent, he said, "He's agreed to be a silent partner in a security business I've been wanting to set up. I just have to choose the location."

"You're asking my permission to get a loan from my brother?"

"No." She'd forgotten how quickly he could move. Suddenly, he stood right in front of her, and his hands encircled her upper arms. "Aria, I tried," he said, gently squeezing her arms. "I tried to walk away—again. I tried to pretend I could let you go, but the truth is, I can't. I can't ignore my feelings for you. I don't want to anymore."

A little spark of something started to bloom inside Aria, knocking down that wall she so desperately sought to build. She began a war within herself. "What feelings, Nick? You've successfully ignored me for four months when I really needed you. You left me alone for all of the briefings and trials and—honestly at many points—accusations."

"I know. I'm sorry. I'm so sorry. I was out of the country most of the time. Hecate and I had to find Roj Singh. That was truly more of a priority than anything else. We had to find the device and the prototype of the shielding he had constructed. We finally ran him to ground in... you know what? I can't tell you about that. Forget I said anything."

"You could have sent me a postcard or an instant message or a text from some obscure or secure phone. But you ignored me and left me alone. You abandoned me. Again." She pulled away. "Jen will take you back on, Nick. Probably promote you. Go back to your life. I just have to figure out some way to live mine without you."

Before she could turn to leave again, he stopped her

by simply saying, "I don't need NISA or Jen, Aria. I need something else."

She closed her eyes and took a deep breath. When she opened them again, he was right back in front of her, his blue eyes pinning hers. "I've spent the last two weeks at my father's house," he said. "I had so much healing to do, so much forgiving to do. I realized something. I realized that I was an empty shell until now."

His eyes swirled with remembered pain and with emotion, and not a small amount of regret. "I wish I could go back and change everything. In a way, I wish I'd have told NISA no in the first place. Just finished my tour of duty and come home to you. You're the only woman I've ever even wanted, Aria. You're the only woman I ever felt like... I don't know how to say this."

A tear slid down her cheek.

Nick kept staring deep into her eyes, not moving an inch as he stood there and spoke with his voice low and urgent. "What we did, what you did, saved thousands of lives. The truth is, it probably saved our very nation. With so much of our elected leadership taken out, we would have been ripe for a major external attack, so you very likely saved millions of lives. The plans they had put in place were solid. If not for you, their plans would have worked. God used you—and He used me—and we stopped them.

"But in the end, it cost us ten years of our lives together." Before she could stop him, he reached out and framed her face with his hands. "I'm so very sorry I hurt you, but if you let me, I'll spend the rest of my life making it up to you. I love you, Aria. I've loved you since high school, since the very first time I ever saw you. I need you. I need you more than anything else in this world. I don't want to live without you, not even one more second."

There were probably a dozen things he could have said that would have done nothing for her, but his sincere words removed all doubt. "Then don't," she pleaded, and suddenly his mouth covered hers, and he kissed her with all the pent-up passion and love that she mirrored for him in her own heart.

She threw her arms around his neck and gave that passion back to him. Her knees vanished, and she felt certain that she started floating above the earth, sailing up into his kiss.

♫ ♫ ♫ ♫

Portland, Oregon
Eighteen Months Later

Through all that Nick had experienced in his life—all the dangers he'd faced and injuries he'd sustained—he never imagined he could find happiness, much less love and contentment. Yet, as he sat and watched his wife cradle their incredibly tiny new daughter in her arms, he couldn't help feeling a complete sense of peace finally settle over him.

He looked down at the worn Bible in his lap and ran his fingers over the stained and bruised linen handkerchief. For the thousandth time, he whispered a prayer of thanksgiving for the blessings God had delivered into his unworthy life.

The entire family had gathered for the birth of this new addition. Retired Army Sergeant Major Jose Suarez had diplomatically suggested naming the baby, "First of many grandchildren to come," though Nick and Aria had politely refused.

As all three of his brothers-in-law entered the crowded hospital room and joined their parents and Nick's dad, one of Aria's brothers slapped Nick on the back. Nick wasn't sure which one it was, but the contact spoke volumes to him.

It said that he belonged, that he was accepted. In the year and a half since he married Aria, Doris had been more of a mother to him than his own had in all the five years he'd lived under the same roof with her. Jose was as much a father to him as he was a wise friend. The slap on the back from one of Aria's older brothers told him that this was his family now. His *familia*.

The brothers took some getting used to, always protective of their baby sister. They had opened up a place in their pack and granted him membership almost without question, knowing that his love for Aria was genuine and—in reality—the only important thing, the only thing that mattered. They said, without saying it, that where he came from, how he lived, or how he was raised meant nothing in the light of that love.

Pain and hurt of the past would heal with time and effort. Somehow, even his own father blended in with this amazing and close family, and in what nonbelievers would only ever perceive as the strangest way, he completed it.

Despite how utterly unworthy Nick felt of accepting

love or forgiveness, for whatever reason, God had decided to bless him. First, He had blessed Nick with Aria. From the second he first ever saw Aria all those years ago, he knew that he had found his reason for living. Every time she spoke to him, every time he fell under her gaze, every time he caught her scent, every time they touched, every time they kissed, he knew that God had made her especially for him.

Then God blessed him with a family that accepted him as one of their own. Finally, God had blessed him with a child of his very own.

Slowly, day by day, God healed him. Nick knew that his amazing wife was the most significant part of that healing. A simple look or touch from her soothed his troubled brow and erased years of pain and remorse. Her prayers lifted him up and kept him safe from the nightmares that only rarely visited anymore. He no longer had to be strong and in control all on his own. He and Aria, his beautiful bride, could be strong together by leaning on the endless strength of their Creator.

Nick turned back to look at Aria Williams, his wife, and their beautiful baby. Aria looked up, perhaps sensing her husband's gaze. As her brown eyes met his ice-blue stare, love flowed between them in a cord of three. He knew he'd finally found the normal that he'd been searching for all his life.

Normal wasn't a swing set in the backyard of a suburb, or a wife in the kitchen making dinner. It was a peace in his heart that told him he was loved, that he belonged, and that he was free to love this woman who had given him their child and given him her heart. He would bask in their love all of his days on this earth. He would put his very life on the line to protect them and provide for them as long as he drew breath. He finally had a family.

"Want to know something?" he asked.

"What's that?" Her voice sounded husky, tired, but incredibly joyful.

"You look terrific, holding little Jennifer Carol, there."

Aria snorted as if he were teasing, then took a second look at their child, a closer look. She looked back at her husband and nodded. "I think you're right. We can call her 'Jaycee' for short."

He nodded. "Want to know something else?"

"Sure," she smiled.

He leaned over and softly kissed Aria. "I love you," he said simply.

She smiled and pulled him back for another kiss. "I love you more," she said, then made to soothe Jaycee, who loudly protested being squeezed between her parents.

The End

Acknowledgments

I love these United States of America, my country. Even today, I believe our nation is truly one of the greatest countries on earth, with so much promise and potential. We live in a land whose shores people actually die trying to reach. Oftentimes I get annoyed at gluttony, greed, laziness, political corruption, entitlement and the like; and I sometimes forget and let those feelings overshadow the fact that there is so much good about my homeland, so much hard work that built this nation.

Anyone who has ever read my blog on Veterans' Day has witnessed my post honoring my family's service to our country (Visit: halleethehomemaker.com/my-veterans-day)

With a great-grandfather who was a World War I veteran, two grandfathers who were World War II veterans, a father who is a retired Army Sergeant Major, a father-in-law who is a Vietnam and Gulf War veteran and retired Army Colonel, a sister-in-law who is a Gulf War and War on Terror veteran and retired Army Colonel, and a husband who is still an NCO in the National Guard and who served in the Gulf War and the War on Terror, patriotism and love for this country is deeply ingrained in my family and me. I am proud of the military tradition of my family. I pray that my sons continue it and continue to stand up for and fight for the idea that is America.

Nicholas "Nick" Williams was molded in my imagination out of the very best of the military legacy of my family. Aria Suarez, her brothers, and Carol Mabry are all Army "brats"—children of career Army soldiers. Their decisions, reactions, and actions throughout this book are seen through the veil of firsthand knowledge and understanding of the sacrifices made by "brats" like me for these United States.

I would love to know your thoughts. I really would.

Writing is often a solitary profession, but it doesn't have to be. I personally read every single book review, positive or otherwise. I'm not exaggerating. It would mean the world to me if you shared your thoughts with me. Hearing from my readers helps me prayerfully craft the next story. An honest review also helps other readers make informed decisions when they seek an exciting, romantic Christian book for themselves. Please use the link, or even your smartphone and the QR code, on this page to share your thoughts and tell me what you liked or didn't like about the story. I would so love to hear from you.

www.halleebridgeman.com/ReviewAria

Yours in Christ;

HALLEE BRIDGEMAN

The Song of Suspense Series

A Melody for James

MELODY Mason and James Montgomery lead separate lives of discord until an unexpected meeting brings them to a sinister realization. Unbeknownst to them, dark forces have directed their lives from the shadows, orchestrating movements that

keep them in disharmony. Fire, loss, and bloodshed can't shake their faith in God to see them through as they face a percussive climax that will leave lives forever changed.

♫ ♫ ♫ ♫

An Aria for Nick

ARIA Suarez remembers her first real kiss and Nick Williams, the blue-eyed boy who passionately delivered it before heading off to combat. The news of his death is just a footnote in a long war, and her lifelong dream to become a world-class pianist is shattered on the day of his funeral.

Years later, Aria inadvertently uncovers a sinister plot that threatens the very foundations of a nation. Now, stalked by assassins and on the run, her only hope of survival is in trusting her very life to a man who has been dead for years.

A Carol for Kent

BOBBY Kent's name is synonymous with modern Country Music, and he is no stranger to running from overzealous fans and paparazzo. But he has no idea how to protect his daughter and Carol, the mother of his only child, from a vicious and ruthless serial killer bent on their destruction.

♫ ♫ ♫ ♫

A Harmony for Steve

CHRISTIAN contemporary singing sensation, Harmony Harper, seeks solitude after winning her umpteenth award. She finds herself amid the kind of spiritual crisis that only prayer and fasting can cure. Steve Slayer, the world-renowned satanic acid rock icon, who has a reputation for trashing women as well as hotel rooms, stumbles into her private retreat on the very edge of death.

In ministering to Steve, Harmony finds that the Holy Spirit is ministering to her aching soul. The two leave the wilderness sharing a special bond, and their hearts are changed forever.

They expect rejection back in their professional worlds. What neither of them could foresee is the chain of ominous events that threaten their very lives.

♫ ♫ ♫ ♫

Available in eBook, Paperback, or Hardcover
wherever fine books are sold.

Excerpt

Please enjoy this exclusive excerpt from the full-length Christian romantic suspense novel, *A Carol for Kent*, part three in the Song of Suspense series.

♫ ♫ ♫ ♫

Birthday girl Lisa Mabry had selected her favorite pizza parlor for her seventh birthday lunch, as she had every year since she could pronounce the word, and brought best friend since kindergarten Amy Bradford along with her, as she also always had since the day they met. The two little girls giggled and whispered as they ate green olive pizza with extra cheese, and Assistant District Attorney Carol Mabry intentionally let the go of the memory of her morning spent at the funeral parlor.

She forced herself to focus entirely on her daughter while they were in the restaurant. By the time they piled back into her Jeep, she had mentally left murder and autopsy reports behind, and transformed from A. D. A. Carol Mabry into just Carol, just Ms. Mabry, just Lisa's mom.

The drive to the ranch took twenty minutes, and the

girls sat in the back seat, continuing their whispered conversation. The whispers got louder until they were full-fledged yells, and Carol finally interrupted them. "Girls! What are you two arguing about?"

"Ms. Mabry, who do you think is cuter? Tim McGraw or Bobby Kent?" Amy asked. Carol felt her stomach tighten.

"I told you, Bobby Kent is way cuter than Tim McGraw. Besides, Tim McGraw is married and has like a dozen kids. Bobby Kent isn't married, so that makes him even cuter," Lisa said. "Plus, he has the same name as my grandma and grandpa. That's even more extra points."

"What do you think, Ms. Mabry?" Amy asked again.

Carol refused to get a headache on Lisa's birthday. Sometimes, tension and stress built up so that she would get headaches that made her have to lie down in a darkened room and fight back tears of pain. But it wasn't going to happen to her today. "I think you two should play rock-paper-scissors, and whoever wins is right," she said, turning onto the drive that led to the ranch house.

The game brought on another bout of arguing, but by then, Carol was out of the vehicle and didn't have to listen to it. She looked around her, but it didn't look as if anything had been done to prepare for the party. Marjorie was so efficient that Carol usually had nothing to do by the time she came over. She began to get worried that something had happened to Robert. She turned to the girls as they got out of the Jeep. "Lisa, go look in on the new foal Lightning dropped yesterday. I'm going inside to see what grandma's up to."

"Ok, Mommy. Come on, Amy," Lisa said, then they

took off at a run toward the horse barn.

"Don't go inside the stall without grandpa. Just look!" Carol called to them, then turned to go in the house. She had her hand on the door when Marjorie opened it and stepped out onto the porch. Carol immediately knew something was very wrong.

"Carol," Marjorie greeted, then she stopped.

"What's the matter, Marjorie?" Carol asked, taking the older woman's arm and guiding her back to the door. "What happened? Is Robert all right?"

Marjorie put her hand over her face and burst into tears. "Oh, Carol. I'm so sorry." Carol steered her through the door and into the kitchen. Marjorie sat in a chair at the table and buried her face in her hands, her body wracking with sobs. Carol looked and saw Robert seated at the table. He looked so frail like a strong wind might just break him to pieces. He reached out to take his wife's hand.

"Robert, what is it? What happened?" she asked. She started really feeling frightened.

"Carol," he whispered, then cleared his throat and stopped. He cleared his throat again, then said in a stronger voice, "Whatever happens, whatever gets said, you have to know that we are truly sorry. Don't let this spoil Lisa's birthday."

"What's going on?" Carol demanded, her teeth set. "Tell me right now. Right this second."

♪ ♪ ♪ ♪

Unobserved until this moment, international Country music superstar, Bobby Kent, studied Carol Mabry from the doorway of his parent's kitchen. The anger at his parents burned through his system slow and low, like an underground lava flow. They'd decided to tell him about two hours ago.

His mind rejected the fact that he had a daughter, a seven-year-old daughter. It was too much to fathom at one time. How could two people who professed to love him have kept that information from him? He hadn't been able to get an explanation out of them yet. Both of them had been too upset to make any sense. But he assumed it had something to do with money. It nearly always did. He figured the woman standing over them at the table could shed some light on the subject for him.

He'd known who they were talking about before they'd even said her name. The moment she spoke, he remembered her vividly. They'd met in a classical violin class at the University of Georgia four weeks before he received the call about his demo and packed his bags to leave. He had been amazed by her musical talent and impressed with her in general. He had asked her out, and they had shared some lunches and a dinner and gone to a movie together on a double date. They had gone to one dance at the student center.

The night he got the call, they had celebrated. They'd sat on the tailgate of his truck and eaten too many Krystal cheeseburgers with way too much champagne. The celebration had gone until dawn. Bobby assumed Lisa arrived a scant nine months later.

He wanted to turn his anger to someone other than his parents, but he couldn't find it in him to force it onto her. The one thing his father, Robert, had been very clear about was that they had misled Carol all this time. All these years.

Years!

Carol believed that Bobby knew all about his daughter, Lisa. So Bobby ran his hand through his hair and prepared himself to face her righteous wrath. He had a feeling it would take some time to convince her that he wasn't the bad guy here.

He stepped fully into the kitchen, his boot hitting the linoleum, causing a sound that reverberated through the room. Carol stiffened, as if she knew who she was about to see, and turned to face him. He watched the recognition come instantly, and suddenly her hazel eyes filled with burning rage so powerful he almost wished he hadn't made his presence known.

"Oh, of course! Should have known," she bit out through gritted teeth. "Exactly what are you doing here? Today of all days?"

He didn't know how to begin, so he decided to start with his defense. From the look on her face, though, he wasn't sure she would even hear his words. "I didn't know, Carol."

♫ ♫ ♫ ♫

Find *A Carol for Kent*, part three in the Song of Suspense series in ebook, paperback, or hardcover wherever fine books are sold.

Translation Key

Military Terms & Jargon

9-line—a Medical Evacuation Request in the military is a report that has specific information in each of nine lines of the request.

brown shirts—(also, brownshirts) The original "jackbooted thugs" the *Sturmabteilung* (SA) functioned as the initial paramilitary wing of the Nazi Party. They played a crucial role in Adolf Hitler's rise to power in the 1920s and 1930s and are famously known for the "night of the long knives" when, in June 1934, loyal but lower-ranking "brown shirts" quietly murdered the entire SA's leadership and at least 84 others who had angered Hitler in the recent past all on a single night. "Brown shirts" is used today as a euphemism for any government-sanctioned agent or agency perceived as capable of "thuggery" and most often used by members of the US Military to describe agents of the Department of Homeland Security (DHS), who purchase things like armored vehicles and heavy weaponry despite legally not having any kind of combat mission.

CASH—Combat Army Surgical Hospital.

CH-47—The Boeing CH-47 Chinook is an American twin-engine, tandem rotor heavy-lift helicopter. Its primary roles are troop movement, artillery placement, and battlefield resupply. It has a wide loading ramp at the rear of the fuselage and three external-cargo hooks.

check your six—watch your back or check your six o'clock; The "clock orientation" originally became necessary to conduct effective, organized aerial combat. When oriented like a clock face with 12 o'clock being ahead of you, six o'clock is directly behind you. In air combat, an enemy below you on the right would be at 3 o'clock low while an enemy to your left and above you would be at 9 o'clock high.

device—a euphemism for "bomb" or "explosive" often used by EOD personnel (US Military jargon).

Duhs—derogatory term for agents of the Department of Homeland Security (DHS), usually employed when DHS agents arrive in foreign combat zones without any prior coordination, legal justification, or real necessity to be there (US Military jargon).

EOD—Explosive Ordnance Disposal

klick—(also, click or klik) one kilometer or 0.621 of a standard mile; 1 mile = 1.609 kilometer (US Military jargon).

LoJack—the Brand name and trademark of the LoJack Corporation (NASDAQ: LOJN) is also common military and law enforcement jargon, used as either a noun or a verb, for any theft prevention system, device, or methodology involving remote geolocation and tracking (US Military jargon).

M-249—The M249 light machine gun (LMG), previously designated the M249 Squad Automatic Weapon (SAW), and formally written as "Light Machine Gun, 5.56 mm, M249," is a gas-operated, air-cooled machine-gun with a quick-change barrel. It is agonistically belt or magazine fed and provides infantry squads with the heavy volume of fire of a machine gun combined with accuracy and portability approaching that of a rifle.

M-4—The M4 carbine is a family of firearms that was derived from earlier carbine versions of the M16 rifle. With replaceable 30 round magazines, the weapon can accurately fire a standard full metal jacket 5.56 NATO round at distances of up to 800 meters in semiautomatic or full-automatic modes of fire.

M-9—The Beretta M9, officially the "Pistol, Semiautomatic, 9mm," is a 9×19mm Parabellum pistol adopted by the United States Armed Forces in 1985. With replaceable 15 round clips, in semiautomatic mode it fires a standard NATO supersonic 9mm machine-gun round at effective ranges of up to 100 meters.

OGA—Other Government Agency; a euphemism for "black" or highly covert government agencies or their agents. Also often erroneously applied to government agents or agencies performing combat roles with no legal charter to do so (US Military jargon)

SAW—Squad Automatic Weapon (US Military); rarely refers to the venerable belt fed M-60 machine-gun, but most often refers to the M-249 light machine gun (LMG).

sitrep— Situation Report (US Military). A report on the current military situation in a particular area. The standard format for reporting enemy information is the SALUTE report. SALUTE is an acronym that stands for Size, Activity, Location, Unit identification, Time, and Equipment.

Computer Terms

CGI—Computer Generated Imagery

ID—Identification or unique identifiers

IDS—Intrusion Detection System (passive)

IP Address—a unique string of numbers separated by periods that identifies each computer using the Internet Protocol to communicate over a network.

IPS—Intrusion Prevention System (active)

GPS—Global Positioning System

MAC Address—A media access control address is a unique identifier assigned to network interfaces for communications on the physical network segment.

micro-SD card—extremely small Secure Digital: a non-volatile memory card format for use in portable devices, such as mobile phones, digital cameras, GPS navigation devices, and tablet computers.

Other Acronyms, Jargon, & Allusions

BOLO—Be On the Look Out; a law enforcement notice

CAC—Common Access Card; a chip-enabled smart card issued to the military, government employees, and government contractors used for identification, 2-factor authentication, and non-repudiation. It is often commonly and incorrectly called a "CAC Card."

DHS—Department of Homeland Security (US); see also "brown shirts" and "Duhs."

DMV—Department of Motor Vehicles (most US States)

DOD—Department of Defense (US)

DOE—Department of Energy (US)

DOJ—Department of Justice (US)

FBI—Federal Bureau of Investigation (US)

FDLE—the Florida Department of Law Enforcement (Florida's State Bureau of Investigation)

JPL—Jet Propulsion Laboratories, a federally funded research and development center and NASA field center near Pasadena, California.

MI-5—Military Intelligence Department Five, the internal security arm of the British Government (Great Britain)

NASA—National Aeronautics & Space Administration (US)

NISA—National Intelligence & Security Agency (Fictional)

NSA—National Security Agency (US)

RFC—Request for Change; a Change Request.

RFI—Request for Information; a formal request for details or detailed specifications.

SBI—State Bureau of Investigation; the criminal justice investigatory body with multi-juristictional responsibilities and authority within a US state.

the Troubles—euphemism for the bloody and violent ethno-nationalist and sectarian conflict in Northern Ireland, which began in the 1960s and ended with the Belfast "Good Friday" Agreement of 1998. At its peak, the British Army and the Royal Ulster Constabulary (RUC) were deeply involved in the violence. The "Ballast" investigation by the Police Ombudsman confirmed that British forces colluded with loyalist paramilitaries on several occasions and were directly involved in criminal activities including murder, abduction, torture, and rape, and later actively obstructed investigations into allegations of those charges. Outstanding allegations of abductions and gang-rape of young Irish girls by British soldiers remain unpunished and sporadic violence as reparation is conducted against alleged perpetrators or their families in the Republic of Ireland, Scotland, England, and mainland Europe to this day.

Treasury—Department of Treasury (US), so called in favor of the acronym DOT to avoid any possible confusion with the Department of Transportation.

Secret Service—From 1865 until 2003, all Secret Service Agents were Treasury Agents. In 2003, DHS took over command and control of the Secret Service as well as the Treasury run Federal Law Enforcement Training Center, along with twenty other agencies including the US Coast Guard from DOD, Transportation Security Administration (TSA) from the Department of Transportation, and NIST from the Department of Energy to name a few. In the months that followed, an astonishing number of Secret Service Agents resigned to take positions within the Department of Justice like the US Marshals Service, or other local law enforcement agencies as far from the DHS political center of gravity as possible. The Secret Service that remained under the leadership and guidance of DHS has suffered one embarrassing scandal after another since then from prostitution rings in Columbia, to agents charged with child predation, to alcohol-fueled sprees on foreign soil.

French words/phrases

communiqué—(both/either) the message and the means of communicating

en route—while on the way, while traveling

ganache—a buttery chocolate sauce

Spanish words/phrases

amigo—friend, buddy

brillante—brilliant

comprende—understand, comprehend

dónde está—where is

Hablo español con fluidez y Puerto Rico el acento de mi abuela.—I speak fluent Spanish with my grandmother's Puerto Rican accent.

Sí. Sambriento.—Yes. Starved.

Vamose a salir de aquí.—Hurry out of here.

Reader's Guide
Luncheon Menu

Suggested luncheon menu to enjoy when hosting a group discussion surrounding *An Aria for Nick*, part 2 of the Song of Suspense series.

One thing I am passionate about in life is selecting, cooking, and savoring good whole real food. A special luncheon just goes hand in hand with hospitality and ministry.

If you're planning a discussion group surrounding this book, I offer some humble suggestions to help your special luncheon talk come off as a success in this section.

When Nick first comes to Aria's house, she cooks him a steak dinner with roasted potatoes and seasoned green beans.

In this section, you will find those recipes the way I imagine Aria would have prepared them. You can pre-slice the steak and very easily feed 2 or 3 people from one steak at a luncheon.

The Steak:

Sizzling saucy oven skillet steak

Nick has spent a decade in and out of third world countries. He's learned to appreciate any good, wholesome meal, and this steak certainly tops that list.

This steak recipe is best done in an iron skillet and is a featured recipe in my cast iron cookbook *Iron Skillet Man, the Stark Truth about Pepper and Pots.* This method is an absolutely foolproof, quick and easy, and simple way to prepare a perfect steak indoors in the oven. No propane grill or charcoal briquettes required. This method takes 15 minutes, tops. It turns out a beautifully juicy, medium-rare steak with crisped and crunchy edges, and so much flavor you will simply feel amazed!

The SECRET to this recipe is to put the salt away and don't touch it until the very end, if then. Trust me. No salt. Seriously.

There are three really nice ways you could serve this steak, depending on your audience.

1) You can serve the steak on a serving tray and let your best carver slice and serve directly at the table.

2) You can slice and serve in a lovely presentation of fanned slices of about 1/4 inch to 1/2-inch-thick strips either on a serving platter or directly onto each plate next to attractive side items. Or,

3) You can do either of the above with the addition of a heavenly skillet sauce reduction either served in a gravy boat with a ladle or poured directly over the sliced steak just at serving time.

If you choose the third option, once the steak is resting (see *Directions*), you can whip up a delicious skillet sauce in no time at all, using the steak drippings still in the pan.

Follow these directions: Bring a burner to medium heat. Put the skillet over the medium heat burner and add about 1/2 cup of (preferably homemade or organic) beef stock and about 1/2 cup of red wine (see note) to the skillet.

NOTE: If you abstain from alcohol even in cooking, you can substitute a 100% pure grape juice (ensure there is no apple juice in it) and one teaspoon of distilled vinegar to approximate the same flavor and properties while cooking.

Scrape up any small bits of steak still clinging to the skillet and whisk until well mixed. Bring to a boil then lower heat and simmer until the liquid volume is reduced by at least half, whisking occasionally.

Once the steak has rested, and just before carving, THEN you may wish to add a dash of Kosher salt to taste. To serve, either let your best carver slice and serve directly at the table, or, using a very sharp knife, slice the steak against the grain.

Slice into 1/4 inch to 1/2-inch-thick strips. Fan these slices out onto your serving platter or onto each individual plate next to your side items.

Pour the skillet sauce reduction into a gravy boat if carving your steak at the table, or, pour the sauce directly over the sliced steak in a nice drizzle just before serving. Then serve immediately.

Here's the steak recipe.

Ingredients

A single high-quality lean ribeye steak cut 1 to 1 1/2 inches thick and about 1 pound in weight (boneless or bone-in makes no difference, though I prefer the flavor of bone-in) extra virgin olive oil to coat (grapeseed oil, butter, or tallow can substitute)

1 TBS Montreal Steak seasoning mix as a steak rub

NOTE: Instead of store-bought, check my website for a great and easy recipe at:

halleethehomemaker.com/homemade-montreal-seasoning

Supplies

10 to 12-inch diameter cast-iron skillet

thick, well-padded oven mitt or pad

long sturdy kitchen tongs

bowls and/or ramekins

timer or egg timer

aluminum foil

whisk

Preparation

Let your steaks fully reach room temperature through and through. Dry them completely with paper towels or a clean kitchen towel.

Place the 10 to 12-inch diameter cast-iron skillet in the oven. With the skillet inside, set the oven to broil, or bring to about 500° degrees F (260° degrees C).

Directions

1) While waiting for the oven and skillet to reach full heat, reserve about 2 TBS extra virgin olive oil in a small bowl or ramekin.

Mix up a generous amount of Montreal Steak seasoning mix.

Brush the oil all over the steak, coating it generously on both sides and on the ends. Once fully coated, generously "rub" the steaks evenly with more Montreal Steak seasoning, covering both sides of the steak, patting it into each steak so that it sticks.

2) When the oven with the skillet inside has reached broil, turn on a stove burner to high heat.

Using your thickest and most reliable oven mitt or pad, very carefully remove the piping hot cast iron skillet from the oven and place it on the High heat burner.

3) Use long, sturdy kitchen tongs and place your steak into the center of the hot pan. It should sizzle immediately.

Cook the steak for 30 seconds on one side, then flip it over. Cook the steak for an additional 30 seconds on the other side.

Turn off your burner.

Immediately, and once again using your thickest and most reliable oven mitt or pad, carefully place the skillet with the seared steak in the middle back in the oven.

4) Using a timer if needed:

*For a perfect MEDIUM-RARE steak, broil the steak in the skillet in the center of the hot oven for exactly 2 minutes. Open the oven and quickly but carefully flip the steak onto the other side using the long, sturdy kitchen tongs. Close the oven and cook for an additional 2 minutes.

**For a perfect MEDIUM steak, add just 1 minute to the cooking time for each side for a total of 3 minutes per side instead of 2 minutes.

Turn off the oven and immediately, using your thickest and most reliable oven mitt or pad, quickly but carefully remove the steak from the oven.

Using the tongs, remove the steak from the skillet and place it on a large cutting board. Cover with aluminum foil and let the steak rest for about 5 minutes before serving.

The Roasted Potatoes:

Roasted fingerling potatoes

Nothing pairs as nicely with a perfectly cooked steak as a potato and Nick knows it. This is a wonderful and simple, hands-off side dish. A light coat of extra virgin olive oil with the simple seasoning of salt and pepper is all you need.

Ingredients

About 12-15 fingerling potatoes
1 TBS extra virgin olive oil
1 tsp Kosher or sea salt
1/2 tsp fresh ground black pepper
1 TBS dried parsley

Supplies

sharp knife/cutting board
measuring cups/spoons
medium bowl
pan
aluminum foil

Preparation

Slice the potatoes into bite-sized pieces, leaving the skin on.

Preheat oven to 350° degrees F (175° degrees C)

Directions

Toss the potatoes with the oil, salt, pepper, and parsley.

Put in pan.

Cover with foil.

Bake at 350° degrees F (175° degrees C) for 30 minutes.

The Green Beans:

Allspice green beans

Aria kept the meal for Nick simple... steak, potatoes, and green beans. This recipe is lovely—fresh green beans with a surprising flavor of allspice. They'll pair perfectly with steak and roasted potatoes.

Ingredients

1 lbs fresh green beans, trimmed and snapped

1 tablespoon extra-virgin olive oil

2 cloves garlic, crushed

½ cup water

2 teaspoons ground allspice

Dash Kosher or sea salt to taste

Dash fresh ground black pepper to taste

Supplies

good sauce or frying pan with a lid

Preparation

Wash and snap beans

Directions

Heat oil in a medium saucepan over medium heat.
Cook and stir garlic until lightly browned.
Mix in green beans and water, and bring to a boil.
Stir in allspice, salt, and pepper.
Cover. Simmer 20 minutes, until green beans are soft.

Reader's Guide
Discussion Questions

Reader's Guide
Discussion Questions

Suggested questions for a discussion group surrounding *An Aria for Nick*, part 2 of the Song of Suspense series.

In the book of John 18:37, Jesus explains that for this reason He was born, and for this reason He came into the world.

The reason?

To testify to the truth.

In bringing those He ministered to into an understanding of the truth, Our Lord used fiction in the form of parables to illustrate very real truths. In the same way, we can minister to one another by the use of fictional characters and situations to help us to reach logical, valid, cogent, and very sound conclusions about our real lives here on earth.

While the characters and situations in the Song of Suspense series are fictional, I pray that these extended parables can help readers come to a better understanding of truth. Please prayerfully consider the questions that follow, consult scripture, and pray upon your conclusions. May the Lord of the universe richly bless you.

♫ ♫ ♫ ♫

Staff Sergeant Thomas Ahearne trained Nick for battle with his father, but he did not actively evangelize him. In fact, the first time Nick ever held a Bible was when Aria gave him one.

1. Do you think Nick would have been receptive to the Word of God if Ahearne had evangelized him?

2. What did you think when Aria gave Nick the Soldier's Bible before he went to Basic Training?

3. Have you ever gifted someone whom you cared about with a Bible?

♫ ♫ ♫ ♫

But I say to you, love your enemies, bless those who curse you, do good to those who hate you, and pray for those who spitefully use you and persecute you… Matthew 5:44

Taken directly from the sermon on the mount, the words of Christ Jesus are unambiguous in both meaning and intent. Even so, Nick struggled with the idea of praying for his own father, even after he became a Christian.

4. How do you think that affected his walk with Christ?

5. As Christians, how difficult do you find it to love your enemies and pray for those who persecute you?

The Bible teaches us to love our enemies and commands us not to murder. Yet, Ecclesiastes 3:3 says there is a time to kill, and the Bible is full of tribute to warriors from David to Deborah.

6. How do you think Nick's career could be reconciled with a Biblical walk?

7. Do you think soldiers who follow orders on the battlefield have broken God's commandments?

♫ ♫ ♫ ♫

Nick realized Aria had nearly reached the end of her proverbial rope, and offered to pray with her in an attempt to help center her. It worked.

8. Can you recollect a time when you used prayer as a means for centering yourself in a stressful situation?

9. What is it about prayer that provides a centering, calming effect?

♫ ♫ ♫ ♫

Aria worked through her broken wrist and the end of her career because Raymond sobered up, came to know Christ, and ended up helping hundreds of boys over a decade of sobriety.

10. Would you have been able to "find the bright side"?

11. 1 Thessalonians 5:18 tells us to give thanks in all circumstances. How did Aria model this to us?

12. Do you think Aria and her family's love and acceptance of Raymond had a direct impact on his lasting sobriety?

More Books

Find the latest information and connect with Hallee at her website: www.halleebridgeman.com

FICTION BOOKS BY HALLEE:

The Jewel Series:
Book 1, Sapphire Ice
Book 2, Greater Than Rubies
Book 3, Emerald Fire
Book 4, Topaz Heat
Book 5, Christmas Diamond
Book 6, Christmas Star Sapphire
Book 7, Jade's Match
Book 8, Chasing Pearl

Love Makes Way 6/2023

Standalone Romantic Suspense:
On the Ropes

The Red Blood and Bluegrass Series:
Black Belt, White Dress
Blizzard in the Bluegrass
Coming Soon
The Seven Year Glitch

Order #1 146 9/2/23

The Dixon Brothers Series

Book 1, Courting Calla

Book 2, Valerie's Verdict

Coming Soon

Book 3, Alexandra's Appeal

Book 4, Daisy's Decision

Virtues and Valor Series:

Book 1, Temperance's Trial

Book 2, Homeland's Hope

Book 3, Charity's Code

Book 4, A Parcel for Prudence

Book 5, Grace's Ground War

Book 6, Mission of Mercy

Book 7, Flight of Faith

Book 8, Valor's Vigil

COOKBOOKS BY HALLEE:

Parody Cookbook Series:

Vol 1: Fifty Shades of Gravy, a Christian gets Saucy

Vol 2: The Walking Bread, the Bread Will Rise

Vol 3: Iron Skillet Man, the Stark Truth about Pepper & Pots

Vol 4: Hallee Crockpotter, and the Chamber of Sacred Ingredients

About the Author

With nearly a million sales, Hallee Bridgeman is a best-selling Christian author who writes romance and action-packed romantic suspense focusing on realistic characters who face real-world problems.

An Army brat turned Floridian, Hallee finally settled in central Kentucky with her family so she could enjoy the beautiful changing of the seasons. She enjoys the roller-coaster ride thrills that life delivers with a National Guard husband, a daughter away at college, and two middle-school-aged sons.

A prolific writer, when she's not penning novels, you will find her in the kitchen, which she considers the "heart of the home." Her passion for cooking spurred her to launch a whole food, real food "Parody" cookbook series. In addition to dozens of nutritious, Biblically grounded recipes, each cookbook also confronts some controversial aspect of secular pop culture.

Hallee has served as the Director of the Kentucky Christian Writers Conference and continues to serve on the Executive Board, President of the Faith-Hope-Love chapter of the Romance Writers of America, and board Secretary for Novelists, Inc. (NINC). She is a long time Gold member of the American Christian Fiction Writers (ACFW), and a member of the American Christian Writers (ACW). An accomplished speaker, Hallee has taught and inspired writers around the globe, from Sydney, Australia, to Dallas, Texas, to Portland, Oregon, to Washington, D.C., and all places in between.

Hallee loves coffee, campy action movies, and regular date nights with her husband. Above all else, she loves God with all of her heart, soul, mind, and strength; has been redeemed by the blood of Christ; and relies on the presence of the Holy Spirit to guide her. She prays her work here on earth is a blessing to you and would love to hear from you.

Sign up for Hallee's monthly newsletter! You will receive a link to download Hallee's romantic suspense novella, On the Ropes. Every newsletter recipient is automatically entered into a monthly giveaway! The real prize is never missing updates about upcoming releases, book signings, appearances, or other events.

Hallee Online

Newsletter Sign Up:
halleebridgeman.com/newsletter

Author Site:
www.halleebridgeman.com

Facebook:
facebook.com/authorhalleebridgeman

Twitter:
twitter.com/halleeb

Goodreads:
goodreads.com/author/show/5815249.Hallee_Bridgeman

Homemaking Blog:
www.halleethehomemaker.com

Blogger with **Inspy Romance** at www.inspyromance.com

Newsletter

Sign up for Hallee's monthly newsletter! Every newsletter recipient is automatically entered into a monthly giveaway! The real prize is you will never miss updates about upcoming releases, book signings, appearances, or other events.

Hallee's Newsletter

halleebridgeman.com/newsletter

Made in the USA
Middletown, DE
29 March 2023